My first thanks are due to members of my family who, on hearing that I was writing this book, presented me with a computer. Then to Julie and Mark Somers, my wonderful great niece and nephew who taught me how to use it and steered me through countless crises when I was tempted to take a hammer to it. Especially to Julie for knocking the manuscript into shape and putting it onto disc. Without their help I doubt if it would have seen the light of day. My thanks are also due to those who throughout my life have provided me with examples of human nature, enabling me to bring to life the characters in this book.

THE HEART ENTRAPPED

'Lonely the heart entrapped in a forbidden love'

THE HEART ENTRAPPED

Mike Soper

ATHENA PRESS
LONDON

ISBN 10-digit: 1 84748 108 6
ISBN 13-digit: 978 1 84748 108 5

First Published 2007 by
ATHENA PRESS
Queen's House, 2 Holly Road
Twickenham TW1 4EG
United Kingdom

Printed for Athena Press

To John,
who shared my life.

All the characters depicted in this book are entirely fictional and bear no relation to anyone known to the author. The exceptions are the author himself, who appears fleetingly on three occasions as himself, and Lenin, who was a very real dog.
The home farm and Barnfield are also fictional.

Chapter One

Dad looked up from the paper he was reading.

'I reckon you've been working on those books long enough, lad, and that you could do with a break. Would you like to go out and check up on the ewes? I don't think that any more are likely to lamb tonight, but you never know. You'll find the torch on the scullery table.'

My father and I were with my mother and two sisters in the sitting room of a long low farmhouse that nestled against the hillside of our Devonshire farm, which by then had increased to 580 acres from the original 200 that my grandfather had bought forty years before.

I was fifteen at the time and revising for my O levels at the grammar school in Norton, our nearest town. Up until then, he might have said 'I'm looking after the calves today, would you like to give me a hand?' during my school holidays. But neither he nor my mother had ever made me feel that I had to become involved in the farm. If, at eighteen, after A levels, I wanted to farm, it would probably be an agricultural college, or perhaps a university. But that would be up to me to decide.

This attitude was probably based on his own experience, when he had been deprived of a college course by the sudden death of his father, who had been tragically killed by being crushed under an overturned tractor. My father was eighteen at the time, and was destined to go to college the following year. There was nothing for it but for him to come back to run the farm and provide a home for his mother and younger sister.

My grandfather had been a first-generation farmer, coming in with a fresh mind and no traditional ideas. On coming out of the army at the end of 1918, he had taken a course in surveying, and then got a job with an electricity company in Devon, constructing power lines in the countryside. In this job, he became interested in farming, and fell in love with the daughter of a substantial farmer in mid-Devon. They were married in 1921, and the following year, with financial help from his father-in-law, he took the plunge and bought our 200-acre farm.

It was a time of depression in farming, and land was cheap. The former owner had gone bankrupt, and the farm was in poor condition, so my grandfather got it for a song. He was left with enough capital to be able to spend money on improving some of the buildings.

Grandfather must have been a pretty shrewd operator, for he realised that relying on horse work was too slow for getting the land back into condition. So the two teams of horses that went with the farm were sold, and in came two second-hand tractors instead. He took on a young man from the village, and taught him tractor work and maintenance, and Jake was still working on the farm when I was a toddler forty years later.

The motley herd of dairy cows was also sold. Grandfather saw how tourism was increasing in Devon as motoring became more popular. Surely, he thought, there should be a good market for quality milk and cream in the summer months? He went up to Scotland and bought twenty-four Ayrshire cows, to which he added six Guernseys to improve the fat content and colour of the milk. He had them tested for tuberculosis, and negotiated a contract with a local dairy to pay him a considerable premium for the milk. Down from Scotland, too, came Gordon, a young college-trained herdsman whom he tempted down with the promise of a good cottage and a larger herd in the future.

In his domestic life, my father, John, had been born in 1922, and his sister, Emily, a year later. In 1934, my grandfather managed to buy another one hundred acres adjoining the top end of the farm, which enabled him to spread his costs. By the outbreak of war in 1939, he was so well established that he was asked to become a member of the local War Agricultural Committee.

Just how the fatal accident occurred remained a mystery, as he was a very experienced tractor driver. He had gone out to turn the hay on the steepest field on the farm, where some trees and a brook kept the surface moister. Perhaps his concentration lapsed, as he thought of a committee meeting that evening and he was going faster than he thought as he came to turn at the bottom of the field. A patch of wetter, previously unturned hay was found with a skid mark afterwards where the tractor had tipped over. My father came home from school to find his future irrevocably changed.

Fortunately Dad seemed to have inherited much of his father's shrewdness. To start with he had help from his uncle, who farmed some fifteen miles away, but he was soon quite capable of running the farm on his own. He had a good staff to support him, and had always worked during his holidays, so he was not left out of his depth.

For the next three years, his mother kept house for him and his sister. He had become a keen member of a newly established Young Farmers Club in Norton, which provided a social life for him. After a couple of years he was elected as chairman, and it was then that another member brought his sister to a meeting, and it fell to him to make her feel welcome.

Mary Sykes was nineteen at the time, and worked for an estate agent in Norton. Not very tall, she had long dark hair drawn back behind her ears, and wide-set grey eyes beneath a broad forehead. A strong chin suggested a determined character beneath her rather shy demeanour. But when at ease, her face would relax, and a smile would light up the eyes, which were such a striking feature of her face.

She came from a very religious family, and was a dedicated churchgoer. She was different from the other cheery, buxom Devon girl members of the club. John was apparently intrigued from the first moment he saw her. As he was serious minded himself, her reserve, in contrast to the extrovert chatter of the other girls, drew him to her. For her part, she said in later life, she was quite bowled over by the way in which this fair-haired, blue-eyed young man, who must have been attractive to other girls, went out of his way to make her feel among friends. For her it was a case of love at first sight. For him, perhaps not quite at first sight, but not far off it.

He wooed her assiduously, and when he was twenty-two he proposed; they were married at the end of the year. His mother and Emily moved out of the farmhouse to a cottage near Norton, and Emily married a north Devon farmer two years later.

Over the next four years three children were born, my sister, Juliet in 1945, Caroline a year later, and then me in 1948. But two years before that a very important event came up in John's life.

The nearest large estate decided to sell off two of its outlying farms. One of these of 220 acres bordered the top end of our farm. Though the farmhouse was a bit small, it had a set of well-maintained buildings, two cottages and good-sized fields of very fair quality land.

The agent called to see my father to enquire whether he might be interested in buying it. He certainly was, as he could see tremendous opportunities. If he got it, he could relocate and increase the size of the dairy herd, which he could not do at home owing to the steepness of the land adjoining our buildings. He could probably double it and also get a lot more land for cropping.

The trouble was that he had no ready cash with which to buy it. Both he and his uncle thought that borrowing money from the bank was the first step to bankruptcy – a view very common at one time. Admittedly his father had done it, but that was rather different as it was in the family.

Dad called in the local advisory officer, as he was always keen to get advice, even if he didn't always take it. Out came the slide rule, and a thorough investigation into the financial aspects revealed that at current interest rates and farm prices it should be possible to pay off the bank after about five years. Off he went to the bank manager, who was only too keen to lend the money to this progressive young farmer. The estate accepted his offer, and suddenly he was farming nearly 600 acres.

The herd was moved up to the new farm, and a milking parlour was installed which enabled Gordon to milk single-handed twice the number of cows he had milked on the home farm. The herd was housed in straw yards, which saved a lot of labour. Gordon moved into the farmhouse, and a new young tractor driver, Victor, moved into his cottage. At the same time, Dad changed the colour of his cows to black-and-white Friesians, which gave a lot more milk than the old Ayrshires had done, though he did lose the quality premium for the milk. This was more than compensated for by the higher yields.

So this was the environment into which I had been born, with two very loving parents, and sisters who tended to mollycoddle their young brother.

Early recollections are all of my mother. Home-loving and rather reserved, she did not go out much, and there were few visitors to the house. After the sisters went to school, all my time was spent with her. I would toddle round behind her as she tended the long flower bed against the wall that separated the lawn from the lane which ran up to the main road to Norton. Another bed ran the length of the house, which had an old wisteria over the front door and yellow climbing roses up the walls. It was a picture postcard of a garden. Beyond the lane, a row of towering elms protected us from the south-west gales blowing in from the distant Atlantic. To the east of the house was the kitchen garden, made fertile by liberal dressings of farmyard manure, and a soft fruit cage. A swarm of bees given to my mother before I was born had now increased to three hives, which was one of the pleasures of her life.

Mother had a strong religious faith, and she really did believe that God had created the world in seven days, a concept that I abandoned when I did biology at school. But I inherited a religious streak from her. Dad was not always to be found in church on Sundays, if there was work to be done on the farm. But generally he would drive us in, because he was still deeply in love with his wife, and knew that it pleased her to have him beside her. He also believed that it was right to bring up his family on moral principles.

So Sunday church services became a feature of my life. I liked the majestic language of the Psalms and the Bible – so much so that religious belief has remained with me, not the unquestioning faith that was such a comfort to my mother, but one which was to be sorely tested on more than one occasion in the future.

My father, as I remember him at the time, seemed tall to me, but was actually an inch or two under six feet, with fairish hair, rather pale blue eyes and a slightly reddish complexion. He must have been attractive to women, but he was much in love with his wife, and I feel sure that he remained faithful to her. They did not display visible affection, for that was not fashionable in that tight-lipped era. When they were together, there was a sense of mutual affection and tolerance for each other's views. I don't think that they could ever have had a row, as they would not want to risk hurting the other's feelings. It was a true marriage of togetherness.

The two girls were completely different from each other, both in appearance and character. Juliet resembled her mother, with straight dark hair, a rather oval face, and with the same distinctive grey eyes. She was like her, too, in temperament: not exactly shy, but never one to push herself forward. She worked hard at school, loved reading, and was clearly destined for an academic career.

Caroline, on the other hand, was clearly her father's daughter. She had his fair hair and blue eyes with full cheeks and a lovely skin. With an extrovert approach to life, she was always bubbling over with enthusiasm for some cause or other. She obviously preferred boys to books, and a hockey stick to a school satchel. When she was thirteen, the alarm bells rang when Mother, to whom lipstick was an unknown accessory, spotted Caroline with lips of a strange colour. It was if Jezebel had stepped out of the Bible and into her home. The riot act was read, though it had little effect as Caroline had already began to show a wilful streak, which caused her parents some disquiet over the next few years – but that was all in the future.

I was about four years old, when Mother suddenly said, when we were in the garden: 'We're going in now. You've got to learn to read and write. We can't have you going off to school unable to write your name.'

She found it hard going to start with, and her patience was sorely strained, but eventually things fell into place. By the time I went to school the following year I had learned to enjoy reading, and was well ahead of most others in the class.

Primary school years fled by and, when the time came, I had no difficulty in getting a place at Norton Grammar School, which had a good academic reputation. There I settled down quite happily, though I found it difficult to make close friends as I was still rather shy, and not interested in the frivolous activities that my classmates enjoyed.

It was rugby that helped me to find my feet. New boys were lined up and made to run five times up and down the field. The faster ones were put in the back division, and the slower ones, of which I was one, were put in the scrum, where I settled down as right front-row forward. Working as a member of the team seemed to give me a boost – especially as, in my third game, I found myself in possession of a loose ball and, dodging two opponents, scored my first try, to the acclaim of my team mates.

There was another reason why I liked the game, the significance of which was not apparent at the time. The hooker in my first year was a rather older boy, called Eric, to whom I seemed to be attracted in some way. As we got down in the scrum, I would feel his right arm clasping me to him, and my left arm would be round his waist pulling him tight to me. Each time I would get a feeling of warmth and security at being so close to his body. It was not actually an erotic feeling, but just one of contentment.

One aspect of playing rugby was a constant worry. Since I had come into contact with other boys in the changing room or the showers, I had become obsessively reticent about revealing my most intimate parts to public gaze. I had not felt this when I was small with my sisters in the bathroom. But when mixing with other boys, it was a different matter, especially as it appeared from surreptitious glances that I was not especially well endowed, compared with some of the others. I would creep into the showers clutching my towel until the last moment. Other boys walked boldly in, flaunting their manhood for all to see. Eric was one of these, clearly proud of what he had to display to anyone who cared to look.

One day, at an away match after I had got into the first XV, there were no showers but a vast tub in the middle of the changing room, into which we had to pile together. Getting to it without a towel was like walking the plank, but once in the tub the contact with so much male flesh was erotically stimulating – almost embarrassingly so. Why was it, I wonder, that I was so squeamish, when in later life I had no inhibitions?

By the time that Dad had asked me to check up on the ewes, my two sisters had begun to go their separate ways, with Juliet shortly off to read law at university, and Caroline leaving school at seventeen to do a secretarial course at the local tech. Parties, dancing and boyfriends, seemingly a different one every month, were the order of her day. At the start of her last term at school, she suddenly said: 'Mark, it's quite time you learned to dance. You're spending far too much time on your books, and you should come out and enjoy life. Claire wants a partner for the Young Farmers' dance on Saturday week as her boyfriend has gone back to college.'

'I don't want to learn to dance,' I said, 'and anyhow I wouldn't have anything to say to her, as I'm sure she's not interested in books or rugby, or farming for that matter.'

'Come on, you'll have to learn sometime or you'll turn into a recluse. We've got nearly two weeks, and I can give you the basics in that time.'

'I just don't want to. I won't have the time now I'm starting on my A levels.'

'Rubbish, I'm taking you in hand and that's that. Dancing today isn't like it used to be, but I'll give you a bit of the old-fashioned stuff, anyhow.' Caroline was a persuasive, not to say a strong-willed girl, and I knew from experience I'd have to give in sooner or later.

She got the old gramophone out of the attic where it had been put when dad bought a television so that he could watch the farming programmes. She also rustled up some Victor Sylvester and Elvis Presley discs. As with the reading lessons from my mother, I found the conventional stuff very difficult to master, and was endlessly treading on her toes. Rock and roll was easier as it seemed that one only had to prance up and down. After ten days, I was passed fit to take Claire to the dance.

I still look back on that dance with horror. Claire was as extroverted as my sister, and chattered away trying to keep the conversation going, but I couldn't think of anything to say. After I had stamped on her toes two or three times, it was obvious that she was bored, and she finally went off with other boys. Caroline, seeing me discarded, rescued me a couple of times, and I had another disastrous attempt with a girl from my school. Thank goodness, it was over at last, and I could go home. Strangely I had got no pleasure from contact with the girls, but thought how much nicer it would be to have my arm round a firm body in the scrum.

From the time that Mother first noticed the colour of her lips, Caroline had been something of a worry to my parents. Mother had led a sheltered life, and had not realised how much the world had changed by the early sixties. She still lived in an era when girls should be safely tucked up in bed by ten o'clock. If they stayed out with boys they might suddenly be pregnant. Dad was more worldly, but was concerned at the frequent changes in the faces of her boyfriends.

Every now and again he would put his foot down with instructions to be home by midnight. It would work for a time, but soon it would be one o'clock again when the current boyfriend would drop her at the gate, and she would creep in hoping that everyone was asleep. But Mother probably would not be, worrying about what Caroline was getting up to. I was never worried about it, as I thought that she was very worldly-wise at a young age, and had no intention of spoiling her happy life by getting pregnant.

She left school at seventeen, did her secretarial course, got a job with an accountant in Norton and at the age of twenty finally got her man in the form of a twenty-five-year-old son of a property developer. Their first son, Daniel, was born a year later, so Mother could rest peacefully at last.

But that was all in the future as I moved up into the sixth form to do my A levels in English, history, economics and biology. I reckoned that the last two would be useful if I went into farming, and the first two if I wanted a job outside. School life got better as I got into the sixth form, and was able to work more on my own. I was aware that one or two girls tried to get a bit too close, but they got no encouragement and soon gave up. I had no intention or desire to get involved in social activities. There was one, however, who always seemed to be in the library when I was, and in whom I felt a slight interest.

Her name was Barbara. She had a slim figure, dark hair always cut short and a rather small oval face beneath a short fringe, which gave her a rather elfin and slightly boyish look. She had well-developed breasts, which didn't seem to match up with her figure quite, and which I found rather unattractive. But she was serious minded, and we used to chat to one another. That was all, and I did not feel sexually attracted to her.

Just before the start of my last term, Dad suddenly said over breakfast: 'Your mother and I think it would be a good idea if we bought you a small car, so that you can get to school under your own steam. You could also stay on to work in the library without having to catch the school bus, or us having to come in and fetch you.'

'That'd be marvellous, Dad. Thanks so much for thinking of it. It'll certainly make it much easier if I want to stay on working.'

Dad had contacts in the trade, and in no time I was the proud owner of a second-hand Morris 1000, with only 6,000 miles on the clock. For the past year I had been driving one of the bigger tractors on the farm, so had no difficulty in passing the driving test. It was exciting to own one's own car, with all the independence that came with it. I called her Bess, and came to love her like a dog, and she never once let me down in all the twelve years that I was to own her.

'We both think it would be a good thing if I gave you a regular allowance instead of you having to come to us if you need anything,' Dad said the following day. 'I'll have a word with the bank manager, and open an account for you. What about £500 a year to start with, and then we can see how it goes?' Up until then they had given me pocket money and Dad paid me something for work at harvest.

'I'm tremendously grateful, Dad. £500 a year sounds almost too much, but I'll accept it all the same. If I don't need it all, I'm sure it will come in useful when I go on to college or university.'

After the exams were over, I had a few days at Aunt Emily's. I got on well with her two boys, who were a bit younger than me, and I always enjoyed visiting her. We got in quite a lot of surf bathing, a sport to which I was becoming increasingly addicted, and some tennis which I had learnt to play at school.

Before we had broken up after the exams, the sixth formers had decided to meet up for an evening party with supper and dancing at a local hotel. I would have preferred just a drinks party as I still didn't enjoy dancing and making trivial conversation with girls. I much preferred a pint of beer with rugby friends.

Shortly before the party, Barbara rang: 'Mark, you will be going to the party, won't you?'

'Yes, of course.'

'Do you think that you could possibly give me a lift in your car as I've got no transport?'

'I'd like to. Where do you live?'

'Out in the country, about three miles west of Norton. If you've a pen handy, I'll tell you how to find me.' So I was committed to taking a girl out for the first time – except for Claire, which hadn't really counted as a date.

Barbara was easy to get on with as we drove to the party, asking about my family and the farm and what I was intending to do in the future. She was going to university to train as a teacher, after a year out, and I told her that I would probably go to an agricultural college as I had not got my name down for a university.

The evening passed quickly as we mixed with the others. As we reached her home, it was in the dark and I remembered that she had said her parents were away for the night.

'Would you like to come in for a cup of coffee, Mark?'

'I think I really ought to be getting home, or Mother will be wondering what I'm up to.'

'It won't take a moment. Come along in. It'll finish off the evening.'

She was so insistent that I gave in. She drew the curtains and sat me down on a sofa while she brewed the coffee. Putting the cups on a side table, she came and sat down beside me.

'This is nice, isn't it? I did enjoy the evening. Thanks so much for picking me up and for taking me. I don't know what I'd have done if you hadn't been there. Probably not gone, I expect, which would have been a pity, as it was a lot of fun.'

'I thought it was a good evening, too, and I'm so glad you rang me. Otherwise I'd have had to go on my own which wouldn't have been nearly so enjoyable.'

'I'd guess that you haven't taken many girls out before, have you?'

'Well, no, not really. Life has been far too busy, what with work, sport and giving Dad a hand on the farm. Anyhow, socialising isn't my scene, it all seems rather a waste of time.'

'If you're going to college, you'll have to get used to leading a more sociable life, won't you?'

'I suppose so, but I don't intend to let it interfere with work, as some people do.'

'Come on, you'll turn into a recluse if you're not careful, and then you'd miss out on half the fun of being at college.' At that, she moved up closer to me on the sofa.

'I don't believe you've ever kissed a girl, have you?'

'No, but then I've never met one that I wanted to kiss.'

'We'll soon put that right, then,' she said as she moved up against me and put her arm round my shoulders, drew my head down and kissed me on the lips. I had not seen her with lipstick before, and somehow it put me off. I kissed her back half-heartedly, as I didn't want it to go any further. I liked her but felt no physical attraction at all.

'That's not nearly good enough. Relax, and let yourself go. What are you afraid of?'

Oh well, I thought, I'd better go along with it and pretend I'm enjoying it. So I held her tighter and kissed her firmly on the lips.

'That's more like it.' But as she kissed me back, she somehow slid under me across the sofa, and I was on top of her feeling her breasts pressing against me as she clung closer. I had a feeling of distaste at this soft body clasping mine, and I had a sudden vision of Eric's arm round me in the scrum. How much more exciting that would be, I thought, than this soft thing.

It was then that her hand went down to my waist, and I felt her fumbling for the zip. As she found it, and started to pull it down, I realised what she was doing, and sprang back off her with a feeling of shock and revulsion. Clearly I was meant to fall in with this attempted seduction, and Barbara was by no means the rather innocent and intellectual girl I had thought her to be. What right had she to invade my privacy like this? It was mine to give, not hers to take. It was not as if she would have found anything to excite her there, as I had not been sexually aroused in any way by this assault on my virginity. It had simply antagonised me.

'I'm sorry, Barbara, I'm not ready for anything like that yet. You see, I don't believe in any sexual relationship before marriage. I want to keep it and wait for someone I love.'

'So you don't care for me at all, then?'

'Of course I like you as we do seem to have quite a lot in common, but it's only platonic. This may sound callous, but I am not attracted to you in any sexual way, I'm afraid.'

I felt rather sorry for her then as I realised that she might have been harbouring some sort of crush on me, and had misread things that I had said to her. If that were so, she would now be feeling humiliated at going so far and being so abruptly rebuffed. This thought was reinforced by her reaction.

'You're really incredibly old-fashioned, you know. We're in the twentieth century, not way back in 1900. Things are quite different now. Surely you want to let your hair down now and again, don't you? I can't think what you're worrying about. You're so cold and inhibited; anyone might think that you're queer.'

'Of course I'm not queer. It's only that I don't want to commit myself to anyone while I'm still so young. It seems immoral to me, somehow.'

'Oh well, if you want to be so pious and live a dull, uninteresting life, it's up to you, but you'll miss the hell of a lot of fun in life if you go on like this.'

I had had enough. 'I really must get home now. Thanks for such an enjoyable evening, Barbara, and I'm sorry if I've disappointed you. We'll meet up again before long, I'm sure.'

Driving home, my mind was in turmoil. Those words 'Anyone might think that you're queer' had hit me like a bullet. What if she was right and I was homosexual? Surely I couldn't be, could I? I was nothing like poor little Adrian in my class at school, with his effeminate speech and mincing walk, who was hopeless at games and whom the boys laughed at.

Nor was I like those comedians on television, Julian and Sandy in *Round the Horne* or other camp actors pretending to be queer. I remembered Mother once saying, as she watched a programme on the box, 'I can't abide those effeminate creatures. I don't know why they allow them on the screen.' If I really was queer, what on earth would she think of me?

And what had the Bible to say about it? 'Man shall not lie down with man'; and what did God do to Sodom and Gomorrah to punish them when they practised it? Clearly He regarded it as a sin. But if I was normal why should I have felt repelled by Barbara's sexuality and the softness of her body clinging to mine? I should have welcomed it and taken her to bed. All my talk about being too young was said on the spur of the moment to get me out of the predicament I was in. If it had been Eric, would I have reacted differently? I felt sure I would.

If I was heterosexual why should I be tempted to look at other boys' bodies in the showers and yet be so reticent about revealing my own? And another thing: those wet dreams that I used to have when I was younger, before I had found out about the relief that comes from masturbation, were always triggered in the last stages by contact with men or boys, and never by girls. Might that be significant?

It was with thoughts like this that I reached home, but they would not go away as I went over the events of the evening. If I was queer, it would mean that I would not marry, as it would not be fair on a girl to do so, if all I wanted was a man in bed.

'Did you enjoy the party?' Mother said over breakfast. 'You were quite late coming in weren't you?'

'Very much, Mother. I'm sorry if I woke you. When I took Barbara back I went in for a cup of coffee, and we stayed on talking longer than I meant.'

'I saw her once at one of your school events, but I thought that she seemed a very nice girl. Quiet, and not made up like some of the others. Will you be seeing her again?'

'I don't really know, but I expect we'll meet up sometime.'

At that moment Dad came in for his breakfast.

'I've decided what I want to do, Dad. I don't want to hang about for a year waiting for a university course. I'm sure that the best thing to do would be to get a place at an agricultural college next year, which shouldn't be difficult with my good A levels. Then after that we can decide, but I don't think that I want to come back to work at home for some time, as you don't really need me. I'd like to get a job to see the world a bit first.'

'That's very wise, Mark. College courses cover a very wide

field these days, with quite a lot of management in them, which might help if you wanted a job outside farming. Which college were you thinking of?'

'I thought I'd write to the four bigger ones, which would include the south Devon one.'

Mother perked up at this. She had looked a bit disappointed at my noncommittal reply about seeing Barbara again. Oh dear, she was probably already thinking about grandchildren; but if I went to the local one, she would at least have me around still.

The next two days were spent in getting a report from school and writing to the colleges to enquire about places. My A levels must have impressed, as three of them wrote back immediately offering me a place in September. With the family not wanting me to go too far away, I chose the local one so that I would be able to get home for weekends if I wanted to.

Chapter Two

When I was packing, I realised that I had never been away from home for any length of time before, apart from spending short holidays with Aunt Emily. We had never had family holidays, as Dad always seemed too busy to get away; and Mother, who had never had them as a girl didn't like the idea of being uprooted from her domestic routine. As children we always had the farm to roam over, and never felt a need to go away.

It didn't worry me, as I would be able to come back at the weekend if I wanted to. The prospect of getting away and making new friends was exciting.

There were about thirty of us entering college, including a few farmers' sons like myself, and it didn't take long to coalesce into small groups with similar interests. We tended to eat together and gather in the college bar for a drink before getting down to work in the evening. But I was not one to linger wasting time on smutty stories, and one drink was usually enough. At home there was never any drinking, apart from a bottle of sherry or whisky on the sideboard brought out on the rare occasions when the parents entertained.

Each of us was allotted a member of staff to act as a course tutor, and I was lucky to be attached to a young member of the farm management team, Richard Sykes, who had been on the staff for only a couple of years. He had a really sympathetic personality, and I liked him from the start. He showed me the ropes, organised my lectures, and kept an eye on what I was doing, treating me as an equal. As it turned out we would remain friends for life, even if we did not see one another much in the post-college years.

It was in the second week that I first saw Simon. I had gone into the bar for a drink with two new friends before going up to my room to work. He was there with two friends talking and laughing.

I noted that he had curly fair hair, a bit tousled, over a wide forehead and tanned, slightly freckled cheeks. A rather long nose prevented him from being really good-looking, but it was his bright blue eyes that caught my attention. Little creases round them made him look as if he were half laughing, as indeed he often was, for he was always happy with himself and the world.

As I was looking at him, our eyes met, and it was as if an electric current had passed between us. I had the sensation that we had met before in some previous existence, and were destined to meet again to renew a forgotten friendship. I was the first to look away, but twice over our drinks I caught him looking at me again. I went up to my room to work, but those blue eyes kept projecting out from the page that I was reading. I seemed to know already that there was some bond between us, and wondered when we would meet again.

I had not long to wait. The following day was the first rugby practice and, as I walked on to the field, there he was.

'Hello, Mark. Good to see you. I hear you played in the scrum at Norton Grammar for two years. It looks as if we could do with you, as we lost a lot of forwards last year.'

'That's right, but how do you know my name?'

He smiled and his eyes seemed to light up. 'Ha, I've got ways of finding out things, if I want to. By the way, my name's Simon Trevelyan, in case you're wondering who I am, and I'm starting on the second year of the diploma course.'

'Where do you play, then?' I thought that by the look of him – he was some two inches taller than me, with a slim figure – that he probably played in the back division.

'Usually left centre, though I do play on the wing sometimes.'

We were divided up into two teams, and at half time, I was promoted to the probable First Team. But not before I had brought down Simon with a flying tackle when he was in full flight.

'That was a tough tackle, Mark,' he said as we got up from the ground, and I detected a note of approval in his voice. It was the first time that I had touched him, but it was not to be the last, by any means. I didn't see him after the game, as we lived in different blocks, where we had our own showers. So it was about four days later that we met outside the dining room after lunch.

'Hello, Mark, how are you getting on?'

'Just fine, thanks. I feel as if I've been here for years already. Hope to see you at the match on Saturday.'

'I'll look forward to it. See you.' With that he was gone, but I felt happy somehow.

Having my own car, I usually went home on Saturday night. I found out that Simon did the same, so apart from rugby games and occasional glimpses over meals I didn't see much of him for the next few weeks. But each time I would feel strangely happy.

It was good to get home for a break on Saturday nights. Dad and I usually walked the farm on a Sunday afternoon, after taking Mother to church in the morning. But as we walked, I found myself thinking how enjoyable it would be to have Simon with us, as I felt sure that he would get on well with Dad, and it would be fun to show him the farm.

Halfway through the term, Simon came up to me after lunch.

'Are you doing anything this evening, Mark? Because if not, James and Andrew and I thought we might go up to take a look at a pub on Dartmoor that has been renovated and which Andrew has heard is quite good, and we wondered if you'd like to join us.'

'No, I've got nothing on, and I'd love to come. Are you sure you've got room for me?'

'Oh yes, there's bags of room for you and Andrew in the back. See you in the car park at half past seven, then. Glad you can come.'

James was in the rugby team, so I already knew him, but I had not come across Andrew yet. They were completely different in character – James tall and dark and a little slow in speech, and Andrew short and chubby with mousy coloured hair and an extrovert – but both of them made me feel completely at ease as we drove to the pub. I had expected Simon to be rather a fast driver, but in fact he was cautious and careful.

The talk over our drinks and a game of darts was mostly of farming and a possible entry to the Common Market, but they also discussed current affairs and other national issues. In the sheltered life that I had led I had never really thought about such things, and felt out of my depth. I resolved that in future I would try to find time to read a national paper in the college library each day, so that I could keep up with them. This outing was the first of what soon became a weekly event.

But every now and again after one of these meetings I would have a nagging fear. If I really was homosexual, what on earth would these friends think of me? Would I have to give up all thoughts of a closer friendship with Simon, and would they reject me? Somehow I thought that Simon might accept it, but I must be careful in future not to give myself away.

It was at the last of these evenings before going home for Christmas that I was jolted back to doubts about my sexuality. Halfway through the evening I had a need to go out to the gents. As I stood to unzip, the door opened behind me, and suddenly Simon was there beside me, and his sleeve brushed my arm. Involuntarily I completely froze up from having him so close to me.

He seemed to have no difficulty in relieving himself, but I couldn't pass a drop and fumbled around trying to get started.

'What's up, Mark, have I frightened you or something?' As he said this, I saw him looking down at my non-functioning organ.

'Go away. I'll never get started with you standing there. I'm always shy with someone close to me.'

'OK, then, I'll go and leave you to get on with it.'

In bed that night the incident kept on coming back to me. Did my freezing up denote a sexual reaction, or was it just my modesty coming out when he was suddenly standing there? But what about him? Had he deliberately followed me in, and what was he doing looking down to see what was happening there? Could it possibly be that he had some sexual interest in me?

Thinking back, he always seemed to be with men friends, and I had never seen him talking to any of the girls, who would surely find him attractive. And what about the various eye contact that we'd had, especially in the bar that first night? Might it be that he had the same feelings for me that I had for him? So might he be homosexual, too?

He had none of the usual symptoms of being 'queer'. But then, I thought, nor have I. If he was, where would that lead us? Physical sex between two men, or women for that matter, was

surely unnatural and wrong in the eyes of God? But that brief
contact with him had stirred up more intense emotions than I had
ever felt before. I realised that what I really wanted was to be in
his arms, whatever the consequence might be for our future
relationship.

I only saw him casually once more before Christmas, but
when the post arrived on Christmas Eve, there was a card.

'Happy Xmas, Mark, and best wishes for 1968. Simon.' I had a
feeling of elation, as I had never had a card before from anyone
outside the family.

It was a very happy time that year, with Juliet home from
university, and Caroline with an older boyfriend, with whom, as
mother said, she appeared to be 'going steady'. It was made even
happier for me by that Christmas card.

The first night back at college, there was a knock on the door.
It was Simon.

'Hope you had a good Christmas. What did you get up to?'

'Nothing very much, just at home with the family. But it was
good, with sister Caroline looking as if she has found her man, at
last. Thanks so much for the card. I did appreciate it, but I'm
sorry that I didn't send you one.'

'I don't see why you should have done, but I thought it'd be
nice to let you know that I hadn't forgotten all about you.'

'What about you? Did you do anything interesting?'

'No, it was just my sister and her family with us. After that I
was rather bored, as there wasn't much to do. Having been away
at boarding school, I've never made any friends locally, and I find
Mother and Father's friends a bit stuffy. If I had known you a bit
better, I'd have rung up to see if you could come over. By the
way, Mother says that she would like to meet you, so could you
come over to lunch one Sunday? I'm sure you'll like her, as she is
terribly easy to get on with.' Like you, I thought, but didn't say it.

'I've never asked you before,' I said, 'but where were you at
school?'

'At a public school in Dorset. My parents believed in boarding
schools as they thought it was good to teach me to be independent and to stand on my own feet. I was sent away to a prep school
when I was eight, and was a bit homesick at first. But I was very

happy at both my schools, and made a lot of friends, though it got a bit boring in the holidays. But sister Margaret was still at home then, and we used to do a lot of things together.'

'So how did you come to land up here?'

'I loved doing biology at school, and didn't like the prospect of a town life like Father's. I decided I wanted something out of doors and was lucky to get a job working for a year on a dairy farm in Cornwall. I learnt an awful lot while I was there as the boss took an interest in me, and I lived in the farmhouse with them. So after next year I shall be out job hunting.'

'What sort of a job?'

'I'd like to get into the Advisory Service, where I could get out on to farms, and be faced with problems to be solved. Failing that, possibly an assistant manager's job.'

'You'd make a good adviser. I remember Dad saying that managers' jobs are risky, so I'd keep away from that, if possible.'

This talk with Simon was the first that we had had alone together, and it left me a bit depressed. It would mean that in about eighteen months he would be off out of my life, unless I found a job near him, which would be extremely unlikely.

Our weekly pub jaunts continued, but now sometimes we would meet up in each other's rooms for coffee and a discussion about all sorts of subject. All three of them had been to boarding schools, and encouraged to take an interest in current affairs, whereas I had been on the school bus home with no further contacts with boys of my own age, which put me at a disadvantage.

One evening in Simon's room the discussion turned to homosexuality as a result of the passing of the bill in Parliament sanctioning homosexual acts in private. 'It should have been passed years ago,' Simon said. 'It's monstrous that people should have been persecuted and labelled as criminals just because they were born to be attracted to people of their own sex. What do you think about it, James?'

'I agree, though I don't know exactly what the effect will be, as it is something that has been going on for centuries in private anyhow. Removing the criminal element should certainly make it easier for homos to meet each other, instead of it all going on underground. As long as the physical side is kept private, it should be fine.'

'That's just the point,' Andrew chipped in. 'Will it stay private once it is all out in the open? I'm all in favour of having clubs where people like that can meet one another, and maybe pubs as well, but I wouldn't want it to get to the point that we'll see men kissing or holding hands in public. That would probably antagonise people, and do the cause of homosexual equality more harm than good.'

'My father once had to defend a local businessman on a charge of indecency after he had been caught by the police,' said Simon. 'Luckily he got off with a fine and was not sent to prison, but the publicity nearly ruined him. If the bill can stop that sort of thing happening, it must be a good thing. Anyhow, what do you think about it, Mark?'

I had been sitting quiet up until then, wondering if all this applied to me.

'I don't really know what to think, as I don't know much about it. I was brought up on the Bible, which says in the Old Testament that "man should not lie down with man", and just look what God did to Sodom and Gomorrah when things were getting out of hand. But biology suggests that all our characteristics are of genetic origin, so some people must be born like it, and it seems wrong that they should be punished for doing something which seems natural to them. Perhaps the Bible didn't get it right.'

'You must admit,' James said, 'that most of what is in the Old Testament is just a fairy story and has no real relevance to the world we're living in today. Much of it was concocted by priests or tribal leaders to maintain discipline – like stoning to death for adultery, or the cutting off of limbs for trivial offences like homosexuality. If that applied today, an awful lot of people would be walking round without limbs, wouldn't they? Then to make their case stronger they invented the idea of a vengeful God raining down punishment on transgressors. For goodness' sake, Mark, don't be swayed by that guff.'

'OK, I'll admit perhaps we shouldn't be influenced by the Old Testament, but what about the New? Surely you can't maintain that's got it wrong, can you? What about all the thousands of people who, in the past, have built magnificent cathedrals, composed wonderful music or painted great works of art as a result of Christianity? Were they all taken in by what the Bible said?'

'That's quite a different matter,' Andrew said. 'We're talking about homosexuality, and as far as I know nothing was said about it in the New Testament until Paul came along later on, and he is the only one on record to disapprove of it. Jesus never said anything about it. In fact, it's quite likely that some of the Apostles may have been queer or bisexual anyway. You can't tell me that a dozen young men traipsing around Palestine in the prime of life didn't get up to something. What about the reference to "the disciple whom Jesus loved"? That sounds suspicious to me.'

'You see, Mark, I don't really think that you ought to worry at all about the few references in the Bible,' Simon said. 'We're living in 1968, and it's marvellous to have everything out in the open, so that quite innocent people can feel safe from prosecution at last, if they are born that way. But I do agree with Andrew that it would be a bad thing if it got out of hand, causing an increase in prejudice, which is bad enough as it is. I just hope that the physical aspects of it will be confined to the privacy of people's homes.'

And so the argument went on, but my mind was in turmoil as I went back to my room. I felt great relief at the liberal attitude that the others had taken. It could mean that if I was queer and they found out, they might still not ostracise me. But all that had been said about the Bible had led me to question the faith that I had been brought up with. If I was in love with Simon, as seemed to be the case, I would obviously have to forgo some of my religious principles.

For various reasons the invitation to meet Simon's parents did not materialise until the last week of term, when I was invited over to Sunday lunch a fortnight hence. I found the house easily – a large, stone two-storey building, probably about 300 years old, set well back from the road by a large lawn and well-kept flower beds. By the look of the large Mercedes parked beside the house, there was obviously no shortage of money in the Trevelyan household. Simon was there to meet me with his usual happy smile.

His mother, Cynthia, was much as I had imagined her – lightish brown hair, just starting to go grey at the temples, but with no attempt to conceal it, and no trace of make-up on her face. She had a broad forehead and Simon's eyes and a lovely warm soft colouring in the cheeks, while her lips, like his, seemed to have a half smile, ready to come out at the slightest provocation. A comfortably upholstered body gave her an air of motherliness which was borne out by her character – warm, outgoing and friendly.

'Do come in, Mark. I'm so pleased to meet you at last, as Simon has told us so much about you. Jack will be in from the garden in a moment, and then we'll have a drink.'

As she said this, she leaned towards me, encouraging me to kiss her on the cheek. It took me by surprise, for never in a hundred years would Mother, with her shyness, have thought of kissing a strange young man on first meeting him. We were in the large drawing/sitting room, which ran the breadth of the house, with French windows opening on to another lawn and flower beds at the back. Beyond this was the vegetable garden and fruit trees, and a tennis court.

'Only a cold lunch, I'm afraid,' she said, 'as we had a meeting after church and there wasn't time to cook.' At that moment, Jack, Simon's father, came in – a tall, distinguished-looking figure with greying hair but still youthful complexion. I noticed that he had the little creases round the eyes that Simon had inherited.

'Glad to meet you, Mark. Now, what about a drink? Sherry, or would you prefer a beer?'

'I'd rather have a beer, if you've got it, please.' I had never tasted sherry before, so played it safe and was glad Simon had the same. They were both such easy talkers that lunch passed quickly. Afterwards I realised that they had got all sorts of information out of me, about my parents and the farm, and how grandfather had acquired it and built it up. Jack knew quite a lot about farming, as his solicitors firm had clients connected with it in various ways.

'I'm going to put my feet up,' Cynthia said as we finished our coffee. 'I expect Simon would like to show you the garden.'

'Yes, and after that I thought that we might go out for a drive in the car, as I don't think Mark knows the countryside round here.'

'That's a good idea. We'll expect you back about half past four for a cup of tea.'

The garden was obviously Jack's pride and joy, and was looking its best with spring bulbs in flower; but the tennis court was neglected and overgrown.

'We used to play quite a bit till sister Margaret got married,' said Simon. 'Since then, I've had nobody to play with, so we've rather let it go. Didn't you say once that you had played at school?'

'Yes, but I never played enough to get at all good at it. But I did enjoy it a lot.'

'I'll tell you what, why don't we get the court back into condition again, and then you could come over for a game? I'm not much good, either, so we could get a lot of fun out of it.'

'That'd be marvellous, because I would like to play more. It's good exercise when we can't play rugger.' The thought of spending whole days with him was almost too good to be true.

'Come on, let's jump in the car, and I'll show you what the country's like round here.'

We drove through the Devon countryside, looking wonderfully fresh with young growth in the pastures, and spring corn just showing through in the arable fields, and daffodils and primroses in the hedgerows. The views were fantastic, with the mass of Dartmoor to the south, Cornish hills to the west and a huge stretch of farming land almost up to the north coast. With the sun higher in the sky, it looked like the Promised Land.

'Stop the car so that you can have a good look without running off the road,' I suggested.

He stopped in the next lay-by, and we got out to enjoy the panoramic view.

'It's a wonderful view, isn't it? I feel that I'd never want to leave it, though I suppose I'll have to when I get a job somewhere at the end of next year.'

'Don't think about that now, it's a long time ahead. Let's make the best of it now while we can, just the two of us together.' I was surprised by what I had said, but the words had just slipped out involuntarily. It obviously surprised him, too, for he turned to me, and looked me hard in the eyes.

'Do you really mean that? I hope you do.' We went back to the car and sat there, saying nothing.

'What are you thinking about?' he asked.

'I was just thinking that I wished we could be here for ever with this wonderful view, and you here in the car with me. I'm sure you must have realised by now how much I value your friendship. You've taken me into a different world, which I would never have found if I hadn't met you. I want you to know just how grateful I am for that.'

'I hope I won't let you down then.'

Before we got back, he turned towards me as he was driving.

'Do you like the theatre, Mark?' For a moment I didn't know what to say, because up until then I had never been to a proper theatre in my life. I had been to school productions and to an amateur production in the village hall, but that was all. If I admitted this to him, would he think me such a hick he'd no longer want to waste time on me when he could be with his more sophisticated friends, or should I fudge an answer? I decided to come clean, for what would be the point of pretending?

'To tell the truth, I've never been to a proper theatre in my life. Why did you ask?'

'I rather thought that might be the case. I love it, though I seldom get the chance of going now. Mother and Father used to take us up to London for a few days before Margaret left home, and we'd always do a couple of shows. I did enjoy it, especially musicals and ballet. I asked because the local operatic society are doing *Carousel* the week after next. We saw it in London, but I'd love to see it again. The story's a bit crummy, but the music is marvellous. Would you like to come with me?'

'Of course, I'd love to go. It'll be the week before term starts, so what about the Tuesday?'

'Should be all right. I'll get moving on it tomorrow and get the tickets.'

'Did you enjoy your day, dear?' Mother said as I got home.

'Tremendously. Simon's parents are awfully easy to get on with. Like you, his mother seems to do a lot in the village. They've got a lovely old house and garden which his father keeps in wonderful condition. They've also got a tennis court which has been neglected. We thought that we'd try to get it back in shape, so that we could use it, as he is keen on playing. It'd give me a chance to get better as well.

'By the way, we're not doing anything a week on Tuesday, are we? Simon has asked whether I'd like to go to the theatre with him to see the operatic society do *Carousel*. He saw it in London some years ago and wants to see it again.'

'No, I'm sure we've got nothing planned. It's the last week before you go back, isn't it? I'm so glad you've found such a nice friend. You must bring him over to lunch soon, as I'm sure your Father would like to meet him.'

'I'd love to. We could go round the farm. I'm sure Dad would like him.'

Simon rang one evening to say he'd got the tickets, and suggested we meet for a snack meal beforehand at a pub close to the theatre. He was in high spirits and chattered away about the show, and others that he'd seen.

'We must go to the ballet one day, if a touring company comes to the theatre. I love watching the dancing. By the way, do you ever listen to classical music? I do enjoy the less heavy stuff, like Beethoven and Brahms. I've got quite a few tapes at home. I'll put some in the car so that we can listen if we're driving somewhere.'

Once again, I had to plead ignorance, as we had never had any music in the family. Mother had taken me to cathedral concerts on a couple of occasions, and I had loved the majestic choral works, but that was the limit of my musical experience.

'I'd like that.'

The thought came to me as we settled into our seats in the theatre how lucky I was to have met someone with so many interests to guide me into this new world. I was excited by the hum of anticipation as the audience awaited the arrival of the conductor and, when the curtain went up, by the vivid colour and movement on the stage and the vitality of it all. Then suddenly something traumatic happened as the tenor playing Billy Bigelow launched into the song:

'If I loved you, words wouldn't come in an easy way. Round in circles I'd go / Longing to tell you, but afraid and shy, I'd let my golden chances pass me by / Soon you'd leave me…'

I felt a firm pressure of Simon's leg against mine. It was as if an electric current had flowed up into me and the blood seemed to be draining out of my limbs. For a moment I thought I might faint, as a vast ache affected the area of my groin. Then it happened – a sudden involuntary emission from an organ which hadn't even yet fully hardened up.

I shrank back into my seat, withdrawing my leg from all contact with him.

'Are you all right?' he whispered.

'Yes, fine.' But in reality I was full of confusion at what had happened, wondering if a wet patch would show up on my trousers at the interval.

As I regained my composure and concentrated once more on the stage, I thought to myself: *So this is it, the moment of decision. Should I commit myself to him, or stick to my religious principles?* There was really only one answer. I moved my leg back against his, and so we sat happily until the interval.

'Enjoying it?' he said.

'Enormously, but I'll have to pay a visit to the gents.'

'OK, but would you like a drink?'

'Yes, a soft one, I think.'

'I'll see you in the bar, then.'

Fortunately there was an empty cubicle where I could clean up, and nothing had come through my pants. He was waiting in the bar with a welcoming smile as our eyes met. Nothing was said then, but we both knew that a milestone had been passed in our relationship and nothing would ever be quite the same again.

The second act passed in a glow of contentment, and the pressure increased as the tenor sang, 'You'll never walk alone…'

'So how did you like your first visit to a real theatre?' asked Simon after the show.

'I loved the music and the colour and the vitality of it all. I shed a tear when Billy was killed, as it all seemed so realistic. Do you think that there might be an afterlife of some kind, in which our spirits can return to be with those we loved on Earth? The Bible talks about resurrection, but says nothing about coming back to Earth, and I don't like the idea of living in marble halls.'

'None of us will ever know till we get there. I do feel that relationships on Earth would be rather pointless if they just finished with death. Perhaps the spirit can move on to exist on another plane and be close to a loved one, until they are united again. What might happen then, goodness knows. Perhaps they both go pop, and start again.' By this time we had reached the cars.

'You don't have to rush back, do you? Let's sit in my car for a few minutes.'

'I mustn't stay too long, or Mother will start worrying, but it'd be nice to talk for a bit.' We sat together in the car with knees touching over the gear change.

'When you first touched me,' I said, 'and I drew back in my seat, an alarming thing happened. I felt a kind of spasm running up into my groin and thought I was going to pass out. Then there was a kind of ache there, and before I knew it, I had shot a load into my pants, which is why I had to go to clean up in the interval.'

'I guessed something was wrong, but had a dreadful feeling that I had gone too far, and that you were repelled by the contact. You can imagine the relief when you came back to me.'

'Of course I wasn't repelled, for I knew for certain then that you felt deeply for me. I still have this feeling that somehow it is morally wrong, but I don't care, as I'm sure now that I do love you whatever the consequences.'

'I love you, too, and think that I have done since that first night when our eyes met in the bar. I felt then that we would be destined to come together sometime. But I could see that you were probably very innocent, and I heard that you were rather religious. So I knew that I must take it slowly in getting to know you better.'

'So I suppose this means that I have to accept that I'm definitely queer, then?'

'Yes, I think it does. If you are not attracted to girls sexually, and you've fallen for me, I guess you're unlikely to change.'

'What about you? How long have you known?'

'Oh, a long time. I was seduced by an older man when I was sixteen, though it wasn't entirely his fault as I rather egged him on. Then I had a couple of affairs at school, neither of which meant anything as we were really just messing around with sex. After that, I had three casual experiences when I was working on the farm in Cornwall, which left me quite cold, and ashamed of myself, as it all seemed so sordid. I've done nothing since I've been in college, having decided to wait till I found the right person. That's my sordid past, and if you don't like it you'd better jump in your car and go home.'

'I don't care about your past. It's the present that matters. I'm quite glad about it, as it means that I'm important to you, and it's not just a casual fling.'

'Mark, you can be sure that this is different to anything that I've known before. I have never, ever, felt for anyone in the way I feel for you. Those earlier fumblings were just getting to know the ropes – a preparation for meeting you. I've felt from the start that I just wanted to know you and to be with you, and the sexual element hasn't come into it, though I admit I'd love to have you in my arms.'

'Me, too,' I said.

With that, he leant over, put his arm around my shoulder, drew me towards him and kissed me on the lips. I experienced none of the revulsion I had felt with Barbara on the sofa, but just a feeling of great happiness and warmth.

'You must get home,' he said, 'as you've further to go than I have, and your mother will start wondering what's happened to you. Let's not hurry this. I'll see you in two days' time back in college. I don't think I'll go home at the weekend. What about you?'

'No, I shan't go back either. Let's spend some time together, shall we?'

'Yes, now drive carefully. There are two of us now, don't forget.'

Mother was waiting up for me when I got in.

'Did you enjoy the evening, dear?' What was the show like?'

'Quite marvellous, Mother. I enjoyed every minute of it, even more than I expected. I'm sorry to be so late, but we had a cup of coffee afterwards and stayed talking over it.' We kissed goodnight, and suddenly I was panic-stricken. What on earth would she think if she knew that, little more than an hour before, my lips had kissed those of a man I was in love with? She must never be allowed to find out, or it might break her heart. I felt as if I were betraying her. What would Dad think if he knew? He might take it better, but they would be saddened that there would be no wife for me or grandchildren for them.

I didn't see Simon the first day back in college, but ran into him at lunch next day.

'What about a drink this evening?' he asked. 'I'll be in the bar at eight o'clock, if that's all right.'

'Fine, I'll be there then.' As we finished our first beer, he said: 'We don't want to stay here all the evening, do we. Shall we go up to my room?'

As we got there, I noticed that he carefully locked the door. So this is it, I thought. This is how one loses one's virginity in the 'queer' world. I'm quite ready.

No word was spoken as he moved towards me, or when we were in each other's arms. Just a huge sigh of relief from me to feel his body close to mine at last. We stayed like it for some moments, lost in the fulfilment of dreams.

Slowly I started to take off his shirt, as he pulled me down on to the bed where we undressed each other until, naked, I could feel the warmth and tenderness of his body against mine.

'Oh, God, Simon, I do love you. I wish we could be like this for ever.'

'I love you, too, I've never felt such happiness before.' Then as our hands reached down to the ultimate parts of our bodies, I suddenly started to tremble uncontrollably, and lay there shaking like a leaf.

'What's the matter? You're shaking all over. Are you all right?'

'I'll be all right in a moment. It's just the excitement of being in your arms at last that's taken me over. It's proved too much.' At that I relaxed and the trembling ceased.

I had never seen him naked before, and had expected him to be very well endowed. To my relief he was not much bigger than I was myself. I had feared that my somewhat modest equipment might be inadequate to give him full satisfaction. Thankfully, too, he was uncut and flexible so that we felt compatible. He was wonderfully tender as he explored every part of my body, as I did his. And so we lay, reaching a climax, which came to me first, but to him soon after.

Then, relaxed in each other's arms, I said: 'Was I all right? You see, never having done this before, I didn't know what to expect, or what you might like from me.'

'You were quite perfect, Mark. I'm sure now that we are really made for each other. I've come to realise that there are two aspects of a truly loving relationship: the purely physical one of sexual satisfaction, which is a bodily function. Then there is the spiritual side – the feeling of deep affection and trust for someone who feels as you do, and the desire to care for and to protect them and to share every aspect of life with them. If one of these is missing, the union will not last. I know now that for me we have both.'

'I feel the same. I have no doubts either. I did worry that you might want to go into me, but I didn't like the idea. It seems unnatural and nasty somehow.'

'Don't worry about that. I let someone do it to me once, and it hurt, and I felt humiliated. Anyhow, it's so unhygienic. To me, it's just crude sex. I suppose if you're a very effeminate type, you might want to be dominated that way by some hairy great male with a beard, but that's not for me. I want mutual love and affection.'

When he said this, I had a great feeling of relief. In my ignorance, I had rather assumed that this was what happened in relationships between men. It was one of the reasons that I was reluctant to admit that I might be homosexual, as it seemed vulgar and to have little to do with real love. Perhaps that was what the Bible thought it was all about – not the sort of love that I felt for Simon. That was so tender that surely it could not be wrong in the eyes of God?

'Are you doing anything tomorrow?'

'No, nothing special. Have you got something in mind?'

'Well, you did say that we might try to get your tennis court back into shape so that we could play on it this summer. If it was a nice day, I wondered if we might go and put a mower over it.'

'That's an excellent idea. I'll ring Father to see if the mower has been serviced. We'd better go after lunch, as Mother may not have food in the house, or they might be out.'

At breakfast next day he said that the mower was ready and they'd expect us after lunch. We had to go over the court twice, and it was very brown and soft, so we gave it a good dose of Jack's garden fertiliser and hoped for the best. That evening we went to bed together again, and it was almost better than the first time as there were no inhibitions now.

When I was at home the next weekend, Mother said, 'Why not bring your friend over to lunch next Sunday, and then you and Dad can show him the farm in the afternoon?'

'I'll ask him, and let you know during the week. I'd certainly like you to meet him.'

Simon was good at talking, so lunch went well, with Dad questioning him about the farm he had worked on in Cornwall, and Mother about the garden at home. Going round the farm later, Simon was firing questions at Dad about the herd, and his management of the pasture, and the crops, and I could see that Dad was impressed and probing him to see if he could pick up any points that might be useful. He was always doing that with visitors.

'I did like your parents,' Simon said that night back at college. 'Your old man is very clued up, isn't he? And I thought that your mother was sweet. I think you're more like her than your father. You've got her type of face and eyes.'

During the week, Simon said that his mother had rung up to say that the court needed cutting. Would I like to go over on Saturday and stay the night so that we could set up the netting and have time for a game if it was fit for play?

Of course I would. So the next Saturday afternoon we got down to work, cutting the grass, repairing the stop netting in places and put the net posts in their slots. By then it was too late to play, so we hoped for a fine day to come. That night, Simon crept into my room to tuck me up with a kiss, but that was all.

He proved to be a rather better player than I was, especially with his serve, but I took one or two games off him, and it was great fun. That was the first of several happy afternoons, during which we both steadily improved – as did the court. Cynthia and Jack were so welcoming that it was not long before I felt one of the family. If Mother and Dad were a bit jealous at my weekends away they didn't show it, as I think they were happy I was enjoying my life so much. As we got back from the second of the weekends Simon said, 'Have you forgotten that you once said that you were keen on surfing, and would teach me how to do it one day?'

'No, I hadn't forgotten, but there's been so much going on I put it to one side. Would you really like to have a go at it?'

'Yes, of course. What about next weekend?'

'That'd be fine. I don't think that we'll go up to Aunt Emily, as the surf isn't always awfully good there. Last year we went down with her boys to a beach in Cornwall, called Polzeath, which is down the coast from Bude, so it's not too far away. We could drive down on Saturday morning and find a B&B for the night. That'd give us two days for you to get the hang of it. We can hire wetsuits and boards down there, so that's no problem.'

Shortly before we got there I spotted a B&B sign outside a small house set back from the road with a nice garden.

'Stop a moment, Simon, let's book in now, then we needn't worry about it this evening. This place looks nice.' I went in and the door was answered by a grey-haired, motherly-looking lady.

'I've only got a twin bedded room available. I'm afraid. Would that be all right?'

'Perfectly, we're used to sharing a room.' She named a low figure, which I accepted on the spot. 'Would you like an evening meal? I'll be cooking tonight and could easily do one.' I looked at Simon, who nodded his approval. 'I'll see you about seven thirty then.'

We were lucky with the weather as a stiff breeze brought up some good surf. After parking at the beach, we got the boards and wetsuits and changed at the car.

I started him off on waves that had already broken, but he got the hang of it so quickly that we were able to move up to where the waves were just breaking.

'Don't go out too far,' I said. 'There's no point, as you want to get the wave just as it is breaking. Those experts out there think they're clever waiting for the big one. When it does come they often miss it, so they're wasting time treading water. Stick with me to start with, and I'll tell you when to jump.'

After three failures in timing, he got a big one just right on the break, and shot past me whooping with delight at the sheer acceleration as it carried him towards the beach. After that there was no stopping him, and I had difficulty getting him out of the water.

You can't stay in the sea all day, so we changed back and bought a pasty for our lunch. Then we walked the cliff path towards Pentire Head, where we lay together on the warm, scented turf looking down the rocky coastline to Trevose lighthouse and the estuary towards Padstow and the Rock sand hills with the distant purple moors behind. Another idyllic memory to be locked away in the nostalgia of first love.

In the evening we bathed again. We had intended to go out for a drink later, but by the time we had finished the large spread provided by Mrs Trewin, and we had helped with the washing-up, it was too late. We discovered that her husband had owned a dairy farm in the neighbourhood, which he had sold at a good price, and they had retired on the proceeds. So the talk was all on farming when they heard we were agricultural students, and we chattered until bedtime.

Actually we had never shared a room before and I was embarrassed. Ever since I was a small boy, I had knelt down to say prayers before bed, as Mother had taught me. Would Simon, who was not religious in any way, think me a complete wimp if I did so now?

'What's the matter?' he asked from his bed as I wandered round thinking what to do.

'Would you think me a sissy if I said my prayers?'

'Of course not. I'd think all the more of you if you did, as long as you don't ask me to get down with you. I wasn't brought up that way, I'm afraid.'

'OK, I'll say a special one for you then.' And I did. After that I bent over and kissed him, and within two minutes his regular breathing told me that he was asleep. I lay there a while relishing the happiness of being there beside him.

Next morning, Mrs Trewin flatly refused to let us pay for the meal as she said that she and her husband had so enjoyed the evening, she couldn't possibly ask us to pay.

'Do come again any time you're here for surfing. We'd love to see you.'

We went into the sea three times next day. On the drive back, he put his hand on my knee. 'Thanks for a fabulous weekend, I've never enjoyed one more. We must do it again.' I thought how rewarding it was that, for once, I should be introducing him to a new experience rather than the other way round.

The next few weeks flew by. Shortly before exams, on the way back from a day trip surfing at Polzeath, he turned to me.

'What are you doing in the holidays?

'I shall have to be at home to help Dad with the harvest in August and early September, and I might go up to Aunt Emily for a few days, but otherwise I've nothing planned. Have you got something we might do together?'

'Well, yes. Five years ago we all went to Switzerland and I enjoyed it so much that I've always wanted to go back, but I've never had anyone to go with. Would you like to go?'

'Isn't Switzerland very expensive? Do you think we could afford it?'

'It needn't be if we took the car and a tent. All these countries have very good campsites nowadays. We could put a lot of food in the boot, so the only cost would be getting there on the boat and petrol and small site fees. That wouldn't cost much when divided by two.'

'It's a brilliant idea, and I'd love to go, as I've hardly been out of Devon before. I could do three weeks early in July after the end of term. Would that be OK for you?'

'Perfectly. I've nothing planned for then.'

Cynthia was delighted when she heard of the plans, as were my parents. She went into Exeter and bought a small tent, two sleeping bags and a groundsheet. To this she added a small gas stove and a kettle. She fished out an old wicker hamper from the attic which she intended to stock up with tins of food. The more I saw of her the fonder of her I became, which made Simon happy.

Exams came and went with results out shortly before we left. Simon had done well enough to come back for the following year for the advanced course, as had James and Andrew, and I had come second in my year. So we could go off assured of returning to college for the next year.

On 2 July we set off, the car loaded down with camping gear and food to last a month. We had decided to go in his car, and to share the driving, so I had done a few runs to get used to it before driving on the wrong side of the road. Simon had also brought along tapes of classical music to introduce me to his favourites.

We spent the first night in a B&B in Dover, so as to be able to get an early boat and a full day's drive through France, which Simon said would be pretty dull. He had decided to make for Strasbourg and the Black Forest. The drive was rather tedious, so he put on the tapes, starting with Beethoven's *Emperor* concerto, which he thought would be a good appetiser, as indeed it was. His main favourites were Beethoven, Brahms and Tchaikovsky, and by the time we had reached Strasbourg on the second night, we had been through most of his tapes, and I was hooked for life, partly, I suppose, because I was sharing his enthusiasm.

We made Baden-Baden on the edge of the Black Forest on the third day.

'Let's stop here a couple of nights,' he said as we booked in at an attractive campsite in woods just outside the town. 'It'll be a change from driving and I do like the look of the place.'

He was right, for the old buildings, beautifully kept gardens and parks around the Casino area, and the classical building housing the thermal baths gave it a kind of Edwardian aura. This was enhanced by the well-dressed ladies sipping their tea outside the Casino listening to the strains of Johann Strauss coming from the nearby bandstand. As Simon said, 'You almost expect German officers in nineteenth-century uniforms to emerge at any moment, it's such a perfect operetta setting.'

Two more days were spent exploring the Black Forest, with its rolling, tree-clad hills and little market towns and lakeside campsites where we experienced the camaraderie and friendliness of camping life.

It was on the road from Basle to Lucerne that I first saw the mountains. 'Stop,' I shouted to him excitedly, and he pulled on to the hard shoulder. 'Just look at that.' Far away to our left, beyond a vista of wooded countryside, towered a massive range of brilliant white peaks framed against the vivid blue of the sky. The sun shining on the snows accentuated the whiteness against the green of the intervening trees. It was a picture that remained etched on the memory for life.

'It's certainly a marvellous view,' he said. 'That's where we're making for.'

In Lucerne we had some difficulty in locating the campsite on the lakeside, which was situated some way out of the city which we explored next day. With its wooden bridges and narrow streets in the old town one felt again transported back in time, except for the presence of hundreds of tourists like ourselves.

'I'd like to stay two nights here and spend tomorrow on a trip round the lake. Do you think we could spare the time?'

'Oh, yes, easily. I'd like to stay here, too.'

Mother had given me a camera before we left – one where you didn't have to fiddle around with exposure adjustments – so on the boat the next day I was continually jumping up and down as new vistas presented themselves.

'You'll use up your films in no time if you go on like this,' Simon said, 'You had better save up some for when we get up into the mountains.' At that I curbed my enthusiasm and sat down to relish the pleasure of sitting there beside him and sharing the day with him. The evening was one to be enjoyed with a good meal in a restaurant crowded with young people like ourselves beside the lake.

'Time to move on,' he said the next day, 'We'll make for Interlaken and you can drive.'

As we came down towards the town, he spotted a campsite sign which took us down to a small site in woods on the edge of the river joining the two lakes, where we booked in. It was as we were walking down the long strip to the town in the afternoon that he spotted a notice of a concert the following evening in the Kursaal.

'Mark, we simply must go. It's got the Bruch Violin Concerto, and Tchaikovsky's Fifth. We can afford to spend two nights here. I'll buy the tickets now.'

'Let's have a day off from driving,' Simon suggested the next day, 'and take the train to Kleine Scheidegg, which lies right under the Eiger and the Jungfrau. We went there last time and it's really spectacular.'

The camera was kept busy as the train wound its way round the bends, every now again presenting stupendous views of the mountains hanging over us. The place itself was a disappointment and swarming with tourists but the surrounding scenery made it with the north face of the Eiger towering above us.

For me it became truly memorable for the photograph I took of him which stands on the desk before me still. A half-length from the waist up, it shows his tousled fair hair and tanned face framed against the backdrop of the snow-clad mountain behind him. At the top is a sliver of deep blue sky above the snow, while the red colour of his favourite jersey accentuates the contrast of the different colours. As so often he is smiling happily.

We were back in time for the concert, and once again I felt the thrill of anticipation as the orchestra tuned up.

'I'm sure you'll like the Bruch,' he whispered as the conductor raised his baton.

He was right. I sat enthralled as the slow movement unfolded with its haunting themes seeming to encapsulate all the love and yearning that I felt for him. The sensuality of the music moved me so much that I had to wipe away a tear that threatened to roll down my cheek. It was almost the same with the Tchaikovsky slow movement, with its undertones of lost love and sadness.

As we walked back to the camp, I took his arm for a moment. 'Thanks for a wonderful experience which I'll never forget whatever happens in the future. I'd never have found music like that if it hadn't been for you.'

'Forget it. You'd probably have found it sooner or later, I expect. I loved it, too.'

We drove up to Grindelwald next day, closely following the railway of the day before. Crowded with tourists, it was obviously a summer as well as a winter sports centre. Counting our money, we decided we could afford the ski lift up high above the town to the top station at First. It was fun sitting beside him on our little seats swinging into space, and once again the camera was busy.

Walking on up the mountain path, we finally found a dry grassy ledge to eat our lunch of ham and rolls. Afterwards we lay together in the sunshine, with the whole majestic panorama of the Wetterhorn, the Munch, the Eiger and the Jungfrau and scores of lesser peaks spread out before us, while ravens, borne up on the draught from the mountain face below, were framed against the deep blue sky. Just he and I together, while all the world stood still around us, and time had no meaning. If there is a heaven, I thought, then this is it.

He must have been thinking the same, for he suddenly said: 'We must make the best of this, Mark. It can't go on for ever, you know. You do realise that, don't you? Next summer, I'll be out looking for a job, and it'll probably be miles away from Devon, and you'll be doing a final year in college or working at home.'

His words struck home, for up until then I had not dared to think of being parted from him. I had vaguely thought that if he got a job, I might get one near him too.

'I've already decided that I shan't go home to work when I finish the course. Dad doesn't really need me. Anyway, I'd like a job where I can be independent and see something of the world that you've shown me exists outside. I'm not ready to bury myself on the farm yet. Perhaps when Dad is older I might come back, but certainly not now.'

'And get married and start a family,' he joked.

'No, I shan't do that. It wouldn't be fair on the girl for one thing – even assuming I could give her what she wanted in bed, which might be doubtful. You see, I know now that it is only a man's body that I want beside me. That feeling would be unlikely to go away, however much I liked her in a platonic way. It would be awful if I were torn between any affection I might have for her or our children, and an aching desire to be with a man. Then supposing she found out – how devastating that would be for her! I could never take the risk of that happening, I'm afraid.'

'That's a pretty unselfish view to take, and you're probably quite right. Basically I feel the same, but I would love to have kids, and I do fear the thought of getting old alone without a partner, if we were separated. People like us tend to retreat into themselves if they have no one to love, and rely on casual sex where there is no love. What would you do, if I were no longer here?'

'Jump into the nearest river, I expect, as I couldn't bear the thought of life without you now.' At that moment, a large cloud which had sprung up from nowhere obscured the sun, and a chill wind blew up from the mountain face and sent a shiver down my back. I hoped it was not an omen.

'Time to be moving,' he said. 'Let's stop for a cup of tea at that café we passed on the way up.' We warmed up on the now sunlit terrace of the café, but some of the sparkle had gone out of the day as I pondered what we had said. Sooner or later I would have to face up to being parted from him. But we had another nine months together, so why worry now? Live for today and to hell with tomorrow!

We tackled the Susten Pass with its hairpin bends the next day to move up the valley to Andermatt. At the top of the pass, he said: 'You can take over the driving now, so that I can have a look at the scenery.' All went well, until on the outside of a bend, a coach came up towards us. I moved over to the verge, to see a sheer drop of hundreds of feet on to rocks below and stalled the engine, leaving the coach driver to get past if he could.

'Can you cope, or would you like me to take over?'

'No, I'm OK now, it was just seeing that sheer drop about a yard away that panicked me for a moment. I've no head for heights it seems.' I drove on, slowly regaining confidence.

Andermatt was a disappointment. Dominated by an army barracks, it was obviously dead in the summer, and we were glad of warm sleeping bags in the chilly night air. Simon looked at his map.

'You know, we're not far from Italy here. It's only over the St Gotthard Pass, and then down a long valley, and we come out near the Italian lakes. It's either that or we drive east to St Moritz. Which would you like?'

'If you think we've got the time, I think it'd be fun to be able to say when we get home that we've been to Italy. But it's up to you, as you're doing most of the driving.'

'We'll go down to Italy then. I'd like to see the lakes.'

I had an idea that he might have rather underestimated the distances, which can look quite short on a map, but which in the mountains are much longer because of all the hairpin bends. But we still had plenty of time, anyhow.

The St Gotthard Pass was cold and bleak, as we looked down the valley winding its way to Italy, and the route was not made easy by massive roadworks for a future projected tunnel through the Alps. So we only reached Lugano that day, which we were surprised to find was still in Switzerland in spite of its Italian name. But with its beautiful lake, its palm trees and its scented shrubs, it didn't much matter what country it was in. But it all seemed rather too luxurious, epitomising Swiss prosperity, so we decided to move on the next day.

'We've got two choices,' he said, looking at the map. 'Either we go to the west to Lake Maggiore, or to the east to Lake Como. Maggiore looks rather large on the map, but Como's quite narrow, and looks more intimate. What do you think?'

'I read once that Como's very beautiful. Let's go there, shall we?'

'OK. Como it is then.'

The road was surprisingly narrow at first, clinging to a mountainside; but then, through a tunnel, we were suddenly in Italy. The long slender cypress trees, the yellow houses with red-tiled roofs looking as if they could do with a coat of paint, so different from those we had just left, told us immediately where we were.

The first sight of Lake Como was breathtaking as we turned the corner at the top of the hill leading down to Menaggio – a very deep blue with almost a hint of grey in it. In the distance we could see Bellagio, lying on its peninsula cutting the lake in two. Beyond were wooded hills and mountains where traces of winter snow still lingered. Fresh vistas unfolded as we negotiated the hairpin bends into the town. The campsite was in woods beside the lake, a perfect setting.

We ate our lunch on a seat beside the lake under oleander trees in full bloom, watching ferries busily traversing back and forth across the water, and small white yachts gathering for a race.

'We must stay here for a couple of nights at least,' Simon said, 'it's quite heavenly. We'll take a trip down the lake tomorrow, and have a look at Como, shall we?'

'I'd love to stay as long as we can spare the time. There must be a lot to explore.'

That afternoon we took the ferry to Bellagio, with its steep, stepped shopping alleys leading up to a higher road, where cars seemed almost to scrape the side of the shops and pedestrians took their lives in their hands. We lazed over a cup of tea under the awning of a small hotel watching the world go by. It looked cool and inviting inside.

'One day, when we're rich, we'll come back and stay in there for a few days,' he said. 'I do like the look of it.'

'I'd love to,' I said – but I was not to know that it would be at least another twenty years before I came back, and then, sadly, it would not be with Simon. Perhaps it is as well we cannot see into the future.

I stood him a good meal that evening at a restaurant beside the lake in Menaggio, and then we lay together in our little tent.

A bright sun brought out the clear blueness of the water, as we sat together on the top deck of the ferry as it zigzagged from one little town to another across the lake to Como next day. Imposing villas, with well-kept lawns, cypress trees and terracotta pots filled with geraniums, alternated with small houses clinging to the water's edge on rocky outcrops. One could see now why it was that, over the centuries from Pliny onwards, Lake Como had become a haven for composers, writers, artists, politicians and in modern times even pop stars. The sense of peace and security was everywhere.

That was the southern limit of our travels for, next day, we headed back north to Switzerland and home. As we took a last look at the lake, he said: 'We simply must come back here. Perhaps not next year, when I think I'd like to go to Venice and the Dolomites, but the year after, if you're still with me, love.'

'Of course I will be. I'm sure you know that.'

Landing at Dover seemed to close a chapter in my life, as if our holiday had been some kind of dream from which one was aroused by the familiar feel of England. But unlike a real dream, which fades with the day, this one would remain a nostalgic memory, especially in view of what lay ahead.

'Thanks so much for everything,' I said as he dropped me at home. 'It's been quite fabulous and unforgettable.'

'Don't thank me; it's you that made it possible by coming into my life to share it. That's the ultimate reward – to share life with someone you love.'

'Would you like to come in, Simon?' Mother said. 'I do hope you had a good time.'

'Absolutely marvellous,' he said. 'The car went like a bomb, and I only had one bad moment when Mark nearly hit a coach on a hairpin bend in the Alps. I don't think I'll stay, thanks, as they will be expecting me at home, and I ought to get back. I'll ring up soon to see if you might have time for a game of tennis.'

'I'd love one,' I replied, 'if we are not too busy with harvest.' Then he was gone, and suddenly I felt completely alone after three weeks with him continuously by my side.

Harvest had just started and Dad seemed pleased with the new combine harvester he had recently bought second-hand. That evening they wanted a full account of our travels, and I told Mother that I had got through seven films with the camera she had given me. When they were developed they could see all the interesting places we had been to.

'I rather envy you,' Dad said. 'Perhaps your mother and I will take a holiday one year and you can look after the farm for us.'

'I think I'd rather like that,' said Mother, 'as we've never had a proper one since our honeymoon in Wales. You could tell us where to go, Mark.' It was clear that I had got her thinking of breaking out of her routine.

Harvest went well for a time, and on slack days I got in two games of tennis and a day trip for surfing. Then suddenly Vic, the head tractor driver who drove the combine harvester, went down with appendicitis at a critical time.

'I don't know whether to suggest this,' Dad said, 'but do you think Simon might like to come over and stand in for Vic? He seems very competent, and might like the experience. He could have the spare room opposite Mark's, couldn't he, dear?'

'Yes, that'd be quite all right,' Mother replied. 'Just let me know, and I'll make up the bed.'

'I'll ring him straight away,' I said. He was delighted and came over that afternoon, as he was always rather bored at home in the holidays.

It was wonderful having him around as one of the family, but frustrating that we never had an opportunity to get together. I would creep into his bedroom to say goodnight, but we had an unspoken understanding not to have sex if our parents were in the house. It didn't seem right somehow. We did have one afternoon, when Mother was with Caroline and Dad at a meeting, and harvest was held up by rain. After lunch we took to my bed and spent the afternoon in each other's arms.

The summer passed too quickly with him staying for a month until Vic was fit for work. That left two weeks, and we spent much of the time together, including a few days up at Aunt Emily's, which he enjoyed.

Chapter Three

It was good getting back to college after the long break, and in no time we were back to the old routine, with the four of us discussing how to put the world to rights.

After lunch one day at the end of October, Simon said: 'Andrew's asked me if I would drive him up to Holsworthy tonight for a Young Farmers Public Speaking. You wouldn't like to come as well, would you?'

'I don't think so, thanks. I've an essay to finish for Richard. I can't spare the time, I'm afraid. Have a good evening.'

Mother had given me a small portable radio the year before, and I liked to listen to the local news as I was shaving and dressing. I wasn't paying particular attention next morning until I heard the announcer say, 'The police are investigating a serious car accident near Holsworthy last night. It appears that a car was forced off the road on a bend. The driver was certified dead at the scene of the accident, and his passenger was airlifted to the Devon and Exeter Hospital where he is in intensive care.'

A terrible chill ran through me. Holsworthy and two people in a car. Surely it couldn't have been Simon and Andrew, could it? Don't be silly, there were probably masses of cars with two people in them in the area last night. But I still had a feeling of foreboding.

Dressing as fast as I could, I went round to Simon's room in the next block. I hammered on the locked door, but there was no reply. Now seriously alarmed, I rushed up the stairs to Andrew's room. His door was locked, too, and there was no reply. In a panic, I hammered on Simon's again. Something must have happened if neither of them were there. The only way to check would be to ring Cynthia, even if she did think I was making a mountain out of a molehill.

The telephone was in the main college building outside the dining hall. Her line was engaged. I waited five minutes; still engaged.

'What's up, Mark? You look like a ghost.' It was James, who had come down to breakfast. I told him of the news item, and that neither Simon nor Andrew were there.

'I expect the car broke down, and they're stranded or something. Anyhow, come in with me and get some food into you, and then you can try Cynthia again.'

I bolted some breakfast as quickly as I could, and tried the phone again.

This time it rang, but it was a long time before Jack's voice answered. It didn't seem like him at all, too harsh and stressed.

'Hello, who's that?'

'It's Mark. I'm sorry to bother you, but I'm very worried about Simon. He went up to Holsworthy with Andrew last night and neither of them are in their rooms, and I heard on the local news about an accident there last night. It wasn't them, was it?'

'Mark, I'm desperately sorry. Yes, it was them. Simon is dead, and Andrew is seriously injured and is in intensive care. Cynthia is distraught and is lying down. Could you ring tomorrow evening, when we'll know more? Try not to take it too hard, Mark.'

James was waiting for me, but he could tell by my face that the worst had happened.

'Simon's dead, and Andrew is seriously injured. I must ring Mother to tell them at home, and then I'll go to my room, as I think that I'd like to be alone. Could you tell the college, in case they haven't heard, do you think? I couldn't face it.'

'Of course. Oh God, it must be a ghastly shock for you. It's bad enough for us. For you it must seem unbearable. I'll pop in later to see if you're all right.'

I got through to Mother straight away.

'Mother, I've some dreadful news. Simon is dead. He was killed in a car crash last night.' As I said this, my throat swelled up and I just couldn't say another word.

'Oh, my dear, how awful for you. How on earth did it happen? He was such a careful driver, you said. Would you like to come home for a day or two? You might find it easier to get over the shock here with us, and I'm sure the college wouldn't mind you missing a few classes.'

'I think I'd rather stay here, thanks. It'll be terrible wherever I am, but there will be more to think about here, instead of brooding at home.'

'You may be right, dear, but do come home if you'd like to.'

I went up to my room and locked the door, and sat down at the desk in a state of shock and frozen disbelief. Surely it must be some nightmare from which I would awake? But all the time I knew it was no dream, for the words 'Simon's dead' kept recurring in my brain. Surely he couldn't be, with all his love of life, his tenderness and thoughtfulness for others? How could that be extinguished at a moment's notice by some crazy driver, who probably contributed nothing to the world? How could a loving God allow this to happen to one so good and kind?

Oh, God, why did you do this to him when he was so happy, and we had so much to live for? You can't be loving at all, but an Old Testament God raining down vengeance on harmless people, and tolerating all the misery and suffering in the world. All these years I've worshipped you, I must have been conned by simple people who have never stopped to question their beliefs. Those rules in the Old Testament must have been dreamt up by priests and leaders to maintain discipline, who invented a vengeful God to back them up. No loving God could ever condone stoning to death and mutilation for adultery and homosexuality.

But if that was so, how can one account for Jesus, and the New Testament? Perhaps he was just a visionary, swallowing previous teaching whole, and adding to it to make it more applicable to his time. Wasn't he, too, abandoned in the end, crying in agony from the cross, 'My God, My God, Why hast thou forsaken me?' Perhaps he had been conned as well.

Another thought came to me. Perhaps if there was a loving but strict God, Simon's death and my misery were just a punishment for our unnatural love. After all, He had punished Sodom and Gomorrah with death. Surely that was different, for then He was punishing carnal lust, and not the kind of deep love that we had for each other. That should never have been punished by death.

As I sat staring into space, I thought: What is the point of going on into bleak years of loneliness, with no hope of ever meeting another Simon? Why not end it now, and be with him still? It would be quite easy – just go out surf bathing and not come back. There would no stigma of suicide, but it would be considered another tragic accident.

Then I recalled reading *Hamlet* for my A levels. He too had thought of suicide but had abandoned it from fear of what might come after. 'For in that sleep of death what dreams may come when we have shuffled off this mortal coil, must give us pause.'

It gave me pause, for then I thought of Mother and of Dad. What awful grief they would feel at the loss of their only son. I thought of Simon, too, on some different plane in the spirit world. He would not want that either. I would somehow have to face life without him, as I had done before we met.

I looked at his photo on my desk, and suddenly the floodgates burst. With head down, I broke into uncontrollable sobbing at the thought that I would see him no more. My whole body seemed racked in pain as the tears streamed down until I could cry no more as the tears ran dry.

This just won't do, I thought. Simon wouldn't want me to show such grief. I must toughen up somehow to face the world. At that I caught sight of the unfinished essay on the desk and realised that if it had not been for that I might now be dead, too, as that was the main reason I'd not gone with them. It was then that I realised that I wanted to be alive.

There was a knock on the door. It was James. 'I've come to take you down to lunch. It'll be difficult for you, but you'll have to face it sometime, so the sooner the better.'

As I was tidying myself up, he said: 'I do know what this means to you, because Andrew and I knew all about your relationship. Simon told me about his feelings towards men in our first year, so when we saw how close you were it was not difficult to put two and two together. It was just great to see you both so happy, as we were very fond of him.'

When he said this, I felt a huge relief that I wouldn't have to pretend any more, and also that they accepted my sexuality without question. It meant that we could remain close friends in the future.

'What about you and Andrew then? Is there anything between you?'

'Good heavens, no,' he laughed. 'We're as hetero as can be. We don't bother about girls. There are far more important things to think about. When we've finished here and got jobs, we'll probably look around and get married, but that can wait for now.'

Lunch was difficult, as I had to pretend that Simon's death was not too important to me. Halfway through, the Principal came in and called for silence.

'I expect that most of you know already that Simon Trevelyan was tragically killed in a car crash last night and that Andrew Mason is in a critical condition. I am sure that all who knew Simon well will miss him greatly, for with his humour and happy outlook on life he made a big contribution to the college, especially on the rugby field. I am sure that you would like me to express our condolences to his parents and to tell them how much we shall miss him. I will put up a notice as soon as we have details of the funeral arrangements, as I expect some of you will wish to go.'

I had survived that ordeal. I felt grateful to James for his support, and somehow got through the rest of the day. It was rather ironic that at bedtime I found myself kneeling to say my prayers as usual, in view of the morning's questioning of the existence of God. Whether He was there or not, I still felt the need to pray that Simon was at peace, and that somehow we might always be together. But once in bed, I had a vision of him lying cold in some mortuary instead of lying beside me, and cried bitterly again.

Next morning there were two letters, and a note. The note was from Richard Sykes asking me to see him at twelve o'clock. The letters were from Mother, Father and Cynthia.

Mark dear,

We were terribly shocked to hear about Simon this morning, and we do both want you to know that we are here for you if you need us. You must be quite devastated at losing him in such a dreadful way, and the shock must be very difficult to bear. We both liked him so much when he was here in the summer, as he was always so happy and full of fun.

The only consolation is that he is now at rest in the care of the Lord, and that you will have happy memories always with you. You are bound to miss him so much at first, but time does heal wounds, even if it does not happen straight away. Before long other things will come into your life to fill the gap that he has left. Try not to grieve too much and remember that God is always there for those who need Him. I do hope that you will be able to get back on Saturday.

Ever, your loving Mother.

Dear Mark,

I am thinking of you and how much you must be missing Simon. We liked him so much and were very happy over your friendship with him. Your Mother and I hope to be able to get to the funeral. Let us know at the weekend whether you would like to come with us.

Much love, Dad.

My dear Mark,

I just don't know what to say, except that we do both feel for you, as you were such wonderful friends. It must be simply awful for you. We are both finding it dreadfully difficult to bear, but some-how we have to carry on. We will hope to see you at the church on Tuesday, but if you thought that it might be too much for you, we'd quite understand.

With all our love, Cynthia.

'Come in, Mark,' Richard Sykes said later that morning. 'I just wanted a word with you about Simon. I know what close friends you had become, and the shock of his death must have knocked you sideways. I know from when my father died from a coronary what a sudden death can mean to you. It can be really traumatic. If you'd like a few days off that would be quite all right with the college. I'm not sure whether you know that we have a trained counsellor on the staff. I'm sure you'd find her very understanding if you felt the need to talk about it. I know that grief is a very private thing but it can sometimes help to be able to talk.'

'Thanks so much, Richard, it's kind of you to think about me. We became close friends during our holiday together, and his death is a ghastly shock – especially as if I'd not had your essay to finish, I might now be dead, too, as he'd asked me to go with them. Yesterday for a brief moment I even thought of joining him. But I'm better now, and think that I can probably cope on my own. If things did get bad, though, I might well go to see if Betty could help. It really is kind of you to think of me. I do appreciate it.'

I rang Cynthia that evening to thank her for finding time to write in the middle of her own personal grief.

'It was so good of you to write when you must have so much to do. His death must be awful for you, as you were so wonderfully close to each other. I'll certainly be there on Tuesday. Mother and Dad want to come as well, as they'd got so fond of him last summer. I don't think that I could bear to go to the crematorium, though, as I might break down and that would be embarrassing. Do you think that it might be possible for me to see him to say goodbye? I'd find it traumatic, but I do want to see him one last time.'

'Jack and I were talking to the undertaker this afternoon, and have arranged to go in to see him at eleven o'clock on Saturday morning. Would you like to come with us, or would you rather be alone?'

'To be honest, I'd rather go alone, as I may shed a few tears. I've just heard that Andrew is better, so I thought that I'd take James in to see him afterwards.'

'I quite understand. I'll tell them that you'll be in to see him at eleven thirty, shall I? He'll be in the chapel of rest, and there'll be someone to show you in. By the way we'll be coming up shortly to collect his things, but I'll give a ring beforehand, to see if there is anything there that you'd like to have. I know that he'd want that.'

'I'll think about it and let you know.'

The news of Andrew was better next day, so I asked James if he'd like to go to see him after I had been to the undertaker. To my relief he said he'd rather not go in with me. He'd prefer to remember Simon as he was in life, laughing.

'You can stay as long as you like,' the young man said as he showed me in. 'I'll be about to show you out.'

The chapel was furnished in bright colours, with none of the gloom that I had expected. His coffin was lying just in front of the altar. If his face had been damaged in the accident, the morticians had done a marvellous job, for he was lying there peacefully asleep, looking just as he had done in his sleeping bag on our holiday, when I would awake first and lean over to kiss him.

'Thank God, you're sleeping peacefully, my love. Thank you for everything. We'll be together always, and I'll never forget you.' I bent down to kiss him one last time. His lips were cold on mine, but I felt that he knew that I was there with him. A few tears rolled down, but I did not cry. He would not have wanted that. I turned as I went out for one last look, before leaving him alone for ever.

James was quiet as we drove to the hospital, sensing that I wouldn't want to talk. We found Andrew looking surprisingly well, with his broken leg sticking out in its plaster. He also had three broken ribs, and had been unconscious for six hours after the accident, but fortunately his skull had not been fractured.

All he could remember was coming up to a bend, and headlights moving towards them very fast. On the bend the other car appeared to be heading straight into them on the wrong side of the road. He just remembered Simon frantically swinging over to miss it, but that was all. In fact, what had happened was that the front wheel caught the edge of a drainage channel cut into the bank, which threw it over in a somersault where it hit a tree. Simon was killed instantly. Luckily a car was behind them and the driver pulled Andrew out, and summoned the emergency services. The other car drove on without stopping.

'I feel terrible about it. I should never have asked Simon to drive me up there, as it wasn't really important. They could have got on without me. I'll never forgive myself for causing his death. You must feel it terribly, Mark, as you were so close to him.'

'Yes, it has been awful, but James has been marvellously supportive. He's told me that you both knew about us, and it's a great relief not to have to pretend any longer, and that I can still rely on your friendship. But look, Andrew, you simply must not blame yourself. It wasn't your fault at all, but just dreadful bad luck that some lout of a driver should have been on the road at that moment. There is no rhyme or reason why good people in the world are taken away and useless ones allowed to survive, but that is how it seems to be. I'm beginning to doubt if there really is a benevolent God controlling things. Promise me that you won't blame yourself, please.'

'Mark's perfectly right, Andrew,' said James. 'You've absolutely nothing to blame yourself for, so let's hear no more about that. Anyhow, are you still in much pain?'

'It's not too bad now, and they give me painkillers if I need them. The worst thing is the ribs, which are still terribly sore, and I can't laugh without terrible pain – not that there's much to laugh about, is there?' At that he tried to laugh, and gave a cry of pain instead.

James continued: 'I've told Mark that he mustn't shut himself away and mope, and that he must come to us if he feels too much down. Simon is gone, and grieving will not bring him back. But now he's not here, we shan't have his car, shall we, so we'll be counting on Mark to get us around.' They laughed at that, except that it was a cry of pain from Andrew.

'Of course, you've only got to let me know if you want it,' I said. 'Anyhow, I hope we can renew our evenings out as soon as Andrew's fit. How long are you likely to be in?'

'They say I should be out in about ten days, though I may be hobbling round on crutches to start with.'

As we left we promised to come in again to see him. I dropped James at the college, and went home for the night, happy at the thought that I need not worry about my sexuality as far as they were concerned.

Taking Mother to church on Sunday morning was not a good experience. The sermon given by a plump, smug priest was all about the love of God, and His forgiving nature, and how lucky we all were to be able to enjoy it. He gave the impression that he had a private line through to the Almighty. It was not at all what I wanted to hear in my rebellious mood, thinking, what does this silly old man know about love? Has he ever had someone he loved snatched away at a moment's notice? Where does the love of God come in there? The more I thought about religion, the more artificial it all seemed.

Then I was on my knees for prayers, which did seem to have

some relevance if there really was an omnipotent God looking down on us, and I prayed for Simon to be at peace. That night, walking past the door of what had been his room, I was enveloped once again in self-pity.

I drove James and two rugby friends to the funeral, leaving Mother and Dad to come under their own steam, though I sat with them in church. Lots of his friends came, and with Jack and Cynthia's friends the church was full. I made up my mind to try to switch off entirely, though it was not possible, of course, when the coffin was brought in.

But as the service proceeded, I had a feeling that Simon was there with us, especially during the address by the Principal. He went up in my estimation by the way he dealt with Simon's life and his contribution to the college. At one stage, I could hear Simon saying, 'Come off it, Prin, you can't be talking about me. I'm nothing like that, and never did much for the college, apart from being myself.' The feeling that he was actually there and not in the coffin was very strong, and I became convinced that life does not end with death.

As we went out I introduced Mother and Dad to Cynthia and Jack.

'We must have a word later on, if you can stay,' Cynthia said to Mother.

'We'll certainly stay on,' Mother said, 'and I would love to have a talk.'

While the family went to the crematorium, we made our way to the village hall for the refreshments.

'I thought it was a lovely service, didn't you?' James said, 'especially the Prin's address. I always thought he was rather a stuffy old boy, but he came up trumps today.'

'Yes, he was good. While he was talking Simon seemed to come through to me saying that it was all a load of rubbish. He couldn't believe it was him he was talking about – and he was laughing as usual. It was an odd feeling.'

So that was it, and I had got through it somehow without losing my composure. I felt he would have been proud of me for that. Cynthia and Mother seemed to get on very well, as did Dad and Jack, and the mothers arranged to have lunch together.

Over the last few weeks of term, I found that I was thinking less of him in the daytime, though he was always in my thoughts at night. Two weeks after the funeral, Cynthia asked me to come over to lunch on the following Sunday.

She was looking strained after the tension of the previous weeks, and over the meal his name was hardly mentioned. When we had finished, Jack said: 'I'll leave you two together, as I've a lot of tidying up to do in the garden.'

'I asked you over, Mark dear, to tell you that we do understand the grief that you must be suffering. You see, we did know about your relationship with him. He told us about his private life when he was eighteen, though I had suspected it before that. One of my brothers is homosexual, and he was caught in a police trap about ten years ago. He was not sent to prison, but got away with quite a heavy fine. He was not important so it didn't get into the papers. But he lost his job because of it. Fortunately he found another one, and then met his present partner, and they have been very happy together for the past ten years. Simon found out about it, and told us he was the same, and that he was very unlikely to marry.

'It was a shock, of course, but it didn't affect our love for him, in fact it seemed to accentuate it. We were rather worried after he left school as he seemed to be getting in with a bad set, but it seemed fine when he went to college. Then he started talking about a friend called Mark, and asked if he could bring him over to meet us.

'We both took to you immediately, and were delighted that he had found someone with whom he was obviously so happy, as you seemed to be as well. When you got back from holiday, he told me how much in love he was, as we had no secrets. I hoped so much that it would last but it was not to be.'

Several times as she was speaking, I felt tears welling up. As she finished, I put my arms around her, but for a moment couldn't speak because of the lump in my throat.

'You can't imagine what a relief it is to know that you knew all about our relationship and you were not worried about it. It's just wonderful to have it all out in the open so that I won't have to pretend. James and Andrew knew about it as well, which means a lot to me.'

I hugged her closer, and saw that she had tears in her eyes as well.

'You're so brave,' I said. 'You put me to shame. Your loss is so much greater than mine, but all I've been thinking about is myself. It's amazing the way you've taken it.'

'You're bound to go through a long period of grieving, dear, and feel that life is almost impossible without him, but it will pass in time and remain as a golden memory. You're at the start of your life with a career ahead of you. There will never be another actual Simon, but sooner or later you will find someone else to love, though it may take years. You're such a kind and loving person, you will find him. When you do you must bring him over to meet us.'

'Of course I will. What worries me is what Mother might think if she found out, as she is so influenced by what the Bible says.'

'I wouldn't worry, dear. From meeting her, it's obvious that she loves you very much. I'm sure that would override any doubts about the Old Testament.'

Once again I thought that if I did not have a mother already, I'd adopt Cynthia.

'We're coming over on Tuesday afternoon to collect his things. Can you be there?'

'I'll try,' I replied, 'but I've got a field class, and may not be back in time. You did ask if I wanted anything of his. I would like the red jersey that he was so fond of, even if it might be a bit big for me. The other thing would be the tapes of classical music that we took on holiday. He taught me to appreciate good music, you know, and I'd love to have those tapes to remind me of him.'

'Are you sure that's all? I'll put them out for you.'

I got back from the class just as they were finishing, though in a way I regretted it. Seeing his empty room and the stripped bed where we had first come together was almost too much to bear. If they had not been there, I would have broken down again. There only remained the photograph of me which he had taken in Baden-Baden.

'What would you like me to do with it?' she said.

'I don't really want it. Would you like to take it?'

'I'd just love to have it. I'll put it beside one of him, so that you can be together.'

'That's a lovely thought.' We closed the door, and a chapter in my life was over.

Christmas seemed dull that year as I thought back longingly to the card that I had got from him that had meant so much to me. It was halfway through the next term that I made the decision that would determine the future course of my life. I made it one Sunday afternoon walking the farm with Dad. I would not stay on at college for a third year. Most of my friends, and especially James and Andrew, would be gone, and there were too many ghosts around to remind me of past happiness.

'I've decided not to stay on at college for another year, Dad. I want to get out and see something of the world. I don't want to come home yet either. You don't really need me here, and I'm not ready for it. I don't know what I'll do, but I'll find something.'

'You're probably right. It'll be good for you to get away and gain experience of working in the world outside. It's probably what I would have done, if I had had the chance.' I was pleased that he had taken it so philosophically, but then he'd always said that it would be up to me to choose what I wanted to do.

It was during the Easter break that Dad was asked by one of the farming journals if they could send a reporter down to write up the farm, as my father had just won a prize for the dairy herd. In due course a youngish man arrived to go round the farm in the morning and then to stay for lunch.

His name was Norman Briggs, about thirty-five, nice looking and easy to talk to. He was about six foot in height, though he looked as if he might run to fat later. I made these observations as I caught him eyeing me up a couple of times over lunch. It seemed that he did a lot of travelling about the country. Suddenly it came to me that this might be the sort of job that I might like. An opportunity to write and one with plenty of out-of-doors work.

'How did you get into your job in the first place?' I asked.

'I did a three-year degree course at Reading, but there was no chance of getting into farming as I had no capital. I got a reporter's job with a provincial paper with a good rural circulation in the eastern counties, and did five years as a cub reporter. Then I got a job as an agricultural reporter with another paper over there. Three years later this job came up, and I was lucky to get it. I've never regretted it, even though it does involve a lot of travelling and I'm away often. But I'm not married so that doesn't really matter.' As he said that, he looked me in the eye with a quizzical stare. I thought that there might be some sort of a message there, but decided to ignore it.

'If you were thinking of it, you'd need to be able to type and do some sort of shorthand, and write decent English, though even that doesn't seem to matter much these days.'

We talked a bit more about it before he left, but I had already made up my mind.

I rang up Caroline next day.

'I want to learn to type and do some elementary shorthand. Will you teach me?'

'Yes, of course, but why? You'd better go out and buy a portable typewriter and a book on shorthand and I'll see what we can do.'

So for the remaining two weeks of the holiday I spent most of the time at her house and, with a background of gurgles from my new nephew, made quite good progress under her expert tuition. Typing was relatively easy, but shorthand more difficult. Back at college, I was just able to take down lecture notes in shorthand, and type them back in the evenings. But then there had to be a break as I had to revise for my finals.

Richard put me under pressure to stay on for another year but, when he realised that I was determined to break away, promised his full support in my job hunting. Exams came and went, and second place overall brought a promise from the Principal to back me up, stressing my writing ability.

The hardest thing was saying goodbye to James and Andrew, who had proved such good friends when I needed them. Both had got jobs, James as assistant manager on a large Cotswolds estate and Andrew with land agents in the North. As things turned out I was destined to see quite a lot of James in the future and we remained friends for life, but sadly I never met up with Andrew again.

I decided that I'd like to work somewhere in the West Midlands, partly because I could get home quite easily, but also because I had liked the look of the countryside when Dad had taken me up to a dairy sale in Cheshire one Easter holiday.

During a break in the harvest, a kindly librarian in Norton had got out a list of the provincial papers in the area. On my new typewriter, I wrote off to six editors offering my services as a junior reporter. Only one replied, from the *Westerton Herald*, asking me up for interview. Might this be the start of a new life for me? Time would tell.

Chapter Four

The editor of the *Herald*, Edwin Mallory, turned out to be a man in his fifties, with hair going grey, and an academic look about him. He had the air of an archetypal Oxford don, but the things that appealed to me about him were his friendly manner and a kind of old-fashioned courtesy, which put me at ease straight away. I felt that I'd like to work for him. With him was his assistant editor, Martin Smith, a much younger man in his thirties, with sandy hair, a sharp face and an air of get-up-and-go about him. They were a strange contrast, but seemed to get on well together.

'Thank you for coming up to see us, Mr Harper,' said Edwin. 'I hope you had an easy journey. So why do you think that you'd like to get into journalism, and why pick on us?'

'I've been interested in books from an early age, and when I was doing my A levels in English, I got interested in writing. Then at college I found that I was quite good at essay writing. As I said in my letter, I'm a farmer's son, and one day I suppose that I might go back to run the farm, but I certainly don't want to go home to bury myself in Devon just yet. I want to get out to see the world first. I'd really like to become an agricultural journalist, but I realise that I must get a lot of practical experience first. I wrote to you because this is an area that I like, and it would be fairly easy to get home if I needed to.'

'You do realise, I hope, that life for a young reporter can be quite tough at times, though it can also be very routine and boring. Life in a city of this size can be pretty rough, and every now and again you may be faced with harrowing and disturbing situations. You are not your own master, and may be called at any time to report on quite horrific incidents. Would you be able to cope, do you think?'

'I think so. I may have led a rather sheltered life so far, but I've already had to face a difficult crisis, and have come through it.

With regard to long hours, I'm not married or tied by any family commitments, so that should be no problem. I would like to have an occasional weekend off, though.'

'Normally you'd be on call for two weekends a month, so that's no problem. Now, can you type, and do some sort of shorthand, and use a tape recorder?'

'I can type reasonably well, and do some rudimentary short-hand, but I've never used a tape recorder. I imagine I could pick that up fairly easily?'

'Yes, we could teach you that. You have got a car, I presume?'

'Yes, my father gave me one for my last year at school, so I've been driving for nearly four years.'

'Have you any particular interests outside farming?'

'I got quite interested in politics at college, especially as it looks as if we might join the Common Market before long. I'm quite interested in sport, having been in my school and college rugby First XV, and I enjoy tennis in the summer.'

'What do you think about the Common Market, then?'

'I don't see much value in joining from an agricultural point of view, as it would throw our markets wide open to the Dutch and the French, and we'd be handing over control to Brussels, which could be dangerous. I can see that it might help some sectors of industry, but on balance I think we should retain our independence.'

'You may be right, but I don't think that would be a very popular view in this area. I hope you realise that a reporter has to be as non-political as possible. This paper has a broad policy of supporting the government of the day, though we are not afraid to criticise if we feel it's exceeding its powers. We are slightly right of centre, which reflects the views of the majority of our readers, especially those in the country area, where the weekly *Herald* has a wide circulation.'

'Have you ever written about sport?' Martin interjected.

'No. I think I know enough about rugby to be able to write about it, but that's the only game I'm really familiar with.'

'That's fine,' said Edwin. 'Now if we were to offer you a job I'd like to emphasise something I said earlier. You could well come up against some very unpleasant aspects of life as part of the job. The city has quite a large industrial population, with some underprivileged areas and a mixed ethnic society. Domestic violence, murder, rape, drug abuse, drunkenness, not to mention a whole range of other petty crimes, are all on the menu. Are you confident that you could handle such issues?'

'I wouldn't know, of course. But I've had to deal with stress. I'm pretty sure I'd cope.'

'Now, have you any questions you'd like to ask us? If not, perhaps you'd be good enough to go out for a few minutes, while I talk to Martin?'

I only had to wait a few minutes before Martin summoned me back.

'Right, Mark,' said Edwin, 'I'm glad to say that we'd like to offer you a job as a junior reporter. We were impressed by the excellent references you enclosed with your letter. Now we've met you, we're satisfied that you'd fit into our team here very well. Obviously you'll need to sharpen up your secretarial skills a bit, and a course at the local tech might help. The starting salary is £2,000 a year, which is the standard rate. The appointment and salary will be reviewed after a year, and there is a three-month period of notice on either side. You can claim a mileage allowance for your car if used for your work. Are you willing to accept?'

'Yes, of course. I'm delighted, and I'm sure I'll enjoy the job.'

'Good, when would you be able to start?'

'I would like two weeks, if possible. We've still got some harvest to finish, and I'll have to find somewhere to live. Would 15 September be all right?'

'Fine. We'll expect you at nine o'clock, and Martin will look after you to start with. Have a safe drive home.'

The first priority was to find somewhere to live, so before I left I picked up a copy of the weekly *Herald*, which had details of estate agents and properties. Mother was delighted to hear that I had got the job.

'Westerton's not too far away is it, dear. You'll be able to get home for weekends quite easily down the new motorway, won't you. That'll be nice for you.'

'We're supposed to have two weekends a month when we are on call, and I expect that there'll be other things cropping up as well, so I may not get back too often.'

I didn't want her to get the impression that I'd be dashing home every other weekend. About once in six weeks was what I had in mind. It was time to loosen the apron strings and move out into the world.

Next day, I rang up five of the house agents to enquire about flats to let. I was looking for one with two bedrooms, if possible, or one larger one, a decent-sized living room, kitchen and bathroom. I drew a blank with the first four and was getting worried, but the fifth did have one on their books, though there was someone after it already. If I was interested I'd better inspect it immediately.

The next day I drove Mother up to see if it might be suitable. It was in a quiet residential area to the west of the city not far from open country, with a playing field in front. It was the top floor of a large Victorian house, which had been converted into three flats. It had its own entrance, using the former servants' staircase to reach the flat. Apart from the sizeable living room there were two rather small bedrooms, a reasonable kitchen with just enough room for a table and separate bathroom and lavatory. There was a view of distant hills from the back window of the sitting room.

It was ideal in many ways, but there was one big snag. The rent they were asking was way beyond what I could reasonably afford on my starting salary, especially as I'd have to spend money on furnishing it.

'What do you think of it, Mother?

'It should suit you very well, dear, and I do like the neighbourhood and that view across to the hills. I think you ought to take it.'

'I do like it. But I'm afraid I'll have to let it go, as I can't possibly afford the rent.'

'It would be a terrible shame to lose it, dear, as I think it'd be ideal for you. I'm sure that Dad would want you to get it. Would you like us to help you with it? The farm's been doing well, so we could afford it and, after all, if you were getting married you'd probably be coming to us to help you with a mortgage. I don't expect Dad will continue with your allowance, now you're earning, so he'd be saving that money. Why don't we go half and half for the first year at any rate?'

'Mother dear, that's really marvellous of you. Of course I'll agree, and we'll look at it again if I get a decent rise next year.'

We clinched the deal with the agent there and then, and I agreed to come back in three days to sign the papers and pick up the keys.

Cynthia was delighted to hear about the job and the flat.

'I've got a spare bed you could have, with blankets and mattress, and a number of other things in the attic that we shall never again use. Why not come down in a day or two, and we'll see what we can find for you.' Mother also had some things in the farmhouse that were not needed which she said I could have.

Fortunately Dad had quite a large farm trailer which he towed behind his car, and I drove this over to Cynthia's. In addition to the bed, she had a carpet which would just about fit into the sitting room, a table for the kitchen and two upright chairs. She also gave me a small desk which had been in Simon's room.

'That'll do for your typewriter and papers. We don't need it and I'm sure he'd like you to have it, now he'll never need it.' I felt like crying, as it was so characteristic of her to think of something I'd use every day to remember him by. She was moved, too, as I saw her wipe away a tear. Even though it was nearly a year since he had died, it was obvious that the wounds were far from healed.

I made a list of things I'd want in addition to those that Cynthia and Mother had given me, and we went off to a sale in Norton, where I managed to pick up two quite good armchairs, a quantity of kitchen utensils and cutlery, and a carpet for the bedroom.

On the Saturday before I was due to start, everything was loaded up and I followed Dad up in my car. It was a struggle getting the bigger things up the narrow stairs, but Dad was pretty strong and we managed it somehow. Mother had brought a picnic lunch, and it was all finished by tea time, when we celebrated the first meal in my new home. One thing I had completely forgotten was pictures, so I was going to live with bare walls for the time being.

When they had gone, I had a feeling of intense loneliness. With all the excitement, I hadn't had time to think what it would be like living on my own. Here I was on the top floor of a house in a completely strange city knowing absolutely no one. I felt almost frightened, and decided that the next day I'd try to establish contact with the owners of the two flats below me, so that if anything went wrong I'd have someone to turn to. Then I caught sight of Simon's photograph, and tears came back.

'Oh God, love, I wish that you were here to keep me company. I do miss you so much.' As I said that, he seemed to smile back, and I felt a little better.

Next day I went to morning service at the cathedral, and prayed that my new life might bring happiness. So much for the doubts that had nearly swamped me after his death.

Later I knocked on the door of the flat below. It was answered by a bright girl in her twenties who was followed by a rather older man in T-shirt and jeans, who invited me in when I told them who I was. Sarah was a nurse at the local hospital and Roger a surveyor with the city council. There was no sign of a wedding ring. They had lived there for two years, and had hardly seen the occupants of the lower flat, who were away a lot. They thought there was little point in me contacting them. It was a relief to know that I had such a nice couple below me, especially as they said, as I left: 'You must come in for a meal sometime, and don't hesitate to knock on the door if you need anything.'

The *Herald* offices were on two floors of a newish office block near the city centre. On the first floor was the reporters' room with a row of desks with typewriters. There were smaller rooms for senior staff. On the upper floor were two areas for the compositors, where the paper was put together: one space for the daily edition, and one for the weekly. Printing was done in a small factory on the outskirts of the city.

Presenting myself on the Monday morning was just like the first day at school all over again. As Martin took me round introducing me to my new colleagues, I felt that I would never be able to remember their names or what they did. It was not made easier by his quick-fire delivery, which gave little time to memorise names or jobs before he moved on to the next one. I was to spend a day for the first week with each of the department heads to get the hang of how the paper was put together each day.

They turned out to be a very diverse group. The head of the news section with whom I was placed next day was a hard-bitten journalist of the old school, in his mid-fifties, with a trace of a Scots accent. He ruled the team with a firm hand, giving praise where it was due, but was scathing about any writing which did not come up to scratch – as I was to find occasionally in the future. It was his job to pick out lead stories, and decide what prominence to give them, subject to Martin's approval. The lesson I learnt from him was to cut out all unnecessary words. It was clear that my leisurely style of writing had no place in journalism.

Of all the heads, I seemed to strike up a particular rapport with the head of the home section, Angela Cantlay, a tall, athletic looking woman in her mid-thirties, I guessed. She had an expressive face with rather high cheekbones and green-grey eyes, closely cut lightish brown hair not tinted in any way, and a very firm mouth and chin. At first meeting I found her slightly formidable, as she was clearly someone who did not mince her words. She hadn't got that chin for nothing.

Unlike some of the others she seemed happy to give me as much time as I might want regarding her full page in the weekly edition and her bits and pieces in the daily. She asked a lot of questions about my background and was obviously interested in me as a person.

'Don't hesitate to knock on my door if you want help with anything,' she said as I was leaving. 'I well remember how lost I was at the start of my first job when I felt I had no one to turn to.'

'I'll certainly take you at your word, and thanks again for giving me so much time.'

There was a canteen in the basement where many of the staff had lunch most days. In my second week, Mike Sayers, who had been very helpful with advice in the newsroom, told me about a tennis and squash club which he belonged to, not far from my flat. I had already decided not to join a rugby club as I did not expect to have enough time to play, but I did want to get some exercise during the winter months, and the thought of tennis in the summer was appealing. I had never played squash but it seemed ideal for the winter.

'I'll tell you what, Mark, why don't you come along to the club with me one evening and then you could decide if you'd like to join? I'd be happy to propose you and I'm sure we could rustle someone up to second you.'

'That'd be very good of you. Mike. If I did join is there someone who could give me squash lessons?'

'Yes, there's a pro, Cliff Jones, who taught me three years ago. He's a good teacher, and he has a small shop there where you could buy a racquet and some balls. Are you doing anything on Wednesday evening? I've got a court booked when I'm playing with my girlfriend, so why not come along then and I'll introduce you to the secretary.'

'I'd love to. About what time?'

'We should be finished by eight o'clock. I'll see you in the bar then.'

My indoctrination under Martin Smith went on for another week. He gave me reports to write, selected from the pile of government documents that seemed to come in daily from the Whitehall paper factory. My job was to distil relevant ones down to a few hundred words according to their importance. Many of them went into the bin if Edwin or Martin did not think them sufficiently newsworthy. I suppose it was good training, but I did find much of it boring trying to make sense out of the jargon in which most of them were couched. He also passed on reports from correspondents, which had to be edited down to a given number of words. It wasn't long before I was quite good at visualising numbers of words as column inches.

I used my second weekend to explore the city more, and on the Saturday evening took myself to a concert in the City Hall by the Birmingham Symphony Orchestra. Emotions were terribly mixed. On one hand I was uplifted by the magnificence of the *Eroica* and the more intimate sounds of a Mozart piano concerto. On the other, I experienced a feeling of great sadness that I was not there with Simon, or with anyone to enjoy the music with. I was suddenly reminded of a saying attributed to Mark Twain, which I had picked up somewhere in my reading: 'Grief can take care of itself, but to get the full value of joy, you must have someone to share it with.' The fact was that I was lonely, and felt there was nothing I could do about it. I decided not to go to concerts alone in the future. It was too distressing.

By the time that I met Mike at the club, I was beginning to feel more at home. There was a good corporate feeling in the *Herald* office, and it was nice to be greeted with 'Hello, Mark' by whoever was about as I went in each day.

The tennis club had four courts and two squash courts, good changing facilities and a large lounge bar. Mike had finished his game when I arrived and introduced me to the professional, Cliff Jones, a lean athletic man of about forty-five, and Sam Roberts, the secretary, short and chubby, usually to be found with a pint of beer in his hand.

'So you think you might like to join?' Sam said as we were introduced. 'I'll get you an application form. Mike says that he'll propose you, and I'm sure we can find someone to second you.'

'Yes. I'd certainly like to become a member, especially if Cliff could give me some squash lessons.'

'I'd be glad to. If you already play tennis, you shouldn't find squash too difficult.'

'I've just had an idea,' Mike said. 'Why don't we ask Angela to second you? I'm sure she'd be happy to.'

'I didn't know she was a member. But there's no reason why I should have done, I suppose. I'll fill up the form now, and you can sign it, and I'll take it to her in the morning.'

Angela was delighted to sign it. The only problem now was the subscription, which was bigger than I expected. I didn't know whether I could afford it, but I decided that I'd have to somehow as I really wanted to join.

When Mother heard about it the following weekend when I went home, she was very enthusiastic about me joining the club. I had an idea that this was partly because she thought I might meet a nice girl there, but maybe that was unfair.

'How much is it going to cost you, dear?'

'Quite a lot, I'm afraid, when you take the cost of the sub, the lessons and the equipment into account. I can't really afford it, but I'll find it somehow.'

'With your birthday coming up soon, I'll give it to you as a present. Just let me know what it comes to, and I'll send you a cheque. Make it a two years' sub, dear.'

'That really is sweet of you, Mother dear. It's a lovely present, and it's one that I can go on enjoying all through the year.'

As I walked past the door of Simon's room, going to bed, I still had an intense feeling of loss. But then I thought that if he had lived, we would probably be apart by now. Sooner or later a break would have been inevitable, and there would only have been the prospect of occasional meetings or holidays together. What had happened was terrible, but I had a new life now, and there was less time to dwell on the past. I felt that he was telling me to get on with that new life, and leave the past behind.

As I walked the farm with Dad next day, he told me there was a rumour that an elderly neighbour was retiring and selling up his farm of about 150 acres. It adjoined the eastern side of our farm, and was reasonably good-quality land, though rather run down.

'Do you think that I ought to make a bid for it, Mark?'

'It all depends on the price, Dad, and how well it would integrate with ours. I think you could probably farm the arable land with our existing machinery, so there'd be no extra cost involved there. You could keep a few more dairy cows if you put a couple of our arable fields back to grass, and grew crops on the new land instead.'

'I'd thought of that. It would mean building some extra cow cubicles to house them, but there is room for them. Perhaps I shouldn't ask you this, but do you think that you might want to come back here to farm it one day, when I'm ready to retire? Your mother isn't keen for me to take on any more land if you're not likely to come back, as she thinks we've got enough already, and that it'll just give me more work for nothing.'

I just didn't know what to say as I was still so undecided about the future, especially as I was getting so involved with my job. If, in time, I'd made a successful career for myself, would I want to bury myself in Devon? And always at the back of my mind was the question whether by then I might have another partner in my life – or if I had not, would I stand any chance of finding one in rural Devon? If not, I could picture myself as a lonely embittered old bachelor dreaming of what might have been. I didn't like the idea.

'I'm sorry, Dad, I don't know what to say. I do love the farm, and it would be a challenge to run it one day, but I can't forecast how I'd feel about it in say twenty years' time, when you might want to retire. But I'm sure you wouldn't go wrong in buying the land, and I don't see that it would really increase your workload at all. I'd go for it if it comes up.'

'I quite understand how you feel, and I shouldn't have asked you. Just forget all about it. I'll make a bid for it when it comes on the market.'

My life as a reporter started on the Monday morning with a visit to the magistrates' court with Jack Ingram, a senior reporter who specialised in crime. He introduced me to a couple of the court officials, saying it was useful, as they could tell you in advance about the more important cases that we might want to feature in the paper.

Being a Monday morning, there were the usual cases of drunk and disorderly arising from weekend excesses and, in addition, one of attempted rape and one of drug possession. As the rape case was contested, it was referred to a higher court, but not before a number of details had been revealed.

'Try your hand at writing up the drugs and the rape cases. They might make the evening edition,' he said, and seemed reasonably satisfied with my efforts.

That evening, at a retirement party for a civic dignitary, I met up with the *Herald*'s photographer, with whom I was destined to work frequently in the future. It had been a rather dull day, but I couldn't complain that Edwin hadn't warned me of that.

It was on the Thursday that I first saw my name in print as a result of my report of an industrial dispute at one of the city's bigger companies. 'By our reporter, Mark Harper.' I felt quite proud.

Pride comes before a fall, they say. Next day, I was severely reprimanded by Martin over a piece I wrote about a company that had gone bankrupt. I had said that among other things it was due to shortage of capital.

'What's your evidence for that statement?'

'Well, none, I suppose, though it's pretty obvious, I'd have thought.'

'You'll land us up in court if you make statements that you can't substantiate. We're living in a very litigious age and newspapers are fair game for any Tom, Dick or Harry with a shady lawyer out to make a quick buck.' It was an important lesson to learn, and I took it to heart. The following day he sent for me again.

'You did say when we interviewed you that you were keen on rugby, didn't you?'

'Yes, that's right. Why?'

'The chap who usually reports for us is seriously ill in hospital, and I wondered if you might like to go along and report on the match with the Saracens tomorrow. Sarah will give you a press pass if you can do it.'

'I'd quite like to have a shot at it, if you think I could manage it. I hope you wouldn't expect too much. How many words would I have?'

'Round about 200, and don't make it too heavy reading.'

It would be a real challenge as I knew nothing of the team, and would have to rely on the programme for the players' names, and hope I got them right.

I felt like a new boy as I entered the box to see three people already there. Two of them at the far end were archetypal ex-players, muffled up in coats and scarves, red in the face from long exposure to the elements and pints of beer. The third member, who I sat down next to, was very different. Tall and thin with slightly shrunken cheeks and large glasses, he looked more like a professor, quite out of place in a press box. But he gave me a very welcoming smile.

'I'm Trevor Inglis from the *Birmingham Standard*,' he said. 'I'm only here to see the Saracens play, as they're playing against us next week.' I just remembered the name as that of an outstanding international winger from the days when I first played at school.

'I'm Mark Harper, and I'm only standing in for our regular man who's in hospital. To be honest, this is the first match I've ever reported. I don't even know the names of the Westerton players, as I've only been here a month.'

'I might be able to help you then, as I know most of them apart from one or two new men in the pack. I could probably give you a few tips about what to include in your article as well, if you liked. You don't want to scribble down too many notes, or you get lost in the detail. Just pick out a few major movements or incidents and base it on those. I remember the first one I ever did, and I just couldn't sort it all out afterwards.'

'I'd be awfully grateful if you could do that. It'd certainly help me to get the hang of it.'

He was as good as his word, every so often saying, 'That's so and so,' or, 'I'd note that movement, it was a good one,' or maybe, 'Make a note of that try.' I soon found I'd got plenty for my 200 words.

'Thanks so much,' I said at the end of the game. 'That was tremendously helpful, and I'm most grateful.'

'Not a bit. I'm delighted to have been able to help. I hope we'll meet up again soon.'

'That wasn't at all bad for a first effort,' Martin said on the Monday morning. 'They've another home game next Saturday. Would you like to cover it?'

So that was how I became the rugby correspondent for the *Herald*, as the regular man sadly died. I drew the line at going away to cover distant matches, for which we used agency reports. That was cheaper anyhow than paying me to travel miles for just a few hundred words, and it gave me freer weekends.

My membership of the squash and tennis club came through two weeks after I had sent in the application, and I immediately fixed up the lessons with Cliff Jones. I found the speed of the ball difficult to deal with at first. Cliff was a patient teacher, and my having played tennis was a help. By the end of the first lesson I was feeling more confident.

'I don't really think you need any more lessons now,' Cliff said after the third lesson. 'What you really want now is practice with other players, and then perhaps a top-up later on.'

After showering down I went into the bar, to see Angela there talking to a young man of about thirty. It was the first time I had seen her in the club.

'Hello, Mark. I don't expect you've met Robert, have you? Robert, this is Mark Harper who has come to work at the *Herald* recently.'

'Glad to meet you, Mark. I'm Robert Mitchell,' he said as we shook hands. 'How are you getting on with your lessons with Cliff?'

'Actually he's just signed me off – saying that what I need is practice with other players.'

'I'll give you a game one evening, if you like. I've only been playing for two years, and I'm not much good. Not like Angela here, who's really hot stuff, and beats the daylight out of me.'

'And so I should be,' said Angela, 'seeing that I've been playing for about sixteen years. I'd be happy to give you a game and will promise not to be too hard on you.'

'I'd love that, but I think we should leave it till I'm a bit better.'

While this conversation had been taking place, I had caught Robert eyeing me over once or twice as I sized him up. Just under six foot, I guessed. He had very dark hair kept rather long, over large dark eyes with silky eyelashes, a long nose and a wide mouth with prominent lips, which gave him a slightly feminine appearance. He was not my type at all, and I felt none of the excitement I had experienced at seeing Simon for the first time, but I was pretty certain that he was eyeing me up with a purpose. I felt no physical attraction, but I did like his friendly manner and his smile, and thought I'd like him as a friend.

'Could you manage next Tuesday for a game?' asked Robert.

'No, I'm tied up on Tuesdays, but I could manage Wednesday.'

'That'd be OK with me. I'll book a court for seven o'clock, shall I?'

'Fine, I'll look forward to it.'

It was probably inevitable that a young, reasonably good-looking unmarried man should attract feminine attention in an office like ours, and it was not long before I became aware of it. One or two of the girls from the secretarial department always seemed more than willing to do jobs for me, or could be found close to me in the canteen for lunch. With Barbara in mind, I kept them at arm's length, and then one day in an inspired moment let slip a remark about a girlfriend in Devon. I reckoned that it might get round on the office grapevine that I might not be available after all. It seemed to work, for their ardour quickly cooled.

Time was passing so quickly that I realised with a shock that it was only two days from the first anniversary of Simon's death. I decided to spend the evening alone in the flat recalling our happy holiday from my photos, though I knew it would be difficult.

Actually it was not, for I got two telephone calls, one from Cynthia and one from James. I was much moved by both of them, especially Cynthia's, who in the midst of her own grief had thought of me. She was deeply interested to hear how I was getting on, and said that I must go see them over the Christmas holiday.

James and I talked for more than an hour about our respective jobs. I was glad to hear that he was very happy with his, and was being given a lot of responsibility by his boss. We agreed to talk about once a month in the future. It was good to recall what a wonderful support he had been in the crisis of Simon's death.

The first game of squash with Robert was enjoyable, even though he beat me easily. We agreed to try to get a game once a week, as he had found it a bit difficult to find partners. I thought that with further practice we could be a well-matched pair. Showering down afterwards, I caught him glancing at me once or twice. Strangely, my intimacy with Simon seemed to have liberated me of the shyness that I had previously had in revealing my nakedness, and I did not mind the thought of Robert giving me the once-over. I registered that he was well endowed, but was not aroused by what I saw, though it was nice to see a naked body again.

Over a drink afterwards, it transpired that he was an accountant with one of the larger city firms. It was fairly obvious that he was not married, but I decided to test him out, all the same.

'So I take it you're not married, Robert?'

'Good heavens, no, and no likelihood of it, either.'

'Why's that? I'd have thought you were about the age to be thinking of settling down to start a family.'

'I'm perfectly happy as I am, thanks. I share a flat with a close friend, who's a doctor, and though we row at times, we do get on well. Why should I want to give that up and tie myself to a woman, and land up with a bunch of kids? Anyhow, now we're on the subject, what about you?'

'No, I've no intention of getting married. I don't think I'm cut out for it, though I do feel that I'd like a couple of kids sometime.'

'Does that mean that you're gay, then?'

'Gay? What do you mean?'

'That's the new word that has come in from the States, instead of "queer", thank goodness. I always hated that word for people like us. It sounded so derogatory and demeaning, somehow.'

'I disliked it, too. Yes, I suppose so, but please don't tell anyone. I suspect that some of the people I work with might be prejudiced, and I wouldn't want to run the risk of my career being nipped in the bud just as it's getting off the ground.'

'The secret's safe with me as I'm in the same boat. Some people may have put two and two together when they have seen me and John, who is ten years older than me, living together, but I don't think anyone at work suspects anything. I must get back now, or John will be wondering what I'm getting up to. See you next Wednesday. I'll book a court.'

It was after our third game that Robert said: 'John's away at a conference in London. Would you like to see the flat, and I'll rustle up a bit of supper?'

'I'd love to.'

It was a large, two-bedroom flat on the third floor of a modern block in the centre of the city, close to the hospital where John was a consultant, and clearly there was no shortage of money, as it was expensively furnished. Robert was a good cook; it didn't take him long to knock up a couple of savoury omelettes, followed by an apple pie from the freezer. As we finished washing-up, the moment that I had rather anticipated arrived.

'Going back to what we were talking about the other evening, I do find you rather attractive, Mark. Would you feel like taking it any further?'

'I thought that might be the case from the way you were looking at me when Angela introduced us that evening, and by the way you looked at me in the showers. I do like you a lot, and I value our friendship, but to be honest I don't find you physically attractive as you're not my type at all. When my lover was killed in a car crash just over a year ago, I vowed I wouldn't go to bed with a man unless I felt I really loved him.

'But I've come to realise that I do feel a need for sexual relief with someone which wouldn't involve an emotional element. If that happened, it would only be in the nature of satisfying a bodily need. In your case, though, there is the complication that you already have a partner of whom you seem very fond. If we got together, I would feel that I was betraying him. But the ball is in your court, really.'

'I do love John very much, and I know he loves me as well. But when you've been together for a long time – eight years in our case – there is a danger that lovemaking can get a bit stale – especially in my case as I had led a rather promiscuous life before I met him. It has nothing to do with the emotional and spiritual love we have – that's quite secure. In a strange way, that seems to be strengthened if one of us has an occasional fling on the side.

'For all I know John may be up to something in London at this moment, but if he is, he'll tell me about it. I'm not sure that I'd tell him about you, if we did anything, in view of our squash connection. He might get jealous in that case, and I wouldn't want to involve you in any way. I'd certainly never have sex with you if he was at home as I really would feel then that I was letting him down. Sounds irrational, but that's how I feel. I've no intention of getting emotionally involved with you, but shall we give it a trial? I won't ask you to go to bed!'

With that we moved together, and for the first time since Simon's death, I experienced the intense physical satisfaction of close bodily contact with another man, and the stimulation of a strange hand caressing my body, and of mine exploring his.

It was clear that he had a passionate nature, and we were both ready for physical relief, so everything happened very quickly, especially in my case.

'I'm so sorry to have come so fast, but it's the first time for over a year, so I suppose it was to be expected.'

'Don't worry about that. I was very ready for it as well, but it's good to find that we're so compatible. We mustn't make a habit of it, but I hope we can get together again if the opportunity arises.'

'I certainly hope so. I'd like it.'

I had expected to feel remorse at what had, after all, been a fairly loveless act. But I didn't at all, because I was fond of Robert and had enjoyed the physical contact after a long abstinence. I had no religious reaction either, as I had already come to the conclusion that if God had provided us with sexual organs, he'd presumably expected us to use them. The fact that he had made me to be attracted to my own sex didn't alter the picture, so far as I could see.

In the months ahead, we would occasionally indulge ourselves if his partner was away, and we became close friends within the limits imposed by his relationship with John.

Edwin Mallory had been right to warn me that a reporter's life could be tough at times. During my first year the routine round of civic receptions, weddings, funerals, council meetings, school events, planning developments, industrial disputes, magistrates' courts, petty crime and so on were the bread of life. But every now and again would come an event to test one's stamina.

I was called on twice to report on horrendous car crashes, one a motorway pile-up with people dead or badly hurt, and the other a three-car crash on a country road with two dead lying beside the road, before an ambulance could get through. Inevitably, this brought back memories of Simon lying dead, and I found it difficult not to break down. Intruding on the grief of the survivors when they were still in shock, in order to get a story for the paper, was worse still.

Then there were the cases of domestic violence, usually in the run-down parts. Westerton was not a large city, but it had its fair share of deprived areas and low-grade housing in the industrial sector. Here it was drug abuse and drunkenness to which most of the violence could be traced. I well remember a battered wife, thrown out of the house by a drunken partner, and seeing the bruises on her arms and legs from being thrown across the room. Or on another occasion, a terrified young teenage boy beaten up by his mother's boyfriend for a trivial remark that had infuriated him. How could human beings do such things to one another, or how could what must have once been love turn to such hate?

Drug addiction was becoming common then, with all its attendant levels of degradation and crime to fuel the addiction. Sometimes I would be appalled at the level of ignorance of the elementary facts of living shown by those I had to interview. How could our system of education turn out such morons of both sexes, and what earthly chance would the children of such people have of becoming responsible adults when they grew up?

I would ask myself such questions as I struggled to write fair accounts of cases such as these. Almost worse was the thought that it was people like this who were breeding indiscriminately with no thought of how the offspring would be cared for. There was the misery, too, of broken marriages and children raised without love – the criminals of the next generation.

This was the seamy side of journalism, and it was something with which I never quite came to terms, though my skin got tougher as time went on. Possibly that feminine element in my genes made me more sensitive to such social problems, for I was never really able to cope with human cruelty.

Christmas had come and gone with three peaceful days at home, after the pressure of getting out a Christmas edition of the weekly. I drove over to see Cynthia and Jack on Boxing Day. Simon's death had clearly taken some of the sparkle out of their lives, and her face was beginning to show a few lines. But she was still her same loving self as she kissed me warmly when I arrived. I got the feeling that she had adopted me in place of the son that she had lost. It was sad to see that the tennis court on which we had spent so many happy hours had quickly reverted to the condition in which I had first seen it.

'I'm coming up to see your flat as soon as the days get lighter in the spring,' said Cynthia. 'Your mother told me how nice it was, when she came over to lunch recently.'

'I'm certainly very happy with it. I have now got it fully furnished, and it's in a fit state to ask people in, though my cooking isn't good enough yet to risk putting on a meal.'

'That'll come quite easily with a bit of practice. Tell me, are you missing him as much as ever?'

'In a way, but I do think of him less during the day, as there is so much going on. But we often have a little talk as I'm going to bed. That's the time when he seems to be around, and I feel sure he knows when I talk to him.'

'I think he's still with us in spirit, and I do find it a great comfort when I'm feeling down.' She gave me a great hug as I said goodbye, and there were tears in her eyes.

It was early in February when Angela came and sat next to me at lunch one day.

'I hear from Robert that your squash is improving rapidly. Would you like a game one evening?'

'Very much, but I'm sure that you'll be far too good for me.'

'That doesn't matter at all, as you know that you can get a lot of fun out of it whether you're good or not. How about Wednesday evening? I'll book a court if that's OK.'

It didn't take long to appreciate the difference between a class player, which Angela clearly was, and a novice like me. Wherever I tried to place the ball, she seemed to be there to whack it back out of my reach. For most of the time she'd be in the middle of the court, dictating the play while I was scurrying round from one side to the other trying to retrieve the ball, only to be bamboozled in the end by a delicate drop shot dying in a corner. I did manage to score a few points off her, though I suspected that she was not playing at full throttle, so to speak.

'Thanks so much for the game,' I said at the bar afterwards. 'You must have been playing a long time.'

'I was lucky enough to go to a good boarding school where they had a couple of courts, so I've been playing since I was fifteen. Then when I was working in London I had a friend who was keen, so we used to play quite a lot. Since I got this job I've not played so frequently as I'm much busier, but I do like a game every so often to keep my hand in. Anyhow, Mark, you seem to have settled in very well. What do you want to do long term?'

'I suppose that ultimately I shall go back to run the family farm, but I certainly don't want to stagnate in Devon for another twenty years, as Dad is still quite young. My real aim is to become an agricultural journalist with one of the big dailies or specialist papers, as that would keep me in touch with farming, if I did have to go back. But I've obviously got to learn the trade first, which is why I'm here.

'I'm very happy with the job, though I'd like to get out into the country more, instead of being stuck in the city most of the time. I realise that Bob Acroyd covers the farming angle, but I do think that the weekly edition might include more on countryside and environment issues than it does now. I'd like to get involved with that.'

'You may have a point there. I'll talk to Edwin about it one day, and see if he might use you more on issues like that.'

She seemed keen that we should have another game, so we fixed one for a fortnight ahead. Although there was an age gap of at least ten years between us, she was so easy to talk to and was so natural and unaffected that I felt there was no age gap at all. One of Simon's legacies passed on to me was his self-confidence and ability to talk easily to people. This had gone a long way towards supplanting the shyness that I had felt as a schoolboy.

Perhaps, too, it was all those evenings spent with him and James and Andrew, when I had been forced to come out with opinions of my own, that had helped me. Whatever it was, Angela and I seemed to get on extremely well. I had already matured a lot, for the face that I saw in the mirror as I shaved each morning had filled out and the chin had become more pronounced. Without feeling too conceited, I concluded that I was not at all bad-looking, especially when I smiled – rather like Mother.

After our third game, I asked her if she'd like to come up to see the flat and have a cup of coffee. Almost as soon as she entered the room, she saw the photograph of Simon, which I had had enlarged and nicely framed, standing on his desk.

'Who's that?' she asked, 'and where was it taken? He's got a charming face.'

'It was taken in Switzerland, and that's the Jungfrau in the background. It's Simon, my very close friend who was killed in a car crash nearly two years ago.' My voice gave out on the last few words as a huge lump rose in my throat. Damn, damn, I said to myself – I thought that I had learnt to conquer emotion when speaking of his death. Clearly I had not.

'Oh, dear, I'm so sorry. You must miss him, Mark.'

'Yes, I do terribly, but I'm gradually getting over it. Coming up here and getting stuck into the new job has helped a lot, as there's so much going on that there is less time to think about it.'

'Were you in love with him?' she asked, looking me straight in the eye. The question took me completely by surprise. I had supposed that I had never given anyone in the office the slightest indication that I might be 'gay', and James and Andrew had said that they would never have suspected it.

'Yes, very deeply, but how on earth did you guess?'

'I really don't know, but when I first met you I had some kind of hunch about it. Then when I introduced you to Robert, I could see the way he looked at you, and you appeared to be sizing him up. You see, I've known about him for quite a time, as he and his partner, John, have a flat in the adjoining block to mine and I've met them socially, quite apart from the tennis club. The other thing was that you never seemed inclined to chat up the girls, which I would have expected a heterosexual man of your age to do. Then I heard about the girlfriend in Devon, and wondered if I might have got it wrong! A clever move on your part.'

'Well, yes, it was done on the spur of the moment, but it worked quite well.' We both laughed.

'So now you know about me, what about you?'

'I'm much the same. I enjoy the company of men, but I've no desire to go to bed with them. The idea of some huge thing being pushed into me by a hairy man revolts me, just as I expect the thought of some clinging woman with large breasts would revolt you. I have a partner, five years older than me, who lives in London, and we meet up about once a fortnight which, to be honest, is quite enough for me. We shared a flat, and she was upset when I got this job, but I was feeling suffocated and wanted to spread my wings. I've always been something of a career girl, I'm afraid.'

'Well, that clears the air, and it's much easier now we know where we stand. It's difficult for a gay man, who's always afraid that women may start fantasising about him, and taking quite innocent remarks the wrong way, thinking they might get you to bed. Not that it would have happened in our case, unless you had a yearning for a toy boy!'

'No risk of that with me. But it's much the same with us. You'd be surprised how bloody tenacious some men are if you're a reasonably good-looking unmarried girl. They just won't take no for an answer, and assume that you're playing hard to get. You can't tell them that you're lesbian, or it'd be round the town in no time. I think it's worse for us than it is for you. To change the subject, have you met Robert's partner yet?'

'No, he seems to be rather cagey about him, so I've not suggested it. Why?'

'I think you ought to know that John has rather a jealous streak, and is almost paranoid that Robert might leave him for a younger man. We were in their flat one day and John started an argument about it, which was rather embarrassing. I'm certain that Robert would never leave him, for he is far too caring and devoted, but John might get the wrong idea if you were seeing too much of Robert. I wouldn't want that to happen for their sakes and yours as well. I've no idea, nor do I want to know, if you and Robert have got up to anything, but if you do, please be very careful, as I'd hate it if it caused a rift.'

'I'd already come to the conclusion that there might be a problem with John. Actually we have got together once, when John was away in London, but Robert has told me that he would never do anything if John was at home. They do apparently have a little bit on the side occasionally, but their partnership is rock solid, and I'd certainly never risk breaking it up. He is not my type anyhow, so there is no risk of me getting emotionally involved.'

'I've been meaning to ask you, Mark, but are you interested in music? I thought I saw you at a concert after you came here, but when I looked for you at the end you had gone.'

'Yes, I was there that night. I hadn't even been to a concert before I met Simon as my family was never interested. But he was, and when we went on holiday he put some tapes in the car, which we played on long journeys. Then in Interlaken he took me to a concert with a large symphony orchestra, where they played the Bruch concerto, and Tchaikovsky's Fifth, and I was hooked. I'd like to go more often, but I decided that going alone was not on after the concert here. You do need someone to talk to about the music.'

'You're quite right. I'd never go alone, either. Janet and I go if there's a concert when she's up here for the weekend. Would you like to go with me, if there's one during the week? Say no if you might feel embarrassed by being seen out with an older woman who is obviously not your mother! It might look like the toy boy thing again.'

'No risk of me being taken for a toy boy. I'm not good-looking enough for that. Of course, I'd love to keep you company if the opportunity arises.' As it turned out it was to be about four months before there was one that we could both manage. She insisted on paying, which was fair enough as she was earning a great deal more than I was. After that we would do about three a year, sometimes at weekends with Janet, Angela's partner.

'How much do you know about the Common Market, Mark?' Edwin asked me towards the end of August.

'I've tried to keep up with the arguments in the press, as it looks as if we shall go in soon, but I don't pretend to know a great deal about it.'

'I'm planning a series of leaders on how it might affect different industries. Would you like to tackle one about the effect it might have on agriculture? I could give you about 300 words, if you took it on.'

One of the last essays I had done for Richard at the college was on the same topic, so I thought that I might as well have a shot at it. If it were acceptable I might get on Edwin's panel of leader writers.

'Yes, I'd like to give it try. When would you want it by?'

'There's no particular hurry. Say in three weeks' time. Remember it needs to be impartial.'

I handed it in a fortnight later, and Edwin seemed pleased with it, only red-pencilling a couple of lines, which he thought too controversial. As I left his office, he called me back.

'You've been with us nearly a year now, haven't you, Mark? Can I take it that you haven't any plans for moving on?'

'No, none at all. I'm enjoying it here and I've made a lot of friends. I feel I'm learning a great deal.'

'I was talking to Martin yesterday, and we both agreed that, although your probation year isn't quite up, we'd like to confirm your appointment as a full member of the staff. It means that your salary will go up by twenty-five per cent, and if you're happy to continue reporting on rugby, we'd pay you an additional £20 a match. Would that be acceptable?'

'Yes, very much so. It's good of you not to wait till the full year is up.'

'Angela was telling me the other day that you want to become an agricultural journalist, and that you'd like to get more reporting on countryside issues. I'm always hearing about concerns in relation to intensive farming and the intrusion of the city into the country, and I think we might pay some attention to this in the weekly edition. I wouldn't want to interfere with Bob's farming column, but I think we could deal with the wider issues without doing that. I'll think about it a bit more.'

So I was now a proper journalist, with a bigger pay packet, and a prospect of rather more congenial work in the future. I went off for two weeks' holiday to help Dad with the harvest, feeling quite pleased with myself. I probably had Angela to thank for some of it.

As the days had lengthened in that first summer, tennis had to some extent replaced squash, though Robert and I still had a game once a fortnight. Mike, who had introduced me to the club, was about my standard, but Angela was way above us. At her instigation we entered for the mixed doubles competition, but went out in the first round as I was no equal for our male opponent, and she couldn't make up the difference.

James came up and stayed a night with me, and we swapped experiences over our respective jobs, which we were both enjoying. He was vastly amused to hear that I had become close friends with Angela.

'Who'd have thought that you'd land up in a platonic friendship with a lesbian, almost old enough to be your mother,' he laughed. He'd kept in touch with Andrew, who was not happy with his job, and thought he'd look round for another one before long. James's love life was still on hold, as most of the girls he'd met were too impossibly horsy, or too much up-market for a mere assistant estate manager.

Cynthia came up and I took a day off to show her round. She thought I was very lucky to have found such a nice flat. When she saw the blown-up photo of Simon, she asked if I could let her have the negative so that she could get one as well. I felt more like a son to her than ever, as she was so much her usual loving self. She had been over to the farm recently for lunch with Mother, and I was happy to know that they got on so well together.

It was good to get back to some manual work over the harvest. The next-door farm was going to auction early in September, and Dad was determined to buy it so that he could expand the dairy herd, whatever the cost. He had had a good year, and could afford to buy it without borrowing much from the bank.

Then it was back to work again, and the realisation that it was a year since I had driven up to Westerton for the interview. What an astonishing year for new experiences it had been!

Already I was feeling about three years older than the rather scared young man who had driven up that day. It was now nearly two years since Simon had died, as well. At times, it seemed almost like yesterday that I had seen him for that last time. At others, I felt that memories were gradually sinking into the past as I got on with my life – which I knew would be what he would have wanted. It was at night that I missed him most, and longed to be with him again.

Chapter Five

Five years passed quickly by as I became fully integrated into the *Herald's* team. Over these years, friendships with Robert, Angela and Mike Sayers (until he married), became closer. A new member who joined the staff also joined the tennis club and provided another partner for both squash and tennis.

But there was no new man in my life. Often I'd feel the need for someone to love and to come home to in the evenings to share that life. But I had more work and social activity to occupy my time and I began to think I was better alone for the time being. An occasional liaison with Robert helped to relieve the sexual pressures for both of us, as we were compatible and got pleasure from the close contact.

For safety's sake I had still not met John, though I had met Janet – Angela's partner – when they invited me to go to weekend concerts together. I found her somewhat overpowering. She was a senior civil servant in a government department, and clearly used to ordering men around. She lacked Angela's warmth, but they came over as a well-adjusted couple and living apart probably enhanced their relationship. I guessed that if they lived together there would soon be a clash of personalities.

Change was in the air in more ways than one. I was now twenty-eight, and, though happy enough in the job, I could see a danger of getting into a rut. I still hankered after an agricultural correspondent's job to keep more in touch with farming. I had considered a BBC producer's post which was advertised, but decided against it as it would have meant relocating to London.

The time was coming when I'd have to make a move.

There was change looming at the *Herald*, too, as Edwin would retire in three months and Bob Acroyd, the farming correspondent, was also going to retire. I thought I would seek Angela's advice.

'I think you should hang on here for the time being, and see what we get as the new editor. I don't think Martin will get the job because he's too valuable in introducing all this new technology. Anyhow, I don't think he's got the intellectual calibre for it. I can understand your itchy feet. Thirty is a difficult age, when people stop and ask themselves if they want to go on doing the same job all their lives. I'd definitely advise you to stay and see what happens.'

'You're obviously right. The sensible thing is to wait and see what the new man's like. He's bound to want to make some changes, and all our jobs may be at risk, anyhow.'

Edwin had been as good as his word; he had been giving me a bit of reporting on countryside issues, and had sent me away on two conferences and published my two reports. So I had staked a small claim in that direction.

When the time came, luck was on my side. The board did not appoint Martin Smith, but the forty-five year old deputy editor of an eastern counties paper. My first impression, three days after he arrived, was favourable. Eric Munro looked a bit younger than his forty-five years, with a high, domed forehead capped by slightly unruly, wispy hair. He had pinkish cheeks and a strong chin. The most striking feature were two very blue eyes that seemed to be looking at me intently when I was speaking to him. He came over as someone of a sharp intelligence but of a warm personality all the same.

'Come in, Mark,' he said as I entered the room. 'I think it's time we got to know one another You're knocking up towards thirty, I see, and you've been with us for nearly six years, and you come from a family farm in Devon?'

'Yes, that's right, the farm has been in the family for over fifty years, and my father built it up considerably over time.'

'Do you intend to go back to run it in due course?'

'I'm not sure. Dad is only in his fifties, and doesn't need me at home, and I certainly wouldn't want to bury myself there just yet. There's far too much going on here to give it up. My aim is to get a job as an agricultural journalist, so that I can keep up with farming if I do have to go home sometime. At the same time I don't want to get into a rut here, and I've been thinking it might be time to move on before very long.'

I had said rather more than I meant to, but I felt I should put my cards on the table.

'I gather from Edwin that you have already been getting more involved in countryside issues, and he's shown me reports you did on a couple of conferences. Did you get much out of them?'

'Yes, a lot. I got to meet a number of people involved, both in the media and outside. It was particularly useful as I was able to sort out the lunatic fringe from those that really matter. There do seem to be a lot of people around with pretty crazy ideas, and axes to grind.'

'That's very true, but you find them in all walks of life, and especially in this field. By the way, are you married with a family?'

'No, I'm still single, and have no ambition to get tied up just yet. I'm enjoying the free life too much.'

'That's good because I'm going to make you an offer which might involve being away from home rather more. With Bob Acroyd retiring, I've decided to increase the emphasis on countryside matters in the weekly *Herald*, perhaps cutting down on the farming side but increasing the coverage of rural affairs in general.

'We've got a very large area of farming country on three sides of us, but the city is beginning to encroach on it, raising a number of new issues, and creating tensions between town and country within a radius of a good twenty miles, I'd think. I have in mind a full, weekly page dealing with all these issues, and also farming matters. I feel that a paper like ours should do everything it can to foster good relations between the two sides. We had something like this in the paper I've just come from, and I don't see why it shouldn't work here.

'Edwin has shown me your articles, and has been impressed by your work. What would you say if I offered you the job of starting up and editing a weekly page on those lines?'

'I'd jump at it, of course, as it's the sort of thing I've had in mind for years. Are you sure I could make a success of it?'

'I wouldn't have offered it if I thought you couldn't. I'm taking a risk obviously in view of your age, and the fact that you've never run a show of your own before, but both Edwin and I feel you could make a success of it. At first you could call on other members of the staff to help you with layout, but it shouldn't take you long to master that.

'To get down to the details: you'll have an office of your own and a personal secretary who can hold the fort when you're out in the field, and you'll have the use of one of our photographers for local items, if you give them notice in advance. I imagine you'll need illustrations to break up the text. Otherwise you'll have to use agency photographs for events further away. Is there anything you'd like to ask me about?'

'There is the question of salary and expenses. Presumably I would be able to claim travel and conference fees?'

'Yes, of course, at the standard rates. As to salary, I'd suggest an extra £2,000 a year, to be reviewed at the end of your first year. Would that be acceptable?'

'Certainly. What about advertising? I imagine the page will have to carry some advertising, but I'd hope that it would not be very much. Shall I have a budget to work to?'

'Obviously we'll need advertising to help to pay for the cost. I realise that you'd like to keep that to a minimum. I'd think about fifteen per cent might be the starting point, and we'd see how it goes. I think it'd be wise to look at the budget after two or three issues, when we can see how it's working out. But yes, we must have one in due course. Is there anything else?'

'How long would I have to get the first one out?'

'I'd think that you could get the first one together in a month, which would take us up to 10 October? Could you manage that?'

'Yes, I think so. One other thing: I'd like to give up reporting on rugby, which I've done since I came up here, as I can't see that I'll have time for it.'

'I agree. We'll have to find someone else to take it on.'

So I had got what I had always wanted; but the more I thought about it, the more alarming the prospect became. It was not as if I were taking over an established routine, but I would have to set the whole thing up from scratch, with no contacts to speak of. The first thing to do would be to have a word with Bob, who presumably had a list of contacts in the farming world, whom he called on for information.

The next thing would be to establish my own contacts in the

environmental field, such as the Farming and Wildlife Group, advisory officers, land agents, auctioneers, machinery dealers and so on. The list seemed almost endless, but I supposed that with the right contacts the information would start to flow into me, rather than me having to go out to look for it.

Eric had provided me with an experienced secretary, Gillian Bennett, who had worked in the *Herald* office for some eight years, and knew the system inside out. About forty-five, she was married to an official in the city's accounts department, but had no children. The great advantage was that she was a Welsh farmer's daughter who had worked on the farm until she left home so she was conversant with farming and its language.

She was a jolly, extrovert woman, always ready for a joke, with rosy cheeks, blue eyes and a pile of darkish hair sticking up from her forehead. As she was a motherly type, but deprived of children, I always felt she thought that I needed protection and encouragement in my first job. She proved to be highly efficient, and from the start was determined to build up our little empire. She held things together admirably while I was away, and very soon became more of a PA than just a secretary.

Bob's contacts turned out to be elderly farmers whom he'd known for years, rather than the younger, progressive ones that I was looking for. My best contacts were the three district advisory officers in the area we covered, who not only put me in touch with the best farmers but also fed in quite a lot of material for my weekly page.

My first editorial set out the objectives of the new weekly page, which, put simply, were to cover all the issues affecting those who lived in the countryside, and especially to show how farming was an integral part of rural life, and how change was affecting the environment in which people lived.

The first issue seemed to be well received, though there was little feedback to begin with, and the circulation didn't increase, which I found depressing after all the hard work we'd put into it. Eric consoled me by saying that he had not expected an immediate response, and said that it would take time for it to build up.

I got out into the countryside as often as I could, to make myself known at meetings of various organisations and the main events. It was not long before material started to flow back, and it became easier to find enough to fill the page with news, quite apart from the special articles and interviews that I commissioned.

The main casualty in the early days was my social life, as there was simply not time for games of squash, or if there was, there could be no lingering in the bar afterwards. I would clamber into bed at night, wondering why I had ever wanted such a job, and think longingly of the time when I had no real responsibility except keeping to deadlines set by others. But by Christmas, things began to ease up, and I was able to build up a bank of material that I could save for future issues.

Three days at home at Christmas were a welcome break, with the usual family gathering. My sister Caroline's three children were growing fast, with Daniel, the eldest, now seven, already showing an interest in the farm. He would demand to be taken up to the milking parlour to see the cows milked, and to be allowed to give the calves their afternoon feed of artificial milk. He was turning into a strapping boy, with a very happy disposition, and was already beginning to look a bit like Dad, who was naturally delighted that he was showing such an interest in the farm – rather as my father himself had forty years earlier.

As usual when I went home my thoughts turned to Simon, and I'd wonder if I would ever find someone to hold and love, and with whom I could relax after a stressful day. Probably not, and even if I did, would I have enough time to give to him in the hectic life that I was leading? Better to forget it for the time being, and get my satisfaction from the challenge of building up my weekly page.

For some years I had read reports of an agricultural conference held in Oxford each January, and the programme for the one this January had arrived on my desk in October. The Minister of Agriculture was billed to speak at the dinner on the first evening. I thought that I would go and make some useful contacts there, as well as pick up material for my page.

I left the office in Gillian's capable hands, and drove over to Oxford in the morning, as I wanted to find my way around before it got dark. I was there by lunchtime and, having located the hotel and conference venues, had time to look into two of the colleges whose gates were open. Immediately I was struck by the tranquillity of the university in the winter sunshine. Everywhere was a sense of history, of permanence and stability. I could almost feel the presence of past generations of students in the dining halls and chapels. I would have loved to have studied in a place like this. But if I had, I wouldn't have met Simon. Perhaps it was as well I had done what I did, since meeting him had transformed my life.

The dinner was in one of the larger hotels and when I got there, in what I thought was good time, the place was swarming with people. Once again I felt like the new boy that I was, and wondered what to do.

'You look lost, Mark, is this the first time you've been?'

It was a relief to see a face I knew: Brian Gilchrist, a journalist with whom I had got friendly at an environment conference the year before.

'Yes, it's my first time. I'd no idea it would be such a scrum.'

'I'll look after you, then, as I'm an old hand. The first thing we must do is to turn down a couple of chairs at the table where most of the press sit, or we'll never get a seat together. It's always a full house. Then we'll have time to get a drink which we can take in if we have to.'

He forced his way through a crowd at one of the bars and emerged with two pints of beer.

'It's a bit like an old comrade's reunion. People come back every year, especially farmers from all over the country, who probably don't see each other from one year to the next. Some have attended ever since it was restarted in 1951. I'm told that several were actually at the first one in 1936.' From the hubbub, I could quite believe it.

A stentorian voice commanded us into dinner, and as we stood waiting for the bigwigs to take their seats I glanced to my right to see who my next neighbour might be. His face looked vaguely familiar, but I couldn't place him. I looked at his name badge and the penny dropped. It was Norman Briggs, the reporter who had come to the farm seven years before to write it up. He recognised me too.

'Mark Harper,' he said. 'I came to your farm in Devon once to see your father. That was a really good day, and I much enjoyed going round the farm, and having lunch with you. Is this the first time you've been to Oxford? If it is, we'd better introduce you to some of the gang, as they can be very useful for networking and exchanging information. Have you met Andrew Marden? He's recently taken over as head of the BBC's agricultural department.'

'No, I've hardly met anyone yet. One reason for coming to the conference was to establish contacts. So far, Brian is the only person I know.'

'Right, we'll make a start, then.' He shouted across the table to a nice, friendly looking person opposite me: 'Andrew! Have you met Mark Harper? He's the new correspondent at the *Westerton Herald*.'

'Glad to meet you, Mark. Hope you're enjoying it. We must have a talk sometime, as you might be able to help me occasionally. I'll look out for you later on.'

Norman then introduced me to two others on the other side of the table, and Brian did the same with a Scottish journalist on his left. It was already becoming clear that Oxford was the right place to meet people.

'Have you joined the Guild of Agricultural Journalists?' Brian asked.

'No, not yet, though I want to soon. I'll need two sponsors, I suppose?'

'I'd be happy to propose you and I expect Norman would second you as well.' He attracted the latter's attention. 'You'd be willing to second Mark for the Guild, would you?'

'Yes, of course. We'll see the secretary tomorrow and get it fixed up.'

After a good deal of three-way discussion, it was time for speeches. I'd been given a handout of the minister's speech but hadn't had time to look at it. That didn't matter a great deal as it was full of platitudes about the Common Market, which Britain had joined two years earlier. I learnt the lesson that ministers seldom say anything of importance in a dinner speech, and rely on smooth platitudes to get them by. This one was typical, but was fortunately followed by a speech from a witty Oxford academic, who made fun of him in a donnish way.

For quite a time I'd been conscious of a continuous leg pressure under the table on Norman's side. Admittedly we were packed in pretty tight, but not as tight as all that. Coming on top of his habit of looking at me a bit longer than was necessary when we were talking, this had raised a few doubts in my mind about his attitude towards me. I decided that I wouldn't draw away for the time being but would wait, as I might be misreading the situation. Time would no doubt tell.

'Where are you staying?' he said as we got up at the end of the dinner. 'Are you in one of the colleges?'

'No, I'm only here for the one night. I've got to get back tomorrow evening, so I managed to get a room at the Northgate.'

'Oh, I'm staying there, too. Shall we walk back there together? We'll get a drink there as it'll be less crowded than here, where it's always a scrum.

'What did you think of it?' he asked as we walked back.

'The minister's speech was a dead loss, and I shan't get any copy out of it. That old don was first class, but I suppose they're used to it in their profession. But the atmosphere is terrific – rather like an old comrades reunion I had to report on once. Everybody seemed to know everyone else.'

'From long experience, I've learnt never to expect much from politician's speeches, unless it's a special press conference. They seldom come clean, though very occasionally they use the event for an important announcement about policy. They always seem afraid of letting some cat out of the bag.'

We had reached the hotel, where there was almost as big a crowd as up at the hotel. Norman introduced me to two more journalists, one of whom was from the same paper that Eric had come from in the eastern counties.

'I think you'll like him,' the journalist said. 'He's extremely bright and go-ahead, and very fair minded. We were very sorry to lose him, and you're lucky to get him.'

'He's certainly made a good impression so far.'

'It's awfully noisy down here, isn't it?' said Norman. 'Why don't we go up to my room and get a nightcap out of the minibar – if you feel like one before bed?'

'Yes, just a quick one, though I don't want to be too late into bed.'

Warning bells were sounding in my brain that he might have an ulterior motive in asking me up to his room. But I might be completely misjudging the situation, in which case it wouldn't matter. If I wasn't getting it wrong and he had designs on me, I would have to decide what to do when the critical moment arrived. I liked him as a person and he'd already been extremely helpful in introducing me to a lot of very useful people so it would have seemed churlish to refuse. He was not my type, but that sort of thing might not be in his mind, anyhow.

'I take it you're not married?' he said as we got up to his room.

'No, and I assume that applies to you too, doesn't it?'

'What makes you think that?'

'It's just the way you've been looking at me both here and at home, and other little signals suggest to me that you may not be entirely straight.'

'Oh, dear, was it as obvious as all that? I'll have to be more careful in future, shan't I? So you obviously know the ropes. I don't know why, but I had some suspicion that you might be gay when I was at the farm that day, even though you don't show any signs of it.'

'I don't know that you do, either, apart from your habit of staring at men as if you were sizing them up for some immoral purpose.'

He laughed at that. 'OK, I suppose that was what I was doing in your case, as I do find you terribly attractive. Meeting you again here brought it back to me. I wouldn't want to push you in any way, but I would love to take you to bed.'

I hadn't been with Robert for quite some time, and although Norman didn't attract me in a sexual way, I suddenly felt a strong physical need to be in someone's arms again, and to enjoy the sensual pleasure of another body close to mine.

'I must tell you that you're not really my type at all, and it would have to be just a one-off, with no long-term implications.'

'Of course,' he said as we moved towards the bed.

As soon as we had taken our clothes off and lay together, I realised that I had made a grave mistake. He was too big for me in every way. When stripped down his body was rather fat and flabby, and he was rough in his eagerness to possess me. He had none of the tenderness displayed by Simon or Robert. I felt that he was rather greedy. To make matters worse for me, it wasn't long before he said: 'Would you like to take it?'

'No, I'm sorry. I'm too tight.' I had no idea whether I was or not, but it seemed as good an excuse as any.

'That's all right. It doesn't matter. I just thought you might like it; and I would have enjoyed it as you really do have a beautiful body. Let's just enjoy being together.'

But I wasn't enjoying it. I hoped that it wouldn't be long before I could give him what he wanted, as I had come quickly myself, and was beginning to think longingly of my own bed.

As we were dressing, he suddenly said 'Have you ever been really in love with someone?'

'Yes, very much so, but he was killed in a car crash about a year after we met. It had happened a few months before you came to our farm. I missed him terribly, and still do, but I'm too busy now to think too much about him. He'll always be with me, though.'

'I'm so sorry. It must have been devastating, but at least you'll have happy memories. I've never had a close relationship, but I do hope to meet the right man one day, though it'll get more difficult as I get older, I expect. I don't look forward to old age on my own.'

I felt sorry for him as he said that, and wondered if I would be saying the same when I was his age.

'Thanks so much, Norman. I enjoyed that. See you at breakfast.'

As I went back to my room, I thought of Simon again, and how I'd sworn to myself after his death that I wouldn't ever go to bed with a man unless I loved him. Yet here I was, jumping into bed at the first opportunity with someone whom I didn't care for physically at all. I felt a deep sense of guilt, and decided to have a shower to try to wash the shame away.

Brian had been right to say the previous evening that those at the conference were a pretty shrewd lot, for a great deal of constructive comment came up from the floor – almost as valuable for me as the papers themselves. Between them, I garnered enough for two future editorials, and later in the day got material down on tape from three contributors. During the coffee break I was talking to a farmer when Andrew Marden came up.

'Glad to meet you last night, Mark. I hope you're finding it good value. I'm always on the lookout for short pieces to put into *Farming Today*, so if you ever have anything on your pitch which you think might be useful, do just give me a ring. I won't guarantee to use it, as we never know quite how much time we have till the last moment.'

'Of course, I'd like to do that, though I'll have to clear it with my editor first. I'm pretty sure he'll have no objection. In principle, I'd like to do a piece now and again.'

Over the buffet lunch, a farmer from Lincolnshire came up.

'I don't think I've seen you here before, have I?'

'No, it's my first time. I've just taken over as agricultural correspondent for the *Westerton Herald*.'

'I hope you're getting some useful stuff for your paper then. What did you think of the dinner last night?'

'I enjoyed the dinner itself, but I was disappointed by the minister, who really said nothing you could get hold of.'

'Quite right. When I was on the committee some years ago, we passed a resolution never to invite a cabinet minister to speak, but the present lot seem to have forgotten all about it. Hey, Mike,' he shouted to an elderly grey-haired man with a file under his arm, who was just passing. 'Mike, this is Mark Harper of the *Westerton Herald*.' It was the conference organiser who had sent me my tickets and copies of the speakers' papers.

'Good to meet you, Mark. I was glad to get your application as we don't get many people from your area, and it might help if you can give the conference a bit of publicity. Roger, here, came to the first one in 1951, and I don't think he's missed once since, have you, Roger?'

'Only once when I was having a hip replacement in 1965 – and of course when it was cancelled that year because of foot and mouth. How on earth do you remember all this, anyhow?'

'I suppose it's because I handle all the applications myself, and it's easier then to remember names and addresses. Anyway, I couldn't possibly forget an old stager like you, especially after your three years on the committee.'

'Talking of that, Mike, what on earth were you doing inviting the minister to the dinner last night? Have you forgotten that resolution I got through that we'd never invite a prominent politician ever again?'

'I certainly hadn't forgotten, but I couldn't stop them from doing it. They seemed determined to have him. I must be losing my grip in old age.'

'No risk of that, I'm sure. You're very much on the ball still.'

As they were speaking, a thought struck me.

'I wonder if I could give you a ring one day to find out more about the conference, and how it got started in the first place? I'd like to do an article on it, and try to get some of our local farmers interested.'

'Yes, of course,' said Mike. 'I'm usually lecturing at nine o'clock in term time, and out on the farm in the afternoon if I haven't rushed off to London for a meeting. Late morning's the best time. Sorry, I must dash and round up the afternoon speakers.'

I didn't see Norman to say goodbye, but he had already signed my form to join the Guild of Journalists, which Brian had also signed, so that was all under way. Driving home, I resolved to come again the following year, but this time to stay in a college, where I would probably meet more farmers rather than my own fraternity. It had been an enormously valuable experience, making so many useful contacts. Gillian had coped well in my absence so I felt I could safely get away more in the future.

Having got on to the conference circuit, I found that the next one was at the end of February in London, the annual meeting of the National Farmers' Union. I still didn't know London well, but Brian had given me the name of a relatively inexpensive hotel where he stayed. I had been up for several day meetings, and once had two full days when Jack and Cynthia had come up for three days and invited me to stay with them. We had been to the theatre twice, and they had shown me the sights, so I could just about find my way around.

It was quite an experience, seeing the leaders of the industry in action – very different from Oxford. I did get a couple of useful articles from it, but there was far too much political belly-aching against what was now called the European Community. Norman was there, but staying in a different hotel. He was very friendly but no reference was made to our brief encounter.

On my getting back from Oxford, Eric had asked me to see him.

'You seem to have got things well under control, Mark. What would you say if I suggested that we produce a special four-page spring issue? It could help to bring in fresh readers, and produce more advertising revenue at the same time. It'd obviously give you a lot more work, but do you think you could handle it?'

'I think I should be able to manage it, as I've got some articles banked that needn't go out just yet, and they could wait till then. It'll certainly be hard work on top of the normal page, though I suppose it could replace it for that week. When do you think it should go out?'

'I'd think the end of March would be about right. That'd give you two months to put it together and to get more advertising.'

'That sounds all right to me. I think it's a good idea.' So I was now saddled with a lot more work just as I had begun to think that I was getting on top of the job.

I focused quite a lot on environmental topics, not only on the farm, but on how change was affecting local communities. There were some good photographs, a couple of feature articles and I wrote a piece about the Oxford conference, having previously got details from Mike, the organiser. I thought it looked well, and hoped that pride wouldn't come before a fall. Robert, who knew nothing about farming, said he was very impressed with it, and Eric was pleased as it generated quite a bit of additional advertising.

'I thought it was a good effort,' he said. 'Why don't we try another one in the autumn, so that we'll have two a year?' So from then on I was saddled with the two special editions. It wasn't long before I was able to put articles that would keep into storage if I thought they would suit the next special. Within a year of starting it up circulation was increasing, which also helped to bring in more advertising.

The summer passed pleasantly enough. I went to the Royal Show at Coventry for the first time, where I met up with press colleagues and picked up some useful information from a number of the technical exhibits. But, livestock aside, it left me a bit cold. It was far removed from our farming at home, as we had never been into the world of wealthy pedigree breeders, and certainly didn't intend to do so. It all seemed too glitzy, and I had inherited Dad's down-to-earth approach to farming.

Most of the holiday was spent at home, helping with harvest and getting my hands dirty. The three days with Aunt Emily were enjoyable. The two cousins drove me down to Polzeath for a day's surfing, which brought back terribly mixed memories of being in the sea with Simon, and lying side by side in hot sunshine on the cliffs. I suddenly realised how much I was missing through not having a love in my life, but there was nothing I could do about it.

Just after that an event occurred that had a significant effect on my future life, though I didn't know it at the time. The World Ploughing Match was being held on a farm that I had come to know well, about twelve miles from Westerton. I thought I'd ring Andrew Marden to see if he might like me to do a piece on it for *Farming Today*.

'Certainly I would,' he said in answer to my query. 'I'd thought of sending someone over but no one was free, so I had decided to leave it.'

'How long should it be?'

'I can only give you eight minutes, I'm afraid, so you'll have to make it snappy. I'll need it by six thirty on Thursday evening.'

'OK, I think I should be able to manage that.' I suddenly realised that I should have checked with Eric first, so I put my head round his door.

'Yes, go ahead, but try to get a mention of the paper into it, if you can.'

It was a lot more difficult than I had expected. I had to introduce a little local colour at the start and include an interview with the president, who that year was a Frenchman. Then I needed a short piece from the English president, and two more from prize-winners. The Frenchman, whose English was poor, went on far too long, as did the English president whom I couldn't shut up. The overall champion, a Dutchman, was much better and spoke good English and kept to time; but the only English winner of a class, from Devon, was not very articulate. At six o'clock I was still wrestling with the tape trying desperately to get down to Andrew's eight minutes. In the nick of time I managed it, by cutting down the Frenchman still further, hoping he'd still be in bed when it went out in the morning, and not get offended. At the appointed time it was down the line to the BBC. I thought it came over reasonably well next day, though I couldn't believe it was my voice talking, as I had never heard it before.

Andrew rang later in the morning to thank me for it, saying that it was a good effort for the first time. That was the start of a long collaboration with him, and my introduction to broad-casting, which led ultimately to television.

Norman had told me about a conference in Brighton each November devoted to the use of chemicals in farming. I thought I should go as it was a subject that kept cropping up in the course of my work. I rather wanted to see Brighton, because Robert and his partner went down there sometimes at weekends. He said that it had become a centre for gay activities. I had no intention of wasting precious time in looking for sex, but I was curious to know if it was very obvious. I was not promiscuous by nature, as Norman appeared to be, and had no desire to pick up a stranger.

It was there that Norman made a tentative approach which I speedily rebuffed. He took it well, and from then on we remained just good friends, as the saying goes.

It was a useful conference from my point of view as it helped me to appreciate the importance of the chemical industry in modern farming practice. It was an advantage that I was able to relate much of it to our own farm, and it provided ammunition when I had to deal with the lunatic fringe of extreme right wing environmentalists – as I had to many times in the future. As at Oxford, I made useful contacts that would be of value if I needed professional advice for articles I might be writing.

Almost before I knew it, Christmas was on us once more. After a happy four days at home, when I found time to go over to see Jack and Cynthia, it was back to work and my second visit to Oxford for the conference, where I had booked into a college for both nights. I wanted to get a flavour of student life, and to meet more farmers over meals instead of mixing with my own fraternity all the time.

I got there early so as to find somewhere to park the car, as colleges built 300 or more years ago were not part of the automotive age. The college porter directed me to my room, two floors up a narrow staircase worn down by the feet of countless undergraduates over the centuries. It was a comfortable sitting room, with a small bedroom leading off, and views across the garden in its winter clothing. There was a wash basin and hot water heater, but no sign of a loo, which I was now in need of. Surely I wouldn't have to walk across a freezing quad in the middle of the night if I wanted a pee?

I found steps leading to the basement at the foot of the stairs. Pushing open the door I found a changing room with showers and, to my relief, cubicles suitably equipped for my immediate needs. Perhaps Oxford was not so primitive after all.

Tea and biscuits were on offer in the dining hall. As I opened the heavy door I was met by a loud buzz of conversation. There was no one there that I recognised, but that didn't matter for, as I took my cup, a large, red-faced, cheerful-looking man turned to me.

'I don't think I know you, do I? Is it your first time here?'

'No, probably not. I did come last year but stayed in a hotel. This year, I thought it would be more fun to stay in college and meet more people. I see from your badge you come from Devon. Are you farming there?'

'I farm about 900 acres with my brother, not far from Plymouth. You know Devon then?'

'Yes, my father farms up near Norton. I suppose one day I may take over from him, but at present I'm an agricultural journalist, as he doesn't really need me at home.'

'Your father wouldn't be John Harper, would he? If so, I've met him once or twice at union meetings in Exeter.'

'Yes, that's Dad. I'm afraid he's not much of a union man. He prefers being on the farm to sitting in meetings, which he thinks are often a waste of time. Have you been coming up here to the conference for long?'

'About fifteen years, I suppose. It's a marvellous way of keeping in touch with what is going on, both in farming and in its politics, as they always seem to get good speakers. You meet farmers from all over the place, which is refreshing, and it helps to recharge the batteries. People are always very clued up, or they wouldn't come.'

At that moment Mike, the organiser, came up with a cup of tea. He looked harassed. 'George, it's good to see you again. How are things in Devon? Mark, I was pleased to get your application, and to see that you're happy to slum it in college. Most of your people prefer the luxury of a hotel.'

'I thought that I'd probably meet more farmers here, and anyhow I wanted to sample student life again. By the way, thanks for giving me so much time on the phone that day. I featured the conference in my spring special, but haven't had any feedback. I'm working on a couple of younger farmers to try to get them to come next year.'

'Got a good crowd this year, Mike?'

'About six hundred plus. Not like the old days when we packed in over a thousand one year, but that was a bit too much of a good thing. Sorry, I'll have to dash and put out the place names on the top table for the dinner.' At that he was away.

'Astonishing how he seems to do it all himself,' George said, and I agreed.

I sat next to Norman again at the dinner, but there was no repetition of the previous year's contact – though he did lean over once and ask in a low voice: 'Have you found anyone special yet?' To which I replied, 'Afraid not.' The speeches were better than on the last occasion, and I did get some useful copy from one of them.

Andrew Marden came up in the coffee break. 'Thanks for that bit you did for me on the ploughing match. Let me have anything you think could be useful. I'll get in touch if I've a job you could do for us.'

I was glad that I had stayed in college, as I met more people than the year before, and came away with several tapes and the names of at least two people whom I hoped to interview in the future for writing up their farms.

So life went on through the spring and early summer, and I had more time for a social life once I had got out the spring special issue. My squash had improved considerably over the years, and I actually got through two rounds of the club's knockout competition. There was an occasional fling with Robert if John was away, and we still played together regularly, though I now had other partners who sharpened up my game.

Cooking had improved to the point that I felt confident enough to ask a few friends like Angela in for a meal. Eric had invited me to his home to meet his wife and teenage sons. They were an easy couple to get on with. Greatly daring, I asked them back for an evening meal at the flat. It was hardly an adventurous menu, but they seemed to enjoy it. He had proved to be an excellent boss, and soon became more of a friend than an employer.

Early in March the phone had rung one morning.

'Mark, it's Andrew here. I wonder if you could do a job for me? There's an environmental conference in Malvern next Tuesday which I'd like to feature, but I've got no one to cover it. Could you take it on?'

'I'd thought of going to it anyhow, but hadn't definitely decided. Yes, I'll do it for you. How many minutes would I have for it?'

'Twelve minutes at the outside, but preferably only ten, and I'll need it by six thirty. Keep off the lunatics if you can.'

'I certainly will. I don't like them any more than you do.'

There were two good speakers, and I got short tape recordings from both of them. This time I was not tearing my hair out at 6.25 as I had been the first time, but gave him a good piece in eleven minutes flat. He was obviously satisfied as he gave two more commissions at events during the summer.

It seemed that my name was beginning to get known, because the producer of *Farming West* rang just before I went on holiday to ask if I could do a report for him on a West Country farmer who had moved up and started a new state-of-the-art beef unit in the North Midlands. It would save him a long journey if I could. It proved an interesting assignment, and I was able to use a bit of it myself later on.

Most of the holiday was spent at home as usual, but I had a few days at Aunt Emily's, which included some surf bathing, and a visit to Polzeath with my two cousins, now grown-up. It was only the second time I'd been back there since Simon's death.

Inevitably, there was a feeling of great sadness that he was not there to share it, though once or twice I actually felt that he was rushing past me, yelling with delight at having caught a big one. I enjoyed it all the same, as it felt good to be on a board again on a good surfing beach.

The harvest period was memorable, too, for Daniel had persuaded his mother to let him come to stay at the farm for a couple of weeks. He was too young, at nine, to help with the harvest, but he was entrusted with feeding some of the calves, and went out with Dad to help with the shepherding. Dad and Mother were delighted to have him in the house, as it brought back memories of their own children.

I had recently got the impression that they had given up all hope of me giving them grandchildren, as they never questioned me about girlfriends. Already I felt that Dad was seeing Daniel as the one to carry on the farming line eventually – which made me happy.

Chapter Six

That summer saw my first appearance on television. I had met the producer of the BBC programme, Alan Buxton, at Oxford once, but didn't know him at all well, so when the phone rang I had to think twice who it was.

'I wonder whether you might be able to help me, Mark. I'm putting together a programme on chemicals in agriculture. I heard your bit about the conference at Malvern, and this one will cover the same sort of ground. I've already lined up an arable farmer and also someone from the fanatical fringe, but I want someone who could act as a kind of middleman to present a really balanced view. It struck me that it might be up your street. Would you like to take it on?'

'Yes, I'd be happy to give it a go. I'm no expert, though if it's just a matter of coming in now and again to present a balanced view I could probably do that all right.'

'Fine. The programme is scheduled for Sunday three weeks from now. We'll need you for a rehearsal at ten thirty in Birmingham. As you know the programme goes out live at one o'clock.'

'I should be able to manage that. Perhaps you could confirm nearer the day?'

'Of course. So glad you'll do it.'

Actually when we did go on air, I didn't get much of a look-in. The two speakers got at each other's throats straight away, and went at it hammer and tongs. But I did break in when the fanatical environmentalist said that fertilisers poisoned the soil.

'If that were the case,' I said, 'how do you account for the fact that crop yields have consistently increased since fertilisers came in the 1840s and are now roughly five times greater than they were then? You're talking rubbish.' To which there was no reply.

I did get in a few more interventions, but I didn't feel that it had got us any further forward. My initial nervousness at being in front of the cameras wore off quite quickly – as Alan had said it would when I had dried up once during the rehearsal. But I decided that live television would be a bit too stressful if I were playing anything but a minor part.

It didn't seem a year since I had gone to the conference in Brighton, but the programme looked interesting and I decided to go to it again, as the whole debate about chemicals in farming seemed to be heating up. This time I drove down to see whether it was quicker than going by train. It worked out at about the same – just under three hours.

By the end of the first day I felt punch drunk with scientific information. After getting my piece off to *Farming West* and having a bit of dinner, a walk was clearly necessary to get fresh air.

It was a warm evening and, as usual, the Brighton air was invigorating as I walked rapidly along the front towards Hove. I had a feeling that Simon was very close, and I told him how much I still missed him. I was so engrossed with my thoughts that I hardly noticed the figure coming towards me, and nearly bumped into him. As we drew abreast I saw that he had a broad, friendly looking face, and fairish hair that reminded me a little of Simon, and then he had passed. I don't know why I stopped and looked back – perhaps it was the hair. He had done the same, and we both stood there for some moments. Then he turned and came back towards me.

'Nice evening for a walk, isn't it?' he said.

'Yes, I'm really enjoying it. The air's marvellous, and I love the sound of the sea.'

'I should think you need some fresh air after sitting in a conference all day.'

'What makes you think I've been to a conference?'

'Well, you don't need to be a Sherlock Holmes to read a name badge, do you?'

We both laughed heartily at that. In my haste to get out, I had completely forgotten to take it off.

'That was a stupid thing to do,' I said. 'It might have been an invitation to some thug to beat me up and steal my wallet, I suppose.'

'No danger of that with me, I can assure you. I'm perfectly safe.'

'I'm sure you are. You've got far too honest a face to beat anyone up. My name's Mark, by the way.'

'I'm Guy.' At which we shook hands, but his handshake lasted a bit longer than it need have done – as mine did, too.

'Do you mind if I join you? It's nicer walking with someone than being on your own.'

'I was just thinking when I nearly bumped into you how much nicer it would be if I had a friend with me. In fact I was talking to an invisible one, which is why I didn't see you.'

'Well, you've got me now, so I hope I'll be a good substitute for whoever it was.'

'I'm sure you will.' There was something about his easy manner and complete lack of reserve that I found very attractive, quite apart from what I could see of his face under the street lights. He had the same self-confidence as Simon, and I felt already that I'd known him for years.

'Where are you staying?' he asked. 'At one of the big hotels, I expect.'

'Well, yes. But I'm not paying, as I'm a journalist and not a scientist, so my paper has to pay for me to be here.'

'What paper is that then?'

'One you've probably never heard of – the *Westerton Herald* – where I'm responsible for the weekly page on farming and countryside issues.'

'No, I can't say I've heard of it, though I did go though Westerton once. I thought it looked a nice kind of city with an old-fashioned feel about it in the centre.'

'It's a good place to live – not too big, but large enough to have plenty going on most of the time. I'm very happy there. What do you do?'

'I'm an accountant with one of the bigger local firms.'

'Do you live here permanently?'

'Yes, I've got a small flat in Hove. It's only about ten minutes' walk from here. Would you like to come back for a coffee or a drink?'

'I'd love to, though I don't want to be late back.'

'I've got the car outside the flat, so I could give you a lift back to the hotel.'

It was rather less than ten minutes, and we never stopped talking all the way, exchanging details about ourselves and our lives. He was two years younger than me and had moved to Hove after doing his training with a big City company. He found commuting to London each day from Croydon, where his parents lived, quite unbearable. He'd been to a public school in Kent, but decided against going on to university as he wanted to start earning as soon as possible. He'd realised that he was gay while still at school, and moved to Hove to be independent, expecting that Brighton would give him greater sexual freedom. But he'd found the local gay scene was not to his liking – too promiscuous, and too strident and flamboyant. All he wanted was someone to love and settle down with, but so far he hadn't found him.

'If you don't like promiscuity, how come you picked me up so readily?'

'Oh, I could tell as soon as I saw you that you weren't in that league, and anyhow that name badge suggested otherwise.'

By that time we'd reached his flat, which was on the second floor of a terraced house on a side road off the main road from Brighton to Hove.

'Coffee or a drink?'

'I'd like a soft drink if you've got one. I've had too much coffee already, and won't get to sleep if I have any more.'

'Only orange squash I'm afraid. I've run out of anything more exotic.'

'It'll do me fine. Just what I was hoping for.'

'So I assume you're unattached, Mark?'

'Yes, and likely to remain so. A girl tried to seduce me once, and I realised that a soft clinging body repelled me, and that confirmed what I had suspected that I must be gay. Then I fell deeply in love with another man when I was at college. I decided that I shouldn't marry, as it wouldn't be fair on the girl, even if I could give her what she wanted, which might be doubtful. I'd like kids, though I suppose I'll never have them.'

In the brighter light of his sitting room, Guy was even more attractive than he appeared under the street lights. His hair reminded me of Simon's, though it was shorter and less curly. But it was his broad, smiling face, blue eyes, wide mouth and well-shaped nose that really drew me to him.

About the same height as myself, he was as near to my type as it was possible to get, short of a reincarnated Simon.

'So what happened to your lover? Is he still there in the background letting you play away if you want to?'

'I'm afraid not. He was killed in a car crash only thirteen months after we had got together, and I've been alone ever since.' I could only just get the last words out, because of the lump in my throat, and I could feel tears very close.

He saw my distress, and came over and put his arms around me, giving me a tight hug, and burying his head in my shoulder.

'I'm so sorry, Mark. It must have been unbearable if you were really in love.'

'It was terrible at the time, and I wondered how I'd ever be able to carry on without him. But life has to go on, and as the years have passed and I've got more and more busy in my job, with more responsibility, memories have begun to fade, though I still talk to him most days. In fact, I was talking to him when I nearly bumped into you.'

We were still in each other's arms, when he said: 'I do find you awfully attractive, Mark. Would you like to take it further?'

'Very much so. I've not met anyone like you since Simon died, and I'm sure we must be compatible.' No qualms this time about going to bed with someone to whom I was not attracted. This was no sudden clinch as it had been with Norman, but a mutual coming together of two people who were instinctively attracted to one another.

We hardly spoke as we got undressed by his bed; then, as the last piece was gone and our bodies merged we both gave huge sighs of relief and satisfaction at exactly the same time. His body was beautifully proportioned, strong in the upper half, slim at the waist, and then broad again at the hips. His equipment was quite similar to mine, which was a relief, as I was never happy with oversized men. Both of us had been starved of sex for quite a time, so it was not long before we reached our climaxes almost together – a rare event, but one that meant that we could both relax together in each other's arms.

'How was it, Mark? Are you glad we met?'

'Quite wonderful. I had begun to think that I'd never find

anyone like you again. We're made for each other, don't you think?'

'Yes, I've never felt so completely together with anyone before. It's miraculous.'

We lay completely happy and I wished that we could be there for ever. After a time, I looked at my watch. It said eleven thirty. Where had the time gone?

'I'll have to be getting back, Guy. It's a long day tomorrow and I must get some sleep.'

'Why not spend the night here? I could run you back to the hotel in the morning.'

I felt sorely tempted, especially by the thought of waking up and finding him there beside me. But I decided I must go so as to be ready for the first session in the morning.

'I'd love to stay, but I must get back. Another time, perhaps?'

'I'll drive you back then.'

We hugged and kissed again as we reached the door, and on the way back, I rested my hand on his thigh – just as I used to do with Simon.

'We can't leave it here, can we?' he said as we reached the hotel. 'I simply must see you again. Give me your phone number, so that we can talk again soon.'

We swapped our numbers, and promised to speak in a few days.

'Sleep well, love, and thanks for a fantastic evening,' he said as I closed the door.

Lying in bed that night and going over the events of the day, I wondered at the sheer unpredictability of life. At one moment I had been walking along enjoying the evening and thinking of Simon; the next moment encountering someone who might conceivably change the course of my life for ever.

The sex that we had had was something I had only dreamed of since Simon died. Could this possibly be the start of a friendship that might equal that first with him? It would be marvellous if it could, but a nagging thought at the back of my mind kept telling me that it might not work in practice.

Driving home in the grey, foggy light of a November after-noon, the doubt returned. In the first place, there were the pure logistics with me in Westerton and him in Hove, nearly 200 miles away. It would not be like Angela and Janet, who had only to hop on a train for a relatively short journey. It would always take us three hours.

Obviously I couldn't move down to be near him, and if he came to live with, or near me, he'd have to find a job, break the ties with his friends, and start a new life, knowing nobody but me. Even if he did, would I really be able, now that I was so tied up in my work, to give him the time he needed? Probably not, now that I was away so much. That could only lead to unhappiness in the end. Perhaps we should call the whole thing off and regard it as just one of those things which might have been if only circumstances had been different.

Two evenings later, the phone rang.

'Where have you been the last two nights? I've rung about five times, and you never seem to be there. Did you have a good drive back on Tuesday?'

'Sorry, Guy. I've been out at meetings. Two nights ago it was an "Any Questions" meeting in a small town miles away, and last night a farmers' meeting at which it was important to show my face to establish contacts. Yes, it wasn't a bad journey, though it took about three hours from door to door. How are you?'

'In a bit of a daze since meeting you. I felt that I just had to ring you to thank you for Tuesday night. It was so fabulous that I can't believe it really happened. It was all so sudden and unexpected, and it was over so soon, it seems like a dream. Yet I feel that I've known you for years.'

'I feel the same, but I've been doing some serious thinking. We simply mustn't allow ourselves to get too carried away, for quite honestly I can't see much of a future for it in the long term. We're too far apart to be able to see each other often enough to sustain a permanent relationship. You've got your base and friends down there, and I have my very busy job up here. I even doubt whether we could manage weekends together regularly.'

'I do realise you're very tied to your job, but I'm not. I could leave mine and nobody would much notice. I could move up nearer to you, even if you didn't want us to live together. I could probably get another job quite easily with my qualifications. I've not many friends down here. I want to be near you.'

'You're getting carried away in the euphoria of the moment. Say you did move to live closer to me, there isn't room in my flat for two of us, so you'd have to find somewhere to live. My job isn't a nine-to-five affair when I'd be able to see you every evening. I'm usually out at meetings three nights a week, and work late one night putting the paper to bed. Then I like to get in a game of squash one evening a week to keep fit. Then I am quite often away at the weekend. Finally, I might have to go back home to run the farm at a moment's notice if anything happened to my father, and you'd be left high and dry. It hurts to say this, but I honestly think we'd be wise to put our phones down and tear up the numbers.'

'You can't really mean that, after Tuesday evening, can you? I may have underestimated how busy you are, but surely we could see enough of one another to hold us together? I played squash at school, so I could join your club, and we could get games together. Obviously we shouldn't rush into things, so perhaps we could have a weekend together before deciding about the future?'

'OK, I could agree weekends, either down there with you or up here with me, but I want an undertaking from you first. Promise that you won't build up romantic ideas about falling in love with me. I've been there once, and believe me, the pain it can bring if things go wrong just isn't worth it.'

'Sorry, Mark. It's already too late. For me it's been a case of love at first sight. It's something completely new, which I've never experienced before.'

'It can't be real love when we've only spent a few hours together. It's a temporary infatuation which won't last long – like most infatuations. You're just falling in love with the idea of love – like that old song: "Falling in love with love is falling for make-believe." It can't be the real thing so soon. Let's leave it for now, and think about a weekend together. I don't think that I can fit one in now before Christmas, and shortly after that I'll be in Oxford for a conference for two days, so it'll have to be a little time before we can meet. I'm sorry.'

'I'll just have to accept that, I suppose. I had hoped that we could meet sooner than that. Can I ring you next week?'

'Yes, of course, Thursday would probably be the best night. Sleep well.'

'I'll try to, but I'll be thinking of you first.'

I realised then that it was indeed too late to break it off, as it would hurt him desperately. In my heart of hearts, I was glad, for already I was half in love with him myself and was impatient to see him again.

He rang the following week, just after I'd got back from the Smithfield Show in London.

'How are you? I hope you've had a good week since we spoke last.'

'Not very good, really. I had to go to London to the agricultural show at Smithfield both to get some copy for my paper and also to record a piece for the *Farming West* programme. It was very crowded and stuffy, and I picked up a cold and am now snuffling and blocked up. How are things with you?'

'It's been a pretty deadly week, with dull work in the office, and counting the days till we can meet again. I was bored, so I went home for the weekend as my brother and his wife were down from Norfolk. I'm going to be an uncle in a couple of months. Are you one?'

'Yes, four times over. The eldest one, Daniel, is nine now and already showing a lot of interest in the farm. I'm hoping that he'll take over from me one day, as I shan't be having any children of my own. What are you doing for Christmas?'

'I'll be going home for a week. My younger sister will be there, and she's a very lively girl, so it shouldn't be too boring. What about you? Will you be going home?'

'Yes, I hope to get four days, and we'll have all the family in on Christmas Day, which is always fun. Otherwise I shan't be doing very much. Soon after that, I'll be off to Oxford for a conference for two days. '

'Mark, you didn't really mean what you said about ending it, did you? It's been haunting me all the week, and I can't bear the thought of it. I'll promise not to be too possessive or make demands on you. Surely we could meet sometimes without complicating things too much, couldn't we?'

'Yes, I expect we could, as I do very much want to be with you again. It's just that I don't want to make you unhappy if we can't see each other very often. If you did get too fond of me, and then something went wrong, I'd have a terrible feeling of guilt that I had let you down. That's the last thing I'd want. It looks as if I've got the middle weekend in January free. What about spending it together? Could you come up here and stay with me?'

'Of course I'd love to. I could get the Friday afternoon off, and drive up. If you're ever staying in London, I could easily come up for the evening, and perhaps we could go to the theatre. Can we talk again on the phone before Christmas?'

'Yes, it'll be my turn to ring you, and I'll expect a full account of what you've been up to.'

'Don't worry. I shan't be doing anything now I've met you.'

'That's enough of that. You mustn't think like that. I'll ring on Wednesday. Sleep well.'

We talked for nearly an hour the following week, though what about it's difficult to recall. The next day I bought my Christmas cards with a special one for him – the first time I'd sent one to a lover, if that was the right way to describe him. I got one back in due course with 'Just can't wait' scribbled across it.

Christmas passed with its usual family gathering. Caroline's family of four were growing up fast, but Juliet and her partner showed no signs either of marriage or having children. So the future of the family line would probably depend on Caroline's brood.

On the farm, Dad was still integrating the extra land that he had managed to buy the year before. This had increased the size of the farm to about 1,000 acres, and he had just finished building additional cow cubicles to bring the herd size to about 180. I wondered what grandfather would have thought of it, if he were able to look down and see how his modest start of 200 acres and thirty cows had blossomed out.

The farm was making a good profit, but already inflation was pushing up the price of everything we bought in, while the prices we got for the produce remained almost stationary. There was a severe cost/price squeeze going on, and this was the theme for the Oxford conference that I went to early in January.

I stayed in college again, and felt quite at home now that I knew the ropes. They gave me the same room in college that I had before. The current occupier was obviously a very different character from the previous one. Gone were the pin-ups of nude bodies, and in their place sober pictures and books on history. Otherwise things were much the same.

Brian and Norman were both there, but I sat at dinner next to the producer of *Farming West*, who promised to give me further commissions if the opportunity arose. Andrew said the same. It was a moderately good conference from which I got some useful material for the paper. That and information gleaned from discussions made it all worth while.

Guy drove up on the Friday afternoon. We had already exchanged photographs. Mine had been taken by Caroline the previous summer, showing me in shirt sleeves during harvest, and looking quite brown. His had been taken on the beach at Hove, in bathing trunks, with his sun-tanned face emphasising his fair hair and showing off his body to perfection. I put it on my desk alongside Simon's.

At the door he looked even more attractive than I remembered from our brief encounter. He was obviously buoyed up by the prospect of a happy weekend ahead. I felt a bit reserved, still plagued by the thought that I must not let it get out of hand. But once the door was closed and we were in each other's arms all that faded away. To hell with it. Let's live for the present, and let the future look after itself.

As I showed him the flat, he saw Simon's photo. 'That must be Simon,' he said 'He looks a lovely person. No wonder you were in love with him. Where was it taken?'

'In Switzerland. That's the Jungfrau in the background. I took it when we were on our camping holiday together.'

'It must have been terrible for you when he was killed. I am so sorry.' With that he put his arms around me, as he had done the first time we met. 'I know that I could never replace him, but perhaps I can help a little bit to fill the gap in your life?'

'Of course you can. I'm sorry to be so emotional, but grief never goes away entirely. People tell you that time heals, and it does to some extent, but the scars remain and can partially re-open at a moment's notice. Thanks for being so caring and understanding. It means a lot to me.'

'Is there anything you can't do?' he said as we finished the meal. 'You can write, you can speak on the radio and television, you play squash and tennis, and now it seems you're a brilliant cook, as well.'

'I'm certainly not that. I've just taught myself how to do a few dishes for special occasions but that's all. I admit I made a special effort tonight as I wanted to make a good impression for your first visit.'

'You certainly did that.'

We continued talking flat-out until eleven o'clock when I said: 'Let's get to bed now, and make the best of the short time we've got together. You'll have to sleep in the spare room, as my bed isn't big enough to sleep two, though it's adequate for other purposes. Not that I've ever had anybody else in it, so we'll christen it tonight.'

The first encounter in his flat had been a never-to-be-forgotten experience, but this time it was even better if that were possible. We were both releasing the physical longing for each other that had built up since we had met two months before. It wasn't just the sexual satisfaction of our bodies being together, but something deeper and more spiritual which I already suspected existed between us. He felt the same, he said, as we lay relaxed together after we had actually come simultaneously – something that had never happened to me before, even with Simon, though it had not been far off at our first meeting.

It was one o'clock before I turned him out to go to his own bed, but it was a happy feeling to be woken in the morning by the sheets being pulled back, and to feel his warm body against mine, and a strange hand caressing me. We had sex again then.

'I do love you, Mark. I just can't help it in spite of what you said about not getting too involved.'

'I think I love you too, Guy. It's like being with Simon again.'

I drove him round the city in the morning and then out to see the countryside, with a snack lunch at a pub I knew well from previous visits.

I had never asked him if he liked classical music, but I thought he might. So I had bought two tickets for a concert that evening in the City Hall. It turned out that his family had not been interested, and apart from one or two concerts at school he had not become interested himself. I was now in the same position as Simon had been when he indoctrinated me. During the interval, we ran into Angela and Janet. She looked at me quizzically as I introduced Guy to them, but there was only time for a few pleasantries before we had to get back to our seats.

'Are they a couple?' Guy asked as we sat down.

'Yes, though you mightn't think so by looking at them.'

'I did think the older one looked a bit butch. She's not your friend, is she?'

'No, Angela, the fairer, athletic one is my colleague, and a very close friend who I play squash and tennis with. I find her partner a bit formidable, as she's a bigwig civil servant, used to ordering men around. They meet up once a fortnight either here or in London.'

The last work on the programme was again Tchaikovsky's Fifth, the one that had moved me so much in that never-to-be-forgotten concert in Interlaken. I could see that Guy was moved by the sadness of the second movement, and I rested my leg lightly against his to tell him that he was not alone.

'I did enjoy that,' he said as we drove home. 'I must get it on tape, and when I play it I'll be reminded of this evening.'

The second night was almost as good as the first had been, and the next morning, being Sunday, we had a long lie-in together to make the best of the short time we had left. He aimed to leave soon after lunch, to get as far as possible in the light as he did not know the road well.

It was difficult to say goodbye at the door of the flat as we had a last embrace. When I got back after seeing him off, the flat was strangely empty, and I felt alone. In spite of all my admonitions to him not to get too involved, I realised that I was doing just that – falling in love again. Four hours later the phone rang.

'I've got back safely and the traffic wasn't too bad. Thank you so much. It was a magical weekend, and I can't thank you enough. I'm feeling very lonely, and the flat seems empty.'

'Mine is too. After you'd gone, everything was silent and I missed your chatter.'

'My chatter? I thought that it was you who did most of the talking. Anyhow, when can you come down to stay with me?'

'Not just yet, I'm afraid. I've a weekend conference in Lancaster next weekend, and I want to go home the one after that. Then the following one there's something on up here, so it looks as if it will be quite a month before I could manage it. But we can talk on the phone in the meantime.'

'I'd hoped we could meet sooner than that, but beggars can't be choosers, I suppose. It does seem to be a long time to wait.'

'It'll pass soon enough, and we can talk each week on the phone. Things may get easier later on in the year.' I felt mean and heartless as I said that, but I just couldn't afford the time to go rushing off to Hove too often. I was also anxious to avoid a regular pattern of visits building up, which could only lead to disappointment and sadness if it couldn't be maintained. I was determined not to let the affair interfere too much with family and other commitments, much as I wanted to be with him. It was not the same as it had been with Simon when we were both free of responsibilities. I was now too involved with work to let love rule my life entirely.

'Who was your boyfriend?' Angela said when I ran into her on the Monday morning. 'He's very handsome, isn't he?'

'Yes, I'm very fond of him. We met down in Brighton when I was down there for the conference in November. Sadly, he lives down there in Hove, so I don't suppose there's much future in it. It's too far away.'

'Oh, I don't know. Janet and I seem to manage it all right.'

'You're a bit different. All you've got to do is hop on a train and you're there pretty quickly. It's about three hours for us whichever way we go. Now that I'm so much busier, I don't see how I can give him the time he deserves.'

'Give it a try, Mark. He looks just right for you, and you need a man in your life.'

'You can say that again!'

It was a month before I could find a weekend to get down to

Hove to stay with Guy. It came up to expectation in every way. The old saying that absence makes the heart grow fonder certainly seemed to apply in our case. Our need for one another seemed not to have suffered from the separation, and lovemaking was just as fresh and rewarding as ever. On the Saturday, he drove me out into the country and the downs, so different from our local Devon. I loved the feeling of freedom and space and the little villages with their flint houses nestling in the hollows. We drove over to Arundel, with its castle dominating the town, and its cathedral towering above the trees. I was immediately reminded of Milton's poem which I had learned at school:

'Towers and battlements it sees / Bosomed high in tufted trees.'

I felt sure that he must have had Arundel in mind when he wrote those words.

That evening we went to the theatre for a performance of Oscar Wilde's *The Importance of Being Earnest*, which neither of us had seen before, and which we much enjoyed.

'What are you doing for a holiday this year?' he asked over a meal before the show.

'I always go home for a couple of weeks at least to help Dad with the harvest in August, and have a few days with my aunt in north Devon to get in some surf bathing, which I love. That usually takes up the time as we only get three weeks in one go. Had you thought that we might go away together?'

'It'd be marvellous if we could, as I've got nothing fixed. I usually go up to my sister in Norwich for a week, but otherwise I don't do much. I've never had someone I wanted to go away with before.'

'I really think that I ought to go back to Dad for the usual fortnight as he'll be counting on me, but I needn't go up to Aunt Emily then. I could always have the odd weekend there instead. That'd give me one free week, but no more, I'm afraid, and it mustn't be too close to our special spring and autumn issues in April and early October. Could you manage a week at the end of June, do you think?'

'I'd hoped that we could get a bit longer so that we could go abroad, but a week's better than nothing. Is there anywhere you'd like to go? The end of June would suit me best.'

'It won't be worth going too far, will it? What would you think about southern Ireland? I've seen photos of it, and it looks very attractive – rather like Cornwall in places. I'd like to take you there one day, and teach you to surf if you've never done it before, but we could do that on long weekends perhaps.'

'I rather like the idea of Ireland. Perhaps we could fly to Dublin and hire a car there, as that would save about a couple of days getting to Fishguard or Holyhead to catch a boat.'

'That's a brilliant idea. Let's do it then, in the last week in June.'

As we lay in bed together on the second night, he suddenly said: 'How do you feel about our relationship now? Do you still feel that it may not last in the long term? I can't get what you said out of my mind.'

'I do think that it'll be difficult for both of us, because of the distance and the nature of my work. But it seems to be working so far, doesn't it?'

'Yes, but you do realise, don't you, that you're in danger of becoming a workaholic? If you go on like this, you'll find it may interfere with your emotional life.'

'I know, but at the moment it's very much a driving force in my career, while I'm still getting established. I do know how difficult it must be for you, and it's not easy for me either, as I do love you. But I have come to realise that love is not the only thing in my life, important as it is, especially in the first flush of an affair. I couldn't bear the thought of losing you but I do have to reconcile that with my future. I'd be very happy with what we've got now, but is that enough for you?'

'I suppose it will have to be. The only alternative would be for me to move up to be near you, but I can see that that might not help much if you're working all the time. So perhaps we should keep it as it is for the time being.'

'I'd like that, on the understanding that either of us might be free to have a casual fling if the need for sexual relief became too great between the times that we can be together. It wouldn't apply to me, I'm pretty sure, but it might to you, and I'd not like you to feel guilty if you were tempted. It'd be something quite apart from our emotional relationship, which is secure, but just in the nature of a temporary physical relief.'

'I'd agree to that. I do feel the need for it sometimes when we haven't been together for some time. If it did happen, it would not affect my feelings for you in any way. I'll still love you just the same. Let's leave it like that, shall we?'

I was glad he'd agreed, for the last thing I'd want would be for him to feel guilty if he'd been tempted to have a casual encounter. After all, he was far more exposed to that in a place like Brighton than I would be. My only temptation might be a quick fling with Robert.

We had another weekend together before the Easter holiday, when he came up to stay with me. We both enjoyed it, especially as Angela invited us out to a meal and the two of them got on very well together, as I had thought they would.

I got four days at home at Easter. On the Saturday, Dad took me into the farm office as he had something important to discuss. He was now fifty-seven, and had recently seen our accountant, who had warned him that if he died suddenly the estate might be faced with very high charges for estate duty, as it was all in his name. He recommended setting up an estate company so that, if Dad did die, duty would be payable only on the value of the shares he owned in the company and any private capital that he had accumulated.

Dad was anxious to know what I thought of the suggestion, and also whether I had now made up my mind about coming back to take over the farm if anything happened to him, as that might have a bearing on whether to set up the company.

Strangely enough, I had been thinking about it only a week or two before, and had rather reluctantly decided that it would be my duty to Mother and the rest of the family to come back home if he wanted to retire. I couldn't possibly contemplate everything that he had worked for being sold off. Daniel was showing such a keen interest in the farm that he might be there to take over from me at a relatively early age, allowing me to stand down and follow my own interests.

'I'd think it'd be an excellent idea to set up the company, Dad.

I've been doing some thinking lately, and decided that I'd definitely like to come back and take over from you, whenever you decided that you wanted to retire – though I'd hope that it would not be just yet, as I'm enjoying life so much at the moment in my job.'

'I'm so glad. As you know, your mother and I have never tried to influence you, but naturally we hoped that it would be your decision to take over from me one day. I've not said this before but we've both really appreciated you coming back to help with harvest every year, and giving up your holiday for it.'

'I've enjoyed it, Dad. Perhaps if Simon hadn't died, it would have been different, but that was not to be.'

'Right. I'll get on to the accountant after the holiday, and get him to set up the company, though I expect it'll take a few months. What we had in mind was that your mother and I would have thirty per cent of the shares each, and you, Juliet and Caroline would have ten per cent each. That would leave ten per cent unallocated, which Daniel could have in due course if he wanted to get involved with the farm. I'd leave you my shares in my will, now I know that you'd be coming back.'

'That sounds fine. I'm doing quite well at the moment with a bit of money coming in from broadcasting, but a bit extra wouldn't come amiss, as I'm thinking of moving to a larger flat before long.'

Guy and I had two more weekends together before the trip to Ireland, one in Hove with him, and one with me, which only served to bring us closer still together. We spent the first night in Dublin after flying out from Birmingham, then hired a car and explored the city.

Then it was off down to Cork and the south-west, round the Ring of Kerry with its spectacular peninsulas jutting out into the Atlantic with a deep blue sea between. It reminded me of Cornwall, and there were times as we moved up the coast when I would have been glad of my surfboard and wetsuit, as huge rollers came in on almost deserted beaches. I promised Guy that I'd take him over to Polzeath one weekend and introduce him to the sport. I was certain that he'd enjoy it, just as Simon had done.

We were lucky with the weather, too, until an Atlantic depression blew in, and we were holed up in Killarney until it had blown itself out next day. We stayed mostly in small hotels and B&Bs, buying picnic lunches each day, lazing together in the sunshine and drawing ever closer to each other. I was amazed at how much we seemed to enjoy the same things, with never a hint of a disagreement. From Connemara it was back across the country to Dublin and the flight home. He spent the night with me before driving to Hove.

'I've never been so happy in my life before,' he said over breakfast. 'It's been just a marvellous holiday. I hope you enjoyed it as much as I did.'

'Of course. Meeting you has been the best thing that's happened since I lost Simon. I now appreciate again what happiness it can be to share your life with someone you care for.'

Alone once more in the flat after he had gone, I felt miserable with him no longer there after eight days continuously together. Perhaps, after all, we ought to be living together, I thought that night, lying in bed. But back at my desk again, or visiting farms and going to meetings, that thought was soon forgotten as I got back to the old routine.

That was the first of the three holidays that we had together. The following year we went to Scotland for ten days, but the weather was bad all the time, with rain and mist obscuring the landscape, which meant that we were trying to find things to do instead of relaxing in the sunshine. Inevitably relations got somewhat strained, but we managed to get through it without getting on each other's nerves. It was a good test for our friendship.

In between holidays we managed weekends together, but on average it only worked out at once in five weeks, though long talks on the phone helped to keep us together. I was still haunted by the fear that this might not be enough for him, but he seemed to accept that it was the best that we could manage under the circumstances.

I had taken him home to meet Mother and Dad for a long weekend soon after we got back from Ireland. Mother seemed to take to him immediately, and made him feel particularly welcome, and I got the impression that she sensed that our friendship was rather as it had been with Simon. He got on well with Dad, too. He knew little about farming, but quizzed him at some length about the financial side of the business, as might be expected from an accountant.

'Guy's pretty bright when it comes to figures,' Dad said on the second evening, when Guy was out of the room. 'I like his attitude to business, and he's very easy to get on with, isn't he? He reminds me rather of Simon in that respect. He was very easy, too. I'm so glad you've found a close friend again.'

It was on his second visit that I took him over to meet Cynthia and Jack, remembering the promise that I'd made her years before that I'd bring over a new love in my life, if I ever found one. Guy took to her immediately, as I was sure he would, and Jack got on well with him, too. In fact, they got talking about business so much over lunch that Cynthia and I felt a bit left out. After lunch we went round the garden with Jack, and then I drove him out to see the countryside that Simon had shown me that first afternoon when we had been together. It looked as beautiful as it had done then, and we held hands in the car where we'd stopped to admire the view before. I felt Simon was looking on approvingly, and that he was not jealous of our friendship but was relishing my happiness.

It was not the right time of the year to think of bathing at Polzeath, so we decided that we would postpone his introduction to surfing until we might get a long weekend in the summer. He came back with me to spend the next night at the flat before driving home, as he had a few days holiday in hand.

'You're awfully lucky with your family,' he said that night. 'Your parents are both lovely, and you seem to get on so well with them. They obviously love you to bits, and you're very close to your dad. I hardly know my father, as we never seem to have anything to talk about. I've never been very close to either of them, actually, and they don't seem to be very interested in my life either. What they'd do if they found out I was gay, I dread to think. Luckily I do get on well with my sister, which does provide quite a strong family link.'

'I don't know what mine would think, either. They might be

rather shocked, but I don't think it'd affect their love for me. They seem to have given up hope of me marrying anyhow.'

The night after I got back Cynthia rang me: 'We did like Guy. He's a lovely boy, and you're very lucky to have found him. I got the feeling that he's very much in love. Is it the real thing with you, too? I am worried, though, that you seem to spend so little time together.'

'I know. It's awfully difficult living so far apart. And I'm so busy with the sort of job I've got – when I don't work regular hours, I have a lot of evenings out. I know very well that he'd like to see more of me, but I don't know how we could manage that. Even if he came to live near me, I'd still be out a lot.'

'I'm sure that it'll work out all right, but I do think you'll have to give a bit more, if you are to hold on to him. It would be terribly sad if you lost him.'

Guy took me up to have lunch with his parents shortly before Christmas, but I found them very stuffy and lunch was heavy going. His father was an elderly retired bank manager, whose life seemed to revolve round the golf course, while his mother was a typical suburban housewife, much taken up with coffee mornings and bridge parties. Neither of them knew anything whatsoever about agriculture and farming, and gave the impression that they didn't want to know about it either. I could well see now why Guy had said that he didn't have much contact with them. I wondered how two such dull, mundane people had produced such a bright son.

It was clear that neither of them had any inkling about his sexuality, as his mother kept talking about his future children, and how she'd like more grandchildren. I fell to thinking what she'd do if she ever found out.

It seemed that I was beginning to be recognised as something of a specialist on the subject of the impact of farming on the environment. It was a subject that was starting to get a lot of attention in the press during the seventies, and various pressure groups were latching on to it. My study of biology at school, aided by practical knowledge gained from the farm at home, allowed me to see things in perspective. I could understand the desire of some farmers to go out for maximum production, but I could also see that this might involve a danger of losing valuable species of plants and small animals.

I was being asked to write articles about it, and these in turn led to invitations to speak at farmers' meetings at quite long distances from home. Eric had no objection to this as long as I got in a mention of our paper. But it meant that I was away from home sometimes in the evening when Guy tried to ring, and it upset him if I wasn't there. It wasn't that he suspected me of infidelity, but rather that I wasn't there to talk to him and he probably felt that I was drifting further away from him, which wasn't the case at all.

That summer, we took my car to Austria for ten days' holiday at the end of June, as he had always wanted a holiday on the Continent. I still felt that I was not ready to go back to Switzerland, as it would evoke so many painful memories, and I wanted this one to be devoted to Guy and not to the ghosts of the past.

We crossed over from Dover to Ostend, making for Cologne, and then down through the Rhineland, on to Munich and then to Salzburg. Remembering the trip with Simon, I put some tapes in the car which we could play on long journeys, which he enjoyed. We were lucky to get tickets for a performance of *Figaro* at Salzburg, which introduced him to opera for the first time.

'I loved it,' he said, afterwards. 'I'd no idea that opera could be such fun. We ought to try to get to one in London sometime.'

He had never been up in mountains before, as his parents' idea of a summer holiday was two weeks at Bournemouth or Lyme Regis, and since leaving home he had never found anyone he liked well enough to holiday with. I would have been the same if I hadn't met Simon.

The result was that he was delighted to spend the whole time round the mountain resorts, and we never got to Vienna as we had intended. The worst moment was when we got stuck in a ski lift near Halstadt. Sitting on our little wooden seats with only a narrow floorboard beneath us and death, we suddenly stopped, swinging in space with a sheer drop of hundreds of feet on to rocks below. It was like one of those nightmares in which one is marooned on a high pinnacle with no means of getting down again.

There we stayed for at least twenty minutes, wondering whether a friendly helicopter might come to lift us off – otherwise we would freeze to death, the only consolation being that we would die together. It was lucky that there were two of us, as neither wanted to reveal just how scared we were. If I had been alone I might have panicked. Eventually, with a sudden jolt, everything swung into action, and with a sigh of relief we reached the top. It was another two days before we felt confident enough to take another lift into the mountains.

The other highlight was when we found ourselves at the shore of Lake Constance at Bregenz when the opera festival was taking place on its platform on the lake. This time it was *Don Giovanni*, so we had our fill of Mozart.

'That was a wonderful holiday,' he said as I dropped him at the flat in Hove. 'We must do it again. Do you think you might get two full weeks next year? I'd have liked to have had longer, both with you and to see more of the scenery as well.'

'I'll see what I can do,' I said, not knowing that there wouldn't be a next time. Just as well, perhaps.

During the autumn that followed our trip to Austria, I had only managed two weekends with him, but that didn't seem important as I was going to stay with him for two nights when I went to the usual conference in Brighton at the end of November. It would now be the fourth anniversary of that first meeting, and I wanted to celebrate it with him.

He was loving enough, but I got the impression that he was not his usual cheerful self.

'Are you all right, Guy?' I asked him on the second day. 'You seem rather down in the dumps, and not quite yourself.'

'Yes, I'm fine. I'm just bored with the job, that's all. It seems the same routine day after day. Although they've given me more responsibility lately and more pay, the thought of doing the same job for another thirty years or so is pretty depressing. I'm over thirty now and feel that life is passing me by, and I begin to wonder what the future holds.'

'Perhaps you ought to be thinking of going out and getting another job, possibly with a big commercial company on the finance side?'

'I've been thinking of that, but it would probably mean moving away and living in somewhere like London, which I'd hate. I suppose it's all right for heterosexual men, as they'll have marriage and kids to look forward to. But for people like us, there is nothing like that, unless you can find someone you want to spend your life with.'

'I'm sure that what you need is a new challenge. I was very lucky to get my chance when I was only twenty-eight, and it came just when I was beginning to experience the first signs of "Thirtyitis" – that infection that's hitting you now, when you sit back to review your life.'

'You were fortunate, Mark. Your job gets you out into the world, and it's creative and stimulating, compared with my profession, which is mostly dull and boring. Anyhow, I'll think about it, and perhaps start looking around after Christmas.'

I didn't realise then that it wasn't just boredom that was worrying him, though I was to find out soon enough.

Christmas came and went in the usual routine, and then it was back to Oxford for the annual stimulation of meeting old friends and having one's batteries charged up by contact with many of the progressive leaders in the industry.

It wasn't quite the same that year, for Mike, the conference secretary for so many years, had retired, and the friendly informal approach that he had brought to it had gone. It was now run professionally in a new venue, sponsored by commercial companies, and there were fewer farmers there, and more people in business suits. But much of the old camaraderie remained, and it was still worth going to.

In February, I was due to go to London for the annual meeting of the Farmers' Union, and to spend a night there. Mindful of what Guy had once suggested – that he might come up from Brighton for the evening to go to the theatre with me – I tried to ring him up the week before. But two nights running he was not there to answer the phone. I felt a slight unease as he was nearly always on the end of the line. I got him at the third attempt.

'What have you been up to? I've tried ringing a couple of times, and you've not been in.'

'Sorry, I've been out with friends the last two nights.'

I left it at that, as the last thing I wanted was for him to think that I was prying into his private life. Anyhow, we had agreed that we should be free to have something on the side if we needed it, and perhaps that was what he'd been doing. But when I suggested him coming up to London to go to the theatre, he became rather cagey.

'I'd rather not commit myself at the moment, as I might have something on. Could I let you know early next week?'

'Yes, of course, but it'll have to be on Monday, as I'm coming up on Tuesday.'

We chatted on for a few minutes, but I was left with a definite feeling that all was not well. This was confirmed on the Monday, when he rang to say that he didn't really feel like coming up on a cold February night, and getting back very late on the last train – which I could understand, though I was naturally disappointed.

The blow fell on the night after I had got back from London when I found a letter lying on the mat as I came in from the office. It was in his handwriting, and I knew instinctively that something was seriously wrong. Why had he written and not rung me up as he always did?

Dearest Mark,

This is quite the hardest letter that I've ever had to write, and I'm only doing it because I know that I couldn't say what I want to, without breaking down. It's not just cowardice, but I know I'd be unable to speak without crying and that would be dreadful for both of us. The fact is that I have met someone else. You were so right, you see, when you said at the beginning that it would be difficult if we could only see one another occasionally, and five or six weeks has been a long time to wait.

It is probably much easier for you since you're always busy writing, planning things or dashing around the country, so you probably don't feel the need for company. It's very different for me with office hours, and the evenings can be lonely when you're not there. I suppose it might be better if I were part of the gay scene down here, but as you know that is not for me. I just want to settle down to a domestic life with someone I care for – someone with whom I can share my everyday life. I doubt whether it would have worked even if I had come up to live near you, as your work would always have got in the way.

Peter is nearly ten years older than me. He's a university lecturer, so he has to be careful not to get involved with the 'scene' either. He's got a nice bungalow in Rottingdean, which he shared with his mother until she died last year. I'm very fond of him, and we are compatible in many ways. Of course, I don't love him in the way I love you, and never will, but I'm quite sure that we could be happy together as he's wonderfully kind and considerate, and I'm the first love in his life.

You see, Mark, I do have to look to the future, and the arrangement we've had just isn't enough for me in the long term. I had hoped that it would get better in time, but that hasn't happened, and I don't want to continue with the loneliness of you not being there for me. Peter has asked me to move in and live with him, and I've agreed. It'll mean giving up my little flat, but that can't be helped.

I have, of course, told him all about you, and he feels, obviously, that we should stop seeing one another. Otherwise he would just become part of a triangle, and that could lead to jealousy and unhappiness all round. It's been a terribly harrowing time for me, as you can imagine, because I feel dreadful at the pain that I know this will cause you. I remember all the happy times and the holidays that we've had together and I feel awful.

I do know just how much you care for me, Mark, and what this is going to do to you, as it will be the second time that you've lost someone you love. But, knowing you, I'm sure you'll realise that this is the best thing for me – and perhaps for you in the long run. You're such a kind and loving person that I'm sure you'll find someone else – perhaps when you go back to Devon to run the farm. You do need a man in your life.

I think that it'll be best if we don't keep in touch in the future, though I'll live in hope of meeting up with you again one day. Please try to forgive me for doing this to you. I'll always remember the happy times we've had together.

With all my love,

Guy

I had always feared that this might happen, and should have prepared myself for it instead of burying my head in the sand thinking that things could go on as they were. In a way, it was not quite so bad as it had been with Simon, as he was dead, and gone for ever, whereas Guy was still alive and there was always the hope that we might meet again in the future.

But the sense of loss was overwhelming as the recognition sank in that I might never hear him laugh again, that I would never have him in my arms again, or feel the warmth of his body as he crept into my bed in the morning after we had made love the night before. Life without someone to love seemed to stretch out endlessly into the future – as surely I could never expect to find a third man in the fickle gay world in which I was destined to live?

As I had done when Simon died, I put my head into my arms, and burst into tears, sobbing with self-pity at my loss. After a time I pulled myself together. *You're thirty-five now. You're far too old to cry like this. Take a grip. You've lived most of your life alone, and got on all right. You'll just have to get used to it again.* And then I thought of Guy, and how awful he must be feeling, worrying whether I'd got his letter, and how I would be taking it. I went to the phone, and he answered immediately.

'I found your letter when I got in this evening, Guy. I'm so, so sorry. It must have been awful for you having to write it. Of course you couldn't have sprung it on me on the phone or you'd have had both of us in tears probably. I do understand that your future happiness must lie with Peter, and I'm just so glad that you've found someone who can give you love and companionship.

'You're so right about me. Work has taken over such a big part of my life that I could never have given you the time you need. I've conned myself into thinking that it was working, without ever stopping to think what the cost was for you. If I hadn't been so selfish and wrapped up in my own world, I'd have realised before this that you were so unhappy.'

'It wasn't that I was really unhappy, Mark,' he replied. 'It was just that I felt lonely when you weren't there, and I wanted to see you more often, and to settle down with you. Thank you so much for taking it like this. It's easier for me to know that you can accept it, and are not blaming me for letting you down. I'm terribly conscious of the pain it must be causing you, and that I'm responsible for you losing the second person you've loved in your life, as I said in my letter. But I'm sure it must be the best to take the decision now. I do love you, and always will. You must believe that.'

'I know you do, and I feel the same, and I'll never forget you whatever happens in the future. You'll always be there, just as Simon has been. Before we say goodbye, will you promise me one thing? If anything should happen to Peter, and you found yourself free, will you promise to ring me? I might be back at the farm by then, but you know the address. I can't really expect to find another person to love now that I'm getting older. Will you promise?'

'Yes, Mark. I promise.'

With that he put the phone down to save what would inevitably have been tearful moments for both of us. Oh God, I thought, why do people made like us get so emotional? I suppose it must be something to do with feminine genes in our system.

In the days that followed, it was difficult to concentrate on work. I'd be in the middle of writing something, when suddenly 'Guy's gone' would flash across my brain, and I'd have to stop to banish the thought before I could go on. The worst time was when I was alone in the flat in the evening, or in bed at night, having to accept that he'd never be there lying beside me again. The second night after he had gone, I suddenly decided to do what I had been contemplating for some time. I'd move out, find another flat, and start again, rather as I had done when leaving college early after Simon's death.

One of the most difficult things to deal with after the break-up was replying to people who would ask how he was. It was easy with Angela and Robert as I could just admit that he'd left me. But when Mother enquired on the phone, I couldn't decide how to play it, and simply said that I hadn't been able to see him lately. It was not until I went home for the Easter holiday that I knew I'd have to come clean about it.

'I probably shan't be seeing him again, Mother. We were finding it too difficult going backwards and forwards all the time, and he's giving up his flat, and going to live with one of his friends down there.'

'I'm so sorry, dear, We both liked him so much when you brought him down to stay for those two weekends last year and you seemed to get on so well together. You must miss him a lot, as you used to stay together quite often, didn't you?'

'Yes, I am missing him, but there's so much going on in the job that I don't have time to think about it.' I did wonder from the tone of her voice whether she might have guessed my secret, and was trying to say so without asking directly, but I didn't feel ready to take it further at that point.

When I told Angela about the break-up, and said that I was going to find a larger flat, she said that there was one coming up for sale in the next block to hers. It belonged to someone she knew who was moving to a job elsewhere. It wasn't officially on the market yet, but she said I should make a bid for it straight away if I was interested, as they never stayed on the market for long. She gave me the name of the agents.

I quite liked the idea of being close to her and to Robert and John, provided that I could afford the mortgage, and decided to make a bid for it if it seemed at all suitable. So next morning I went round to the agents, and arranged to see it later that afternoon.

It had a large living/dining room with plenty of light, two bedrooms, the smaller one of which would be large enough to house my computer and other gear, and for a bed if I had a visitor. The kitchen was large and well equipped, and the bathroom and loo perfectly adequate for my needs. On the third floor, it looked out to the west over some rooftops, but sadly I would lose the view of distant hills which I had in the old flat. It was all a bit pricey, but the agent said he could arrange a mortgage, and with the money I was getting from my shares in the farm I could quite easily afford the interest payments. I accepted the asking price, and almost before I knew where I was, I was the proud owner of a new flat. Another big advantage was that it was only about ten minutes' walk from the office, and had underground parking, so I could leave the car at home if I wasn't going to need it during the day.

I had by now accumulated too many possessions for Dad to do the move with his trailer, so I had to get professionals in, but Dad and Mother came up to help put things in the right places.

Over Easter, Caroline came over with the children, Daniel,

Harriet, Maud and Jonathan, all of them growing up very fast. The year before there had been a lot of discussion about Daniel's future education. Geoffrey, my brother-in-law, had been keen that he should go to a boarding school, but Caroline and Mother were not too happy about it, so I was brought in to give my opinion. Bearing in mind the maturity and self-assurance that I had noted in Simon, James and Andrew, and later in Guy, all of whom had been to boarding schools, I had come down strongly on Geoffrey's side. In a moment of inspiration, I brought Cynthia into the discussion.

She arranged a visit to Simon's old school with his former housemaster. Daniel himself had been a bit unsure as he'd not seen a boarding school before but he and Caroline came back converted. His name had been put down, he had passed the entrance exam the previous summer, and he'd now been at the school for two terms and was loving it.

Now fourteen, he was big and tall for his age – almost as tall as I was. He was astonishingly mature, and already into rugby, playing in the back row of the scrum. So we were able to talk rugby as well as farming, and it wasn't long before we felt like a couple of brothers rather than uncle and nephew.

He still seemed as keen as ever on the farm, and was now big enough to drive a tractor and take on some of the lighter farm tasks. He was coming to look more like Dad as he got older, and was turning into a real chip off the Harper block, which pleased Dad enormously, as he could see him carrying on the line when I gave up. It pleased me too, as I thought that he might take over from me while I was still relatively young, which might allow me more freedom if I were ever lucky enough to find another partner in my life.

Over the next three years, I continued happily in my job at the *Herald*. Fortunately nothing ever stands still in the farming world, so there was always plenty to write about if one kept one's ear to the ground, especially as I was concentrating more on the countryside and what was happening there.

This was certainly the case as we entered the eighties and farming began to go into a decline, largely as a result of overproduction and increasing pressure from Brussels. The first sign of the shape of things to come was the imposition of milk quotas on all dairy farmers. It was fortunate that we had completed the expansion of the dairy herd a year or two earlier, so we were given a quota that would be adequate for our needs for a few years to come. Cereal prices were also falling so our profits were beginning to be squeezed.

Now that Guy was no longer part of my life I was going home more often at weekends. As a result Dad was consulting me more on policy matters. My work brought me into contact with many of the most progressive farmers in the Midlands, and this was quite a help when we had to discuss developments on our own farm, as I could draw on their experience.

I remember one conversation in particular I had with Dad about modernising the operation of the farm. 'Dad, have you thought about getting a computer for the farm? I was on a farm the other day where they had installed one, and I was amazed at the amount of information that can be stored.'

'I had thought of it, but was afraid that I'd never be able to get my head round it,' he replied. 'Could you look into it for me, and find out the best model for the farm, and whether you can get ready-made programmes for it?'

'I'll certainly do that. The one I saw had special software for both arable and dairy programmes, as well as for the farm as a whole.'

Soon after that conversation, I was playing squash with Robert, who was a bit of a computer expert, and also a farmer I'd recently visited. Between them, they came up with the answers, and within a month we had bought a computer for the farm, and Dad was trying to get to grips with it with the help of Ian Marshall, the head herdsman who had succeeded Gordon two years before when he retired. Dad had been lucky to get him, a young man of twenty-five, college trained, who had coped with the increase in the size of the herd admirably. He took to the computer like a duck to water, and soon had Dad conversant with it as well. When I next went home, Dad said he didn't know how he'd ever got on without it.

Dad had always been right on the ball in adopting new techniques, and it was good to see that he was showing no signs of sitting back as he passed his sixtieth birthday. One of the major changes we had made at the start of the eighties had been to substitute a winter diet of forage maize silage for the dairy cows in place of most of the grass silage that we had previously used. This had only become possible because a local contractor had invested in the harvesting machinery, which we could not afford on our own. It also saved us the cost of having to replace our own grass harvester, which was showing signs of age. The change in the diet had improved milk yields, and the cows definitely preferred it.

One result of absorbing neighbouring farms over the years had been the acquisition of six farm cottages, which we did not need for our own employees, since we were able to farm the extra land with our existing larger machines or contractors; so didn't have to increase the labour force.

Dad decided to take a leaf out of Grandfather's book and make a profit out of the tourist industry, which had expanded enormously over the years. Three of the cottages had been occupied by retired employees at very low rents and eventually became available as the old people died or moved out to be nearer to shops. From 1975 onwards, Dad had done up one cottage each year to make it suitable for holiday lettings, and by now all six cottages had been converted.

Of course there was the updating and furnishing to be paid for, but Dad had learnt the lesson that it was usually cheaper to use the bank's money for improvements like this. In each case he'd been able to pay off the loan after five years from the rents he received. So from then on, they brought in quite a tidy income, as they didn't require much maintenance. This source of income became increasingly important as the squeeze on farm profits began to bite.

Gradually over time the memories of happy days with Guy began to fade, but I did find that after the years of sexual freedom that we had enjoyed, I was missing the physical side of sex. Robert provided an outlet very occasionally, but his John was seldom away, so relief from that quarter was rare. With the sexual liberation of the sixties, both in the hetero and the homosexual world, it had become much easier to find relief if one knew where to look for it in a casual encounter. I never did anything near home, and only very rarely if I was away somewhere on a visit, but in one's thirties sexual urges are strong, and sometimes the temptation was too powerful.

Each time it happened, I'd feel pangs of conscience and sometimes even of disgust with myself if it had been with someone who was not remotely attractive. It felt a bit like it had been that first time with Norman at Oxford, and again I'd feel I wanted a shower to wash away the guilt. I suppose that in the back of my mind was the thought I might find another Guy, for that, after all, was much the way in which I had found him. Of course, I never did, for those who frequent the cruising world are seldom looking for a long-term commitment. Lust is in their mind rather than love!

Socially, the years across my middle thirties passed pleasantly enough after the break with Guy, and it was probably as well that I had no new partner in my life. The move to the new flat widened my social life as I got to know some of the other residents, largely through Robert and Angela. Invitations to meals or evening drinks became a feature of life and, in return, I had to learn how to become a host myself, and became sufficiently skilled in the culinary field to put on a modest meal from time to time.

I had finally met Robert's partner, John, the year before the split with Guy, so he knew that I was gay, and didn't feel threatened by my friendship with Robert as he was aware that I had a partner. I found him a charming, cultured man, quite a bit older than Robert, and I could understand what Robert saw in him, though he wasn't my type at all. He suspected nothing, which was the truth, for anything between Robert and me was just a matter of physical relief for both of us, and not emotional in any way.

The main feature of those years was an increasing involvement with the media, mostly through sound radio on regional programmes. It was a time when alarm bells were ringing about the increasing pressure of urban expansion on country areas, and the need for more housing for the burgeoning population. Strident pressure groups were gaining an increasing grip on some sections of the press, and these, in turn, were starting to sour relations between town and country. There was a need for someone to try to hold the ring between the different factions and I seemed to be slipping into that role.

Andrew, who had now moved from sound broadcasting to television, gave me a small part in two programmes, and I really began to feel that I had arrived when, as I had my hair cut one day, the barber said: 'Didn't I see you on television on Sunday?' Such is fame!

The final accolade came with an invitation to read a paper at the Oxford conference under the heading of *Farming and the Countryside*. I had come a long way since that day ten years earlier when Brian had encouraged me to attend, and Norman had succeeded in seducing me at the same time. The paper seemed to be well received, but I was, after all, speaking mainly to the converted.

Chapter Seven

It was now nearly sixteen years since I had come to work at the *Herald*, and almost ten since I had taken on the job of countryside correspondent. I had established a very comfortable niche for myself, and had no ambition to move on. It had been a challenge setting up the weekly page and the special editions, but it had paid off in increased circulation and more advertising. Eric was pleased with the way it had gone, and left me very much to my own devices, with freedom to get away to events in the field. He was also happy for me to pursue my work with the media. So, even though there was still no man in my life, I was happy in the job and looked forward to more years in the same vein. But, as so often happens in life, just when one sits back in a mood of contentment, fate steps in to take a hand.

It was in April in the year that I had read my paper at Oxford, and I was sitting in my office after lunch writing an editorial for that week's paper, when the phone rang.

'Mark, it's Caroline. Can you come home at once? Dad is very seriously ill and is in intensive care with a stroke, and they are doubtful if he'll ever regain consciousness. Mother's with him, and I'll be going into the hospital later.'

'I can't come immediately as I've some writing I must get finished here first. But I can get away later in the afternoon. Tell Mother I'll get down as soon as I can. What happened?'

'He was in the yard this morning when a lorry with a load of feed for the cows drove in. Though Victor was there to help unload, Dad, being Dad, couldn't stand by while others worked, so he took off his coat, and had unloaded four bags. Walking across the yard with the fifth, he suddenly collapsed with the bag on top of him. When they got to him, he was unconscious, and has been in a coma ever since. It doesn't look good I'm afraid.'

'I'll get down this evening. Have you been in touch with Juliet?'

'Not yet, but I'm going to ring her now.'

It was difficult to concentrate on finishing the editorial, as all kinds of thoughts kept on intruding as the implications of what had happened began to sink in. But I got it finished somehow, and then discussed with Gillian the final layout for that week's page. Fortunately by now she was almost as competent as I was, and I felt safe in leaving it to her.

Eric was very understanding when I looked in to ask for a few days' leave until we knew better what the outcome was likely to be. Neither of us said it then, but I think we both knew that my days at the *Herald* were probably over. I rushed in to ask Angela to keep an eye on the flat, leaving her a key for it. Then, after going back to tidy up and pack a bag, I was off on the road home.

Mother was surprisingly calm when I got in at about eight o'clock. She had a great inner strength, founded on her deep religious principles. She had left the hospital, as he was still in a deep coma, and they said they would ring if there was any change in his condition. Juliet arrived later, and I was relieved to have her there to comfort Mother if the worst happened. I think we all felt that he would probably not pull through, and, in a way, perhaps it would be best if he didn't. The thought of Dad, with all his energy and vigour, lying paralysed, and maybe unable to speak, was just too horrible to contemplate.

The hospital rang in the morning to say there was no change in his condition, but that we should prepare for the worst. In the afternoon they rang again to say that his condition had deteriorated, and we should come. It was all I could do to restrain tears as we stood and looked down at him lying there so helpless, though mercifully he looked completely at peace. Then, quite suddenly with a great sigh, he was gone without pain or struggle, and we were left alone without the one who had been such a powerful influence in our lives.

He had always been there for us – strong, reliable, and loving – and it was almost impossible to believe that he would no longer be at hand to talk to and to come to for advice. It was a shock to realise that it would now be me who would have all the responsibility for family matters, and for looking after Mother, and I felt ill equipped to do so.

In a way, perhaps, it was as well that he had lived for just that extra day, for it had given Mother time to prepare, so that when the moment came it was not too much of a shock. But I could not begin to think what it must be like for her to lose the one she had loved so devotedly for forty years, and on whom she had relied so much. He had always taken the lead, and she had been more than happy to follow. Now she would have to face the future alone – a bleak and lonely future it must seem to her. Thankfully she'd have Caroline and the grandchildren close at hand, and presumably me to look after now that I would be back at home again.

For me, too, the shock had been intense. The previous morning I had set off for a normal day in the office, content with my independent life and with few responsibilities. Suddenly, within the space of twenty-four hours, all that was gone for good, and I would have to start a completely new life as a Devon farmer, tied to a home life with an elderly mother, with all my freedom gone. It was not as if I had a wife and family to share that new life with. I would be a lonely gay man with little prospect of ever finding another partner.

But there was no time to brood on my personal problems with so much to do in the aftermath of Dad's death. Fortunately Juliet was able to get two weeks off, and she was a tower of strength in making most of the arrangements for the funeral, while I shuttled back and forth to Westerton preparing for the next two issues of the weekly page. We had not seen much of one another since she had gone to university, but it was rewarding to find out how well we got on together. We had shared quite a lot of Mother's genes, while Caroline was definitely her father's daughter. I guessed that Juliet had sussed me out long ago, though nothing was said about it. She was clearly sympathetic, having presumably had experience of gay issues in her professional life as a solicitor.

The funeral was arranged for a week ahead at Norton parish church, as we expected a big attendance from the farming world, where Dad was highly respected. He had never been interested in farming politics, because of his aversion to sitting on committees, but he was very well known throughout the country for the quality of his farming, his willingness to throw open the farm to visitors and his readiness to pass on what he had learnt to others.

The church was full. We had asked the president of the County Union to give the address, and I paid tribute to Dad as a family man, who had been such a role model for us all, and to Mother who had been such a wonderful support to him for over forty years. She bore up remarkably well with the support of Juliet and Caroline and the grandchildren.

'It was a lovely service,' Cynthia said as we got back from the crematorium. 'He was a great character, and I'm so glad the president of the union brought out his contribution to agriculture in Devon so well. He was an example of all that's best in farming. How are you feeling about coming back to take over?'

'Terribly mixed up at the moment, to be honest. It's been an awful shock having to give up my previous life at a moment's notice, as I was enjoying it so much. But I've been so encouraged by all the goodwill shown to the family over the past week, that I'm not so concerned now that I'll be disappearing into some country backwater. People have been wonderfully kind, and have offered help if I need it while I'm finding my feet.'

'You'll be all right,' Jack said. 'I can see a lot of your father in you, so you won't go far wrong. And all the experience you've had in your job will be a tremendous help. You must come over to see us as soon as you've settled in.'

I was particularly pleased to see Richard Sykes, my college tutor, there.

'Richard, it's so good of you to have come. I'd much welcome your advice when I've been able to take stock of things. Would you like to come over one day and go round the farm? Perhaps you could bring your management students over as well for a farm management exercise to see if they might come up with some useful ideas?'

'That'd be an excellent idea. Just give me a ring when you're ready.'

Two days after the funeral, I had driven up to Westerton to sort things out with Eric. It was obvious that I couldn't do both jobs, and I'd have to hand in my resignation. But I was worried about the three months' notice in my contract, and hoped he'd agree to release me straight away.

'Of course,' he said when I raised it with him. 'There's no

point in you trying to do both jobs, and it'd be better from our point of view to find someone to get stuck in without delay. Young Malcolm Williams has got a country background, and he's a bright lad. I'll sound him out about it, and if he agrees I expect you could give him good advice and contacts to set him off?'

'Yes, of course, I'll help him all I can, and Gillian will be there to nurse him to start with. She knows the job backwards by now. I think he'd be up to it.'

So that was settled to my considerable relief. There only remained now the problem of the flat. At first, I had thought that I'd like to keep it on so that I wouldn't have to sever all links with my friends. After sleeping on it, I decided that I'd never be able to find the time to justify retaining it. But I felt I'd like to hold on to the furniture for sentimental reasons, and also in case I might want to set up house on my own one day, if I ever found someone I wanted to live with.

The agent sold the flat within a week, and I came out £20,000 to the good due to the boom in house prices since I had bought it. The furniture went into store, and the last links with Westerton were broken, except for telephone calls to Angela and Robert, to start with at quite frequent intervals.

I had come away from the funeral feeling inspired by the expressions of friendship and offers of help. Perhaps I wasn't burying myself in the backwoods after all. It would now be a matter of getting into a farming routine of early rising to put the men to work in the morning, going round the different units to see that all was well and taking over the shepherding that Dad had continued to do right up to his death. One advantage was that I now had Mother to get my meals and do the shopping, so that relieved me of those chores. But the first thing to do was to get on top of the farm accounts, and see if there were any changes that we should be making.

I found when going over the figures for the previous three years on the computer that the profits, though still satisfactory, had been more or less static, because of the price squeeze that I had already been writing about in my job. We would soon have to find some economies, or alternatively generate extra sources of income, if we were not to go into reverse. I concluded that we were safe for the next year or two, but the situation would have to be monitored closely.

When I took over we were farming some 980 acres, of which about eighty were the steep fields at the back of the farmhouse, which were really only suitable for grazing sheep or beef cattle or young females being reared to come into the dairy herd. Dad had kept the ewe flock at about 300, which was a convenient size for him to manage with extra help for special jobs from one of the tractor drivers.

We were employing five men. Ian, the young man Dad had taken on five years earlier to replace Gordon as head herdsman, had turned out well, and he now had full responsibility for the dairy herd. He was also very competent on the computer, which by now played an important role in managing the herd.

His assistant, Duncan, a young man whom Dad had taken on straight from college two years before, was also responsible for the rearing of the young animals. When he was relief milking, that job was done by Stephen, one of the older employees, who also helped with the sheep flock and drove a tractor at busy periods. Then there was young Cecil, also a tractor driver, who was a skilled mechanic and spent a good deal of his time in the workshop, which Dad had gradually built up over the years.

Finally, there was Victor, the head tractor driver, who had been with us for years and who had stood in for Dad, if he was away. It was a very good, quite young team, whom fortunately I knew well from working with them at harvest.

Dad had been a good employer, giving the men plenty of scope and paying well above the standard wage. He had always ensured that their cottages were kept up to date. He had a favourite dictum: 'You can't expect a man to work happily unless he is well housed' – a precept with which I fully agreed. Dad had left each of them a legacy in his will, which they had much appreciated.

The summer before he died, Dad had taken on Daniel, then seventeen, as a full employee over the harvest period, and he lived with us in the farmhouse, which made Mother happy. He was astonishingly mature for his age. Getting into his school rugby team at sixteen, he had been appointed captain for his last year, and a school prefect. He was also keen on squash and tennis, which pleased me. He was already showing a healthy interest in girls, so it was quite on the cards, looking to the future, that he might provide an heir to carry on the farm – assuming that he was willing to take over from me when I wanted to give up. I felt that I didn't want to remain a farmer for life, though for the time being I had to be just that. We noticed during that summer that he would often sneak off in the evenings if we were not working late on harvest. Caroline told us that he was friendly with the daughter of a family they knew well. She was only sixteen, but was planning to go to university to train as a teacher when she left school.

He was now coming up to his last two terms at school, and had just faced up to the same dilemma that I had – where to go next, agricultural college or university? He'd made the opposite choice to me, and had already been given a place at Reading starting in October for a three-year degree course. The deciding factor was probably that he thought he'd get better rugby. He was already committed to working on the farm over harvest, which was a relief to me, as otherwise I'd have been very short of labour.

After taking stock of the farm and deciding that no immediate changes in policy were needed, the next thing was to contact the county branch of the Farming and Wildlife Advisory Group, or FWAG as it was called, to ask if one of their staff could come out and suggest ways in which we might be able to increase the wildlife on the farm.

I'd already seen them in action, and had written up a couple of case studies of farms where they had advised improvements. I thought that there must be scope for us to do something on the farm to increase the numbers of birds, and perhaps butterflies, which seemed to be disappearing fast from the fields. Dad had been a member of the Group, but an inactive one. In the sixties he had grubbed out some of the hedges to make the fields larger and more suitable for the larger machines, and I wondered whether we might plant one or two new ones in strategic places to restore the balance.

The following week, I spent a whole day going round the farm with a young man, who was the officer for our area, by name

Tony Wilkes. He had been to my college as a student and knew Richard well. He was very thorough and the following week presented his report, with a series of recommendations.

The first, a generalised one, was not to trim the hedges down each year, but to let them grow up higher for about three years, so as to provide better nesting sites for birds. He suggested a three- or four-year rota for cutting. It seemed a very sensible idea.

The second was to leave three-metre-wide margins round the cereal fields, and to plant these up with grasses and wildflowers. When I protested at the waste of land involved, he pointed out that these areas close to hedges seldom produced much of a yield, for a variety of reasons such as soil compaction from tractor wheels turning, bird damage as the crop ripened, and so on. They seldom earned enough return to pay for the fertilisers and sprays and tractor time spent on them – something that I'd never considered before.

The third suggestion was to increase considerably the size of one of the two stagnant ponds we had in the corners of two of the fields. The areas round them were always rather wet and never produced good crop yields, and again didn't justify the money spent on them. We could afford to give up about half an acre to enlarge one of them to attract waterfowl, and even to create an island in the middle which would provide a safer nesting place for birds with less risk of eggs being stolen by predators. The other one would not have an island but would be large enough to attract waterfowl.

Another recommendation was to round off several sharp corners in the fields, where it was difficult to turn tractors or the combine harvester. These would be planted with trees to provide nesting sites and straighter runs with machinery. Finally, he recommended two new hedges across pasture fields, which wouldn't interfere with grass cutting machines but which would provide more shelter for the livestock in rough weather, and also nesting sites.

I discussed these suggestions with Daniel when he came to stay for harvest. I had resolved not to make any changes without consulting him first, since he would have to live with them if he did decide to come back to run the farm one day. I had also decided not to discuss that possibility with him until he had been at Reading for at least a year, when we might make him a director with the ten per cent of shares that Dad had left unallocated.

He was very much in favour of the suggestions, except the one about field margins, where he thought we'd lose too much land. I managed to persuade him that the advice on this was pretty convincing.

We agreed that we'd make a start by leaving the field margins unsown when it came to planting the wheat in the autumn, and that I'd get a contractor in to dig the ponds in October. We'd leave the planting of the new hedges and rounding off the corners until the following year. In the meantime, I'd have to get out proper plans so that we could claim grant aid for the improvements. That gave me something to get my teeth into.

Over the years, I'd kept in touch with James on the phone, and had looked in to see him a couple of times when I had been on visits to the Cotswolds gathering material. He had finally found the right girl, and was the proud father of twin sons. He was still very happy in his job. I asked him down for a day to go round the farm to see if he had any recommendations about its future management.

'I honestly don't think that there's much that I can suggest,' he said. 'You seem to have got things pretty well under control and the crops look fine. What I think you may have to do before long is to increase the size of the dairy herd by about thirty or forty cows. It looks as if you'd have room for more without having to spend too much money.'

'I had thought of that, as I can't see the price we get for milk increasing much in the future, and more cows might be the answer. I'll discuss it with Daniel when he comes here for the harvest.' I enjoyed seeing him again, and we decided to get together more often.

So Daniel left school, and after a holiday with Janet, his girl-friend, came to work for us for the harvest, where he more than earned his keep and wages as the relief combine harvester driver, and mother was pleased to have him to look after. Outwardly, she seemed to have taken Dad's death surprisingly well, but there were times when she was obviously missing him terribly. She'd then take herself off to church which appeared to provide comfort. I felt helpless, as there is so little that one can do to relieve another's grief, which must be borne alone – as I had discovered after Simon's death.

Harvest went well, with above-average yields, so that the financial situation was quite good. I had discussed the question of increasing the size of the herd with Daniel, and we mutually agreed to postpone a decision until the following autumn, and try to build up capital to help pay for the expansion.

I gradually settled down to my new life through that autumn, as I got to know neighbouring farmers better. The process was helped by the discovery of a new country house hotel, some six miles away, where the old stables had been converted into two squash courts. A club had been formed which I had joined. It provided not only a chance to get right away from the farm for a time, but also to enjoy the company of people of my own age. They were mainly youngish businessmen, most of whom were married, and none of whom was remotely attractive, so there was no Robert there. I managed to get games about once a week, which was a welcome break from the farm routine.

After Christmas I took myself off to Oxford once more, as things were slack on the farm and Ian and Victor were perfectly able to cope for a couple of days. But I did ask Daniel, who was still on holiday, to come over to stay with Mother while I was away, with instructions to ring me if anything were amiss on the farm.

It felt strange not being there in a professional capacity, and being able to sit back without the necessity for taking notes or seeking interviews on the tape recorder. My old friend Brian did me what was to be a good turn by introducing me to Adrian Newbold, the recently appointed agricultural editor of the *Western Times*, the leading daily newspaper in the West. He had recently moved down from a paper in the North, which is probably why I hadn't met him before. He knew of me from articles I had written and asked if he could come over one day to go round the farm. Andrew also said he had a television programme on the drawing board on pesticides which he might want me for. I came away feeling that I was not entirely forgotten in my rural backwater.

Three weeks later, the phone rang.

'Adrian Newbold here. You may remember we met at Oxford. Could I come over to see the farm one day soon?'

'Of course. When were you thinking of?'

'Would next Tuesday be all right? If so, how do I find you?'

'It'd suit me fine.' When I gave him instructions, he said he'd be there about eleven thirty, so I asked him to stay for lunch.

I guessed that he was a few years older than me, tall and thin, with dark hair and eyes and a pale face. He looked a bit lugubrious until he started to talk, when his face lit up and became animated, and he was clearly very much on the ball.

'It's good of you to come. Is there anything special that you'd like to see?' I said as he got out of his car.

'I'd just like to get a view of the whole farm if you've got the time.'

'Fine. We'll start at the buildings and the herd, and then hop into the Land Rover, as it'd take a bit too long to walk it.'

It felt strange to be on the receiving end of a visit like this, as it was usually I who would be doing the questioning instead of him asking me for details. As a fellow professional, I was impressed by the depth of his knowledge and the way he was probing me, especially on the plans we had for increasing the wildlife.

Fortunately the contractor had finished the digging out of the small lake and the smaller pond. The previous week we had planted the bushes on the small island and, though the whole thing looked an awful mess, one could already begin to assess what it might be like in a couple of years' time.

'That's very impressive,' he said. 'Can I come back again before long to see how it's settled down?'

'Of course, and by then we'll have some idea of how the other plans are working out, though I don't expect any spectacular results – not for a long time, anyhow.'

'Tell me,' he said as we drove back to the farm for lunch, 'did you find it easy giving up your job with the *Herald*, and coming back here to farm?'

'To be honest, it was extremely difficult at first. I missed the pressures of the old job – the full diary, the writing, the farm visits and also the social life that I had in Westerton, which I was enjoying so much. All that was gone in a moment of time and it was very hard to adjust to this sort of life. I felt isolated, and that I was getting out of touch with what was happening in the world outside. But I'm settling down, though I do miss the challenge of writing.'

'Would you like to get back into journalism, then?'

'Very much, though it would depend on how much time was involved. The farm would obviously have to remain my first priority.'

'I've got a proposition that might interest you then. My editor has agreed that we should have a fortnightly article, possibly entitled *Farmer's Diary*, and I'm looking for a farmer with some writing experience to do it for me. I wouldn't want it just to be an account of what is happening on that farm, though that would come into it. It would be more a commentary on what is happening in agriculture, both at home and abroad, and how that might affect the working of the farm in question. You've got the range of farming enterprises here and you've got the writing experience. Would you like to take it on?'

'I'd jump at it. It's just the sort of thing I need to keep me in touch. I'm hoping to bring my nephew into the business in a few years' time, and that might give me more time for outside work. But for the moment a fortnightly article would suit me fine. About how many words had you in mind for it?'

'About five to six hundred. Does that sound reasonable?'

'Actually, it's a bit more than I thought you'd say, but that'd give me scope to cover two or three different topics, which would be fine.'

The fee he offered was quite acceptable, and as we arrived at the farm, we shook hands on the deal.

'What a charming house and garden,' he said as we went through the gate. 'Do you think that we might have a photo of it to head up the article? We could change it about four times a year according to the season.'

'I'd have to ask Mother about that, as the house belongs to her, and she's also the gardener.'

'Mother,' I said as we entered the house, 'this is Adrian Newbold from the *Western Times*. He's just offered me a job to write a fortnightly article for him, and he'd like to have a photo-graph of the house and garden to head it up. What do you think?'

'I do hope you'll agree, Mrs Harper,' he said as they shook hands.

'I'm so glad about the job, dear. It should really suit you, and give you an interest outside the farm. I'm not sure about the photo, though. I wouldn't want a lot of cars coming down the lane and parking outside while they gawped at the garden. I'd want to preserve our privacy.'

'I don't really think there'd be much risk of that, Mrs Harper, as we shan't be saying where the farm is, and anyhow any visitors go up to the farm office, don't they?'

'I think that's probably right, Mother, as I always see visitors up there.'

'All right, then, we'll risk it, but on the understanding that if people do come down, you'll stop using it, Mr Newbold.'

'Thanks so much, but do call me Adrian – everyone else does.'

Mother, in spite of her natural shyness, was always good with visitors and lunch went well as we found out more about him and his family. Over coffee, we discussed further details about the articles, about which we saw very much eye-to-eye. This was the start of a collaboration that was to last for the next twenty years. Occasionally he would red-pencil something that I'd written, but that was his job, and I had often done the same in my past life.

I was still a member of the Guild of Journalists, which gave me access to government publications, and I had joined the Farmers' Union, so I had no difficulty in getting adequate material for my articles outside what we were doing on the farm. It was just what I needed to settle me down.

Daniel came to stay for harvest after his first year at Reading. I decided it was time to talk about the future, so that we could get on with changes, such as increasing the number of cows, which there wouldn't be much point in doing if he wasn't expecting to run the farm in the future.

'Daniel, before we go any further with expanding the herd, I think I'd like to know whether you might be interested in taking over the farm one day, because if you're not, I'd think twice about doing it. If you did want to come back sometime, we could bring you in as a director of the company, and you could have the ten per cent of the shares which haven't been allocated. What would you feel about it?'

'Naturally I've thought quite a bit about it already, and the answer is probably yes. But I'd like a day or two before deciding, as I ought to discuss it with Janet first. You see, we both think that we have a future together, though we're not engaged and don't intend to be just yet. If we do marry, as I hope we will, she obviously ought to be consulted as it will be her future as much as mine that would be involved.'

'Of course, there's no immediate hurry to decide. You might feel that you'd like to get out and get more experience first, and that there would not really be enough room for both of us here at the same time. It'd be a very long term decision, obviously, but I feel it's something we should decide on in principle before long.'

'I do agree, Mark, and it's great that you're thinking about it now. I do appreciate that.' I'd noticed for some time that he'd dropped the 'Uncle' bit when talking to me, and it made us feel more like brothers, which was good.

That evening over supper, I thought I should see what Mother thought about it.

'I asked Daniel today, Mother, whether he could see his future here on the farm, as it would be important to know that if we were thinking of doing any long-term improvements. It's rather what Dad was asking me about twenty years ago. If he did say yes, it might mean that he'd want the farmhouse, as he and Janet would probably be married by then. What would you think about it?'

I got the shock of my life when she replied. 'Naturally, dear, I've thought quite a bit about it since your father died. I'm not getting any younger, and I'm beginning to find the garden quite hard work, though the house is easy enough to manage. But the time will come when I'd probably like to move out to a smaller place in the village nearer the shops. Then you probably won't want to live here alone, will you, as you won't be getting married.'

'What makes you think that I shan't be getting married?'

'Well, you're not made that way, are you, dear?'

'Do you mean to say that you've guessed about me? How long have you known?'

'Oh, a long time, dear, quite soon after Simon was killed. I began to wonder about you that summer when he was working here. I saw the way you looked at each other, and how happy you were together, and how dreadfully distressed you were when he died in that awful accident. It did seem a bit more than just a normal friendship. Of course, I didn't really know much about that sort of thing at the time, only what they said in the Bible.

'When I got friendly with Cynthia I asked her about it when I was having lunch with her one day. She was very cagey to start with, and tried to put me off, as she was afraid I might take it badly. When I pressed her, she told me all about Simon and her brother in London and how much in love with you Simon had been, and how happy you had made him. It was rather a shock at first, because of the Bible and the sort of jokes they make about it on television.

'But she explained it all so sympathetically, she convinced me that it wasn't sinful in any way for two men, or two women, for that matter, to fall in love with one another, if they were made that way. She said it would seem just as natural to them as it would be for us to love our husbands. If God had made you and Simon like that, we should be thankful that you had found one another, and be happy for you. Naturally we were both sorry that you wouldn't have the joy of a happy marriage and having children, but there was nothing we could do. If that was God's will, then we should accept it.'

'Why on earth didn't you tell me at the time that you knew?'

'I discussed it with Cynthia, and she was afraid that it might somehow create a barrier between us, so we decided to put it off for the time being and tell you if a suitable opportunity occurred. But the longer we put it off, the more difficult it became.'

'What did Dad think about it?'

'Of course he knew rather more than I did about it. He was disappointed that you wouldn't be having a happy family life and children, and a son to follow you in the farm. But by then Daniel had been born so that wasn't quite so important to him. But I can assure you, dear, that it made no difference to his love for you, and he became increasingly proud of you as you made such a success of your job. When you brought Guy down to meet us, we both hoped you'd found happiness again, and we were going to tell you then, but he left you before we got round to it.

'We were so sorry when that happened, as we both liked him so much, and you appeared to be so happy together.'

'It was hard as we were very fond of one another,' I replied. 'But it couldn't have worked in the long run. We were too far apart, and I was so tied up in the job I could never have given him the time he wanted, even if he'd come up to live near me. In the end, he found someone kind and loving who could give him that time, so I couldn't expect him to turn his back on it. Perhaps one day we'll see one another again.'

'I'm sure you will find someone else one day, perhaps when you least expect it.'

'I hope so, but until then, Mother dear, I've got you to look after me, and thank you so much for taking this as you have. I can't tell you what a relief it is to have it all out in the open at last, and I won't have to pretend any more.' With that I put my arms round her, and gave her a hug and a long kiss – something I hadn't done in years.

Three days later, Daniel came up with his decision, having talked it over with his parents and with Janet. They had decided that he would definitely like to become more involved with the farm and to take over from me one day. But he'd like to get a job after he finished at Reading, so as to get more experience, and see more of the world before he and Janet settled down. He would only come back when I was ready to hand over control. In the meantime, he'd like to join the company as one of the directors. We agreed that we'd do this on his twenty-first birthday in a year's time. It was a relief to feel that the future of the farm was now secure.

One wet day during harvest, I got him and Ian together to discuss the proposal to increase the size of the herd. Fortunately when Dad had put in the new milking parlour he had allowed for a possible increase in cow numbers.

'I think that we could probably manage another thirty cows to bring them up to 210,' Daniel said. 'Do you think you could manage that, Ian?'

'Easily, the figure I had in mind was 220, as we could then add four rows of ten cubicles each on to the existing lines without too much expense. The parlour could easily cope with the extra forty cows, though it would obviously increase the milking time, but I'm sure it'd be worth it. Can the farm afford it, Mark?'

'Of course, if we're going to increase, we might as well do it up to the limit which you think you could manage, and I think your plan for expanding the cubicles is a very sensible one. So can we agree on 220? It'll mean growing a smaller cereal acreage to provide more maize and grass for the cows. But with cereal prices dropping it's probably wiser to concentrate more on milk. The bigger problem is going to be disposing of the slurry in the winter months. The lagoon isn't big enough, is it, Ian?'

'No, but I think we've got enough room there to bulldoze out some of the bank at the side away from the buildings to make it big enough. If not, we'll just have to empty it twice over the winter.'

'I'd rather not have to do that, as it's expensive and would be messy in a wet winter.'

'I've got another proposal,' Daniel interjected. 'While we're doing all this, wouldn't it be sensible to change the feeding system at the same time? We're going to have to extend the feeding passage and the mangers to provide room for the extra cows anyhow. Why don't we go over to feeding a complete diet with a mixer wagon, and cut out the feeding of the concentrates while the cows are being milked? It might save Ian some time when he's milking as well.'

It so happened that shortly before I'd left Westerton I'd visited a large dairy farm which had just adopted that system, and had been impressed with the results, but I hadn't actually thought of doing it at home.

'You may be on to something there, Daniel, but it'll cost quite a bit on top of the other expenditure. Do you think it'd be worth it? Would it put up yields enough to justify the cost?'

'Yes, it should, but it might mean we'd have to change the type of cow as well. It might mean going over to leaner Holsteins, as our existing Fresians might get too fat on the system, and Holsteins give more milk, anyway.' We'd started out on what seemed a simple proposal to keep some more cows, and here we were, already landing up with a mass of other proposals as well.

'Perhaps before we go any further, we ought to run a few different scenarios through the computer,' I said. 'I wouldn't want to commit myself to spending all this extra money without some more concrete evidence. Could you two get your heads together, as I expect you've some figures from Reading, haven't you, Daniel?'

'Yes, I think I should be able to dig some out of my notes, which should be reliable enough to form a basis for the calculations.'

'OK, let's leave it for now and we'll come back to it later.'

The computer suggested that we should be able to pay off the money invested in about five years if we could increase the milk yield by ten per cent, as a result of the new feeding system. By then yields should be increasing anyhow as the new Holstein crosses ought to be milking. As soon as we had decided in principle to increase the herd size, we picked out the one hundred highest-yielding cows and inseminated them with semen from Holstein bulls. The calves born next autumn should be the first crossbreds, finishing their lactations in about four years time. Such is the long-term planning needed in farming.

Before we came to a final decision to spend the money, I wanted to know what Richard Sykes might think about it. He brought up his class of final year students to do an exercise on it. They spent the better part of the day with us, and Mother put on a good buffet lunch, as I remembered how much I had enjoyed similar occasions when I was a student myself.

Three weeks later, Daniel came down from Reading and we went to the college to hear what the students had come up with. The four teams varied quite a lot in their proposals, but the consensus was that it was a feasible proposition if we could increase yields by six to seven per cent. This tied in well with our own assessment, so we decided to go ahead.

The visit to the college was the first I'd made since I finished my course some twenty years before. Inevitably I found it emotionally disturbing. Simon's face seemed to be everywhere still, bringing back nostalgic memories of that happy year together, but also the trauma of his death. I felt a deep longing to have someone to love again in my life, and blamed myself for losing Guy. The years were passing me by, and the chances of finding someone were certain to diminish as I got older. I'd just have to fill my life with developing the farm, and try to get more outside work.

Before we could go any further a visit to the bank manager was required, and it resulted in a specialist officer being sent down to see me. He thought the scheme was perfectly sound, and was happy to put up the money, which I found reassuring. So that winter was spent getting out the plans, and securing the authority to go ahead, so that we'd be ready to get the builders in as soon as the cows had gone out to grass for the summer.

I was not having any difficulty in finding enough material for my fortnightly articles, and the plans for the herd gave me something to write about on the farm. I was surprised at the amount of feedback that I was getting. Most of it was reasonably complimentary, but some was highly critical, mostly from people with obvious chips on their shoulders or with axes to grind in relation to farmers and their subsidies. It was useful to know that people were reading it. The fear that the picture of the farm might bring sightseers didn't materialise.

When the cows had gone out to grass, the builders moved in to start the expansion of the cubicle house, and enlarging the lagoon for the slurry. We ploughed up two grass silage fields and sowed them to maize, ready for the new feeding system the following autumn.

Daniel stayed with us over harvest, providing a vital pair of hands on the combine to relieve Victor at meal times, and giving me a break on the grain dryer. Thankfully yields of wheat were higher, to help toward paying the interest on the money we'd borrowed for the building.

Cows are creatures of habit, and do not take kindly to changes in routine. They staged a rebellion at the change in the feeding system, when they were deprived of their concentrated feed of dairy nuts in the milking parlour. Ian had to have help in persuading them to go in for milking for a couple of weeks, though they were happy enough to scoff down the tastier silage ration in the long feeding manger, where they were fed their ration of nuts mixed up with their maize silage, and their milk yield declined dramatically. Gradually it returned to normal, then rose above its previous level. The cost of the feed had increased slightly as they were eating a bit more, but on balance it looked as if the new system would pay off, as the genetic influence of the Holstein crossbreeds made itself felt in the future. It also helped us in the first year to pick out those cows that were converting the extra food into body fat instead of milk, and they had to be sold.

We always calved about two thirds of the herd in the autumn and the rest in the spring, as this took a little pressure off Duncan in not having to rear too many calves at once. So that autumn all the cows were inseminated with semen from the bulls of high-yielding Holstein cattle. It would take about five years for the results to show through, but we were both confident that the change in the system would finally pay off.

Daniel was now in his last year at Reading, and he had gained a tremendous lot from his course, not only in technical and managerial terms but also in the development of his character. He had been elected as president of the students' union for his final year, which had given him poise and an aura of authority, and an ability to get up and speak in public on a wide range of topics. He was becoming a distinct personality, and I could see a bright future for him in some aspect of public affairs. Whether this would be in farming politics we would have to wait and see.

James rang up in April, as we hadn't spoken for quite some time, and he wanted to know if I was settling down all right.

'How are you doing, Mark? I hope things are going well on the farm. When are you coming up to see me? Now you're just a farmer, you should have plenty of time.'

'I don't know about that. The days seem pretty full, somehow. We're just starting on a big herd expansion, adding another forty cows, and that's been taking up a lot of time. The builders are due in as soon as the cows are fully out at grass. What about next Wednesday? That's a free day at the moment, and the builders won't be in by then.'

'That'll be fine. I'll expect you in time for lunch.'

'I've got one bit of news,' he said as we were going round the estate after the meal. 'My boss is retiring at the end of September, and I'm hoping that they'll give me the job, though it's by no means certain. The boss says that he'll recommend me for it, but I've an idea that the owner might want to put one of his son's friends in. We'll just have to wait and see, but it won't be decided until July.'

About five minutes later, I had an idea.

'If you did get the job, presumably your assistant's job will be vacant? Daniel's finishing at Reading in June, and though he's coming back to work over harvest, he'll be looking for a job after that, as he wants to get more experience. He's a very bright lad indeed, and he's done very well both at school and at Reading where he's been president of the students' club.'

'That's quite an idea. If I did get the top job, I'll certainly be looking out for someone, but of course I can't promise anything as the owner might have a candidate lined up for it. But I'll definitely keep it in mind, and let you know as soon as my own position's clear. We could have him up for interview then, and he'll have to take his chance.'

I mentioned it to Daniel at Easter. He was very enthusiastic as there weren't many jobs about in his field.

One morning early in May I was going over the results from the herd with Ian to compare them with the previous winter. We had earlier rung the vet as we had some cows that needed attention. As he hadn't arrived by half past twelve, I said to Ian: 'You go off and get your dinner. I'll deal with the vet when he comes.'

About ten minutes later a car came into the yard; however, it wasn't our usual vet, but a much younger man.

'Mr Harper?' he said as he got out of the car, 'I'm David Watson, and I've just joined the practice in place of Jack Smart, who's retired.' As we shook hands, I could see that he was looking at me intently in an appraising way, rather as Simon had done across the bar at our first meeting. It was only a short stare, but in those few seconds a message seemed to pass between us, and I found that I was still holding his hand as he hadn't let go of mine. Then it was over as he walked round to the boot of the car to put on his Wellingtons and protective overalls.

'I hope you'll enjoy working down here. Where were you before?'

'Up near Newcastle, but I was getting too much cat and dog work, instead of farm animals and dairy cows, which is what I'm really interested in. I decided to come down into a proper farming area, and also to be near my parents, who are getting on in years, and live in South Wiltshire.'

By now he'd got his gear on. 'Right, so what have you got for me today?'

'One lame cow, one which hasn't cleansed properly and three for pregnancy diagnosis. Where'd you like to start?'

'Let's get the messy one over first. Then I'll have the lame one, and we'll do the PDs last.'

I was very impressed by the way he went about the job, obviously competent and wasting no time, but very gentle in his handling of the cows, which responded as if they trusted him.

'Have you found somewhere to live?' I asked as he injected the lame cow with an antibiotic.

'Yes. I was hoping to find a small cottage, but the only one was far too expensive, so I've settled for one of the new flats in Norton, which will probably be far more convenient anyway.' I noticed that he always said I and not we, so I decided to settle that issue without delay.

'So you've no family then?'

'No, I'm afraid I haven't even acquired a wife. I've never seemed to find time for it.'

'Oh well, that makes two of us then, as I'm in the same boat.' At that, our eyes met again, and another unspoken message passed between us.

It was nearly half past one by the time he'd treated the last of the cows. 'Would you like to come back down to the farm for a bit of lunch? It'll only be cold ham and bread and cheese, as we never have a cooked lunch, I'm afraid.'

'I'd love to. I can't stay very long as my next date is at half past two.'

'Good. Just follow me down; it's only about a quarter of a mile.'

As we returned to the house I introduced him to Mother: 'Mother, this is David Watson, who's just joined the vet practice. He'd like a bit of lunch before going on to his next job.'

'I'm glad to meet you,' Mother said as they shook hands. 'Can I call you David? Mr Watson sounds so formal, doesn't it? It's only ham and salad, I'm afraid, as we gave up a cooked lunch long ago. I never knew when my husband would be coming in and now Mark is much the same.'

'That'll do me fine. It's far better than a rather stale pub sandwich, I can assure you.'

'David has moved into one of those new flats in Norton which Geoffrey's lot built. He says that he's very pleased with it. Geoffrey's my brother-in-law, David, and he works for the firm that bought the site when the market closed some years ago.'

'They're well designed, with plenty of room, and being on the third floor I've got a good view over the town. You must come and see it sometime if you haven't been inside one.'

'I'd like that.'

'Where did you get your training?' Mother asked him.

'I was lucky to get a place in the vet school at Cambridge. It was good, as it was quite a small school, and we had all the advantages of the university thrown in.'

A sudden thought struck me. 'I suppose you didn't play squash when you were there, did you?'

'Well, yes, I did play quite a lot at the time, but I've not touched a racket for twenty years. I've never had an opportunity in my previous jobs. Why did you ask?'

'There's a country hotel about six miles from here, where they've converted the old stables into a couple of courts, and set up a club which I belong to. If you played, I wondered if you'd like to give me a game sometime?'

'I'd love to take it up again. I'm getting out of condition with all the driving I do and the exercise would do me good, quite apart from the enjoyment I'd get out of it.'

'I'll give you a ring in a day or two, then, to fix up a game, and then I'll book the court. If you haven't got a racket you can buy one there.'

'Good, I'll need a new one as I've no idea where the old one's got to. I'm sorry, Mrs Harper, but I'll have to rush off or I'll be late for the next visit. Thanks so much for the lunch. I do love your house and garden.'

'You must come in again soon, David. We don't get many visitors, and it'd be nice to see you. There's always lunch if you want it.'

'I'll give you a ring soon about the game,' I said as we went out to his car.

'Yes, do, I'm looking forward to it already.' We looked into each other's eyes as we shook hands, and again something seemed to pass between us. He waved from the car as he drove off up the lane, and I walked back, feeling elated.

'He seems very nice,' Mother said, as I got back to the house. 'I do hope you'll get on well as it'd be good for you to have a close friend again, wouldn't it?'

'Yes, but it's early days yet.'

Is this it? I thought to myself as I lay in bed that night. He had given out all the usual signs, and seemed to have registered mine. I found him physically attractive, if not in quite the same league as Simon or Guy. But I was older now and less likely to be bowled over as I had been by both of them.

He was so different in appearance, with brown hair and eyes which seemed to have flecks of green in them – not the blue eyes and fair hair of the other two. But I liked the proportion of his features, as he was good-looking in a classical way, with fine eyelashes and a broad mouth which broke into an attractive smile on the slightest provocation. I liked, too, his personality which made him so easy to talk to. I felt I knew him well already, which was a good sign, and meant that we were likely to get on well together.

I waited three nights before I rang him up, as I didn't want to appear to be chasing him.

'What about that game of squash, David, is it still on? Would Thursday evening about seven o'clock be convenient?'

'That ought to be all right, as I'm not on call then. Will you let me know the exact time when you've booked the court?'

'So glad you can manage it. I'll let you know, and how to find the place tomorrow evening.'

Once he'd acclimatised to the feel of a racket again he turned out to be a pretty good player, and beat me, but not by too much. We had some excellent rallies in a fast game.

'I did enjoy that,' he said afterwards 'I can't think why I didn't keep it up when I left university. I suppose it was because I didn't have anyone to play with. I must apply for membership if you'll support me.'

'Of course I will, and we'll probably find someone to second you. I hope this'll be the first of many more games to come.'

'So do I, it was great fun.'

By this time we were in the showers, and I couldn't resist a glance in his direction. He had a lean athletic body, wide at the chest and hips, with not a trace of flab. He was rather better equipped than me, but not markedly so, and I was glad to see that, like me, he was uncut. I caught him sizing me up, which removed any possible doubts that I had about him.

At the bar afterwards, we got hold of a membership form, though I warned him that it was quite a hefty sub.

'I expect I can afford it. They pay me pretty well in the job, and I've no expensive tastes. I gave up smoking years ago, and drink very little, and not having a wife helps.' We laughed at that.

We arranged to play again the following week. As we were leaving, he said: 'Would you like to come and see the flat and have supper next week after the game?'

'I'd love to. It'll be interesting to see what sort of a job Geoffrey's people did.'

The flat when I saw it the following week consisted of a large lounge with dining area included, two bedrooms, a decent kitchen and lots of cupboards. David was clearly no modernist, as his furniture was old and well worn, and there were family photos and pictures of the countryside on the walls. It had a warm, well lived-in feeling about it, and I immediately felt at home there.

'I do like it, David. It's so nice and homely. I hate all this modern furniture, and that view over to the hills reminds me of the one I had in my little flat in Westerton.'

'Glad you like it. Now what about some food?'

He'd prepared a cold meat and salad supper with apple pie to finish with, and we talked continuously throughout the meal. He wanted to know why I hadn't gone back to work at home when I'd finished college.

'I suppose it was because my close friend Simon had opened my eyes to the world outside, and showed me that there was so much more to life than just farming. Then he was killed in a car crash, and I was devastated, and felt that I wanted to get away and start a new life. I knew by then that I was gay, and I thought that the chances of finding another partner buried down here would be remote in the extreme. Anyhow, Dad was still quite young and didn't really need me at home. As I have always enjoyed writing, journalism was an obvious choice of a job. When did you realise that you were gay?'

'Finally when I was on the vet course at Cambridge. I was a day boy at a good public school, where I had a real crush on another boy, but I don't think he suspected anything and he certainly wasn't gay himself. Then in my second year at university, one of the third year students fell in love with me – or said he did. He managed to seduce me, although I have to admit that I didn't need much pushing. I didn't find him particularly attractive, but I did enjoy the sex part. Then he left and got a job and I never heard from him again. After that I had one or two casual affairs which left me cold, and I've done nothing much for years, accepting the fact that now I've just passed forty it would be celibacy for me in future.'

'Life begins at forty, so they say, so you certainly shouldn't give up hope yet.' As I said that, I looked at him and he smiled back.

By now we'd finished the washing-up, but I was still unsure whether he'd want to take it further. I guessed he might not wish to take the lead. Even though he was a bit older, I was probably the more experienced. After all, I was one of his clients, and he'd not want to risk a false move, which could affect our professional relationship. There was little point in putting it off any longer.

'Do you want to go any further, David? Or would you prefer it if we just remained squash-playing friends?'

'Of course I do. I was hoping against hope that you'd say something. I couldn't, as it wouldn't have been professional conduct. But I think you ought to know one thing first. I'm not into anal sex. I suppose it may be something to do with my training in physiology and hygiene, or that I'm dealing with disease all the time which puts me off it.

'Apart from that, though, it seems rather a sordid business, involving domination of one of the partners, whereas my feeling is that love should be entirely mutual. Of course, we're all different, and some may like it that way, but it's not for me.'

'Don't worry. I'm the same. There's a feeling of Sodom and Gomorrah about it. That's just sex and not real love to me. I may be over-fastidious, but that's how I feel.'

He led me to the bedroom, where we fell into each other's arms, and for the third time I felt the exhilaration of a new love in my life – if love it was to be.

I had been right in my assessment of him when he was handling the cows. He was unbelievably tender and gentle as we caressed and explored each other's bodies. Then suddenly it was all too much for me, and I started to tremble uncontrollably, just as I had when I had first been with Simon.

'Don't worry. I'll be all right in a few moments. It's just that all the longings to hold someone again have proved too much coming all at once.'

I felt him holding me tighter, and slowly the shaking ceased and I relaxed, savouring the pressure of his body on mine, and secure in the knowledge that our reactions to each other were similar. We were, as Simon once said, compatible in bed, with mutual give and take cementing the relationship. As with Guy that first night, we had been deprived of sex for so long that we both came rather too quickly to get the fullest enjoyment from the act. No matter, there would surely now be many more occasions that we could enjoy.

'Mark, those were the best moments of my life so far. Was it good for you, too?'

'It certainly was. It's just so wonderful to be with someone you care for again.'

'So you care for me a bit, do you?'

'Of course I do, but what about you?'

'It's a bit more than just caring with me, I think. I've never experienced real love for anyone before, but it must be awfully like what I feel for you now, I imagine.'

'You mustn't allow yourself to get too carried away in the euphoria of the moment. We really hardly know each other and it may just be a flash in the pan. We may find we don't get on as well as we think. It's early days, though I do feel it may be the real thing.'

It was inevitable, I suppose, that I should compare my feelings now with those I remembered when I was with Simon and Guy for the first time. With the former it had been the sheer adolescent exhilaration of being in love with someone that I looked up to. Then love seemed to be the only real thing that mattered in the carefree life we led, and Simon took the lead as he was so much more experienced than I was. With Guy there had still been an element of youthful enthusiasm about it, but there was also a sense of maturity, where I was slightly the dominant partner, generally taking the lead. I felt more responsibility towards him because of that.

Now, what about David? The physical side of our sex was just as good as with the others, and I knew that this was reciprocated. But now there seemed to be even more of a protective feeling of tenderness towards him and a sense of complete equality in the relationship. But after the experience with Guy, I felt wary of complete commitment, as I didn't want to be hurt again. No doubt, if things went well, that feeling would soon fade as we got to know each other better. For the present, I would simply savour the pleasure of having a new man in my life again.

'Thank you, Mark,' he said as we got dressed. 'You don't want it to end there, do you?'

'Good heavens, no. We may not be able to get together too often, as we're both busy people, and I wouldn't want to do anything at home with Mother in the background. But that may be a good thing, as it'll be all the better when we can have it, and we can always keep in touch on the phone. What about a game of squash next week?'

'Fine, Wednesday's my best day. Will you book a court?'

'I'll bring the membership form and you can sign it.'

'Did you enjoy your evening, dear?' Mother asked when I got home.

'Yes, we had a close game though he beat me again. Those flats Geoffrey built are very nice and roomy, and he's got a good view over the town. I'll take you up one day, as I'm sure David wouldn't mind. Sorry if I'm rather late, but we got talking and I didn't notice the time.'

'Would you like to ask him to lunch one Sunday soon, and then you could show him the farm in the afternoon?'

'That'd be nice. We're playing again on Wednesday, and I'll ask him then.'

By some sort of unspoken understanding we didn't go back to his flat after our next game of squash. It was as if both of us had decided not to rush the affair, but would rather let it develop naturally. I signed his application form for membership, and fortunately another member I knew was in the club who seconded it, and he was duly elected.

On the following Sunday, he came to lunch, and we walked the farm in the afternoon. He suggested we put in a footbath for the cows to go through after milking, as his practice was getting a lot of cases of lame cows from bacterial infections on the bigger farms. He was also concerned that our individual cow cubicles might be too small by the time the herd would consist mainly of larger Holstein cows; but that would have to wait, as we had no money to spend on making them bigger, and it might not prove necessary anyhow. It was a happy afternoon reminiscent of those spent with Simon long ago. He stayed for supper, and I'd have loved to have gone back to his flat with him, but felt that I couldn't leave Mother. It wouldn't be fair on her.

'I do like David,' she said after he'd gone. 'He's got such an active mind and a nice sense of humour to go with it. In some ways he reminds me of Simon, though he doesn't look anything like him, of course. Do you think he might take Simon's place with you, dear? I'd be very happy for you if he did.'

'You're an old matchmaker, Mother dear. I've no idea yet, but we do get on very well, and he seems to like me, too.' I left it at that, but it was fairly clear that Mother was pretty much on the ball as far as our relationship was concerned. I was only so thankful that everything was now out in the open.

Angela came down and stayed for a long weekend during the summer. I'd intended to ask her before but wanted to get settled in first. Our friendship had been one of the things I'd missed most, and though I'd seen her twice on flying visits to Westerton we hadn't really had time to talk properly. I asked her whether she thought it would be safe to ask Robert down for a weekend. She advised against it, as she felt that his John would be unhappy about it, as he now knew that I was gay and would suspect Robert of playing truant. He was still jealous of him, she thought.

It was the first time Mother had met Angela, and they struck up a relationship immediately. Mother knew what a good friend she'd been to me in the early days, and wanted to show Angela how much she had appreciated it.

On the Saturday night there was a good concert with the Bournemouth Symphony Orchestra in Exeter, which I thought Angela would enjoy. David suggested that we should get Mother to come as well. At first she was very reluctant, saying she didn't like going out in the evenings now, but we thought the real reason was that she feared she'd be thought too old for us youngsters, and might feel out of her depth.

'Look, Mother,' David said. 'I'm sure you'd enjoy it. It was only the other day you were saying that you used to like the choral concerts in the cathedral, so you ought to like this one as well. We're certainly not going to leave you behind, are we, Mark?'

'Yes, do come,' Angela said. 'They're playing one or two pieces that I'm sure you'd like. You won't have to dress up, as everybody goes in ordinary clothes these days.'

'Oh well, all right, I'll go then if you're sure I won't be in the way.'

'Of course you wont, Mother. I'll ring up for tickets in the morning.'

I took them all out to dinner before the concert, and as I'd anticipated Angela and David hit it off immediately. It was a light-hearted evening and an excellent concert and when we got back, Mother said: 'Thank you so much, dear, I can't remember when I enjoyed an evening more. The music was so good. We must go again if there's another one sometime.'

I wasn't surprised that she'd enjoyed it, as she and Dad had probably never gone out to a concert in their lives. The height of their social lives would have been the local farming club dinner. I resolved that I ought to take her out a bit more while she was still young enough to enjoy it.

The following day I took Angela over to lunch with Cynthia, as they'd never actually met before. Driving over, she told me how much she liked David, saying that I must hang on to him at all costs. I must never risk losing him as I had lost Guy, to which I replied that there was no risk of that as we were going to be together for life.

Cynthia was now just seventy, and grey hair suited her well, as she had retained her wonderful complexion, which was enhanced in some way by the paleness of the hair. Over the years I had told each of them so much about the other that they said they felt almost like old friends. They chattered away together over lunch, leaving Jack and me to talk farming. He had now retired officially, but still acted as a consultant and went to his office about twice a week, looking after the affairs of some of his old clients. He still spent a lot of his time in the garden, which was as spick and span as ever. I was glad to see the tennis court back in condition as it was being used by the grandchildren.

Angela went back next day, saying how much she'd enjoyed the visit, and berating me for not having asked her down to stay before. I promised her that she'd get another invitation before long, and asked her to tell Robert that I was in love again.

Shortly before harvest, James rang up.

'Good news, Mark, I've got the job. My boss told the owner that the other chap they had in mind wouldn't be up to it, and strongly recommended me. I've always got on well with the owner, and I think that settled it.

If Daniel is still interested in my job, he'd better apply immediately, as there's someone else in the field. Do you think he could come up next Tuesday?'

'I'm not sure as he's just gone away for a few days with his girlfriend. I think Caroline will know where they are, so we'll try to get hold of him. I'll ring you to confirm tomorrow.'

Caroline managed to locate them that night, so the following week Daniel went up for interview. He'd just missed out on a First at Reading, but had come away with glowing references, so we kept our fingers crossed.

After an anxious week, James rang again to say that Daniel had made an excellent impression with the owner and his agent, and he could have the job if he wanted it – which of course, he did. He would have a cottage on the estate, and would be content to look after himself for the first year. Janet still had a year to do on her teachers' training course at Reading, but I suspected she would be down with Daniel most weekends. They had announced their engagement and intended to marry when she had finished her course.

It was a tremendous relief that he'd got the job, as I was sure he'd get on well with James. Fortunately the new job didn't start until October, so I'd have him for harvest, but after that, I'd have no one to bring in at rush periods.

During that summer, the friendship with David deepened until we seemed to be almost part of one another, anticipating what the other was about to say. He spent an increasing amount of time on the farm when he was not at work. He helped Mother in the garden, and became very interested in her bees. We bought him a veil and protective gloves so that he could help with the honey harvest, carrying the heavy crates to the kitchen where the honey was extracted. It was a job that was getting a bit too much for Mother. She was coming to regard him as a second son. We'd get together in his flat after games of squash, but it wouldn't be more often than about once a fortnight, which was a bit frustrating for both of us.

In August he was away for a fortnight driving his parents up to Scotland for their holiday. I felt ridiculously alone, and it brought home to me forcibly how much a part of my life he'd become. We were in the middle of quite an early harvest, so I didn't have much time to brood over it. It was good to get a phone call one might to enquire whether I was all right.

'Oh, God, I do love you,' he said as we lay together after he got back. 'You won't ever leave me, will you, Mark? I missed you dreadfully while I was away, and thought about you every day.'

'I thought a lot about you as well. Don't worry, I'd never leave you now. We're made to be together, and all those wasted years were just there to make it all feel so much better now.' I felt a great wave of tenderness as I looked down at his face on the pillow – just as it used to be when I'd look at Simon in his sleeping bag on our camping holiday, and I thanked God for giving us such happiness.

By the end of the first week in September, the harvest was safely tucked away in the grain store, and it occurred to me that I hadn't had a holiday since I came back to the farm.

'Have you any holiday left, David?'

'About a week, I think. Why? Had you something in mind?'

'Well, yes. With harvest over so early, I think I might be able to get a week away, before the cows start calving in October. Daniel will still be about till the end of the month to keep an eye on things, and I'd like to get right away if you could get the time off.'

'I'll see the boss tomorrow and let you know. Like you, we shouldn't be too busy till October, so he might be able to spare me for my final week. After all, I am entitled to it. What had you in mind and what would be the dates?'

'The sixteenth to the twenty-third. You did say once that you'd not done any surf bathing, didn't you?'

'No, we always had our holidays on the south coast as children, so I never had the opportunity. Is that what you were thinking of doing?'

'Yes, I learnt up at Aunt Emily's in North Devon when I was still at school as her two boys were mad on it. One day they took me down to a beach in North Cornwall called Polzeath, where the surf is generally pretty good. It's about halfway down the coast. Simon and I used to go there, as he'd got to love it, too.'

'It sounds a marvellous idea, as I'd love to learn. I'll do my best to get time off.'

David's senior partner fortunately enjoyed surfing himself, so gave him the week off. I'd made a note of the hotel on the cliff facing the beach when we had dropped in there for a drink one day after our bathe. I rang them up to see if they might have a twin-bedded room available for that week. I thought they might as the schools would have gone back by then.

'Yes, we've got one. It's facing the sea, so it's a bit more expensive.' She quoted what sounded to me a very reasonable price which I accepted on the spot. Daniel agreed to look in to see that Mother was all right and that there were no problems on the farm, so we could go away with a clear conscience.

The thought of going away for a week together, just the two of us, was really exciting. We went in his car, and as we came up to the little B&B where we'd stayed, on the spur of the moment I asked him to stop. The sign was gone, so I thought they had probably retired.

Mrs Trewin answered the door, looking much older and rather frail.

'I'm afraid we don't do B&B any longer, if that was what you were wanting.' Then she looked at me closely. 'Haven't you stayed with us before, a long time ago? I'm sure I know your face. I remember now. You had another very nice young man with you and you were agricultural students.'

'Gosh, you have a marvellous memory, Mrs Trewin. Is your husband still alive? I remember so well the long talk we had with him about farming.'

'No, I'm afraid I lost him four years ago, and I stopped the B&B then. I'm selling up very soon, as it's very lonely here on my own. I'm going to live near my daughter in Bodmin. How's your friend getting on?'

'He was killed in a car crash not long after we stayed here with you, which is why we never came back to stay again. I've not been back since then, as I couldn't face it. I've got a friend now who wants to learn how to surf, so we're having a week's holiday at Polzeath'.

'Oh, I'm so sorry, my dear. It must have been a terrible shock for you. He was such a nice boy, and you seemed such close friends.'

'It was awful at the time, but it's nearly twenty years ago now, though I still remember those days as if they were yesterday. It's so good to see you again, and I do hope you'll settle into your new home all right.'

'Goodbye, my dear, I'm so glad you looked in. Have a good week.'

The surf looked good as we turned the corner close to the hotel, and the sweep of the beach came into view, with the mouth of the estuary and the Atlantic to our right.

'What a wonderful place. I can't wait to get into the sea. I've never seen anything like it.'

'I hoped you'd like it, but you'll have to wait till tomorrow. It's too late now to get fixed up with wetsuits and surfboards. That's our hotel on the left, so you'd better get into the first parking place you can see. Then we'll go in to find our room.'

The view from the bedroom was even better still, as the extra height revealed more of the beach, and the estuary down to Padstow and the Rock sand hills and the outline of the moors behind. I couldn't get David away from the window to unpack. After dinner, we strolled around the cliff, watching fanatical surfers still in the sea in spite of the fading light. Lying together that night, with the sound of the breakers on the rocks below as the tide came up the beach, was the nearest thing to heaven that I could think of.

'Happy?' I asked.

'Utterly and completely, love.'

The surf was at its best in the mornings the week we were there, so we bathed then for about two hours. David got the hang of it very quickly. He loved it when he got the timing right and would hurtle past me shouting with joy. I felt huge pleasure that he was enjoying it so much. Then it would be a pasty for lunch on the beach and in the afternoon walks along the cliffs to the headland, or further north with magnificent views to Hartland and Lundy Island on a clear day.

We'd rest our legs lying on the scented cliff-top turf, listening to the roar of the sea meeting the rocks below. Seagulls floated effortlessly upwards, silhouetted against the blue of the sky, borne up on the draught from the cliff below. It was just him and me sharing our lives while the world seemed to stand still around us. I felt then as I did on that Alpine pasture high above Grindelwald with Simon, but this time the sun did not go in, which I took to be a good omen.

Mid-September can be a wonderful time of the year if the sun shines. It has that special golden glow that is missing in the brighter light of high summer. That year was no exception, and I kept being reminded of the lines from *September Song*: 'And these few precious days, these golden days, I'll spend with you' as we lay together on the cliffs. But that is a sad song about the passing of a life, whereas in our case I hoped it was the beginning of our lives together.

On the third afternoon we went the opposite way, taking the cliff path to Daymer Bay, immortalised by John Betjeman in *Summoned by Bells*, walking across the little church once covered by blowing sand, where the poet lies in peace under the shelter of the tamarisk-topped stone wall. We rested for a time on the seat above the church, savouring the tranquillity and the view across the golf course to the sand hills and the estuary beyond. We might just as well have been a honeymooning couple, spending their first holiday together – which I suppose we really were. Walking the path across the golf course, David said, 'I think I'd like to learn how to play this game.'

'Perhaps when we begin to feel we're a bit too old for squash. The only thing is that I might be too busy to play very often as it must take up a lot of time.'

'It would probably be good for you by then, as it might slow you down a bit.'

The next morning we awoke to find a gale battering the windows, and squalls of rain blowing in straight off the Atlantic. White horses tossing plumes of spray crashed halfway up the cliffs. Only two hardy surfers were to be seen and the beach was deserted.

'A bit too rough for us today, Mark, don't you think? What shall we do instead?'

'Didn't you say that you'd been reading an article about some lost gardens being restored in the south of the county? Shall we look it up on the map, and if it's not too far, we could go over there? The rain may ease off later on, with luck.'

'Good idea. The article did sound very interesting.'

We found out where the Heligan garden was. The hotel receptionist had been there in the spring, and recommended it.

We spent the afternoon there after a pub lunch on the way, fascinated by the reclamation, which was still in its early stages.

'We must come back again in a few years' time. It looks as if there's still masses to do,' David said.

By the time we got back, the wind had dropped, and a watery yellow sun was struggling to get through the last of the clouds, before it disappeared below the horizon. A crowd of surfers were making the best of the huge waves still rolling in.

By the next morning the sun was out again, and the surf was stronger in the aftermath of the previous day's turmoil. We had some long runs right up the beach, and got in one more bathe before leaving for home after lunch next day.

'That was terrific,' David said as we drove home. 'I think I'll retire early and then I could do it every day, and play golf when I'm not in the sea.'

'You'd probably get tired of it quite quickly if you could do it every day. It makes it all the better if you can only manage it now and again. Like most things in life you can have too much of a good thing. But we must certainly do it again, and come over for the day, as Simon and I used to do. It's not really very far.'

'Thanks for a wonderful week, Mark. It's been by far the happiest time in my life, and I owe it all to you. I can't thank you enough.'

'Nonsense, it's just as much due to you coming into my life, when I thought I'd never find someone to share things with again. We're just so lucky.'

'Do you think we might get a longer holiday next year and go abroad, perhaps?'

'I'd been thinking about that myself, but I'm not sure whether I could manage it. Now that Daniel won't be there any longer, I haven't got anyone to look after the farm if I'm away. You did say once, didn't you, that you hadn't been to Italy or Switzerland? I'd love to go back again and see some of the places I went to with Simon. I'll have to think seriously about the farm situation, as I can't be tied to it all the time.'

'I'd love to go. Let's think about it over the winter, shall we?'

He dropped me off at home, and as Mother was out he came in for a final hug. It was difficult to say goodbye, but as we did so we both said simultaneously, 'Thanks for everything.' I took this as a measure of how close we had grown to one another.

Chapter Eight

While I'd been away Daniel had been amusing himself on the computer analysing the profitability of the smaller units, such as the sheep flock, the rearing of beef calves and rearing and selling of surplus dairy heifers. None of these seemed to be contributing much to overall profit. If the price obtained from the sales of lamb was high there was a reasonable profit, but in a poor year we scarcely broke even. The same thing applied to the beef unit, except that if prices for beef were low we were definitely making a loss.

'What do you think, Daniel?' I asked. 'Should we be thinking of making any drastic changes?'

'No, I don't think so. We've got those steep fields, which are too far away to be reached by the cows, and are too difficult to plough, so sheep or beef are really the only option. We ought to consider whether we can keep more sheep, and cut out the beef altogether, selling those calves soon after birth.'

'I wouldn't want to keep many more ewes. I don't want to commit myself to working long hours on the flock, and I don't imagine that Stephen does either. If we doubled the size of the flock, we'd have to employ a full-time shepherd, and the wage bill is high enough already. We might manage another eighty or so, but that's the limit.'

'I agree, the returns wouldn't justify employing an extra man. That means that we'll have to stick with rearing beef cattle.'

'Yes, so the answer must be to get a better price by producing as good a quality beast as we can. I don't think we've paid enough attention to that in the past. We should inseminate all the cows we don't need to breed from for herd replacement with semen from a high-quality bull of a Continental breed, like a Charolais.'

'You're right there. I'd forecast that quality will become more important in the future.'

The next day we updated Ian's list of elite cows from which to breed our herd replacements, paying special attention to what each cow was costing in veterinary attention. Much as I loved David, I didn't want to pay his firm more than I needed to, by keeping cows with bad feet or those prone to udder infection.

Next we spoke to Stephen about having a few more ewes. He wasn't too happy about it, but agreed that another sixty wouldn't make much difference to the workload. The next job was to buy some in without delay, as we'd want to get them settled in before being put to the ram in October. I got them off a dealer who'd just brought a load of crossbred hill ewes down from Cumbria. They looked strong and hardy, and I was pleased with them, especially as they nearly all held to first service when the rams were put in.

During that autumn and winter I found I was getting more invitations to speak at conferences and farming dinners as a result of my fortnightly column in the paper. I enjoyed conferences and the discussions afterwards, and I had to learn to think fast on my feet. But I could often find something to write about as a result of such meetings.

Dinners were another matter, because I was never good at telling funny stories. There is nothing worse for one's confidence than a so-called joke that falls flat. The other problem over dinners when I was first invited was to know what sort of an audience one would be speaking to. I came a bit of a cropper twice: once from having prepared a serious speech only to find the audience dressed up to the nines for a dinner-dance; and once just the opposite, a light-hearted speech for a leaden audience. After that, I always asked what sort of audience it was likely to be.

Increasingly I was out in the evenings, often getting in after Mother had gone to bed. It meant, too, that I was seeing less of David than I would have liked, and having difficulty in fitting in games of squash. The next winter, I resolved to cut down on accepting invitations too far away from home.

The following January saw me back at Oxford once more. Nothing much seemed to have changed, and the old buildings which had enthralled me at my first visit still retained their charm. It was nice meeting up with former colleagues from the press, though both Brian and Norman had just retired. It now gave the impression of a highly professional event, and there were fewer farmers there. It was probably getting too expensive for some of them as harder times were beginning to bite. It was still a sounding board for what was happening in Brussels, and worth going to for that reason.

The most useful contact was Andrew Marden.

'I'm under some pressure to change the nature of the programme,' he said. 'They want less farming and more issues relating to the environment like global warming, carbon dioxide emissions and things like that. I'm perfectly happy about that, but I'm determined that farming should remain the main ingredient.'

'I hope you'll be able to manage it, but the environmental lobby is getting very powerful and vociferous, as you probably know.'

'I certainly do. I'm planning a big series of programmes which will include the scientific issues like climate change and so on, but also programmes about the effect such changes will have on farming practice. I'll be looking for two chairmen to act as anchormen. One will be a scientist and the other a farmer. I've already got one person in mind for that, but I'm not really sure he's right for it. I suppose you wouldn't be interested, would you? You've got experience of television, and you are actually farming which would be a great advantage.'

'I'd certainly like to be considered, provided it wouldn't entail too much time away from the farm. I'm virtually single-handed as far as management is concerned, so the farm must always have priority.'

'It would only mean coming up to Birmingham once a fort-night to record the programme, and possibly spending a few hours at home getting on top of whatever the topic was that you'd be dealing with. I'd be able to help you there, probably with some literature beforehand.'

'OK, then, you can count me in, though I'd not be too upset if you decided to give it to the other chap.'

'What I'd probably do is to give you two programmes each and then decide on one of you for the rest of the series. It'll not happen for probably six months. I'll give you a ring.'

'What about that holiday we talked about in the summer?' David said over supper in his flat one day before Easter.

'I hadn't forgotten it, but I don't know whether I'll be able to fit it in. I certainly can't be away for a couple of weeks to go abroad, now Daniel's gone. There's no one to leave in charge. I'm afraid it'll have to be a week only this year. I do realise how disappointed you'll be, but I can't see any alternative.'

'I do understand. A week away is better than nothing. I did so much enjoy it last year.'

'The best time for me would be early July, as we'll have got the first cut of grass silage in by then, and Ian and Victor have asked for holidays in June, so they'll both be back to hold the fort. Can you get a week away then?'

'I think so probably. The boss goes away in August and Chris takes the last fortnight in July. I ought to spend at least a week with Mum and Dad, as they like me to drive them away somewhere for their holiday, as his sight's getting bad. Have you any ideas?'

'Not really. It shouldn't be too far away, as we don't want to lose precious days travelling, do we?'

'What about a week in Cornwall again? I did enjoy it last year.'

'I was rather hoping you might suggest that. I do like it there, and I'm sure that there's a lot more to explore, in addition to the surfing. Do you think we might find a holiday cottage and look after ourselves, rather than staying in a hotel? I expect the agent who looks after our holiday lettings will know someone local there to contact.'

'I like the idea. You contact your agent to see if there's anything suitable available for the first week in July, and I'll confirm that I can get that week off.'

I rang our man the next day, who put me in touch with a local agent. The only thing he could offer was a converted barn on a farm some three miles inland from the coast, which he could recommend. I booked it and hoped it would be all right, though it was a bit further from the sea than I would have liked.

I had become increasingly concerned as to how we might get on at harvest without Daniel, and decided I'd ring the college to see if they might have a student looking for harvest work.

'Richard, I suppose you wouldn't have a student looking for a job over the harvest period, would you? Now Daniel's got a job, I reckon I'll need another pair of hands.'

'Not on the spur of the moment I'm afraid, but I'll put the word around and see if I can find anyone for you. I expect you'd want someone with a certain amount of experience, wouldn't you?'

'Yes, the important thing is that he should be able to drive a tractor without smashing into something, and that he's got a certain amount of common sense.'

Three nights later he rang to say that one of his first year students who wanted a harvest job might be suitable. He didn't know him well, but he seemed a nice, well-adjusted lad, not in the top bracket intellectually but quite sound. The boy had a car, so should he send him up to see me?

'Yes, send him along, please, but ask him to give me a ring first.'

He turned up a week later, a big strong looking lad, by name Martin Kennedy, with a mop of fair curly hair, blue eyes and a broad, happy-looking face. Mother took to him straight away, and I liked his open, easy manner. I thought we ought to get on well.

It transpired that he'd worked on a dairy farm for a year before going to college, but now wanted experience of arable farming. He was delighted to hear that he would have to help me with the sheep, as he'd not worked with them before. We arranged that he'd come for the last week in July, so as to get settled in before harvest. With that decided I could go away for the holiday with David without having to worry about it.

The barn when we found it had been well converted, with a nicely furnished lounge, two twin-bedded rooms (though we needed only the one) and the usual domestic offices. The only snag was that it had little view, but that shouldn't matter much as we planned to be out most of the time. The farmer's wife who welcomed us was a cheery-faced lady in her fifties, who told us to knock on her door if we wanted anything.

We did miss the sea and the sound of the waves we had enjoyed at the hotel, but it was quite fun being together in our own little temporary home.

Unfortunately the surf wasn't as good as it had been the year before. We had picked a week of very calm hot weather, with little wind, and some days the sea was as flat as the proverbial pancake. But we did get in three days when it wasn't too bad, and we decided that we'd equip ourselves with our own boards and wetsuits.

When there was no surf we explored the coastal bays, having a conventional swim at some of them or lying on the cliff tops listening to the lazy sea below. On two occasions we went up to the moors, climbing the two highest hills in Cornwall. A drink in a friendly pub in the little village usually rounded off the day after our evening meal.

We didn't meet the farmer until the day before we left. I had deliberately not told his wife that I was in farming when we arrived, as I wanted a busman's holiday. We spent the last evening with them talking farming. They were a very pleasant couple whose family of two had already left home. He milked about seventy cows himself on 120 acres of moderate land. I couldn't understand how he could make a decent living out of it until I realised that he had very few outgoings as he did nearly all the work himself. She had a job in the local town four days a week, and the holiday lets – as I appreciated – brought in a tidy income, now that they had paid off the loan for the conversion. I used some of the material for one of my articles dealing with the survival of the small farm.

So after a very happy week together, it was back home to find that Ian and Victor had got on perfectly well without me, as I thought they would.

Martin turned up two weeks before the first crops were fit to cut. I put him to work mainly with the sheep to help Stephen and myself. We were going through the flock, foot trimming and dipping, as we didn't want to waste valuable time over the harvest period dealing with ewe problems that were avoidable with a little forethought.

It was a new experience for me, as I'd never been in the position of instructing a novice before. Daniel had picked up everything from Dad at an early age, so I hadn't had a hand in training him. I was enjoying passing on all the experience I had gained, and responding to the questions that Martin kept asking me. From the start he was very keen to learn, and not afraid to ask simple questions about things I'd always taken for granted, without ever stopping to ask just why we did things in a certain way. It did me good having to justify them. Often when we were working he would be asking questions about the farm, or even farming politics and Brussels. Becoming a teacher was rewarding, I decided.

Fortunately I felt no physical attraction to him at all, and possibly my being gay helped to establish a personal relationship between us. That feminine element in many of those who are gay can lead to a more caring attitude to others than is to be found in those governed entirely by testosterone. Whether that was so, it was the case that quite soon he was calling me Mark, which put us almost into an elder/younger brother situation, which I enjoyed.

I had warned David he would be meeting a quite good-looking young man, but he mustn't get ideas into his head, as I had already found out that Martin had a girlfriend on the college course. Her parents lived in Exeter, so he was off there occasionally after work. I told him that once we were into harvest it would be sixteen hours a day and seven days a week if things were going well.

David came in to supper a couple of times, and they got on well. It was now he who was in the firing line on veterinary questions rather than me. Whether Martin suspected there was something between us, I couldn't guess. It probably wouldn't have mattered if he had as times had changed so much since my student days and many young people seemed to regard gay relationships as quite normal.

It turned out to be a wet and tricky harvest. As soon as the corn began to dry out, along would come another shower or a night's rain to wet it all again. Some of the grain had to be put through the dryer twice before it was dry enough to store. It was all the more annoying as the yields were good, and one could see the profit from that slipping away in increased drying costs. I was pleased to have Martin there to relieve me on the grain dryer.

When we had at last got most of the grain in I persuaded

Victor to let Martin have a couple of sessions driving the combine harvester, though Victor stayed in the cab to make certain there would be no accidents. We couldn't afford expensive repairs that would eat up all the profit. But after all, Martin was with us to learn, and it was only right that he got all the experience we could give him.

He stayed until the end of September, though we could have done without him for the last two weeks. His parents lived in a town, and he had nothing to do if he went home, so he was grateful for the extra time – and of course the cash to help with his college expenses. He was no intellectual, as Richard had said, but his enthusiasm, practical ability and cheerful outlook on life was worth a lot more than a bit of extra brain power.

'Would you like to come back in the Easter holidays to help with lambing?' I asked him as he was leaving.

'I was just screwing up the courage to ask you whether I could come, but I didn't want to run the risk of being turned down. You and your mother have been so good, and I've learnt so much that I'd love to come. You've really made me feel one of the family. Thanks so much.'

The house seemed quite empty when he had gone.

When I rang Richard to give him a report on Martin a few days later, he said, 'I was just going to ring you, as I've a proposition that might interest you. There's a farmer vacancy on the governing body of the college, and I'd like to put your name up for it. It would mean you'd have to serve on the farm subcommittee as well, but they always meet on the same day. How would feel about it?'

'It would depend on how often I had to come down for meetings. As you know, I'm quite tied up here and don't want to spend too much time away, or things might start to get out of hand.'

'That shouldn't worry you as the committee only meets three or four times a year.'

'In that case I'd very much like to be considered, but I'll quite understand if they want someone else.'

'I don't think they will, but I'll be in touch after the next meeting.'

About a month later he rang to say that I had been elected – which gave me great pleasure, as I was very fond of the college quite apart from memories of Simon.

During the years since I had dug the ponds and created the field margins, I had kept in close touch with the officer from the Farming and Wildlife Advisory Group. He had been out several times to see how we were getting on, and on two occasions had brought over other farmers who were thinking of doing the same. He'd also come out to do a butterfly survey in the summer, which he proposed to do every two years to see if he could register an improvement. The ponds had certainly created a lot more wildlife, and I had the impression that there was more birdsong in the spring.

In the autumn he rang to ask whether I'd like to have my name put forward for the county FWAG committee, as they had a vacancy. I welcomed the idea, as it would give a better chance to get round farms to see what other people were doing. So quite suddenly I was on two interesting committees dealing with subjects I was especially interested in. I resisted all attempts to get me on to any of the union committees as I wanted to be free to criticise them in articles if I didn't approve of their policies.

The main event that autumn was Daniel's marriage to Janet, of whom we had become very fond. She was a very bright, down-to-earth girl, with a loving nature, and we were delighted to have her as a member of the family. It was a big, full-dress affair as both families were well known in Norton and Caroline was very much in her element. It was a strain for Mother, who disliked finery and had to buy a new dress and hat for the occasion. She looked very smart in spite of saying that she felt highly uncomfortable, and couldn't wait to get back into sensible clothes again. But it was good for her to see all the grandchildren together – though I guessed that secretly she was thinking of Dad and how proud he would be if only he could have been there.

Seeing Daniel walk down the aisle, I was again struck by how like Dad he had become as he'd got older. His features were a bit thinner, which made him better-looking than Dad had been. In fact, he had turned into a very confident and handsome man.

I had to say a few words, which I found difficult as it was out of my line of speech-making. I took Mother home as soon as I decently could, so that she could cast off her glad rags with a sigh of relief. The young ones kept it up into the small hours with a disco, which was not our line of country at all. I felt glad that I'd not had to get involved in marriage.

I gave Oxford a miss again the next year. It had become very expensive, and the programme for once looked rather dull. I'd have liked to have seen Andrew to ask about his proposed television series, but supposed he'd ring me in due course if it was going ahead.

I needn't have worried for in February he rang up.

'Would you be available to chair a programme early in June, and another one in July?'

'Yes, that should be perfectly all right. I'm not planning to go away then. I think I warned you that I'd be away in the middle of September, if you did want me to do some more.'

'Fine. I'll be in touch in the middle of May. I'm not doing the programme in August, and wouldn't need you till the end of September, anyhow.'

Daniel and Janet were at home for three days over Easter, and we went over the recent accounts together. Profit margins were nowhere as good as they had been a few years before, and the prospect was that they would get even slimmer. Daniel said that James was quite concerned as well, and was looking at ways to increase income from the estate.

I was pinning my faith on getting higher yields from the cows as the crossbred Holstein heifers came into milk, though that wouldn't start until the autumn, and the full effect wouldn't be apparent for at least four years. I was also hoping to cash in on grants that were being talked about to encourage the sort of thing that we'd been doing to improve wildlife habitats. It seemed likely that these might be introduced in place of subsidies for growing crops. If that did happen we'd be very well placed to benefit from them, in the light of what we had already done.

Janet and Daniel seemed to have settled down very well. She'd got a teacher's job locally, and he and James got on well. He told me that they were not planning to start a family for the time being.

Martin came and stayed for a month to help with the lambing and spring work on the farm, and proved himself as useful as he had been in the summer.

'Would you like to come back again for the harvest?' I asked him before he left.

'I'd love to. I was hoping you'd offer me a job then. I'd have to find one somewhere, and I'd much rather work for you than anyone else.'

'That's settled then. I'll expect you about the end of July. While we're on the subject, I'd very much like to get away for a couple of weeks in the middle of September. How would you feel about being left to hold the fort here while I was away? It would be before you'd be going back to college, and I'd be ringing up quite frequently to check that everything was all right.'

'You mean take full charge? Do you think that I'd be up to it? I've had no experience of management before, and would hardly know where to start.'

'I think you could manage it. You get on very well with the other men, and both Ian and Victor, as you know, are very competent and can work without supervision. I'm sure they'd accept it as long as you didn't give them the impression that you're trying to boss them about – but I'm sure you're too sensible to do that. The main thing would be deciding on what fieldwork jobs should be done, and I'd leave a list for that before I went. You could discuss with Victor which would be the most urgent. If you were in doubt you could leave it till I phoned.'

'If you're quite sure, Mark, I'd love to take it on. It'd be a wonderful opportunity to get experience of actually managing something.'

It was a relief to know that he'd agreed to do it. It meant that I could go away knowing that there was someone to take care of things, and also that Mother would have someone in the house. I was always a bit worried about leaving her alone even for a night.

She was now nearly seventy and beginning to slow down. Years of stooping in the garden had begun to affect her lower back, and she was resting more. Stephen's wife now came in twice a week to do the housework, but she still insisted on doing the cooking, though she'd sometimes allow David to prepare supper if he had been with us for the day. He was virtually a second son to her by now. He had never been close to his own mother, it seemed, and he came to regard her as a substitute.

I drove her to church most Sunday mornings, and she remained convinced that she would be reunited with Dad when the time came. I still enjoyed a good church service though my faith was not as strong as it had been before it had been so shaken by Simon's death. It had also been severely tested by several experiences in my journalist days, when I saw the harsh and brutal side of life which was so difficult to reconcile with a vision of a loving God. But I still felt the need for a religious belief.

Finding happiness with David seemed in some way to restore my faith. He wasn't religious in any way and never went to church. But he had very high ethical standards by which he judged his own and other people's lives – which is almost the same thing as following Biblical principles.

Shortly before the first television programme, Andrew sent me details of what he wanted to include. It was going to be an easy run-in to the series as a whole with no controversial issues. He wanted me to take part in the discussions with the two speakers, rather than just act as a chairman.

The rehearsal took a fairly short time before the recording, as it was largely a factual presentation, but I nearly dried up at one point as I had done in my first TV show. Andrew had warned me that I must watch the studio clock like a hawk, and go out dead on time after trailing the programme for the following week. In the rehearsal I had trouble closing down the last discussion, looked at the clock and saw that there were only some eight seconds left for the trailer. In a panic, I couldn't recall the name of one of the speakers I had to trail, and for a few seconds was tongue-tied. By the time I got it we had overrun by six seconds.

'Don't worry,' Andrew said. 'That's why we do a rehearsal. You'll be perfectly all right when we record it' – and I was. It was a salutary lesson, and in future I kept a list of names I might need on my knee under the cover of the studio desk.

The second programme in July was far more difficult to handle, as I had to keep two aggressive and opinionated personalities, who obviously didn't like one another, in some sort of order. They constantly tried to interrupt each other, and I had to be very firm in stopping them from hogging the whole programme. There wasn't much opportunity for me, as chairman, to do anything else but prevent them from having a fight. It must have impressed Andrew, for he asked afterwards if I would chair the remaining six programmes in preference to his other presenter.

It seemed that I had earned my spurs, so to speak. Some programmes were more difficult than others, but I quite soon became acclimatised to a television studio. The fact that everything was pre-recorded made it far less stressful than my first live appearance had been.

It was good having Martin back in the house again, when he turned up shortly before harvest.

'How did the exams go?' I asked over supper the first evening. 'Did you do well enough to go back next year for the advanced course?'

'Yes, thank goodness. I made an awful mess of the economics paper, but I must have done well enough in the others to get me through. In fact I got much higher marks than I'd expected in the paper on crops. It must have been all you taught me last year that helped. I did well in the animal paper as well, thanks to you and all the info you gave me on sheep. I'm really grateful, Mark.'

'I'm so glad you'll be able to go back next year. It ought to make all the difference when you're looking for a job at the end of the course. I'm delighted to hear I may have helped you a bit. I can tell you I've enjoyed it, too.'

As harvest went on I gave him rather more responsible jobs than I had done the year before, and Victor was happy for him to share some of the combine harvester driving at meal times and on long fine days. I hadn't told any of the staff about my plans to leave him in charge while I went away for the holiday. I thought I'd leave that until a couple of weeks before, so that I could show them that he was capable of handling the more difficult jobs and was a full member of the team.

When the time came, I asked Victor and Ian to see me in the farm office.

'As you know, I've hardly been away since I came back here after Dad died, and I do want to get a proper holiday. I'm planning to go away in a couple of weeks' time for a fortnight abroad. You're both perfectly capable of running your own units, but obviously there must be somebody overall in charge in case of emergencies. I think very highly of Martin, and he'll be living here with Mother till the end of September. I've asked him whether he'd be willing to hold the fort. I shall leave him a list of all the work that's coming up, and I'll be ringing up every two or three nights to check on things. I realise that he's still young and not very experienced, but he's got a good head on his shoulders, and I feel that you all get on with him pretty well. He won't be bossing you about, or anything like that, but simply be there to keep an eye on things overall. Are you both happy about it?'

'I'm perfectly happy,' Victor said. 'He's a very keen lad and a great worker. There'll only be straw carting to finish, and the autumn ploughing, and maybe getting the fields ready for wheat, but I expect you'll be back before we want to drill them. You deserve a bit of a holiday, and you can count on us to keep things going.'

'I'm quite happy about it as well,' said Ian. 'I haven't had a lot of dealings with Martin, but he gets on very well with everybody and doesn't throw his weight about. I can see that there must be somebody in charge, and with you on the end of a phone I'm not worried in the least.'

'Thank you both very much. I hoped that you'd take it like that. I'll tell the others in the morning, and we'll have a final get-together before I go.'

The other three said that they'd be quite happy with the arrangement, so I felt that I could get away without running the risk of rancour building up while we were away.

There was a last-minute snag when David, who was doing the bookings, discovered that the last overnight car train to Milan from Calais left on the tenth. I'd have to take a risk on harvest being virtually over by then, or else lose two days of the holiday driving down to Italy instead of putting the car on the train. I decided that we'd take the risk and the train.

In the event, there were still two fields of beans left to cut, but I believed they shouldn't cause too many problems for Victor and Martin.

The train from Calais deposited us in Milan at six o'clock in the morning, but it was nearly two hours before David was allowed to drive his car off the car transporter. No one seemed to be in a hurry on a Sunday morning. We decided that we'd take the motorway north to Como and find a service station where we could get a decent breakfast. We were nearly back in Switzerland before we found one, but it was worth it.

'I think we'll make for Bellagio, and see if we can get a room in that nice-looking hotel where I had a cup of tea that day with Simon. If we can't get a room in Bellagio, we can cross over on the car ferry to Menaggio on the opposite side where there are lots of hotels, but we'll make for Como first.'

'Sounds all right to me. I'm in your hands now.'

We spent a couple of hours exploring the town, including taking an expensive cup of coffee while watching the world go by. It was a strange feeling sitting back with absolutely nothing to do, when time was unimportant.

'You can do the driving up to Bellagio,' said David. 'I want to be able to look at the scenery, and you've seen it all before on the lake trip you told me about.'

'OK, that's fair enough. We'll take the road up the east side, as it'll save having to take the ferry across to Bellagio, even though it looks a bit twisty.'

Twisty it proved to be, and it wasn't long before I was regretting that I'd agreed to drive David's car, which was a little bigger than mine. The narrow road, cut out of rock in places, wound round endless sharp bends, plunging up and down to little lakeside towns and villages with hardly room to pass cars parked by the roadside. All the time, impatient Italians in their little Fiats tailgated this bigger English car, until a few straight yards of road ahead encouraged them to take their lives in their hands to dash by.

It was made worse by shouts from David. 'Stop the car, Mark, I must get a photograph of that.' But I couldn't stop with excitable natives on my tail and no lay-bys in sight.

At last there was one, high above the lake, where we could pull in to eat our lunch out of the boot. Here he could take photos to his heart's content looking down on the blue translucent waters of the lake across to the mountains on the other side. Below us on a small promontory was a yellow house surrounded by tall cypress trees pointing to the sky, their outlines reflected in the water. Further out on the lake a group of small yachts with white sails gathered for an afternoon race. Towards the north, the deep blue of the water assumed that misty blue-grey tinge so characteristic of Como.

'Satisfied?' I asked him as we leaned, our arms touching on the parapet, watching lizards basking in the sun on the stone below.

'It's just like a picture in a glossy travel brochure. It's quite perfect.'

'Time to be moving on. We've got to find beds for the night, so the sooner we book in somewhere the better. We'll try Bellagio first.'

It was swarming with people when we got there, with locals out for Sunday strolls adding to the normal tourists, but we were lucky to find a parking place as someone pulled out almost opposite the hotel where I hoped to stay.

The foyer with its marble floor was cool and light as we went in. A small elderly lady in a black dress was counting notes at a small desk and a younger woman was sitting behind a computer. I decided to approach the older one first, and speaking very slowly said: 'I wonder if you might have a twin-bedded room facing the lake available for two or three nights?'

She looked up rather disapprovingly I thought. An idea flashed through my mind that she might not like two men sharing a room together, and would turn us down accordingly.

'Yes, I think we've still got one available, but it'll cost more with a view of the lake. Number thirty-four isn't booked is it, Maria?'

The other girl looked at her computer. 'No, it's still free.'

She mentioned what seemed quite a reasonable price for the

two nights. 'You speak very good English,' I said.

'So I should, as I was born in Oxford. I married my late husband after the war, and I run the hotel now with my son and his family. Have you got your passports, as we shall need them?'

'I'm afraid they're in the car, but we'll bring them in with our bags. Will the car be all right parked outside overnight?'

'It should be, but you must lock everything up and not leave anything on the seats, and bring in anything of value. Perhaps you could give the passports to Maria, and Giovanni will take you up to the room.'

As we handed the passports to Maria she said: 'Will you be wanting dinner?'

'Yes, please, what time does it start?'

'From seven thirty, and the dining room is on the first floor. By the way there's a sun lounge on the roof, if you'd like to lie out there before dinner.'

It was a large room with two windows facing the lake, cool and dark behind its curtains and closed shutters. I went to one of them, drew back the curtains and opened the window and one shutter – to be met by a cacophony coming up from the landing stage below, where a ferry had just discharged a boatload of tourists.

'I hope it won't be as noisy as this all the time,' David said. 'We'll need the windows open tonight.'

'I expect it'll quieten down later on by the time we want to go to bed. In the meantime, I feel like a cup of tea. We can get it in the arcade outside where Simon and I had it before.'

After tea, we changed into shorts and took our books up to the sun deck, where some ten residents in various states of undress were either cooking their well-oiled bodies in the sun, or sitting reading or dozing in easy chairs. We chose to relax in our shorts on sunbeds after the pressures of the day and a somewhat sleepless night in the train. I couldn't believe that it was only that morning that we had been decanted on the platform at Milan. It seemed as though days had passed. We lay there until the sun disappeared behind the mountain on the other side of the lake.

'Time for a bath before dinner. Do you want to go first or shall I?'

'I'll go first, if you don't mind my soapy water. You can go first tomorrow,' David said. As he stood drying himself by the bath, and I waited to get in, I marvelled once again at the perfection of his body, the broad shoulders tapering to the waist, his broad hips, neat bottom and strong thighs and legs, with no sign of fat or flab anywhere.

'God, you've got a perfect body, David. How amazingly lucky I was to find you.'

'You're not so bad yourself, you know.' At that he held me tight against him, and there we stayed, hugging as if we'd never been together before. At last, I pushed him away.

'Get some clothes on or you'll catch a chill, and let me get in before the water's cold.'

'Would you like dinner on the balcony or inside?' the head waiter enquired as we entered the dining room.

'Let's have it outside. It's still quite warm and we can look at the lake while we eat,' David said, and I agreed.

As we ate, the waters below gradually dimmed as the last of daylight died behind the mountains, and rows of lights appeared on the opposite side of the lake on the road to Menaggio. Ferries were still busily bustling their way hither and thither, little groups of fairy lights floating on the darkening waters. Overhead an almost full moon shone brightly down, its rays reflected on the surface of the lake. It would have been impossible to conjure up a more romantic setting.

Halfway through the meal, the owner's son came to our table to introduce himself and to enquire whether we were enjoying the meal – a touch that made us feel we were welcome.

As we lay in bed together, David said: 'Thank you so much, Mark. I'd never have come to a place like this if I hadn't met you. You've changed my life, you know.'

'Don't thank me. It's Simon you should be thanking, for it was he who brought me to life in the first place and opened my eyes to the world outside Devon. If it hadn't been for him, I'd never have emerged from my provincial shell. I'm rather surprised that your parents didn't take you out into the world a bit more.'

'It was partly because they were fairly old when I was born.

Mother was thirty-eight, and Father forty-six, so that by the time I was growing up they were getting very set in their ways. A trip to Eastbourne or Bournemouth was the limit of their ambition. I've never really got to know my father, as he's always been very reserved and doesn't talk much. Mother always seemed busy with a social life, and never showed any emotion when I was a boy, so I haven't known her well, either. She wasn't warm like your mother is. The result was that I never had the happy childhood that you had, or much real love, I'm afraid.'

'Well, I hope I can make up for that now.'

We were awakened about six thirty by loud clanking noises and engines being started up as the ferries moored outside sprang into life ready for another busy day on the lake. Then there was silence, and I was just drifting off to sleep again when I felt the sheets move. Then a warm body was against mine, something hard was pressing against my back, and a gentle hand was caressing my cock which had suddenly sprung to life.

'Do we have to go tomorrow, Mark, or could we have another night here, do you think?' he said, as we lay together, relaxed after we had come together.

'No, I don't see why we shouldn't stay, though it'll mean one less night somewhere else. But I can't think that there is anywhere to beat this, so let's ask Maria after breakfast if we can keep the room for another night.'

Going in to breakfast it was good to see the elderly lady, and two younger ones and four presumed grandchildren, all having breakfast together with the guests. It was obviously very much a family business. Maria pulled a long face when we asked if we could have the room for another night.

'I'm afraid it's booked for a couple who come every year, and ask for that room. I have got a smaller one on the same floor, but it doesn't look out on the lake. Would you like to move into that one for tomorrow night?'

'Yes, that'd be fine. We could easily shift our bags over in the morning after breakfast. Can you book it for us then?'

So we had an extra day, and decided that we'd take the car over the lake that day to Menaggio and see some of the sights, such as the gardens at the Villa Carlotta, and then spend the following day going round the lake.

We ate our picnic lunch on exactly the same seat under the oleanders where Simon and I had sat some twenty years before, and where we had said that one day we would come back. Perhaps it was as well that we couldn't see into the future then. Little could I have guessed that it would be so long before I did come back, and that when I did, it would be with another man with whom I was equally in love. It was pure sentiment, of course, but I felt that Simon was there with us, and I wanted him to know that I was happy now, but that he was not forgotten.

'I'm sorry, David, it must seem that you're having to compete with a ghost. But he meant so much to me at the time that I can never forget. It doesn't mean that I don't love you just as much. Of course I do, perhaps more so in a mature way. I just want him to know that a small part of him is still with me.'

'I don't mind sharing him with you in the least. I guessed when I first saw that photo of him in your bedroom that he'd always remain part of your life. Actually I feel I owe him a great debt of gratitude for teaching you what love can mean to people like us. Without him, you might not have become the wonderfully kind and sensitive person that you are. You could so easily have become a repressed, inward-looking, gay middle-aged man looking simply for casual sex. I would probably have become like that, too, if fate hadn't brought us together. I don't resent him being with us in the slightest. In fact I respect you all the more for keeping his memory so much alive.'

'Thanks, love. You can be sure that when I'm in your arms, it's you I'm thinking of, and not his ghost.' I looked round to see the coast was clear, and rested my hand on his thigh.

I was driving back from the campsite where we had stayed, when he spotted a house with a yard full of terracotta pots of all shapes and sizes.

'Stop here, Mark, I'd like to go in and look at some of those pots. If they're not too expensive I'd like to buy one to take back for your mother's garden as she's been so good to me. Do you think she'd like one for the front lawn?'

'I'm sure she'd love one. We'll have to find one that'll fit into the boot, though.'

We chose a big oval-shaped one which we could just squeeze into the boot, and in the adjoining shop we couldn't resist buying Italian china pot-holders for her indoor plants as well.

We were back in Bellagio in time for a cup of tea and a session in the sun on the roof terrace until it was time for me to run a bath.

After we had finished our soup at our table on the balcony, two men came in and were shown to the next table, which was so close that I had to move my chair a little to allow one of them to get in.

'Thanks so much,' he said in English.

They were an elderly couple; one of them short with grey hair and slightly bald who I guessed might be in his early seventies. The other was taller and heavily built and probably about ten years younger. As the meal progressed, I heard the older one of them mention Oxford, and caught him looking at me quite intently several times. Finally, he leaned over.

'You must be Mark Harper, aren't you? I'm sure I've seen you recently on the box a couple of times chairing the environmental programme, haven't I?'

'Well, yes, I'm afraid so. Am I as notorious as all that? I'll be getting a swelled head if I'm not careful.'

'I'm afraid it's an occupational hazard. I did some programmes once in the days of black-and-white and found that people were coming up and saying 'Where have we met before?' when I didn't know them from Adam. Is this the first time you've been here?'

'I did come to Bellagio once twenty years ago, and always wanted to come back again, but it's taken me all that time to manage it. What about you? By the way the head waiter greeted you, I imagine you've been here before.'

'I suppose we must have stayed here at least fifteen times, haven't we, John? The first time was about twenty-five years ago.'

'Yes, it would have been at least that. I must look it up in my diaries when we get back,' his companion replied.

'Have you been holidaying together for as long as that?' David interjected.

'Oh much longer. Forty-three years now. We used to go scurrying all round Switzerland, Germany and Italy until we found the places we really liked. For the last ten years or so we have concentrated on those. This is one of our favourites.'

It was noticeable that each time he said 'we', so there was no doubt in my mind that they must be a gay couple, though no one would have guessed it from looking at them.

'Did I hear you mention Oxford earlier on? I go there for a conference most years, and love the place. I always wish that I had been a student there.'

'Neither of us actually live in Oxford, but about ten miles away, but I worked in the university there for over thirty years. It was certainly a lovely place to work and easy to get to London if you got involved with outside work. How long are you planning to stay here?'

'We were going tomorrow, but we like it so much that we decided to stay another day, though we've got to move to a smaller room for tomorrow night. We thought we'd take a trip down the lake to Como tomorrow, and perhaps drop off here and there on the way.'

'We might see you then, as we had thought of doing the same. Where are you planning to go after you leave here?'

'Venice for a couple of days, and then up to the Dolomites, and from there the long drive home taking about three days.'

'You'll find the Dolomites quite fantastic. We've been there four times, and stay at Cortina, which is a good centre. It's a bit of an opulent place, but we stay at a family hotel about a mile out on the road north. Can you remember its name, John?'

'Afraid not, but it's got a large apricot tree growing up over its front wall. I wouldn't advise you to eat them if you did stay there. We tried one once and it tasted very bitter.'

By now, the meal was finished, but we stayed on talking for another ten minutes or so. As we got up, the older one said 'My name's Arnold, by the way, and as you've probably gathered, this is John.'

'As you know, I'm Mark, and my partner's David.' It was the first time that I'd ever referred to him as my partner, but as it was quite obvious that they were a gay couple there was no point in trying to conceal the fact that we were gay, too. It might make it easier if we did meet up with them the following day. I hoped we would as they were both so easy to get on with, and it was good to be able to talk with English people. They might be able to give us some tips about places to visit.

'Would you like to link up with them tomorrow?' I asked David as we went to bed.

'Yes, it'd be nice to spend the day with them. After all we're not likely to meet up with two gay Englishmen anywhere else, are we, and they're too old for you to try to get up to anything.' We laughed at the idea.

Lying in bed, he suddenly said: 'Do you think we shall be together and in love still forty years on, like those two are? I find seeing them together very encouraging.'

'I very much hope so. I know that if we're both spared I'll love you then as much as I do now, and I suspect you might feel the same.'

'Of course I do, but it's sad that we're starting so late. If only we'd met sooner, we'd have had those extra years. As it is we'll be in our eighties by then, which is a bit depressing. I wonder how old those two are. We must try to find out tomorrow if we meet up.'

They'd almost finished their breakfast by the time we got in for ours. We had noticed the previous day that most people said good morning to other guests as they came in, so we did the same. They stopped at our table as they went out.

'John's going up to see if the papers are in. Would you like him to get one for you?' asked Arnold.

'Yes, please. The *Times* if they have one, but if not the *Telegraph* would do. Would you like one as well, David?'

'No, don't bother, I'll share yours Mark. We're in room thirty-four, John, if you manage to find one.'

'We've decided to take a trip down to Como on the lake,' Arnold said. 'If you were thinking of going, the boat leaves at eleven o'clock, so we might see you there then.'

Not long after there was a knock on the door, and John came in with the paper, and a bag of ham and rolls which he'd thoughtfully bought for us, while he was buying theirs.

'Don't worry if you don't want them. They'll come in handy for our lunch tomorrow. I just thought you might be getting low on fresh food. We always take our own, rather than wasting time in restaurants. Anyhow, it's nicer to eat in the fresh air.'

Up until now, John hadn't said very much, but on his own he opened up. We both got the impression that he took the back seat when in the company of his more extrovert partner. If I had been of a jealous disposition, I might have been concerned at the way he seemed to be eyeing up David, but I knew I was quite safe there, as he certainly wasn't David's type.

We thoroughly enjoyed the day with them, lazing in the sun on the upper deck of the ferry, with David continually jumping up and down to take photographs of the changing scenery of the lakeside. It was even more beautiful than I remembered it from that trip so long ago with Simon. Once more, I had a feeling he was with us, happy that I'd found someone to take his place.

We got off the boat at one of the small towns, and ate our lunch under the trees beside the lake, surrounded by brilliantly coloured flower beds. We were back at the hotel in time for tea, and then the four of us retired to the roof to sunbathe until it was time for baths.

We had been quite wrong about their ages as Arnold was already past eighty and John in his early seventies, though you'd never have guessed it from their conversation and the way they behaved. Arnold, as an Oxford don teaching biology, had lived a very active life, being involved in committee work in London. It appeared that he'd led a promiscuous life before he met John when he was nearly forty. He seemed highly knowledgeable about the gay world and affairs in general – as I supposed might be the case for an Oxford don.

They had never actually shared a house, but had spent almost every weekend for forty years together at Arnold's house.

'I think the recipe for a successful relationship is to give each other plenty of space,' Arnold said, 'and even give your partner a little freedom to play away occasionally, if you feel a sexual need for something different. If you're really deeply in love emotionally, it doesn't matter at all. In fact, it can often make the union stronger, as it helps to prevent a relationship from getting stale. That probably sounds odd, but I'm sure it's true. So many unions break down from being stifled through close continuous contact.'

'I think that may be right,' John said, 'but you do need to be honest with one another, and never allow a casual fling to become something deeper, which is where so many heterosexual relationships come unstuck.' That sounded fine, but I felt that perhaps we hadn't really heard quite all of John's side of the story.

I thought Arnold might be right in a way, though I couldn't contemplate ever having even casual sex with anyone else as long as I had David. But perhaps as we got older, David or I might want something different. We'd have to wait and see, but I decided then that I'd give him the option of playing away if he ever felt the need. I knew that our love was strong enough to hold us together emotionally for the rest of our lives – but that was love, not just the physical side of sex, which was something quite different.

We shared a table at dinner that night, and David questioned them on the places they had visited over the years, and asked if they could recommend some for us.

'I can't give you any advice about France, I'm afraid,' Arnold said. 'Neither John or I like the French very much, and apart from a trip to the Riviera, which we found hot and crowded, we've never had a holiday there. We always concentrated on Switzerland, Germany and Italy, and Austria occasionally. We always finish up in Holland, as John has friends there whom he made when he was in the army and liberated them at the end of the war.'

'So where would you suggest?'

'Well, in Italy you must go to Florence, but try to avoid it in a heatwave, as it can get quite sweltering. Then you must go to Rome, of course, and you'll need several days there. But the Amalfi coast, south of Naples, would come first on my list. Would you agree with that, John?'

'Yes, I'll never forget the week we spent in that hotel built into the cliff between Positano and Amalfi, literally hanging over the sea, with its views down the coast and across to Capri. We did all the usual trips from there – Vesuvius, Pompeii, Herculaneum, Capri and south down the coast to Paestum. Or you could stay in Sorrento, though that's rather crowded and touristy now. Then we drove down the Ligurian coast from Genoa to Rome a couple of times. That's a wonderfully scenic drive. There's a terrific lot to see in Italy.'

'What about Venice?' I asked.

'We've been there twice, once staying there for a couple of days, and once for a day on an Adriatic cruise. To be honest I think Venice is almost better seen in Canaletto's marvellous paintings, though the buildings are magnificent, of course. Perhaps we were unlucky, but when we were there it was awfully hot with a sticky heat, and the crowds of tourists everywhere were overpowering. I don't think we'll go back again, shall we, John?'

'No. I'd far rather be in Switzerland or up in the Dolomites.'

'Where do you go in Switzerland?'

'We always spend three days in Interlaken, as it's such a good base for visiting all sorts of other places. The only snag is that it's full of tourists as well. But we always stay at a nice family-run hotel near the east station on the river between the two lakes. If you get a room facing away from the station, it's very quiet and it's patronised by older people.'

'I wonder if that's the one we could see from our campsite when we stayed there?' I said. 'It's close to the bridge coming down into the town, isn't it?'

'Yes, that's the one. We've stayed there umpteen times by now. The other place we really like in Switzerland is Lucerne. It's a lovely city, with historic old buildings, a beautiful lake and another good base for day trips. There's a very nice hotel, standing back on the hillside from the main road south out of the town, with probably the most extensive views you'll find any-where, across the lake to the mountains beyond. It's kept by a very friendly couple, Charles and Albertina, and if you mentioned our names, I'm sure they'd give you a good room.'

'We spent two days in Lucerne on our camping holiday. We thought it was a lovely city and I've always wanted to go back there to see it again. Perhaps we'll make it next year, David. I'm sure you'd love it. Thanks so much, Arnold. It's been very helpful. You've given us enough for at least ten years, I should think.'

'I only hope you'll enjoy it as much as we have. We've had some wonderful holidays together, haven't we, John? I only hope we've still a few more to come.'

By now we had finished dinner, and we sat talking afterwards. The conversation got round to what it was like being gay in the years when gays were classed as criminals and ran the risk of being arrested and put up in court – days which we had hardly known.

Arnold admitted that he'd taken ridiculous risks in view of his position, as there were no pubs or clubs that he knew of where he might have met a partner. Even if he had, he doubted if he'd have used them for fear of being recognised by his students, or people that he knew. He didn't want to run the risk of being joked about by students, as one or two notorious gay dons in Oxford were at that time.

'I was nearly beaten up twice, and was mugged on a couple of occasions, while blackmail was a constant risk for someone in public life. I had an uncle who was blackmailed for life in the early part of the century, as he couldn't risk going to the police. As a result he finally committed suicide after becoming a drug addict. I personally knew two people who took their own lives rather than appearing in court. It was not an easy time.'

'I'd no idea it was quite as bad as that,' David said. 'Thank goodness for the climate we've got now. But both Mark and I have to be very careful, as we suspect that some of my clients and his friends might still be homophobic. It's probably just as well that we don't live together.'

We said goodbye to them at breakfast next day after exchanging telephone numbers. John had told us where to go for food and papers, if we came back again, as we said we intended to do.

'I did like those two,' David said as we drove off. 'I had quite a talk with John last night after you and Arnold had gone down for your baths, and he really opened up. He said he was pretty innocent when he first met Arnold in spite of having been all through the war. It was almost a case of love at first sight, and had remained so in spite of having to accept that Arnold couldn't resist occasional flings with other men. At first he had been terrified that Arnold would leave him for a younger man, and that fear has never really left him. Over the years he has learnt to live with it, and to accept that Arnold had played around so much before they met that he couldn't get it out of his system. It didn't seem to make any difference to their love for one another, and after a time he found that he enjoyed a very occasional fling himself, though he always had a feeling of guilt afterwards.

'The other thing he said was that over the whole of their forty-three years together they'd never had a serious argument about anything. Neither of them would ever run the risk of hurting the other's feelings. I found that very touching. Do you think it will apply to us if we live that long?'

'I don't see why not. We're both pretty easy-going types, and there's no reason why we should have a row. If we ever did look like having one, we'd need to think of those two first.'

We had thought of spending a night in Verona, but decided to push on and catch up with our schedule after the extra night at Bellagio. Maria had given us the name of a quiet three-star hotel on one of the smaller canals leading off from the Grand Canal, and had rung through to book a room for two nights, which saved us the trouble of hunting for accommodation. We found it easily, a former palazzo converted into the hotel, which still retained some of its former character and sense of history. By the time we'd settled in it was bath and dinner time.

It was hot when we emerged from the cool of the hotel next day – a humid, sticky heat that had us sweating before we had got very far on our sightseeing tour, for which David had bought a map in the hotel. The trouble was that several thousands of people from all parts of the world seemed to be doing the same as we were. By the time we got to St Mark's Square, it was packed with tourist parties with guides speaking a dozen different languages. It was as if the Campanile was a descendent of the Tower of Babel.

But the buildings and the architecture were certainly magnificent, and it was good to have seen them once. By lunchtime we both felt exhausted by the heat and the crowds and, over a snack lunch in a small café, decided we'd take a boat over to the Lido in the afternoon in the hope that it might be a bit cooler there. Thankfully it was, and we spent a relaxed afternoon on the beach, which wasn't exactly seeing Venice.

The storm came soon after we'd got back to the hotel,

with spectacular thunder and lightning and torrents of rain. It was lucky that we had got back in time.

Though the storm had cleared the air and it was cooler next day, we thought we'd get up into the mountains, rather than have another day among the crowds. Perhaps Arnold and John were right about Venice.

I'd seen photographs of the Dolomites on the holiday with Simon, but nothing could have prepared us for the first sight of them as we rounded a corner on the road from Venice to Cortina. A series of high, white jagged peaks towering up into a bright blue sky over a foreground of deep-green trees confronted us, previously hidden by an intervening mountainside. David was driving, and I shouted to him to stop so that we could get it on film to fix that moment for all time. Though they were probably still twenty or so miles away their dramatic whiteness made them seem much nearer.

They kept on reappearing as we drove in and out of woods or round hillsides, getting even more spectacular the closer that we got to them.

'I think I'm going to enjoy the next few days,' David said as we approached the town.

The hotel that John had told us about was found without difficulty, and we were given a room with a majestic view across a valley to the mountains behind. The apricot tree was still there, but without much fruit on it that year, so that we weren't tempted to reach out for it.

As the 'boys' – which is what we had begun to call them – had said, the town had an opulent feel about it as we took an evening stroll. It was obviously geared towards winter sports as befitted a place that had once hosted the Winter Olympics.

Four happy days were spent exploring the area, with drives up into the mountains, and walks along forest trails. One afternoon it was a cable car up to a high peak where the snow had only recently melted, leaving a surface like that of the moon.

'I believe the Americans must have faked the whole thing,' David said. 'You can just picture Neil Armstrong stepping out of the module on to this surface. Nobody could tell the difference.'

When the hotel owner heard that I was a farmer he said his

brother owned a small farm further up the valley, and asked if I would like to see it. So on the third morning he drove some five miles, coming with us to act as interpreter as the brother spoke little English. It was about fifty acres in size on which he milked twenty Brown Swiss cows, and grew ten acres of barley to provide winter feed. I couldn't understand how he could possibly be making a living out of it until it transpired that he was getting about twice the price for his milk than we were, and that he spent three days a week as a forester in the adjoining woods. The milk was subsidised so as to encourage farmers to stay on the land, while his wife had a part-time job in Cortina.

It made me realise how ridiculous it was for the European Community to try to devise a policy that would fit both me with 200 cows, and him with only twenty under completely different conditions. It gave me an idea for my next fortnightly article, so the visit was worthwhile.

It took us four days to get home, and I couldn't resist the temptation to digress through the Black Forest to show David Baden-Baden. It had changed little in the twenty years since I had last seen it, except that everywhere seemed more crowded. Smartly dressed ladies still sipped their tea outside the Casino, and the band still played Strauss and Léhar in the nearby band-stand, and the grass and flower beds were as well manicured as ever.

'What a marvellous place,' David said. 'It's like a time capsule, except for the noise of the traffic in the town. I'd like to come back here again one day to explore the town properly.'

'Why not? I'd like to come back as well.' Another place to revisit in the future.

Then it was back home after a wonderful holiday during which we had grown even closer together, if that were possible. It was quite clear now that we'd be together for life.

Mother was delighted with David's present of the terracotta pot, and we mounted it on a raised paving stone in the centre of the front lawn, which gave an added dimension to the garden and the house behind.

During the holiday, I had rung up Martin three times to check that everything was all right on the farm, and was reassured each time that all was well. The last two fields had been harvested, and they were well ahead with getting land ready for the autumn sowing – otherwise there was nothing to report. I felt now that I could safely go away on holiday as long as Martin was there to keep an eye on things. That ought to be for another two years now that he was staying on at college for the extra year. He seemed quite committed to working for me now, and had become almost part of the family.

Life was busy as I took up the reins again, with the next TV programme on getting energy from crops due in two weeks, and my committees all starting to meet again after the harvest recess and summer holidays. Life was as good as it had ever been.

Chapter Nine

Four years passed by in something of a flash. By now Daniel and Janet had a daughter, Maud, and a second child was expected shortly. He was still very happy in his job with James, and I was rather worried that he might not want to come back to the farm if I wanted to hand over to him. I now had a number of outside commitments, and had almost decided that I'd go before I got to fifty in two years' time, to free myself from some of the more tedious practical jobs, such as the shepherding, on the farm. Though I still enjoyed working on the farm, my mind was frequently on other things.

I had just been elected chairman of the county Farming and Wildlife Advisory Group, and also of the farming sub-committee of the college governors. Though the earlier series of TV programmes was finished, I was occasionally asked to do a radio broadcast and still had the fortnightly article for the *Western Times*. In addition I was getting an increasing number of invitations to speak, mainly on conservation issues at farmers' meetings. So life was busy.

Two years previously Victor had retired, after almost a life-time's service to the farm as head tractor driver. Martin was just finishing his college course at the time, and he agreed to come and work full time as tractor driver and my assistant, until such time as he found a better job as an assistant farm manager. Nothing better had turned up for him, and he had married his long-term girlfriend and moved into Victor's house, which was one of the smaller farmhouses taken over in a previous expansion. They, too, were expecting a baby shortly so I was hopeful that he'd not want to move on for the time being.

Meanwhile, the friendship with David remained rock-solid. He was now busier than before, after having been made a senior partner in the practice, which involved more time in administration. It meant that we saw less of each other during the week, but we spent most weekends together on the farm, and got in games of squash about every two weeks, after which we'd get together in his flat. His own mother had died three years before, and his father was now in a home, so he had few family commitments to take him away. He'd come to regard the farm as his second home, as he and Mother got on so well.

With Martin available to hold the fort, we had been able to get abroad for holidays each September on the Continent. One year we had taken the advice of 'the boys' and driven down the coast to Rome, and another year even further, to the Naples area, where we had found their cliff-side hotel near Positano, each time having a wonderfully happy holiday together.

We had been back to Bellagio once, and overlapped with Arnold and John by one day, which we'd spent with them on the lake. They had changed little, with Arnold still his extrovert self and full of wisdom and enthusiasm, in spite of being now well over eighty. I promised to look them up if I was over in Oxford for the annual conference, which I was intending to attend the following year.

In the event, I did not get to it. I had noticed for some months that Mother seemed to be slowing down, but put it down to the fact that she was now seventy-five, and that the years of stooping in the garden and running the house were beginning to take their toll. In the autumn, she seemed to be losing what little weight she had and was complaining of a pain in her back, which she put down to arthritis. I tried to get her to see the doctor, but she wouldn't go, saying: 'Doctors can't do anything about arthritis, it's just old age'.

Finally I brought David into it, as I thought she might listen to him.

'Look, Mother, if you don't get an appointment with the doctor, I'll ring him myself and make one for you, and get Mark to drive you in.' The strategy worked, and I took her in, as she was finding that driving made her back worse.

I could see from the doctor's face that he was worried.

'I don't think it's arthritis, but we'd better have a scan to check.'

It took another two weeks to get the scan result, and when it came it confirmed my worst fears. Cancer, which had probably started in her ovaries, had spread out extensively and had now reached her liver. There was little that they could do, as it was too far advanced to operate or even to try chemotherapy. All they could do would be to try to alleviate the pain as much as possible, and they could only give her about six weeks to live.

We decided that she should be told, as she had great strength of character and her faith would see her through.

'Don't worry, dear, I suspected that it was that all along, and I'm quite prepared for it. We all have to go sooner or later, and I've had a lovely life and I'll be with John again.' I almost cried when she said that. It was so typical of her reliance on her faith to carry her through.

I arranged extra help for her, and Stephen's wife, who had been a nurse, came in twice a day. One day a week I drove her to the hospice in Norton which had been opened some years before, and I arranged for her to be admitted when it was near the end. I had alerted Cynthia about the situation, and she'd drive over twice a week to sit with Mother, though she was now nearly seventy-six herself.

Six weeks from the day that it was first diagnosed, we moved Mother to the hospice, and she died there peacefully four days later. The day before she was quite lucid in spite of the drugs they were giving her to relieve the pain.

'I'm quite ready to go, dear. I know John's waiting for me on the other side, and he's had to wait for so long. Thank you for being such a wonderful son, and for looking after me all these years. I'm just so thankful that you've got David now, and that he's giving you so much happiness. Stay with him, dear, he's so kind, and he's been like another son to me. He'll look after you now I'll not be there.'

'Of course we'll stay together now for life. Thank you, Mother dear, for everything you've done for me. You've been a wonderful mother and thank you especially for accepting David, which made our life together so much easier. I'm just sorry I couldn't give you any grandchildren, but that wasn't to be, I'm afraid. But that doesn't matter now with Daniel there to take on from me. Now, get some rest, as Caroline will be in to see you later.'

That was the last time we spoke, but we were all with her next day when she gave a great sigh of relief, and at that moment I seemed to see her spirit slip away to be reunited with her beloved John. Though there were tears in my eyes, I was left with a feeling almost of relief that her battle was over and that she was now at rest.

It was when I got back to the empty house that the feeling of loss really hit me, and I felt all alone in the world, like a small boy again. Since my earliest recollections she had always been there for me, and the loneliness I felt was almost overpowering. Now she was gone. There was a feeling of sadness that she'd never again see the garden that she had loved and cared for over so many years. I consoled myself with the thought that she might still be able to enjoy it from the spirit world of which I felt sure she would now be a part.

It was a comfort to have Juliet there for a few days, but it was when she had gone and I was alone in the empty house that I took the decision to move out and find a smaller place of my own, as I had done once before. I'd ask Daniel to come back and take over, and go into semi-retirement, spending more time in writing and public work, free of the day-to-day chores of running the farm. The house was far too big for me to live in alone. It needed a young family such as we had been some forty years before. Daniel came back for the funeral, and it was time then for decision-making.

'I want to hand over to you now, Daniel, if you feel ready to come back. I can't go on living in the farmhouse on my own, and anyhow, I'd like more time for my other work. What do you think? Are you ready to take over now?'

'I hadn't expected to come back quite so soon. I didn't think you'd want to hand it over just yet, as you're still so young. But, yes, I'd welcome it, on the condition that you'll still be on hand as a partner in the business, as I'll need your advice and experience.'

'That's what I hoped you'd say. What I'd like to do would be to find somewhere to live not far away, so that I'd be available to keep an eye on things if you wanted to be away, and to act as a kind of senior partner, with you in full charge of the day-to-day management. I'd like to have more time for my outside work, and perhaps do some writing, but be there to give you a hand if you needed it.'

'That sounds an excellent arrangement as far as I'm concerned. To be honest, I don't quite see myself as a small practical farmer spending all my time working on the farm. I'd probably get frustrated if I did, and anyhow it'd be rather a waste of all the training that I've had. So it might mean I'd want to be away a bit, and would need someone to hold the fort.'

'Right. That's settled. I thought that the end of September might be a good time to hand over as I'll need time to find somewhere to live. Would that suit you?'

'That'd be ideal for me, too, as I ought to stay with James till after harvest, and I'm supposed to give three months' notice, which would take us up to August. Let's say the end of September, then.'

So that was that. My future was now decided and I felt relieved, and excited at the thought that I should have time to enjoy a more leisurely existence and possibly see more of David than had been possible of late.

He'd come up to see me the night that Mother died, and put his arms around me in a big hug.

'I'm so sorry, Mark, we're going to miss her terribly. She had become a wonderful mother to me. Perhaps I shouldn't say it but I feel her loss more than I did when my own mother died. You must be feeling it dreadfully after a lifetime together. You know that I'll always be there for you if you need me.'

'I know that, and it's a great comfort. Goodness knows how I'd have coped if I was still on my own. It would have been unbearably lonely. I've decided to hand over to Daniel as soon as it can be arranged. I couldn't bear the thought of living in the farmhouse alone as it would be so much associated with memories of her and the past. It's time to make a change.

'I shall look for a place of my own again quite close to the farm, if possible, as I'll still be involved with the farm as a senior partner in the company. Sometime in the future, perhaps, we might consider living together, if you'd like that, but now is probably not the time to be thinking about it.'

'I'd like to, but not just yet. It'd be a big step giving up one's independence, and anyhow it might not be very wise politically. In both our jobs we're involved with people with very conservative views and, though they mightn't be actively homophobic, they might start putting two and two together if they found out we were living together. It seems perfectly all right for people like actors or MPs to come out these days, but I'm not quite sure how some of my clients, or people who sit on your committees, might take it. They obviously know that we're close friends, and it's probably better to leave it like that – till I retire, anyhow.'

'I'm sure you're right, and it works all right as we are. One day when we're old and grey like Arnold and John it would be nice to be together all the time.'

Juliet came to stay for a few days and with Caroline took a lot of the responsibility for the funeral arrangements off my hands. I was surprised how many there were at the funeral, as she had never led a public life. But she had a large number of friends from the religious side of her life, and also the older generation of farmers who'd known my father well. I was suddenly assailed by grief when the coffin was brought in, and had to wipe my eyes. The thought that I'd never see her again and the memory of all the love she'd given me was just too much. I suppose that close relationship that many gay men have with their mothers applied to me, though I'd never been consciously aware of it in her lifetime.

Cynthia gave me a tight hug and a kiss. She and Mother had become close friends over the years, which had kept us in touch since I'd come back to the farm. Jack was beginning to show his age, and had become rather stooped, but she still looked remarkably young for her age. It made me happy that she'd taken to David immediately and had told me to hang on to him at all costs – something that I knew in any case.

Mother and I had never discussed her financial affairs, as she had Dad's accountant who had always handled them. I assumed that she would be quite well off as Dad had left her the residue of his estate, which had come to about £200,000. We'd shared the household expenses since my return to the farm, and we'd never entertained, and she spent little on clothes. Nonetheless I was still rather staggered when the estate, which included the value of the shares in the farming company, came out at just under a million pounds. Her shares in the company went to Daniel as had originally been agreed when he said he'd come back to the farm. She left me £200,000 with the wish that I should use it to buy a house for myself. The residue was left to Juliet and Caroline, with each of the grandchildren getting a small legacy.

There remained the problem of finding somewhere to live. I wanted to be near the farm and considered one of the holiday let houses, but decided against that as I felt that Daniel would feel that I might be treading on his toes. The specification was that it should be within a four-mile radius of the farm, have three bedrooms, one of which could be used as a study, a decent-sized lounge, a kitchen large enough to eat in and a fair-sized garden.

I looked at about half a dozen houses, none of which, for one reason or another, was suitable. Time was going on, and by the end of June, I was getting worried as to whether I'd find anything ready to move into by the end of September. I rang the agent again.

'I suppose you wouldn't consider a bungalow?' he said. 'I'm just putting one on the books, and I thought it might suit you. But I've got two other people wanting bungalows, so if you did consider it you'd have to move fast.' I said I'd ring him back.

I had never really thought of a bungalow, having lived in houses all my life. But the more I thought about it, the more attractive the idea became. It might be easier for a single man to manage, and there would be no stairs to climb if I was still there when I got older.

'I'd like to look at that bungalow, as I think I might consider it. Could I see it this afternoon?'

We arranged to meet at three o'clock when the owner, who had recently lost her husband, would be there to show us round.

It was just on the outskirts of a little village, Steeple Ashton, about two and a half miles from the farm and six miles from Norton. About thirty years old, it was in excellent condition with a well-maintained garden. Set well back from a minor road out of the village on the top of a rise, it had a lawn in front and a small stone wall along the road. It had a large double bedroom and two smaller ones, a decent-sized kitchen, and a rather small lounge and dining room combined. Behind was the vegetable garden which backed on to the grass fields of a dairy farm. By far its greatest asset was the panoramic view from the front to the south-west across valleys and tree-topped hills into the distance with not a house in sight. Never having lived in a house with a real view before, I was almost entranced by it.

But there was one big snag: the living room was too small and it only had one quite small window facing that view, which made it feel rather dark and poky. I told the agent that I'd have to turn it down because of that.

'What I'd do if it were mine would be to throw out an extension to the front. That'd give you a larger room, and you could have a large glass picture window instead of a wall to make the best of the view. There'd be plenty of room for a patio there as well for the summer without losing too much of the lawn.'

He was quite right, of course. I could see myself behind that window writing, or having meals there watching the sun go down beyond the hills. I did a quick calculation. With Mother's money and some of my own, I could quite easily afford to buy the house and pay for the extension.

'I think I'd like to make an offer, but I'd like to get a second opinion. How long can you give me?' I thought I must get David's views on it before clinching the deal.

'I'd like to have a definite offer by noon tomorrow, as I ought to be letting the other people know if it was on the market, as soon as possible.'

'I'll definitely give you an answer by then.'

I managed to get David on his mobile and arranged with the owner to see it again at seven o'clock that night.

We were there as the sun was getting low in the sky, casting a golden glow over the hills and throwing the valleys below it into shadows.

'I love it,' David said. 'I can just picture the two of us eating a meal there behind the window watching the sun go down. All very romantic. But seriously, I think you should go for it, as it's got great potential, and I don't think you're likely to find anything better, especially as time is beginning to run out. It's quite close to the farm, but not so close for Daniel to feel that you're sitting on top of him.'

That clinched it, and first thing next morning I rang the agent, offering the full asking price, which the widow accepted with alacrity. When I took Caroline and Geoffrey to see it, he said I'd paid too much for it. But I expected that. After all, he was a property developer and beating people down on price was part of his philosophy. He wouldn't have been the successful operator he was if he were not like that.

I was going to have to move fast if the building was to be finished by the time I wanted to move in at the end of September. Plans would have to be got out, a builder found to do the job and, most important of all, planning permission secured.

Fortunately the architect who had done the plans for the last dairy building was back from holiday, and agreed to give it priority to have plans ready at the end of the month. Joe Simmons, our builder, thought he could get it done in time if he could start by the middle of August. Then it turned out that we'd just missed the last meeting of the planning committee before it went on holiday, and it wouldn't meet again until the first week of September. There was absolutely nothing we could do then but wait.

'I'm sorry, David, but I'm afraid we'll have to cancel the holiday this year. I can't afford to be away while the building is going on, as Joe is bound to have queries from time to time. If we could have got on with it straight away it might have been OK, as he would have completed the main work. But now they'll be in the middle of it just when we meant to go away.'

'I quite understand. Perhaps we could have the odd day off when you've finished harvest, go over to Polzeath to get in some surfing, and then find a week in the winter after you've settled in to go off to somewhere warm, like the Canaries.'

'That's a brilliant idea. It would be marvellous to get away for a bit of sun, now that I'm not going to be tied to the farm so much.'

Daniel came down for a fleeting visit one day just before harvest, as Janet wanted to measure up for things like carpets which she said were too old and shabby. She also had designs on a new kitchen, though it seemed perfectly all right to me – but then women always seem to feel they must have a new one when they move to a house.

'Has Martin any plans for the future, Mark? I don't think there'll be room for the two of us when I take over. All I'll need will be a competent tractor driver, and not another manager. That'll save us some money as well. Do you think he might be up to taking on my job? James hasn't taken any steps to replace me yet, though he was talking about advertising for someone earlier in the week.'

'I'm sure he'd jump at it. He's had itchy feet for some time, though he didn't want to move till the baby had arrived. But the child is three months old now, so he'd be ready to go. I couldn't ask for a better or more reliable worker – I wouldn't have employed him for so long if he hadn't been – and I'd give him the strongest recommendation. He's coped perfectly well when he's been in charge when David and I have been on holiday, and he gets on splendidly with the men. He doesn't try to throw his weight about, and is ready to muck in on any job that needs doing. He's not the brightest brain on earth, but his common sense and enthusiasm more than compensate for that.'

'I'll speak to James about it, though I can't guarantee anything, of course. Perhaps you could sound Martin out about it and, if James is willing to consider it, he could come up for an interview and meet the boss and his agent. It'd be a good thing to have it settled before we get too busy on harvest.'

James was definitely interested, as was Martin. I gave James a strong written testimonial to show the owner, stressing that I'd left him in charge of the farm on several occasions, and that he'd coped confidently in my absence.

James said that he came over well at the interview, where he was put through his paces by the agent, and they offered him the job to start in October when Daniel would be taking over from me. Martin was over the moon, and was almost embarrassing in his thanks for all that I'd done for him over the years. For my part I was delighted that he'd turned out so well. I rang Richard to tell him as he was always keen on keeping up with what his former students were doing. When the time came to say goodbye to Martin, it was an emotional moment for both of us.

It was another rather messy harvest that year, and it was lucky in a way that we'd cancelled the holiday, as the last field wasn't cut until the third week in September. It meant that the building of the extension to the bungalow was also held up.

To my relief, planning consent had been granted at the end of the first week in the month. Joe had got off to a flying start in demolishing the front wall, laying the foundations and building the new side walls. But then the weather broke and September gales set in. We realised now that a price had to be paid for that wonderful view to the south-west, as it meant that the site was fully exposed to gales blowing in from the distant Atlantic over Devon and Cornwall. With the gales came driving rain, and the front remained sheeted up for nearly a week while I fretted over both the building and the last of the harvest.

Eventually the builders got going again and finished the main structure quite quickly, except for the sliding glass windows opening on to the non-existent patio. Then followed the usual delays while plumbers waited for electricians or vice versa, and the decorators had to wait for both. Then the windows, when they came, didn't quite fit, which meant another week's delay while that was sorted out. In the end, it was just finished enough for me to move on 1 October, the date when Daniel was due to move into the farm house.

Daniel and Janet wanted to bring down a lot of the modern furniture they had acquired, and asked me to take what they didn't need from the farmhouse. But I didn't want much, as I had all mine from the fiat at Westerton which I'd kept in store over the years, and which was more suitable for the bungalow than most of the heavy pieces from the farm. In the end, I took a few of them that had a sentimental value. We put the rest into a sale, where it made a surprisingly large sum of money, going mostly to antique dealers.

The night I moved in, David came up for a meal and we opened a bottle of wine.

'Here's to the future, love, and perhaps to the day when we'll finally move in to live together, whether it'll be here or some-where else. I would like to do it one day before we get too old.'

'I would, too, Mark. I think it had better wait till I retire, though. Thank you for everything, and the wonderful life you've given me. Now come to bed, I want to tell you how much I love you still.' We made love as if we'd never been together before – a marvellous start to my new life.

I had expected to have time on my hands when I was relieved of the daily tasks on the farm. In the event, Daniel wanted me there most days while he familiarised himself with all the farm details and records. When he was ready, he suggested that we ought to sit down to review policy for the future, as we hadn't done that fully for some years, and we both felt that leaner times might be on the way. We decided to defer that until after Christmas when we had analysed the accounts for the year that had ended at Michaelmas.

I decided to go back to the annual conference in Brighton, which I hadn't been to for several years. I wanted to catch up with what was going on in the agrochemical world, not only to keep my writing up to date, but also because as chairman of the Farming and Wildlife Advisory Group I needed to be aware of chemical issues in relation to wildlife on farms.

Though several old friends had retired, there were still enough former press colleagues around to make it enjoyable. While I was there I was terribly tempted to look up Guy's number in the book, as I wanted to let him know that I now had David in his place, and to find out if he was still living with Peter. I guessed he would be, for he was not the sort of person to play fast and loose in a relationship, even though he had dumped me – but that was quite different. I desisted, but walked along the front that night. No strange man emerged from the darkness, and I doubt if I'd have stopped if he had. I had David now.

That Christmas was the first I'd ever spent without Mother, and I couldn't help looking back nostalgically to past ones when Mother and Dad were in their prime and Caroline was a bright young thing, instead of the middle-aged grandmother that she now was. We spent the day with her family, as she had thought-fully invited David as well. His father was now in a home with Alzheimer's, and no longer recognised him, and he didn't want to traipse up to Norwich to spend it with his sister. From the very start of our friendship he was accepted as one of the family – a kind of honorary uncle, which had made life easier for us.

Whether they knew we were a gay couple, we didn't know, but with so many people now coming out it was probably pretty obvious that we were. We had always been discreet so it probably didn't matter anyhow.

Having more time to spare, I also went back to the Oxford conference in January to get a rather different slant on what was happening in the global industry. Though there seemed to be some optimism among the more progressive farmers there, the general feeling was that the industry would be facing harder times, and prices for milk and wheat – our two main products at home – would be unlikely to rise, because of surpluses and New Labour's apparent lack of interest.

I had kept Arnold's telephone number and, because the conference programme on the last afternoon looked a bit dull, I thought I might go out to see him at his home near Oxford.

'Of course I'd love to see you I've moved to a small house on a retirement estate, but it's a bit nearer the city. I'm not sure whether you'll have heard, but John died suddenly in November, so I'm afraid he won't be here.' His voice broke as he said it.

'Arnold, I am so sorry. No, we hadn't heard. I must definitely come to see you. You must be devastated. How do I find you?' He gave me directions.

He looked much as I remembered him, though a little older. But he had the same friendly, outgoing smile, mental alertness and apparent zest for life that had made our previous meetings so memorable.

'It's awfully good of you to come to look me up. Life can get a bit boring in a place like this, surrounded by old people, although everyone is very friendly and we have a good warden to look after us if we need her. But it's good to see a new face now and again. How's David?'

'Fine, thanks, and he wishes to be remembered to you. Tell me about John; it must have come as a dreadful shock after so many years together. You must miss him terribly.'

'It was ghastly at the time, as it was all so sudden. He was half undressed getting ready for bed, when his aorta ruptured, and mercifully he must have lost consciousness in a few seconds. I'd been rather worried about him for some time, but he just wouldn't go to the doctor. I was very busy just then finishing something off to a deadline, otherwise I'd have rung the doctor myself to make an appointment. I blame myself for not doing anything till it was too late. I still miss him all the time, as he'd always been there beside me for those forty-seven years. We'd become part of one another, and when it happened it felt as if part of my own body had been torn away from me. It was quite extraordinary.'

'I know the feeling. I don't think I ever told you, but I lost my first partner suddenly. We were students at the time, and were both deeply in love for the first time. He was killed in a car crash. I don't know now how I got through it, but I had a very supportive family – though they had no idea that I was gay – and his mother, who did know about us, was wonderful. He's still with me at times, even though it's nearly thirty years ago now.'

'I'm so sorry – it was cruel losing him so soon. At least John and I were lucky to have had nearly fifty years together. The strange thing was that at the beginning I had grave doubts about the relationship, as he wasn't my type at all. But I'd had nine years of promiscuity when we met, looking for real love and never finding it. At that time, as I told you once, we took absurd risks of prosecution, blackmail or being beaten up, and I was longing to settle down to a domestic life, especially at weekends, and I was very lonely.

'We met a few times and seemed to be sexually compatible, and I learnt what a wonderfully kind and caring person he was. By the third time, I realised that he'd fallen hopelessly in love with me, and that it would break his heart if I called it off. I couldn't have done that, and thank goodness I didn't, for it wasn't long before I had come to love him very dearly for all the things he was. I realised that it didn't matter a damn that he wasn't some Adonis with a marvellous figure. It was probably just as well that he wasn't as he might have walked out on me after a few months if he had been. I was nearly forty at the time, so I wouldn't have been able to hold on to a good-looking young lover for long. We came to share everything in life, and never in all those years did we have a serious disagreement. We could never have run the risk of hurting one another in any way.'

'That's exactly what John told David when they got talking together on the second evening at Bellagio when you and I had gone down for our baths. David told me and asked me whether I thought it might apply to us as well. I said I hoped it would, as we'd never had an argument either.'

'I'm still full of remorse, as I know that I made John deeply unhappy at times. He never really got over the fear that I'd leave him for a younger man – which I would never, ever have done, but sometimes he'd put two and two together if he saw me with someone and make six out of it. He suffered for years once without saying anything, when he got the wrong end of the stick over a platonic friendship I had with a younger man whom I used to think of as the son I would have liked to have had. The thing I really regret about being gay is not having had kids. Anyhow, I'm quite certain that he has forgiven me, though I'll feel guilty till the day I die for making him unhappy. He loved me too well, I'm afraid.

'Mark, I'm terribly sorry to have unloaded this on you, but living in a place like this there is no one I can talk to, as I have to keep up the pretence of being a confirmed old bachelor. I do have one or two friends I can talk to on the phone, but that's not quite the same.'

'I'm just glad that you can talk to me. When my second love affair broke up because we lived too far away, and I couldn't give him the time he needed, I had no one to talk to except for a close lesbian friend. She was very understanding, but I'd have liked to have had a man to share my unhappiness with. I'm sure gay men, if they're not in a relationship, do need someone with whom they can share their problems now and again, as many of us still have to be careful if we're living in a possibly homophobic environment. The general public still seem to think that gays are either very camp, feminine "queers" or rampant sodomites, neither of which helps the image of people like us, whose lives are not governed entirely by thoughts of sex. I don't know what we can do about it. Nothing, I suppose, except wait for society as a whole to become more liberal minded, which, thank goodness, does seem to be happening now.'

'Yes, things are moving unbelievably fast compared with forty years ago. To change the subject, are you still happy with David? We both liked him so much, and thought that you were an ideal couple. You must stick with him.'

'We're still wonderfully happy, and we'll always be together. You see, both of us had rather given up hope of finding anyone to love again at nearly forty, and then suddenly, out of the blue, meeting someone so compatible was almost a miracle for both of us. I think that as with you and John it's a good thing that we don't actually live together yet, but only get together at weekends, so that we're not on top of each other all the time. My mother died recently and I've moved into a bungalow on my own, so we'll probably see more of one another now. We'll move in together when he retires, I hope.'

'You're wise to live apart for the time being. So many relationships break down both in the hetero and the homosexual world from people being too much on top of one another. They need space. When John and I first got together I insisted that we should each continue with our working lives, and not share a house, which is what he'd have liked at the time. The trouble was that I'd already become rather a workaholic before we met and kept taking on outside jobs, so I never gave him enough of my time. He never complained, but I do regret it now he's no longer there.'

'I know what you mean. Guy lived down in Hove, and I was in Westerton, so we only saw each other about once in five weeks. He did suggest that he might come up to live near me, but I was afraid that if he did he'd still not see much of me, as I was out a lot in the evenings. He'd give up his friends, move to a strange place where he knew no one and I'd be out most of the time. I was just getting established in my career, and wasn't prepared to sacrifice anything. It was selfish, and the inevitable happened. He found a man in Brighton who fell in love with him and was prepared to give him all the time he wanted. It was his future happiness at stake, and I was glad for his sake. But I was terribly upset at the time.'

'It must have been awful being dumped, but it was a good thing in the end as it left you free for David. It's sad that so many gay men become self-centred when they're young, possibly because they find it difficult to fit into the laddish society of the young heterosexual world. They then tend to withdraw into themselves, and finally get drawn into the shallow sex world of clubs and pubs, where sex is everything, rather than commitment to a long-term partnership.'

'You're probably right there, but I never moved in that sort of a world, so I wouldn't know. All I ever wanted was a close loving relationship with another man, which I got right at the beginning, which has probably coloured my attitude for life. I do have to admit, though, to have been excited by some of the other sexual experiences I've had with men, such as Robert, a Westerton friend.'

'Both of us have been fortunate to have found loving partners. Over my life, I've met quite a few men who'd have loved to have settled down in a partnership but never met the right man or experienced the happiness of a loving partnership. I do believe that a deep same-sex union is usually stronger than a heterosexual one, simply because both partners tend to have the same interests and outlooks on life. Most men and women have completely different interests, and once the first flush of sexual attraction has worn off there may be nothing left of mutual interest, and they get bored. To be really cynical, I'm often surprised that many marriages last as long as they do.'

'Did you and John continue to enjoy sex for the whole of your forty-seven years?'

'Yes, in a way, but naturally it changed as we got older. The first thrill of it wears off before long, to be replaced by the sensual satisfaction of being together and enjoying mutual masturbation. Neither of us were ever into anal sex, though I think he might have enjoyed it with me. I became impotent from prostate cancer treatment fifteen years before he died, and he had a problem ten years later, but we still loved being in bed together, even if we couldn't have an orgasm. The physical pleasure of close bodily contact never wore off, and we were in bed together the night before he died. That is one of the things I've missed most since I lost him. Bed can be a lonely place after sharing it for nearly fifty years.'

'There's still one thing that rather puzzles me. You said that you allowed each other to have casual sex outside with other men if the opportunity arose. I just don't see how you can reconcile that with a truly loving partnership, which ought, surely, to be monogamous?'

'I know that must sound odd, but as I said earlier, it did seem to work for us all right. Men are not naturally monogamous – few animals are. Throughout history men have had mistresses, and always will have. Variety is said to be the spice of life, and this applies to the sexual act just as much as it does to other things in life. Every now and again it's human nature to want something a bit different, but then it's nice to return to the thing that one is used to. Maybe it was because I'd led a promiscuous life for too long before I met John, but I admit to feeling the need sometimes for something more exciting because it would be strange. But that would only lie in the pleasure of the sexual act itself.

'Once when I had met the same man, I think it was four times, and we were very compatible, I realised that he was getting too emotionally involved and that he was at risk of falling in love with me, I had to break it off immediately. I felt that I'd be letting John down, and that it wouldn't be fair to the other man either, as I would never have left John. I would never have allowed myself to get mixed up in an eternal triangle, when a man won't leave his wife for his mistress. I have to confess that I don't think John liked the idea to begin with, but as the years went by, I know he derived temporary sexual satisfaction from an occasional fling. After his death I found evidence of this. The fact that we had been to bed together the night before he died – and enjoyed lying in each other's arms – is proof that it did work. Strange as it may seem, it appeared to strengthen our love for one another. Enough of this, have you time to stay for a cup of tea?'

'I'd love one, but I'll have to be on the road after that. I've never had the opportunity of talking like this to anyone before. It's been really rewarding. I only wish you lived closer, so that I could bring David into it as well. You simply must come down to see us one day. There's always a bed now I'm in the bungalow, and I'd like to show you the farm.'

'If it was twenty years ago, I'd have taken you up on that, but lots of things are going wrong with the bodywork, and I don't go away now. Why don't you and David come up to Oxford one day, and I'll hobble round with you to show him the sights?'

'Yes, we'll certainly do that. Now he's a senior partner he can get away more easily.'

Over tea, the discussion turned to farming, as with his inquisitive mind, he wanted to know what was happening, His brother had owned a farm in Suffolk, and he used to stay there in the past, so knew quite a lot about it.

As I was leaving, I felt I had to say something about John.

'Look, Arnold. You simply mustn't be too hard on yourself about making John unhappy. Even if you feel that sometimes you didn't give him enough of yourself, he would be the first to understand. It was quite obvious to both David and I that he loved you deeply, and that you were a wonderfully devoted couple. We said to each other after we met that we could only hope that we'd be the same if we lived to your age. The past is past and there is nothing you can do about it now. He'd never want you to feel remorse. I know it's easy to feel it if you lose someone you love – to keep saying, "If only I'd done this or that". But it's pointless, because you can't bring back the past.'

'Thanks, Mark. I'll try to bear that in mind. I know in my heart that he's forgiven me for everything, but it's so difficult to lose guilt. Give my love to David, and keep in touch, please.'

As I went to the door, I took him in my arms and gave him a big hug and kissed him to show him that he was not alone. There were tears in his eyes as I left.

When I got back I told David about the visit, and how much I'd enjoyed listening to Arnold's wisdom. We agreed that when the days got longer we'd go to Oxford, and get Arnold to show us round, so that David could compare it with his Cambridge.

Early in February, we managed to fit in the week's holiday which we'd missed in the summer. We flew to Gran Canaria to a nice holiday hotel with a large swimming pool, where we lazed in the sun, or took long walks along the sands, or explored other parts of the island. It was wonderfully relaxing, but it didn't take us long to discover that if we had wanted some sexual satisfaction on the side, it would be perfectly easy to get it.

On the second evening, bearing in mind what Arnold had said, I broached the subject.

'If you'd like some time off away from me to explore the local scene, I wouldn't mind too much. You might feel the need for something a bit different for a change.'

I knew quite well that even if he did, he'd be back with me again, and it wouldn't really affect our relationship. I trusted Arnold's wisdom – if that was what it was.

'Of course not, I'm very content with what I've got. I'll let you off the lead for a couple of hours, if you need a run, though.'

'No, thanks, the grass isn't really any greener on the other side of the fence, even though you may think it is sometimes. I'm very happy with the grass this side.' We both laughed, though it didn't stop us from admiring the local talent.

Back home the word seemed to have got around that I'd handed over to Daniel, and various people came out of the woodwork to enquire whether I wanted to take on other responsibilities. I was pressed to stand for the county council on the grounds that they needed more farmers. The Farmers' Union wanted me to stand for an office in their organisation, but I resisted all these blandishments as I still wanted to be able to criticise them in my writing if I thought it necessary. I did agree to join the committee of the Norton Hospice as they had been so good with Mother, and to become a churchwarden for our little village church which I'd started to attend after I moved. It had a service only once a week, being part of a group of four parishes, and I liked the vicar in charge.

Before Daniel and I met to review the future of the farm, I sat down to think what we might do to maintain our income if prices for milk and cereals didn't increase in line with the rate of inflation, which we both thought would be the case. I had come up with three possibilities. One was to take one or two of our lowest-yielding arable fields out of production and plant them up with trees. In one of the earlier TV programmes I'd chaired, a forestry expert had discussed this, and I thought we could call him in to advise us as he only lived in Dorset. The second idea was to turn one of the fields into a lake, stock it with trout or other fish, and let it out for fishing. The third was to set up a nature trail, which would be easier now that we had the field margins. It would cost little, and we could make a small charge for it to be used by school parties, countryside groups or even visitors to our summer let cottages.

'What do you think of these ideas, Daniel? I'm sure that it's going to become more difficult to make profits out of the straight farming operations, except perhaps from milk if we get the higher yields from the Holsteins.'

'I think you're right there, and I'd agree we ought to be looking at things outside straight farming. I quite like the idea of planting trees. We've got that ten-acre field down near the big pond which never seems to yield as well as the others, and if there is a further squeeze on prices, it'll hardly pay its way. We could get quite good grants for planting it up. Though you probably wouldn't see a return from timber in your lifetime, I might, and that little boy that Janet's expecting any moment might really cash in on it. Another thing is that if we did do that, it'd fit in well with a nature trail round the ponds. I like the idea.'

'So do I. Shall I ring up the forestry man in the morning and ask him to come out and advise us? I thought he seemed very sensible and balanced in his views.'

'Yes, if you could. I'm all in favour of the nature trail, too, and I'm sure Janet would be pleased as she was involved in taking schoolchildren out for nature study in her last job. I don't think I like the idea of a fish pond. We might have difficulty in keeping it full in a dry year, and we'd have to employ someone to take the money, which might eat into any profits we might make from it. I think it would be too risky.'

'I'm inclined to agree. Anything we do shouldn't involve employing more labour. I've a feeling that farm wages are going to rise quite considerably in future, and our labour bill is high enough as it is.'

'I'd quite like to add a few more cows to the herd, but I can't see quite how we could do it at the moment without spending rather a lot of money on new buildings and waste disposal, and we really haven't enough grazing land if we continue rearing all our young stock. I'd like to have another look at the possibility in a couple of years when we'll be in a position to judge how successful the switch in the breeding policy has been.'

'I agree, Daniel. I'd not want to do anything with the dairy herd for at least two or three years. We might know a bit more about the level of milk prices by then, too.'

I managed to contact the forestry consultant the next day, and he agreed to come out the following week to look at the possible site for a new wood. 'I think the farm would be perfectly suitable for growing trees,' he said after we'd looked at several possible sites. 'With your rainfall and fairly mild climate they should grow fast, and by the time that they're mature I guess the world might be getting short of timber at the rate forests are being destroyed. I'd certainly go ahead if I were in your place.'

We picked a ten-acre field, not far from the two ponds, which had one side bordering a minor road on the north side of the farm. We planned the planting scheme with him then and there. With a future nature trail in mind, we left rides which would have easy access to the road. As the field was cropped, we wouldn't be able to do anything until the autumn, when he said he'd be on hand to advise on the planting. It would be a mixed wood of both soft and hard woods.

It was to become one of the pleasures of my future life watching it grow into a wood, attracting all sorts of wildlife to the farm.

The following year, I devised a nature trail incorporating the new wood and both ponds, and also some of the small plantings that I'd done to round off corners, where the trees were now quite big. I spent any spare time devising noticeboards describing what parties should look for when going round. Janet was a great help here with her experience of school parties.

Though she'd known nothing about farming when she met Daniel, she had quickly adapted to life in the country. She had a warm, loving and friendly nature, with something about her of Cynthia as I first knew her. She had fairish hair standing up from her forehead, blue eyes, rounded, slightly rosy cheeks, a healthy complexion and a smiling mouth. Daniel had picked well, and the family took to her from the start. By the time the wood was planted in the autumn, she'd given Daniel a son and heir whom they christened Charles after her father. Then fifteen months later, a second son, John, arrived so it looked as if the future of the farm might be assured. They decided to stop there.

For some years David had wanted to go over to California to visit his cousin Charlotte whom I'd met when she came to stay with him for a couple of days when visiting England. I'd never had time before to go away for the three weeks we had in mind, and we'd decided to go in the middle of September after I'd given Daniel a hand with harvest.

A week before we were due to leave, I'd just got in for tea when the phone rang.

'It's Captain Davenport here, Mark. I've something I'd like to discuss with you. Could I come to see you?'

'Yes, of course, I'll be in all the evening. Come along now, if you like.'

He was the owner of the 200-acre dairy farm at the back of my house, and I'd met him and his wife quite a few times at church and at village meetings. He'd bought the farm when he came out of the army about twenty-five years before. He was employing two men but only milking about eighty cows. David, who was his vet, and I had guessed that he must be losing money on it. Ten minutes later he was round.

'I thought I ought to let you know that we've decided to sell up,' he said as he sat down. 'Neither Claire nor I are getting any younger, and the garden and house are really too big for us now. We're moving down to Cornwall to be nearer the grandchildren. There's no money in milk now, nor likely to be under this damned Labour government, which doesn't seem to care in the slightest about agriculture, as you were saying in one of your articles recently. I'll be glad to get out of it. All the pleasure's gone out of farming.

'Our agent has advised us that it'd be best to divide it into three lots; the land and buildings, the two cottages, and the house and garden. It's not on the market officially yet, but I thought that you ought to know about it, as you might possibly be interested in buying the land. It's only about two miles from your place, isn't it, and you might find it useful as an outlying farm for young stock – or most of it's ploughable if you've got the tackle.'

'It's awfully good of you to let me know about it. I don't know what to say at the moment. I can see that it might have considerable advantages as we are heavily stocked at home. As you probably know, Daniel is in charge now, so I'd have to talk it over with him before deciding on anything. At first sight it would seem to be an attractive proposition, but obviously it would depend finally on what sort of a figure you're expecting to get for it.'

'Our agent thinks that it'd fetch £2,250 an acre if it went to auction. That might sound a lot but it would include the farm buildings, which I've kept in good repair.'

'I doubt very much if we'd be able to find that sort of money. It's a lot for bare land without a farmhouse to go with it. I can't see how we could justify a price like that for just a stock-rearing farm. The figures just wouldn't add up. But I'll go down to talk to Daniel this evening, and get him to put some figures through the computer. The trouble is that I'm off to California for the better part of three weeks in a week's time. If we were interested, when you would like to know?'

'We'd need to know much sooner than that, as the agents want to get it on the market before things go quiet in the winter. I'd think we'd need to know within a week. If you left it, it could be sold by the time you get back. To be honest, we'd like you to have it, as I know you'd farm it well. If it went to auction, it might well go to some up-country woman who knew nothing about farming and who'd buy it for some horse enterprise, and you know what a mess horses can make of pastures. I don't expect you'd like that much at the back of your house either.'

'You're right there.'

He was obviously putting on the pressure, but in a nice way. I'd always known him as a very straight-dealing sort of man, and I was sure that he genuinely wanted us to have it. At the same time, a straight sale would save him a lot of hassle and money as well, if he didn't have to put it up for auction.

'I'll go and talk to Daniel straight away. I'm so sorry you're leaving, as you've done a lot for the community round here, and you and Claire really will be missed. But I can see that you both want to wind down a bit. After all, that's what I'm doing myself, and I'm a lot younger than you. Thanks again for letting me know. It's very good of you.'

As I expected, Daniel was very excited at the prospect of getting more land. His grandfather and great-grandfather had both been expansionists in their time, and he wanted to follow in their footsteps – and he'd learnt to think big from working with James. But at the same time his training in economics and natural shrewdness didn't allow his heart to rule his head.

'It's a great opportunity, Mark, but we mustn't get carried away. It'd be marvellous to have another couple of hundred acres so close to the farm, but land prices are pretty silly at the moment, and I don't need the computer to tell me that you couldn't justify the price he's asking if we just used it for rearing young stock, especially as we both think that prospects for farming are not particularly rosy. What do you think?'

'I suppose we could plough up at least half of it, but there again, the price of cereals at the moment wouldn't justify it. I doubt if the profit from wheat would cover the interest charge. As I see it, the only possible justification for that outlay of capital would be if, by moving all or most of the young stock up there, we could increase the size of the dairy herd down here to about 250 cows. But as we said last time we discussed it, that'd mean spending more capital on new buildings and slurry disposal. You'll have to put the figures through the computer to see if that would be justified.'

'I certainly wouldn't want to try to grow corn up at Barnfield – that's the name of the farm, isn't it? – I don't think it'd be worth the hassle of moving the machinery up and down. I agree with you that the only possible justification for buying it would be if we could increase the size of the dairy herd at home. I'll put some figures through the computer for different options tonight. Then we can decide in the light of what comes out. Perhaps we might have a word with Alan Holmes then to see what he thinks. He's seems a wise old bird, and I'd respect his judgement.' Alan was an old friend of Dad's who had been our land agent for many years.

'That's a good idea. He'll have his ear to the ground in regard to land prices, and could let us know whether he thinks we'd be justified in making an offer.'

David was coming over to a late supper that night, and I was keen to hear what he might think about the wisdom of buying it.

'I can't give you an opinion about the price, though it does seem an awful lot of money. But I do know the farm, as the Captain has been one of our clients for years. It's a good clean little farm and, as it's ring-fenced apart from the bit at the back of the bungalow, there's little risk of stock picking up diseases like TB from a neighbour. It's a high farm, and the cattle always seem very healthy there. I'd judge it to be an excellent rearing farm. I can tell you that all the vets round here are getting very concerned at the spread of TB. So the price of heifers to replace cows that have to be slaughtered ought to remain high, and you should be able to cash in on that.'

The following morning we went over the figures the computer had come up with. Daniel had tried to estimate just how much extra capital we'd have to find to convert the buildings at Barnfield for calf rearing, and also to provide for another thirty, or at the most forty, cows at home. As the first of the Holstein cross heifers had shown an increase of about five per cent in yield over the pure Friesians, he built in an extra eight per cent for milk income from either 240 or 250 cows, and an increased income from the additional beef cattle and heifers that would be available for sale.

The upshot was that it would be safe to pay only £2,000 an acre if we could milk 250 cows and increase their yield by at least eight per cent, and also increase income from the extra cattle by some twenty per cent over the existing figure. There was no way in which we could afford the full price of £22,500 the Captain was asking.

That afternoon we got an interview with Alan Holmes.

'It'll obviously be a gamble, Mark. Prices for land are stupidly high in relation to what you can get out of it. It's being bought for prestige or leisure purposes, such as horses, and there is a lot of money sloshing around. I could see one of these up-country people buying both the land and the house for an equestrian enterprise if it went to auction. I couldn't possibly advise you to pay more than £2,000 an acre, and that's really rather too much if it's to be used for farming. But if you can increase the income from the home farm substantially from having this extra land, it might just be worth it.

'It's difficult to say where land prices will go in the future. If they continue to rise, you'll have made a good investment, but I think we'd better leave that out of the calculation. I'm sorry I can't be more specific than that. I'd offer him £20,000, and say that's a final figure. Whatever happens, you'll have an uncomfortable flight to California. If he accepts, you'll be worrying that you've paid too much. If he doesn't, you'll feel you've missed a good opportunity. If you'd like me to act for you, just say the word.'

'Thanks, Alan, of course I will.'

'Well, I don't know that we're much further forward,' Daniel said, 'but at least it confirms what we thought. Let's go and see the bank manager and ask what we'd have to pay for the loan.'

We were welcomed with open arms as one of his best customers, as we'd always managed to pay him back quickly in the past.

'Of course, we'd be glad to loan you the money,' he said after I'd explained the situation. 'It's quite a good time at the moment with interest rates down so much on what they were. I could let you have the money at five and three-quarter per cent, as it's quite a sizeable sum. Would that be acceptable?' Daniel had based his calculations on a six per cent charge, so it meant that our figures now looked a bit more favourable.

'Yes, I'll let you know in a couple of days if we're going ahead with it.'

'So what about it, Daniel?' I asked. 'It's your future that this is all about, and your children in due course, I expect. It ought to be you to take the final decision, not me.'

'You're the senior partner, so I'd like to know what you think first. You've got a lot more experience than I have.'

'I'd offer him the £20,000, saying that's our top limit. But if he turns it down, that's that. I don't think we could afford to go above it. If it was auctioned, we might get it cheaper.'

'That's my feeling, too. Will you contact him?'

'I'll ring him tonight. I expect he'll want time to contact his agent, but we should get an answer before we go away next week.'

I managed to get him on the phone that evening, saying that under no circumstances would we go any further than £2,000 an acre. He promised to let me know within three days after discussing it with Claire and his agent. He came through two days later.

'We've talked it over, Mark, and we've decided to accept your offer, even though our agent thought we'd get more if it went to auction and wanted to stick out for his original figure. But I've always held to the maxim that a bird in the hand is worth two in the bush, and if you had it it'll save all the uncertainty of going to auction. We both felt that we'd like you to have the land as we know you'll farm it well, especially as you're living on the spot.

'If it'd been auctioned it might have gone to some dealer who'd have no real interest in it or, as I said before, to a riding stables, who'd make a mess of it. I may be sentimental but I'm very attached to this place, and feel a certain amount of responsibility for its future. I've always admired your family's farming, and enjoyed your articles in the paper and what you've said on the box. I've only met young Daniel once, but he reminds me of your father, and that's a pretty good recommendation. I know it'll be in safe hands, and we'd both like to wish you good luck.'

'Naturally I'm delighted you've accepted the offer. We wouldn't have gone any higher as all our calculations showed that it was the ultimate limit, and even now it'll probably be quite a few years before it'll show any profit. I'm asking Alan Holmes, our agent, to get in touch with your man to settle all the details, and I hope everything will be in place by the time I get back from the States in three weeks' time.

'I hope you may be able to find time to look us up one day to see how we're getting on.'

Chapter Ten

Alan had been quite right when he said I wouldn't enjoy the flight to Los Angeles, as I'd be worrying whether we'd done the right thing in borrowing so much for only a marginal return in the immediate future. I felt that I'd been precipitated into a decision without having had time to think it through properly. Then I consoled myself with the thought that the family hadn't got it wrong in the past and that Daniel had wanted to take it on. It was his future that mattered and the decision had been taken, so there was no point in worrying about it.

I always had ambivalent feelings about going away for more than a few days. I didn't like the disturbance to the regular routine, or all the packing up and flight arrangements, even though David had taken care of that this time. I had to get two articles written for the paper, as I felt that 'Mark Harper is on holiday' somehow denoted laziness. Was it really worth all the hassle of preparation to see overcrowded beauty spots around the world?

But this time the other half of me was buoyed up by the prospect of nearly three weeks with David beside me. We still had reservations about living together permanently but the idea of being in his arms each night, and then back in my own bed waiting to hear his measured breathing tell me that he was peacefully asleep, was exciting. Holidays like that were certainly to be savoured; but if we had it every day would familiarity breed contempt or, if not contempt, boredom, so that the pleasure of holidays when they came would be largely lost? Perhaps we shouldn't live together yet, but wait until we were older.

We'd arranged to stay the first four nights with Charlotte at her home in San Diego, down near the Mexican border, then fly back to Los Angeles where we'd hire a car and drive up the west coast to San Francisco, stopping to look at two big dairy farms on the way.

She was there to meet us at the airport, a short, plumpish, highly extrovert lady of about sixty, who always dressed in rather voluminous clothes that somehow gave her an appearance of width. That was how I remembered her from the brief visit she'd paid to David on a trip to England soon after we had got together. With her was a tall, distinguished man whom she introduced as Frank, who drove us back to her house in one of the wealthier suburbs of the city.

'Frank's my neighbour,' she said. 'He's going to do the driving for the next few days, as my eyes are getting rather bad.' It turned out that he was a retired general, recently widowed. Charlotte had lost her husband, a stockbroker, seven years previously, but had stayed on in her house in a wide street lined by huge palm trees.

'I've only got one guest room, I'm afraid,' she said, showing us into a large en-suite room with two beds. 'So you'll have to share but at least it's not a double bed if one of you snores.' By the way she said it I guessed that she'd probably sussed us out when she was in England. 'We'll have some supper when you've had a wash and brush up.'

Ten minutes later she fished a tasty beef casserole out of the oven, and we sat down to a welcome meal fortified by a bottle of excellent Californian wine. Neither of us had to do much talking, as she seemed to have an endless list of topics up her sleeve, one of which she'd produce as soon as the previous one showed any signs of flagging. Every now and again her flow would be supplemented by an off the cuff remark from the General delivered in a dry, deadpan West Coast drawl. It was quite a hilarious meal, as she was a good raconteur who clearly liked to entertain her guests. After we'd finished our coffee, she said, 'Now you two get off to bed as soon as you feel like it. You must be feeling exhausted. I always want to sleep for a week after that tedious flight from London. There's no hurry in the morning. There'll be some breakfast about nine o'clock and Frank will be round about eleven, and we'll play it from there.'

'Thanks so much, Charlotte, for that lovely meal. It was just what we needed after that long day. I think we'll take you at your word and get off to bed, shall we, Mark?'

'I'm certainly ready for it. Good night, Charlotte, and thanks, too, for an enjoyable supper. Good night, Frank. Thanks so much for picking us up. See you in the morning.'

'I think we're going to enjoy this trip, Mark,' said David as we prepared for bed. 'Charlotte's great fun, isn't she, and the General's quite a character as well. I'll let you off tonight, I'm far too tired for any further activity.'

'Me, too.' After a goodnight hug, I was asleep within a few minutes of my head hitting the pillow.

Waking up next day, I felt completely disorientated, and couldn't believe that we were about 8,000 miles away from where we'd been yesterday morning. I was glad to have David there as a connection to my former life. His presence gave me a feeling of security. He said he felt the same when I woke him from a deep sleep. This was jet lag, we supposed.

'Slept well, I hope?' Charlotte said, as we appeared for breakfast on the patio at the back of the house. 'It's a glorious day and the forecast's good, so we'll get out and show you some of the sights when Frank comes round.'

'Slept like logs,' we said in unison.

There followed three days of typical Californian hospitality and sightseeing organised by the General with almost military precision.

San Diego, with its scenic waterfront and fine harbour, its huge bridge across to Coronado Island, its world-renowned zoo, art gallery and Elizabethan Old Globe theatre, and countless other attractions had much to offer, and Frank knew it all. The preserved old town took one back to the days of the colonisers and western film sets. One expected to see Gary Cooper ride out, guns blazing, at any moment. The contrast with the downtown skyscrapers next door to it was a breathtaking example of the rate of change, and one couldn't help wondering what it would look like in another hundred years' time.

Days of sightseeing were followed by dinners with Charlotte's friends, all extremely hospitable. There was a slight feeling that we were rather like a couple of new arrivals at a zoo – strange creatures from another world who had to be inspected by the natives. A few who hadn't 'done' England seemed to think that we were living in some strange backwater of the Middle Ages, especially when it emerged that I was a farmer. I felt they were looking for straw in my hair or wheat growing out of my ears. Even those who had been to London for two days, and had done Windsor, Oxford and Stratford-upon-Avon on the third before leaving for Paris, were almost as uninformed. Then I realised that I was just as ignorant about California as they were about England, and felt chastened in view of their kindness.

As Charlotte saw us off at the airport, we promised to come over again before too long after pressing her to visit us again in England. She had been a wonderful hostess, and the General a most accomplished guide as well as a man of humour and wisdom.

We hired a car in Los Angeles and spent a couple of nights at a motel in Hollywood, as Charlotte had advised us not to waste time seeing LA. Then it was off on the road north to San Luis Obispo, close to which were the two dairy farms I'd arranged to visit. David volunteered to drive so that I could inspect the countryside, but as it consisted mostly of dried-up pasture populated by a few Hereford cattle, there wasn't much that was worth seeing.

At the first dairy farm next day they had about 2,000 cows, kept on bare feed lots of about one hundred cows each, fed on alfalfa hay and soya bean-based concentrate, and milked three times a day by immigrant Mexican workers. It seemed that England wasn't the only country that employed migrant labour for the dirty jobs. For David the visit was more interesting than it was for me, as he spent a lot of time discussing veterinary problems. I switched off early on, as the system was such that I'd be unlikely to learn anything from it and, anyhow, it appalled me by its apparent inhumanity, when animals were treated as inanimate units rather than living organisms. The second farm, though smaller, worked on the same system, so we cut the visit as short as we decently could and got back on the highway north, calling in on the fabulous Hearst Castle on the way.

This time the view was much more worth seeing as the road skirted the Pacific, plunging down almost to the sea, and then up again round mountains and canyons, where stunted pine trees seemed to sprout out of bare rock. The Big Sur country certainly was big, reminding us of the Amalfi coast road from Sorrento that we'd driven two years before.

Two nights in Monterey gave us the chance to visit Cannery Row, now transformed into a glitzy tourist attraction, though the preserved section showed what it must have been like when it was immortalised by Steinbeck. The second day on the Carmel peninsula was memorable for its spectacular coastal drive beside the ocean, watching seals and sea lions basking on the rocks, while myriad sea birds kept up a continuous cacophony.

On the landward side were the famous golf courses of Cypress Point and Pebble Beach. 'Let's have our lunch down there on the rocks,' David said. 'It reminds me of Cornwall, without the steep cliffs. Do you remember seeing that seal one day, when we were on the coastal path near Lundy Bay? Only one, compared with the hundreds here, and look at all this wildlife.' We sat not far away from the lone stunted tree at Cypress Point – that most-photographed tree close to the famous short hole across the creek.

'We did say that first day we went to Daymer Bay, and sat in the churchyard, that one day we might learn to play golf. D'you remember?'

'Of course I do,' I replied. 'One doesn't easily forget one of the happiest days of one's life. I think of that week as a sort of honeymoon. It's probably about time we did learn to play the game, if we're ever going to. We don't seem to get as much squash as we used to, and it'll get a bit too strenuous before we're much older. I don't quite know how I'll find time to play, but you'll need something to keep you occupied when you retire. Yes, let's talk about it when we get back.'

'I'm so glad you feel like that. I'm sure we'll get a lot of fun out of it as we get older. People go on playing into their eighties, I'm told. One of my partners was almost born with a club in his hand in Scotland, so I'll pick his brains when we get back.'

It was at about five thirty next morning when I was woken up, and thought that David must be trying to get into my bed, which seemed to be rocking about. *What on earth is he up to?* I thought. Then the light went on as he reached the switch; my bed moved violently again, a glass of water fell off a side table and a chair started moving across the room.

'What shall we do? Should we get out in case the roof falls in?' I asked.

'Let's stay put for the moment and see if we get another shock. If it's no worse than the last one, we'll probably be all right, as I think I read somewhere that the first one or two are usually the worst. Don't forget that we're very close to the San Andreas Fault here. The Big One will come one day, I expect, but I don't think this is it.' He was right, as there were no more.

San Francisco turned out to be just as beautiful a city as it was cracked up to be. We found a modest motel on the road out to the Golden Gate Bridge, for the three nights we thought we would need to explore the city and the surrounding countryside. There was something almost mystical about the place, with its hilly streets and its wooden houses in the older districts. The view from the bridge across the blue waters of the bay down to the city skyscrapers in the morning sun was magical.

We did all the things that tourists should do, including the boat trip round Alcatraz, the ride on the trams, a meal at Fisherman's Wharf and a drive to the Redwood National Park – and even a gay cinema on the edge of Chinatown, which left us both unmoved. This was followed by two days in the wine country and a drive to Yosemite National Park for a night. That proved something of a disaster as it was very hot and a forest fire up in the mountains produced a pall of smoke over the valley, which trapped a revolting smell of burning fat from the barbecues of thousands of Americans getting back to nature, or to their roots. Whichever it was, we beat a hasty retreat back to San Francisco next morning for the last two days of a marvellously happy holiday.

We were lucky to get seats for a performance of *La Bohème* at the Opera House on the penultimate evening and for a concert by the SF Symphony Orchestra where they played my beloved Bruch Concerto on the last night.

'We'll make a resolution to do more of this when we get home,' David said. 'Even if it means going up to London for it. I can get an occasional day off now, and so can you.'

'I'll hold you to that.'

Daniel had driven up to Heathrow to meet us, and filled me in with developments on the way back. Everything had gone smoothly over the purchase of Captain Davenport's farm at Barnfield, and we'd be signing contracts shortly, but otherwise the news was not good.

He had been up to assess what would be needed to convert the buildings into a calf-rearing and young stock-rearing unit, and reckoned that it would cost quite a lot more than we'd estimated. In addition he'd had second thoughts about the labour that would be needed to run it. We had rather assumed that Duncan, the young man we'd taken on to look after all the young stock when Jake had retired would be able to run the new unit from home. Daniel now realised, as we should have done at the beginning, that with the number of calves going up to about 250 each year, it would be essential to have someone living on the spot to look after them, both for security and health reasons.

'Of course you're right. We ought to have given it more thought to start with. If it hadn't all been so rushed we obviously would have done. What do you suggest?'

'We've only two alternatives as I see it. Either we go to the auction and buy one of the cottages, or else we try to get planning permission to build a house for a stockman up there. That'd take months and probably cost more than one of the cottages at auction. I think we'll have to buy one of them whatever the cost, but that's going to add to the size of the bank loan considerably.'

'That's right, but we'll just have to face up to it. We had better keep very quiet about it, and ask Alan to go the sale and bid for it on our behalf. If people knew we had to have it, they'd probably push the price up.

'Have you said anything to Duncan about it yet? He may not want to live up there, and if he doesn't we've got a crisis on our hands.' He'd recently got married and settled into one of our better cottages, and I was afraid he wouldn't want to move. He had proved to be a very reliable worker, and was in some ways a key member of the farm staff.

'I've an idea which might go some way to easing the financial situation,' Daniel said. 'If we can persuade Duncan to make the move, we won't really need his house for another worker. It's quite a good house with a nice bit of garden, and we could probably let it out for quite a high rent to someone in Norton who wants to get out of town to live in the country. I'd guess that we might get more from the rent than the interest charge on the loan to buy the Barnfield cottage.'

'That's a brilliant idea. It'd maybe mean losing that cottage for a long time, but I don't see how we could ever afford to employ another person on the farm, so it shouldn't be needed in the future. We'd better ask Alan to look at both the cottages and advise us as to what we might have to pay for the better one.'

Duncan pulled a long face when we told him about the plans for Barnfield in the office next day. He pointed out that they'd only recently finally settled down in their cottage, and had spent quite a lot of money on carpets, curtains and household things which might not fit the other house. It would be a bit further for his wife to get into Norton each day for her job, and would mean leaving the friends they'd made among the other staff members and their wives. He'd need to discuss it with his wife before coming to a decision.

We had expected him to make these objections, but hoped that he might be tempted by the prospect of having a substantial enterprise of his own to look after and a very considerable increase in salary, which we should be able to afford from the increased output from the farm in terms of milk and meat. We gave him two days to think it over, and waited with bated breath for his decision. He finally agreed reluctantly to move after he and his wife had taken a look at the better of the two cottages. He said what had finally swayed him was the prospect of running the unit more or less on his own, and he welcomed the responsibility. Though I was living virtually on the farm myself, I was determined not to saddle myself with daily routine jobs again in view of my other commitments. My role in it would be purely a supervisory one under Daniel's direction.

We managed to buy the cottage we wanted at the sale, though it cost a couple of thousand pounds more than Alan had expected. However, we were already so deeply committed that we had to have it, and Daniel was convinced that in the long term Barnfield would turn out to be a very substantial asset to the farm business, and in course of time he was to be proved right. He and Duncan managed to do some of the conversion themselves over the winter which saved us some money.

By the time of the spring calving there was enough accommodation ready for housing the new-born calves. We gradually moved more young stock up there as grass became available, until by the autumn the unit was fully operative. It had all cost a lot of money, but we were confident we'd done the right thing in setting it up.

'What about golf?' David said over supper one Saturday night at the end of April. We'd got in the habit of meeting then if he was not on call from his surgery, and he'd spend the night if he had Sunday free as well. He'd taken over one of the spare bedrooms and kept pyjamas and shaving gear there, so that he could stay if he wanted to. It was almost a preparation for living together permanently.

'I think we'd better get on with it now, and make the best of the summer. Have you had a word about with the partner you mentioned?'

'I was talking to him yesterday. He's a member of an old established club up in north Devon, but he advised against trying to get in there as there's a long waiting list for membership, and it's pretty expensive as well as being too far away for us to get to easily for lessons and practice. He said that the new course up at Thistledown isn't at all bad, and the young pro there is meant to be a good teacher. Being quite a new club, they might still be looking for members, so that we could probably get in there straight away. I suppose it's about eight miles from here, isn't it?'

'About that, I'd think, though it's not an easy road. Shall we drive up there tomorrow afternoon, if you've nothing else planned?'

'No, there's nothing on the books. In that case I'll spend the night here. I'd like to have something nice and warm alongside me tonight. It must be ten days now.'

The older we got, the more like a happily married couple we became, though our love was still as fresh as ever. Sometimes, remembering the past, I'd feel that it was too good to be true, and wondered how I could ever face life again if anything were to happen to him. The mere idea of it was too frightening, and I'd try to shut it out of my mind, as there was no point in worrying about such an eventuality unnecessarily.

The next afternoon we drove up to Thistledown to look at the course and enquire about membership. It had been constructed out of two small farms on the edge of moorland and had magnificent views from several of the holes. A lot of trees had been planted, and were now growing sufficiently large for it to look like a golf course rather than a cow pasture. It had the promise of becoming an attractive course in a few years.

The clubhouse had been adapted from one of the farmhouses, and the outbuildings converted to a pro's shop, so there was a comfortable, established look about it. The secretary was out, but the steward showed us round saying that there was no waiting list for membership. He suggested we had a word with the professional, Colin Smart. A youngish-looking man of about thirty, his surname suited him, and I caught David eyeing him over with obvious appreciation.

'Surely you must be Mark Harper, aren't you?' asked Colin, looking at me closely. 'I recognise you from those television programmes on the environment a while back. I always tried to get in to watch them in my lunch hour if I could. When are going to do some more?'

'There's nothing on the stocks at the moment, but I hope there'll be another series before too long. It's good to know someone is watching them, anyhow. This is my friend David, and we're thinking of joining the club. Neither of us have played the game before, so if we did join we'd need lessons. Would you be able to give us some?'

'Of course, that's what I'm here for. I'd be pleased. Have you played other games, like cricket?'

'I was hopeless at cricket and took up tennis as soon as I could. You were the same, David, weren't you?'

'Yes, I never took to cricket, but we've played a lot of squash in the past, though not so much lately. Why did you ask?'

'Many people who've played cricket find golf quite difficult at first, as the arm action is so different. But if you've played squash, that's fine, as you'll have good arm and wrist muscles, and should have no difficulty with the golf swing. If you do join, just let me know. Would you like to come together to start with, while you're picking up the basics? It would be cheaper for you, and it'd save me from having to go over it twice.' He gave a short laugh.

'I think that's a good idea, don't you, David? Let's have the first two together anyhow, and see how we get on.'

'What do you think about it?' I asked him as we drove home.

'I liked it. The course looks interesting, and the clubhouse has a nice homely feel about it – not too modern or glitzy. The sub seems a bit high, but I suppose it's in line with others of its type or it wouldn't get any members. The pro makes it worth joining, if nothing else.'

'I hope you noticed the wedding ring. It's probably just as well, or I'd have had to keep my eye on you all the time.'

'Yes, I did see it. Sad, but that's life, isn't it? It doesn't matter, as we can still enjoy a bit of stargazing, and I've got a nice farmer to be going on with.'

When we started filling up the application forms for membership, we found that we had to be proposed by two existing members of the club who knew us – and of course we didn't know anyone. Angus, David's work partner, belonged to a different club so probably wouldn't be acceptable. I rang up the secretary next day to find out if there was a way round the problem.

'Could you come up to see me one day soon, and I'll ask the captain to meet you? How about Saturday morning? I know he'll be in then.'

'That'll be fine, and I'll bring my friend along as well if he's free then.' I thought he sounded friendly, and anyhow they would be unlikely to turn down two new members.

When we got there, the captain turned out to a substantial landowner from the north of the county, whom I'd not met, but whose estate I'd visited on a FWAG visit the year before. He knew me as he apparently read my articles in the paper and had been to a meeting at which I'd spoken.

'Glad to meet you,' he said. 'I always enjoy your articles, and I feel I almost know your farm by now. I'd like to come down and go round it one day if you could spare the time.'

'Of course, I'd love that. Just give me a ring. I've got a bit more time now I've handed over the day-to-day management to my nephew. About joining the club – neither David nor I know any members, so what can we do?'

'Oh, that'll be all right. I'd be only too happy to propose you both, and then we can rustle up a couple of members to second you. I'm sure we'll have one or two who'll know your name, even if they haven't actually met you. Just let Jack have the forms and we'll put them before the committee at its next meeting. I'm delighted you've decided to start playing. You're wise to do it now before your muscles begin to get weak. You should have about thirty years of pleasure out of it, if you're lucky.'

'Thanks so much. That's extremely helpful. We were a bit worried as to whether we'd be allowed in. We both liked the look of the course so much with its marvellous views, and we'd have been very disappointed if we couldn't have got in.'

'We'll be glad to have you. Now, what about a spot of lunch if you've got time?'

'Thanks all the same, but I'm afraid we've got to get back as I've got someone coming to see me – perhaps another time when we've become members.'

'Well, that was all a lot easier than I expected,' David said as we drove home. 'It obviously pays to be something of a celebrity if you want to get things done.'

'I'm not sure that celebrity is the right word. Perhaps a notorious character might be more appropriate. They seem a very friendly lot and I feel we ought to enjoy it there, if we can find the time to play often enough.'

We were duly elected and then fixed a date with Colin for our first lesson, when he gave us the basics of how to grip the club, how to swing it, how to stand up to the ball and how essential it was to keep one's head still. I found the close contact with him stimulating, as he was not only extremely good-looking but also appeared to radiate a kind of sympathetic warmth so that you felt he was enjoying contact with you. If it hadn't been for that wedding ring, I would almost have suspected him of being one of our fraternity. I discussed this with David afterwards, and he said that he got the same vibes as I had.

To begin with, the bit I found most difficult was the grip on the club, which hurt my fingers. But it wasn't long before they appeared to get used to it, and in the effort to remember all the other things one should be doing any little discomfort in the fingers was forgotten.

We both found it terribly frustrating when we hit every ball either hard on the head so that it scuttled along the ground like a rat bolting for a hole, or sent it flying off sideways at a tangent right or left. But every so often, the ball would fly off the centre of the club and go sailing straight down the practice ground with no effort at all. I would get just the same feeling of satisfaction then as I did when getting the break of a wave just right, and hurtle towards the distant beach on a surfboard. Then all the bad shots would be forgotten in the realisation that it could be done, and that one day it might be possible to string such good shots together and do a good round without too many stupid mistakes.

After two lessons together, Colin took us separately, insisting that we then spent another hour on the practice ground. After six lessons, he said: 'That's about all I can do for you at the moment. You'd better try to get in as much practice as you can. Then I suggest that we play a round together, and I'll try to correct your faults as we go along.'

The main problem we had was getting enough time to get over to the club to use the practice ground. I solved this by cutting a level piece of field at the back of my bungalow, and when there were no cattle grazing the field I'd sneak out and hit a hundred or so balls up the field. David would pop over and do the same when he could find time. In this way, we were both able to get into a reasonably grooved swing, so that when we got out on to the course for a game, there were not too many wild shots; and by the autumn Colin expressed surprise at how well we we'd got on.

In the spring after we'd got possession of the new farm, I invited my friend the FWAG adviser to come out and advise on what we might do to improve the environment so as to encourage more wildlife, of which there didn't seem much. I'd already noted that the grass didn't start to grow as early as it did on the home farm, and concluded that this was because we were several hundred feet higher up. It was rather exposed down one side to winds from the east and north, and the existing hedges were low and full of gaps.

His advice was to plant a 350-yard-long shelter belt of trees right down the exposed side of the farm, which would eventually cut off the cold east winds in the spring, and lead to a warmer microclimate where the grass would start earlier in the spring. This would need to be some fifteen to twenty yards wide to be fully effective. It would mean that we'd lose quite a bit of grazing land, but it ought to pay off in the end, by giving us more productive pasture. We could get a substantial grant for doing this and maintenance payments as it was getting established. I wouldn't see much benefit in my lifetime, but Daniel would as thinnings became available, and Charles or John certainly would if one of them eventually took over the farm. I would only be doing what countless landlords had done over the centuries in planting trees for the future.

The adviser also suggested grubbing out three rather scrubby hedges round smaller fields, and planting two new ones to give bigger areas in which our silage contractor's very large machines could work more effectively. Even with our size of farm, we could no longer afford to buy expensive machinery that was only used for short periods each year, and we were increasingly relying on contractors for the bigger jobs.

We couldn't do everything at once. We decided on the shelter belt as a priority for the first year, and replanting the hedges the following one. If we could do the planting with our own labour in the late winter when things were relatively slack on the farm, the grant should easily cover the cost. We decided on a mixture of softwood and hardwood species, which should provide some income a bit sooner, and included some flowering trees such as cherries and sweet chestnut to provide more food for the wildlife.

The planting proved to be a massive task, but Daniel and I got our coats off alongside Duncan and other members of the farm staff and the job was finally finished by Easter. I felt a huge sense of satisfaction at having planted several thousand trees myself, rather than employing a contractor as we had for the ten-acre wood on the home farm.

Later, when the trees had established, I got in touch with a biologist from the university. I suggested that he might like to have a project for his students to come out twice a year to do counts of birds, butterflies and moths, and small mammals for the next ten years or so to try to get a measure of what the biological effect of such a planting might be. I did this because I had been unable to find any reliable figures anywhere that could tell me whether what we were doing was actually worthwhile. The biologist, Tom Wilson, was fortunately enthusiastic about the proposal, and that was the start of a collaboration which lasted until he retired twenty years later.

As things turned out, it was to be about five years before Tom was able to get any very significant increase in any of the species on his list. But as the trees grew, and we let the new hedges grow taller in the fields to provide more shelter for the grazing cattle, the bird population definitely increased, and I could hear more birdsong from my bungalow. It became one of the pleasures of my life to walk up to the buildings along the shelter belt on a sunny morning to check with Duncan that everything was all right, and to hear birds singing lustily in the fast-growing trees. When we had reached that stage, I rang up Captain Davenport and invited him and Claire to lunch so that they could see what we had done. They professed themselves delighted that they'd encouraged us to bid for the farm, as it would have been so different if it had gone to some cattle dealer with no real interest in it.

In June, I invited Angela down to stay for three days, as she had only once been down since Mother died. David took a day off, as I wanted to take her down to Cornwall to see where we bathed and to look at the little church. We put the wetsuits and the boards in the car in the hope that the surf might be good.

Polzeath was looking at its best, and biggish rollers were breaking well out from the beach. It was too tempting, and we left Angela sitting on the rocks to watch while we enjoyed ourselves for an hour getting in some really long runs.

'I simply must have a go one day,' she said as we changed out of our wetsuits by the car. 'It looks really exciting. I'm sure I'd pick it up quite easily. Can I come and stay again before long? And I'll bring a bathing costume next time.'

'Of course, but you'll need rather more than one day to really get the hang of it. I'll tell you what. David and I have decided not to go abroad this year, and we planned to come here to stay for a week, just as we did soon after we first met. Why don't you come down and stay for a few days? It'd be great fun to have you with us, and it'd give you more opportunity to pick up surfing.'

'When were you thinking of coming? I'd love to join you if we're not doing anything then.'

'We were planning to be here from 16 to 23 of September, if the hotel could take us then. Could you manage a few days that week?'

'I'd have to ask Janet, of course. We're booked to go to Italy early in August, but I don't think there's anything on in September. If I can borrow your phone this evening, I'll give her a ring to find out.'

'Of course you can. Why don't we go up to the hotel now to enquire about rooms?'

'Hello, Mr Harper,' the elderly lady at the reception said. 'We haven't seen you for a long time. Do you want to come to stay again?' I was astonished that she'd remembered my name, as we had only been into the hotel a couple of times for a drink and some food since we'd stayed there.

'How on earth do you remember my name? Yes, we wondered whether you might have a room for David and me for 16 to 23 September, and also possibly a single one for three nights in the middle of that week.'

'I'll just have a look. Yes, I could manage a double for you two for that week, and it'd be facing the sea, which I expect you'd like. I've got a single free that week as well. It doesn't face the sea, but it's quite a nice room. Would you like me to hold it for you?'

'Yes, if you could. I should be able to ring you tomorrow to confirm it. Would that be OK?'

'Yes, of course.'

'Now we're here why don't we get something to eat at the

bar?' David said. 'Then this afternoon perhaps we could walk round the cliff to Daymer, and show Angela the church.'

We had a drink and a sandwich at the bar and, leaving the car on the beach car park, walked round the cliff path past Greenaway with its views down the estuary to Padstow and the moors beyond. On a sunny afternoon, with the incoming tide rapidly covering the sandbanks in the estuary, it was an idyllic sight.

'It's just lovely. I can understand why you two seem so happy here,' Angela said. 'I just can't wait to get back here in September.'

She was equally enchanted with the little church and its setting. As before we sat on the seat above the church where ten years before David and I had sat, on what I still thought of as a kind of honeymoon. It was wonderful to realise that all the hopes we had then were being fulfilled, and that we were still as fond of each other now as we were then.

As the tide was up round the rocks, we walked the cliff path skirting the big round hill and then back down the golf course, the full extent of which we'd not seen before.

'Now we know how to play the game, we must definitely come down and have a round here one day,' David said. 'It really looks exciting and challenging.'

'It certainly does. We'll find a day in the autumn, now that we're not going abroad this year. We should have some spare days then.'

That evening Angela got through to Janet, who confirmed that the three days in September were free, so I rang the hotel and booked her in.

Daniel was still glad of an extra pair of hands at harvest, and he and the tractor driver, Paul Westcott, whom he had taken on in place of Martin, drove the combine, while I took over on the dryer and storage of the grain in the silos. Now that we'd got up to nearly 250 cows, the acreage under corn had dropped considerably as more land was needed for summer grazing and growing maize as feed for the winter. Even so it was a tricky harvest that year, and we only finished a few days before we were due to go to Polzeath, and there were still a lot of straw bales out in the field when we left. Fortunately the new type of straw baler which wrapped them in polythene meant that they could be left out in the field without damage. We then employed a contractor to transport what we needed up to Barnfield for wintering the calves and young stock.

We enjoyed some excellent surf on the two days before Angela joined us, but it moderated then, which made it easier for her first lessons. We hired a suit and surfboard for her for the three days. She'd always been a good athlete, so she took to it quickly, showing considerable skill in picking a good wave and timing the launch accurately. By the end of the second day she might have been doing it all her life, and we had the greatest difficulty in getting her out of the sea by the time we'd had enough. Our routine was bathing in the mornings on the incoming tide, and sightseeing in the afternoon to places that we'd discovered over the years. It was great having her for meals with her tales of experiences she'd had in journalism, and in fending off importunate men without letting them know she was a lesbian.

'I want to ask you both a question,' she said over coffee after dinner on the second evening. 'Do either of you regret having been born gay?'

'I did when I was growing up and had to come to terms with it when I was an undergraduate at Cambridge,' David said. 'It's difficult when you find yourself round a bar with a group of heterosexual men swapping stories of sexual exploits with women, or telling dirty stories. You can feel terribly out of it. At those moments I envied them. The only homosexual people I was aware of were the notorious, very camp feminine types who I didn't want to be associated with in any way as I didn't feel I had anything in common with them. Then you couldn't meet the sort of gay person you'd like to meet because they were lying low as well. It wasn't till this older student said he was in love with me, and seduced me, that I began to feel more comfortable about it, as he told me how common it was below the surface.

'Then later on I saw friends getting married and having kids and I was envious as I would have loved to have had children. But by then I'd realised that it might be a terrible mistake to marry, as it wouldn't be fair on a girl not to be able to give her the full love she deserved, quite apart from the sexual act itself, which I felt I probably couldn't handle. So I more or less retreated into myself, as I was never tempted by promiscuity. I just lived on having casual sex occasionally, hoping that one day someone would turn up. Then Mark appeared, and suddenly life was transformed, and I'm sure I'm happier now than I would ever have been as a heterosexual married man. So, on the whole, I don't regret it.'

'What about you, Mark?'

'Rather the same in some ways, I suppose. But my actual situation was rather different. Meeting Simon while I was still very young and innocent, and falling in love with him so intensely gave me a different start to David's. I learnt about emotional love at the same time I learned about sex. With many gay men, I think sex is the dominant factor in the early stages, and they come to imagine that it is the only thing that matters and don't consider commitment at all.

'When Simon was killed, I'd already realised that what I wanted in life was a stable relationship, but I couldn't contemplate that in marriage when women didn't turn me on in any way. Like David, I envied heterosexual men who could marry and have a family as I, too, would've loved to have kids. But kids grow up and often seem to be a disappointment to their parents, so perhaps that was an illusion, too.

'Then when I was a reporter I saw so many distressing cases of matrimonial breakdowns, and the havoc they caused to wives and children, let alone to fathers, I began to think I was better off being single, even if it meant loneliness at times. Then I had the trauma of losing Guy, and felt that life might be easier without the stress of a relationship at all, and I ceased to envy heterosexual men. In my heart, though, I still really wanted love and commitment to another man, which eventually came with David. No, I don't regret being born gay. It's your turn now, Angela. We've bared our souls, what about you?'

'I was never cut out for matrimony. I've never been maternal, or longed for kids, and even if I'd been straight I rather doubt if I'd have made much of a mother – or a wife for that matter. I'm far too strongly opinionated, and think that I'm always right, and that wouldn't have gone down well with a man. I expect there'd have been a lot of arguments if he was the kind of man I might have married – a strong character. If I'd married a mouse, that wouldn't have suited me either, as it would have been no fun living with a man who agreed with me all the time. I'm far better off with Janet, as we're both strong characters with some soft sides to our natures. If we do have a row we always patch it up quickly, as we do need one another just as you two do. So I'm perfectly happy with my sexuality, thanks.'

'I suppose it all boils down to whether you're lucky enough to meet the right one early enough in life,' I said. 'When I hear of gay men who've never experienced a happy relationship – perhaps because they've always set their sights too high – I realise how astonishing it is that I've actually met three men with whom I'd have gladly spent the whole of my life.'

'That's because you're such a nice caring person, and good-looking into the bargain,' David said. 'It probably wouldn't have been so easy if you were short and ugly. Many gay men are terribly influenced by looks, instead of taking time to assess the character behind the face, or the body for that matter. They look for perfection, and if they don't see it they scamper off and try to find it elsewhere. The result can be that they never do find love, and end up embittered, disillusioned and self-centred, haunting gay bars and clubs every night for easy sex.'

'You're right about looks, David. Janet and I wouldn't have been together all this time if I'd been swayed by looks when we first met, as she certainty wouldn't have qualified for the front page of a glossy magazine. There was something about her face that attracted me, because it denoted character and personality. It must have been the same with her as well, as I was certainly no oil painting myself. We took time to get to know each other, and found that we had interests in common, quite apart from being attracted to other women.

'When we were living together in London, we were too much on top of one another, which is why I moved. To be honest, I was a bit worried as to how we'd get on living together when we retired, but it's worked out well, as we've both mellowed and neither could contemplate life without the other. We've different interests to keep us occupied. Me being here with you for three days is an example. Janet's interested in archaeology, which bores me stiff, and likes to go away on digs, while never in a hundred years would I expect her to want to go away surf bathing. At the end of the day, it's all a matter of give and take.'

'Good,' I said. 'It looks as if we're all three happy gays together then. It's a lovely evening, let's go out for a stroll on the cliff before bed.'

We really missed her when her three days were up.

'I've really enjoyed this tremendously,' she said as we saw her off. 'Thank you both so much. I think we ought to make this an annual visit, don't you?'

We spent another four days of our holiday in London. Recalling how much we'd enjoyed the concert and the opera in San Francisco, and our resolution then to try to get a bit more entertainment into our lives, we thought that we'd give London a try. David knew it a lot better than I did, having been brought up in the suburbs, whereas I only knew it from going to meetings and conferences, and the three days I'd spent there with Cynthia and Jack. He enjoyed showing me the sights, and we went to concerts or the theatre every night, starting with a Beethoven concert at the Albert Hall.

The highlight on our last evening was seeing the Matthew Bourne production of *Swan Lake* with its gay undertones, and fabulous dancing by the male swans to Tchaikovsky's magnificent score.

'We'll just have to see that again,' David said as we came out. 'It's so moving and the music is terrific. I feel I could go back and see it again tomorrow.'

'You can't do that, I'm afraid, as we're off home, in case you've forgotten. But I'd love to see it again. Perhaps it'll come to Bristol if it goes on tour. We must remember to watch out for it.' The trip to London was such a success that we decided to do it again the following year.

Autumn turned into winter, and soon another year had gone by, and I was back in Oxford for the conference. I realised with a pang of remorse that we'd never fitted in the visit with Arnold that I'd promised him the previous year. I'd thought about it once or twice, but one or other of us always seemed too busy to fit it in.

I rang him. 'Arnold, it's Mark here. I've a terribly guilty conscience that we never came up to see you last year as I said we would. We always seemed to have so much going on that we never managed to find a date. How are you? I do hope things are going all right.'

'Apart from getting bloody old, I'm more or less OK. Lots of things are going wrong with the bodywork, and I'm getting dreadfully lame, but at least the brain still seems to be functioning reasonably well. Are you coming to see me?'

'I'm afraid not this time, as I've got to get back after lunch on Tuesday, but I promise that we'll come up to visit you as soon as the evenings get lighter in April. David sends his best regards, by the way.'

'Sorry you won't be able to make it, as it would have been lovely to have seen you. If you don't ring me by early April, I'll be ringing you. Give my love to David.'

'I will. Look after yourself, and be good!'

Chapter Eleven

In the middle of March, I had a letter from Andrew at the BBC to say that he'd got a series of three programmes on the drawing board about growing crops for renewable energy. Would I be interested in chairing them? They'd start in May and go out at fortnightly intervals. Daniel had once raised the question of growing oilseed rape on the farm if biodiesel seemed likely to get off the ground. The programmes would be a good opportunity to learn more about it, so I readily agreed.

The first one centred on getting bioethanol from cereal crops, which was being done in America. I thought this might help us if it increased the price of wheat. I came away from that one disappointed as it appeared that the Government was highly unlikely to invest the capital to get processing plants off the ground. The second one was about rape for biodiesel which looked more promising, though it was not of much interest to me personally as we'd decided it would be a risky crop to grow under our conditions. The third one was on other crops that might be grown to provide energy, though none of them seemed a likely starter because of transport or processing costs.

I had to admit that I hadn't learnt a great deal from the programmes, but it was good to get back into a TV studio again and to meet some of the others taking part, and if nothing else it gave me material for a couple of articles in the paper.

At the end of April, we'd finally managed to fit in the visit to Arnold at Oxford, meeting him for lunch at a country pub just outside the city. He appeared more lame than he'd been when I'd seen him fifteen months before, but otherwise was the same lively, rather extrovert character, so easy to get on with.

We did a tour of some of the colleges, including his own, and it was fascinating to hear first-hand historical details about buildings that I'd admired in the past, but about which I knew nothing. He was an inspiring guide with all sorts of amusing stories about Oxford characters from the past.

David was clearly impressed, though he couldn't get himself to admit that Oxford was better than his own Cambridge. Arnold, who'd been at Cambridge before moving to Oxford, had to agree that there were certainly some outstanding buildings in Cambridge such as King's College chapel and the Backs, but that was about the lot. Oxford had more depth to it, and was a much better place to live, with a surrounding countryside of greater interest and beauty. Exhausted by sightseeing, we drove back to Arnold's house for tea.

'What's it like being nearly ninety? Don't you get bored now that you can't get around like you used to?' David asked him as we sat down.

'Not really. Time still seems to go remarkably fast. You just have to learn to accept that you can't do the things you used to do. John and I used to just jump into the car and go off up to London to the theatre, or drive down to Cardiff for lunch with friends. I'd still like to be able to do it even though it wouldn't be the same without him. But I keep fairly busy with reading and writing. The essential thing above all others is to keep the brain active, and then to some extent the body looks after itself – or that's my philosophy, anyhow.

'I've still got some gay friends from long ago, and they need to talk on the phone sometimes. One has just lost his partner after forty years, and needs comforting. Having been through that myself, I think I've been able to help him a little.'

'Do you still miss John?' David asked him.

'Yes, just as much as ever. You can't be together with someone for nearly fifty years without them becoming part of you. You just don't realise how much you love them till suddenly they're no longer there. Of course he's still there in a way, as he comes back into my thoughts several times a day, and I talk to him most nights. I can't see him or feel him, but he has come back to me four times now through different mediums, so I know that he's still concerned about me, which I find comforting. That saying, "To live in hearts of those we leave behind is not to die," is one of the truest – and most consoling things – ever written.'

'It's marvellous that you're able to keep his memory alive like that,' I said. 'When I lost Simon in that accident, I still felt that somehow he was close to me and concerned with what I was doing. Then as time went on and I became very busy in my job, he came back less often. I felt that he was happy when I met Guy, for he more or less disappeared then. I suppose he realised that I didn't need him, until Guy left me, and I became aware of him again. It's the same now I've got David. It's silly, but there it is.'

'No. It's not silly. I can quite understand how you feel about it. Once you've really loved someone, it never completely leaves the system. I'm too old now ever to find someone to love again, so I'll have John there till my time comes, when I can only hope we'll be together again. But that's enough of that. It's been lovely to have someone to talk to. It's one of the disadvantages of living in a heterosexual world that there is no one to talk to about intimate things. I just hope that you and David will have as long together as we had.'

We could have gone on much longer, and I felt desperately sorry for Arnold. But he was such a resilient character that we both felt he could cope pretty well on his own. It was probably better, if one of them had to go first, that it was John, as he'd have been left terribly adrift if Arnold had gone first.

'Thanks so much, Arnold,' I said. 'It's been a wonderful day for us, and I hope you've enjoyed it as much as we have. Do come down and stay with us for a couple of days before the old legs pack up on you. A change would do you good. We'd come and fetch you.'

'I'd love to, but I don't really like going away now. Perhaps I could give you a ring if I wanted to change my mind.'

We both gave him a big hug as we left, to show him we really cared.

In June that year, Charlotte came over from San Diego, and David took a week's holiday to show her round. She stayed with me in the bungalow as there was more room there than in David's flat. I had to leave him to play the host on some days as I was tied up with meetings, but did find time to go with them on longer trips to the Eden Project, and the hidden gardens of Heligan, to Polzeath where we bathed, and to other tourist attractions. She was the easiest of guests to entertain, with her enthusiasm and extrovert nature.

She thought it would be her last visit, as the macular degeneration in her eyes was slowly getting worse, but she gave us orders to report back in San Diego the following year. We really missed her when she had gone, as she entertained us as much as we did her.

As David had already used up a week of his holiday, we didn't take our own car abroad that September, but did a fly/drive ten-day holiday to Zurich. We explored parts of Switzerland we didn't know and travelled down to Lake Garda, but still finding time for two days in our usual room at Bellagio. It was just as attractive as ever, and it felt nice to be welcomed at the hotel as Arnold and John had been, though we would never equal their record of visits.

All through that year, David seemed to be finding more time for golf than I could manage, and was getting quite hooked on the game. He'd made a few friends at the club, and played in competitions, and had got down to a handicap of fifteen, which was good considering the time that he'd been playing the game. I played with him mostly at weekends, and took out enough cards to get a handicap of eighteen, which was unlikely to get any lower unless I played a lot more. But I enjoyed the recreation without ever becoming as enthusiastic as he was.

Having handicaps meant that we were able to play on some of the better courses. One day that autumn, we took a day off to play a round on the course at Daymer that had first given us the idea of taking up the game. It turned out to be a wonderful seaside course, quite different from our own, and kept in excellent condition.

'That was a marvellous experience,' David said as we drove home. 'It was even better than I expected, and the views of the estuary and the sea were brilliant. I think it must be just as good as those two we saw in California. We must come down again and play in the spring – if we can afford it, that is. It's pretty pricey compared with ours at home, isn't it?'

'Yes, but it's worth it once in a while. It's just such an attractive setting apart from the quality of the course. I'll bet it's tough in a south-west gale like the one we had that day when we first stayed at Polzeath. We'd better pick our day carefully when we come down next time.'

It was in November when the phone rang just as I was shaving. I hardly recognised the voice as David's – it was so croaky.

'Mark, you couldn't come over, could you? I'm feeling awful. I had a dreadful night and I'm sure I must be running a temperature. It's probably only flu, but I'll ring the doctor as soon as the surgery is open. I've never felt so ill before.'

'I'll be right over as soon as I've finished breakfast. Just stay in bed and keep warm and ring the doctor.'

He looked dreadful when I got to the flat, with a flushed face and a very hot forehead, and a temperature of 102°F. He'd not felt quite right the previous day, and had begun to feel really ill just before going to bed. He had hardly slept, and coughed a lot during the night. He just felt terrible and couldn't bear the thought of food. I made him a cup of tea, and helped him to the bathroom, and while he was washing, rang up his surgery to say he was unlikely to be at work for several days.

The doctor's diagnosis was flu, and he was put on antibiotics to cope with possible secondary infections. It was the first time either of us had been ill since we'd met, and I was frightened that night when his temperature went up to 103°F and he still wouldn't eat. I spent the night in his spare room listening for any untoward sounds, and worrying about pneumonia, and how it could kill people, until I drifted off into a fitful sleep. By the morning his temperature had dropped by two degrees, and he managed to get down some bread and milk, which I remembered Mother giving me once as a boy. By the evening he got down a little boiled fish and milk pudding, and his temperature was down to 99°F. I took him back to the bungalow on the third day until he could find his feet again, but it was another ten days before he was fit to work.

'Thank you, Mark dear, for looking after me like that. I really thought I might die that first night, and I think I might have done if you'd not come to the rescue. You'd make a wonderful nurse if you were ever looking for a second career.'

'You'd have done the same for me if it had been the other way round. But you did give me a fright when your temperature went up on the first night, and I was afraid you'd got pneumonia. I realised then just how much you meant to me, and how devastating it'd be if I ever lost you.'

'I kept thinking of that, too, and how alone you'd be if anything happened to me. Thank goodness it didn't, so let's forget about it. The thing now is to get fit again and back to work.'

Not long after he'd taken over from me Daniel had joined the local branch of the National Farmers' Union, and after only three years they'd elected him as chairman, which gave him a seat on the county executive committee. His experience of leadership, which had started with being captain of his school rugby XV, followed by chairing the agricultural club at university had equipped him well for public work. He needed more intellectual challenge than that provided by just running the farm – rather as I had. Unlike his grandfather he seemed to enjoy committee work and trying to influence policy through debate and reasoned argument. He may have got some of this from his father's family of businessmen having inherited genes that promoted executive ability, which blended well with those from our down-to-earth family. Whether that was so or not, he was developing into an assured and confident personality who seemed likely to go far in public life.

Within two years of joining the county executive, he'd been elected as a county delegate to the national council in London, which entailed visits to the capital, and speaking engagements in the county.

I was well aware of the risk that things might begin to get neglected on the farm if he were away too much, so we came to an agreement that I'd try to be around to keep an eye on things if he was to be off the farm for more than a day at a time. It did mean that I was having to spend more time on the farm, for example getting out in the morning to organise the day's work, than I did following him taking over. I didn't mind this, as I was now getting fewer speaking engagements, and the men in charge of the three main units on the farm – the dairy, the arable and the calf unit at Barnfield – were all very competent by now. But it was still important to have someone there to take spot decisions and to maintain an impression of corporate unity. As time went on, Daniel got more involved with farming politics, but if he was planning on being away he always left me with a list of jobs to be done. There was no question of me taking over a managerial role again, and he remained the boss.

Anyhow, I had my own work to keep me comfortably busy, as the FWAG committee was becoming a bigger job, as more farmers became aware of environmental issues and the possibility that there might be payments in the future. The college committee was facing problems with the sharp fall in the numbers of workers on the land which was leading to fewer students applying for college places. It was going to mean change and diversification.

I had known for some years that there was a national award for farmers who had made a marked contribution to the conservation of wildlife on farms, as my committee had been invited to send in the names of anyone in the county they might think worthy of an award. I'd never considered this for our own farm until the secretary of the committee told me that some of the members thought that I ought to allow my name to go forward, in view of what we'd done at home and more recently at Barnfield. I was reluctant to agree as I didn't want to be nominated and then turned down. I asked Daniel what he thought and he was very keen that I should agree to be nominated.

So I told the secretary of the committee to go ahead and put our name forward, and thought no more about it. Then a couple of months later we received a large form on which we had to detail everything we'd done over the years – from the digging out of the first pond. It turned out to be quite an impressive list when it also included what we had more recently been doing at Barnfield.

About a couple of months later we got a letter from the organisers of the scheme to say that we had been placed on a shortlist and would be visited by three judges in July. I was pleased to see that I knew one of these, whom I'd met a couple of times at Oxford.

They duly arrived and spent nearly a whole day going round the two farms. I gave them the most recent report on the bird populations from the university biologist, which had shown a small increase in numbers on the home farm, but nothing as yet at Barnfield. This seemed to impress them, as did the nature trail, which was now getting established. Janet put on a good lunch for them, and altogether it was an excellent day and we felt quite optimistic.

It was a disappointment when we heard about two months later that the award had gone to a farm in Yorkshire, and that we had come second. I was then rung up by the judge I knew, who told me that it was a very close decision, and that we ought to apply next year, when he implied he thought that we'd get it.

This we did, and after another full inspection from a slightly different set of judges, we were given the award. That meant a trip to London for Daniel, Janet and me for an excellent lunch and the formal presentation of what was called the Silver Lapwing Award. The only snag was that it meant I had to make a speech after the presentation by a member of the Royal family. Thirty years earlier, I'd have been terrified at the prospect, but the shy young man that Simon had brought out into the world had changed a lot since then, and it was not much of an ordeal.

The sequel was that two years later I was invited to become a national judge myself, which involved a most enjoyable week travelling all over Britain to assess shortlisted farms. It provided an opportunity to see parts of the country I'd never visited before, and in addition to pick up some useful tips to take home. It involved a three-year stint as a judge, and it was one of the most rewarding jobs I ever did.

A constant threat hanging over the farm was the risk of the cows becoming infected with bovine tuberculosis. This had been spreading rapidly in the South West, after having nearly been conquered in the sixties. The sad thing was that it was never quite eradicated, and the infection spread into the local badger populations which were increasing rapidly as a result of protective legislation. This had been introduced largely as a result of a series of television programmes depicting them as nice cuddly little animals with pretty faces.

I knew otherwise. Coming home late one evening from a meeting, I hit one in the car. I went back with a flashlight to see it lying apparently dead in the middle of the road. As I bent down to move it to the verge, it suddenly reared up, and would have had my fingers off, or even my hand, if I hadn't snatched it away. Luckily I was left with only a slight graze on one finger. Badgers have lethal teeth and jaws, and are certainly not nice-tempered cuddly pets. We kept a very close watch for any signs of them encroaching on the farm, and if they had moved in, I'd have been sorely tempted to gas them in their burrows in the dead of night when no one was looking.

Barnfield was ring-fenced by roads, so there was no risk of infection from neighbours' cattle. But at home one field had a common fence with a next-door neighbour, so I told Daniel to erect another fence on our side to keep the cattle well apart.

I'd written about the problem twice in my fortnightly articles, and received support from a considerable number of correspondents. These I sent to the Department of Farming and Rural Affairs, as the Ministry of Agriculture was now called, asking for stricter legislation to control the disease, but all to no effect.

When Daniel and I had completed our last review of future policy, we had decided that we'd finally dispose of the sheep flock, which had never made much of a contribution to the overall profits. It took up quite a lot of Daniel's and my time, and Stephen, who had acted as part-time shepherd for so long, was coming up to retirement. Now that we were milking far more cows, there were enough cattle being born to graze the steeper fields which we were unable to plough for cropping, as well as the new land at Barnfield.

If we were going to continue with sheep, we'd have to triple the size of the flock to about 1,000 ewes so as to justify employing a full-time shepherd, and neither of us thought it would be worth it. I was sorry to see the sheep go, as they'd been part of the farm for the whole of my life, but times change, and small enterprises didn't fit in with the modern world of specialised production. As we were now inseminating half the herd with semen from bulls of a beef breed, there would be something like 120 beef-type cattle to be finished for the market each year, if we kept all the calves, rearing them to start with at Barnfield. So when we had weaned the lambs off the ewes that summer, we sold the flock in time for the new owner to get them into lamb in the autumn. It wasn't until they were gone that we realised just how much time we'd been spending on them.

In September that year we spent the whole of our holiday in Switzerland, mainly exploring areas that we'd not visited before. David, with his new enthusiasm for golf, wanted to spend a day watching the Swiss Championship at Crans-sur-Sierre on the spectacular course in the mountains, with its fabulous background of the snow on the Eiger and the Jungfrau.

'That's about it,' he said. 'I thought Pebble Beach in California and the course at Daymer had it all, but this is quite magnificent. We must put our clubs in the car another year and come and play here. Just look at that view. It's quite breathtaking. I bet the ball goes miles in the thin air up at this altitude.'

'It'd be quite an idea, and we could play on some other courses, too. I've always wanted to explore that one up at the back of Menaggio in Italy. There are probably some other good ones around if we knew where they were.' We made a good resolution to take our clubs another year.

On the way back, we put in three days at Interlaken at the 'boys'' hotel on the lakeside, and drove up the valley to Grindelwald. I retraced our steps of thirty years before from the end of the ski lift at First. I found the identical spot where Simon and I had eaten our lunch and speculated about the future. It was a perfect day and nothing seemed to have changed except that far more tourists walked the mountain path. This time, the sun shone continuously and no dark cloud and cold wind blew up to presage a disaster as had happened on that occasion.

'I wonder what would have happened if Simon hadn't been killed in that accident,' I said to David as we lay side by side after lunch enjoying one of the most spectacular mountain panoramas in the world. 'Do you think he and I might still be together?'

'Pretty unlikely, I expect. Passionate first adolescent love affairs seldom stand the test of time. You'd have been separated fairly soon by getting jobs, possibly distant from one another, and as you found with Guy, it would have been difficult to have maintained a close relationship. You might have remained faithful, just meeting up now and again and having an occasional holiday together, but from what you've said about him, I rather suspect that Simon would have felt the need for more frequent sexual activity than that.'

'You're probably right. In a way, he was rather more highly sexed than I was. He was certainly more experienced, so he'd have needed more, just like Guy did, though I don't think he'd have hankered after a quiet domestic life, which is why Guy left me.'

'Possibly not. It's difficult to speculate. People like us are all so different in what we want from sex – and life – for that matter. You've only got to look at the gay scene to realise that. We seem to vary from the wildly promiscuous who don't understand the word commitment and have no desire to settle down, to those like us who are perfectly content with sharing every aspect of our lives together, and to whom one's partner's life and happiness is just as important as one's own.'

'I suppose if Simon had found someone else when we were living apart, it's possible that we might still have met up from time to time. We might have had the same kind of arrangement that Arnold and John had, whereby they allowed each other latitude for extramarital sex. I feel sure that Simon would still have wanted to be with me occasionally. I hope so, anyhow.'

'And what would have happened then after you'd come back to the farm, and met me? Would you have been so ready to jump into bed with me, or would you have regarded me as just another vet looking after your cows?'

'Gosh, I hadn't thought of that. It would certainly have been a complication. I suppose, in a way, it would have depended on how close Simon and I still were. If we had still been close, I would have just thought to myself, Blimey, he's nice looking. I wouldn't mind going to bed with him, and I'd have looked forward to you coming to the farm so that I could fantasise about how nice it would be to have you in my arms.

'But if I was only seeing him very occasionally, I'd certainly have fallen for you, as I'd have been more hungry for sex and in need of a full-time partner again. I would then probably have sought a dispensation from you to be free to see him very occasionally, as he would have had sought from his then-partner, presumably. Would you have given it to me?'

'Of course, I would, though I might have been a bit jealous. I'd never have risked losing you because you wanted to spend a night in bed with an old flame now and again. I love you far too much for that. Thankfully, the situation never arose.'

'Thank you, my love, for that, and thank you for making my life the happy thing it is.' As no one was looking, we held hands for a few moments, savouring one of those moments that stays in the memory for ever. A moment of complete togetherness in a wonderfully scenic setting.

We were just into the new millennium when an official-looking letter dropped on the mat one morning. It was from the Prime Minister's office. In rather flowery language, it said that he had been considering the names of those who had been nominated as worthy of recognition for a contribution to some sector of industry or public life. He would like to submit my name to the Queen for the award of Officer of the British Empire for services to environmental conservation. Was I willing for my name to be submitted? I knew perfectly well that the PM, who was probably then flying off to Japan or New York, had nothing to do with it, and that the decision had been taken by a small group gathered together in a dusty Whitehall office.

But I was flattered all the same that someone should have put my name forward to Downing Street, though I couldn't think who it could have been. Perhaps it was the Lord Lieutenant, a prominent landowner in the county, whom I'd met a couple of times, and whose estate we'd visited for a Farming and Wildlife meeting.

I didn't particularly want the honour, but it would have been churlish to refuse it after someone had recommended me, so I wrote off accepting nomination.

About two months later I was commanded to present myself, accompanied by two guests if I so desired, at Buckingham Palace on a certain date. The two guests presented a bit of a problem, as I would have liked to have taken David as one of them. Rather reluctantly I decided it would have to be Daniel and Janet, as she was already involved in running the nature trail, and anyhow it was the sort of occasion a woman would love.

'I'm so sorry, David, I would have loved to take you as one of my guests, but I think it's really a family affair. You do understand, don't you?'

'Of course you must take Daniel and Janet to a do like that. It's a family thing. In any case, it'd hardly be the done thing to take your boyfriend to meet the Queen would it? Naturally I'd have enjoyed being there, but I'll come over to supper when you get back and you can tell me all about it, and we might celebrate in an appropriate way afterwards.'

The three of us went up to London the night before, and stayed in the hotel where David and I stayed when we went up for our concert or theatre trips. I picked up a hired morning suit complete with a top hat from a well-known outfitter before going to the theatre to see a musical which I thought Janet would like.

They separated us as soon as we got into the inner courtyard at the Palace, and it seemed a long wait for the recipients sitting in the ballroom before things got moving. I found myself sitting with a rather dull civic dignitary from the North on one side, and a motor racing driver whose name was vaguely familiar on the other. Fortunately the latter was easy to talk to, so the time passed quickly.

We had the Prince of Wales doing the honours, as the Queen was abroad on a foreign tour. He'd obviously been well briefed beforehand, as he congratulated me on what I was doing for conservation in the West Country, and said he read my articles from time to time. I really felt that I had arrived, so to speak.

Daniel took us to lunch at the Farmers' Club, which he'd joined recently to provide him with a base on his increasingly frequent visits to London for meetings. To round off the day David came over to supper to get the low-down on the day, and we went to bed to celebrate.

Whether this award had anything to do with it or not I was unsure, but within six months of getting it I received another official letter – this time from the Department of the Environment. For some time, there had been a lot of debate in the Commons about future sources of renewable energy in the light of carbon emissions from fossil fuels and their influence on global warming. There was also the question of how long it would be before supplies of fossil fuel ran out. The Government had shilly-shallied for a long time, but had finally agreed under pressure to set up a Committee of Inquiry to make recommendations for future action.

The letter said that the committee of sixteen would consist largely of scientists whose research was concerned with different aspects of the problem, but the Environment Minister wished to have two farmer members: one from the East, where it was anticipated that most energy-providing crops would be grown, and one from the West, where wind or wave power might be possible sources of renewable energy. My name had been suggested as a suitable member from the West, among one or two others. Would I be willing to serve if my name were to be approved when it went to higher authority? It was anticipated that the enquiry would take about two years, and it would involve meeting in London for a day each month.

This came right out of the blue, and I was very uncertain as to whether I should take it on. I was not a scientist, and was no expert on the subject, though I'd picked up quite a lot of information through chairing the various TV programmes. I might find myself completely out of my depth when it came to scientific discussions between professors. On the other hand it would clearly be very important that farmers' views should be heard, and I might be able to bring a certain amount of commonsense into it if discussions became too airy fairy.

'What do you think I should do, David?' I asked when he came up to treat some cows next day. 'I do feel there's a serious risk of finding myself out of my depth with a lot of scientific boffins arguing among themselves over my head.'

'I don't see why you should feel that. They're only human beings like the rest of us and, after all, you've had to deal with quite a number of them when interviewing them on your programmes, and you've never come unstuck. I think you should accept.'

'Of course you must take it on,' Daniel said when I asked him what he thought. 'It's terribly important that we get farmers' voices heard on every possible occasion. You probably know as much about it as any other farmer they could find, and a lot more than most. After all, you've been writing about things like this for years, and you're well known from your TV programmes. I'd say you're just right for the job, and you'd be excellent at bringing some of the more extreme so-called experts down to earth as you've got bags of common sense and you're not afraid to express your opinions. You simply must accept.'

On the strength of their opinions, I wrote to say that I'd be willing to serve, and got a letter back to say that I'd been appointed. The meetings were held in a government office in Whitehall, and fortunately did not start until eleven o'clock, so I was able to catch an early train up and get back home the same day. I wouldn't have wanted to spend a night in London each time. There was always a mass of papers to read before each meeting so the journey passed quickly.

For the first two meetings, I felt like a new boy on his first day at school, in the presence of a phalanx of distinguished scientists, all of whom seemed to know each other already. They obviously wondered who this stranger from the backwoods was, and what he was doing there at all. My fellow farmer, who came from East Riding in Yorkshire, admitted to me over lunch at the second meeting that he felt out of his depth to begin with.

He was a typical Yorkshireman, plain speaking, and very much down to earth, but not too dogmatic. I came to value his opinions, often delivered with a minimum of words, very highly. He'd had a long experience of committee work, and came straight to the point every time. We both found some of the woolly and meandering statements of one or two of the scientists hard to bear. They never seemed to commit themselves to a definite opinion, but always hedged them round with ifs and buts. Every so often, my colleague would intervene in a typical Yorkshire accent with: 'Mr Chairman, can we get back to the point at issue, please?'

After a couple of meetings, when we had got to know each other better, especially over the buffet lunch which was provided, things became much easier. I felt more confident in expressing my own views, especially on subjects such as wind power, which had become a hot topic in the South West. Daniel and I had looked at the possibility for increasing income from a wind farm at Barnfield, with its relatively exposed position. We had decided against it for two reasons. First, there would have been a lot of opposition on scenic grounds, and I didn't want to upset our neighbours. Second, I felt that the turbines might adversely affect the build-up of the wildlife on the farm which I was trying to establish. I hadn't any evidence about this, but just had a hunch that birds might be discouraged by the whirring of the blades – or be hit by them. A third reason, of course, was that I didn't want them close to my house, either. So we decided against it.

The evidence for using crops as a source of energy was very compelling, especially in view of the surpluses of cereals that had built up and which were responsible for the low prices we were getting for them. If we could use the land for growing non-food crops, it would reduce surpluses significantly and give farmers the chance to grow crops that were not subject to the whims and pressures of international markets. The evidence showed that Britain was lagging far behind some other EU countries in growing rape for biodiesel, for example. The two of us managed to persuade the other members that if Britain were to meet its commitments for reducing carbon emissions, the growing of crops for energy would be essential – which was one of the recommendations made in the final report.

Often I would look at waves breaking when we bathed, and I'd think to myself, if only we could harness all that power in the sea, as tides come in and out, we could surely solve our energy problems at one fell swoop. Just as mountainous countries used their rivers to generate hydroelectric power, why couldn't we use our sea to do the same? When our committee was hearing evidence on using water as a source of energy, I made a strong plea for much more money to be spent on research. The experts assured us that the technical problems were immense, even in an obvious case like the Severn Bore in the West Country. Perhaps they were right, but I couldn't help thinking that those problems might be solved if more effort could be put into it. I felt certain that one day wave power would become a major contributor.

The two years of the enquiry passed quickly by, and when it ended we somehow felt deprived. It was a bit like closing down a club of which we had all become close active members, especially over the buffet lunches, where we had got to know each other personally. Even one or two of the professors who at the start had seemed aloof became human and friendly.

From the farming angle the report came down strongly in support of building a number of processing plants for crops such as rape and wheat, perhaps with a mixture of private and public financing, to provide energy – rather as it had done eighty years before to stimulate the nascent sugar beet industry. When it came to wind power, we stipulated that future plants should be built offshore, and that research be initiated to find out if such platforms could be used to harness power from the sea at the same time. We were less enthusiastic about getting energy from very bulky crops, since the cost and waste of energy in getting them to processing plants might outweigh the advantages of an initially cheap source. In all we made twenty recommendations, most of which were accepted by the Government.

It was fortunate that, by the time it was published, more scientific evidence of melting glaciers and global warming had become available, so the powers that be were more ready to take notice of it. At the end of the day, we felt that we'd done a good job, and I had no regrets that I'd agreed to play a part in it. Having inside knowledge on some of the topics we covered proved very useful for my press articles. It had involved many hours of reading scientific jargon, much of it conjectural, because hard facts were still difficult to come by. It also illustrated how contradictory the views of so-called experts can be, but I'd learnt that lesson as a young reporter listening to expert witnesses in court cases many years before. Overall, I had enjoyed the experience, but was glad to be free of monthly trips to London.

Chapter Twelve

Four more years passed by at an astonishing speed. I'd always assumed that time would drag with advancing age, but the reverse was proving to be the case, and here I was in my late fifties still feeling about thirty. David, two years older than me, had had nearly enough of his quite stressful job, and decided to pack it in when he was sixty. He would have a good pension and money left by his parents, so he'd be comfortably off. When the time came, he got a part-time voluntary job with a charity in Norton to keep his brain working. That, and golf three days a week, kept him occupied.

I didn't have time for that, but we always tried to get a game together at the weekend. He had developed into a useful player with a handicap of ten, but, with less time to play, I never got any better than sixteen.

We had maintained our enthusiasm for surf bathing, and contrived to spend a week at Polzeath each year, where Angela would join us for three days. Each time she'd say it was her last because she was getting too old, but come next year she'd be back. We thought that part of her pleasure was being in the company of men for a time, as a change from Janet. Once again, we'd discussed buying a bungalow in the area, which we could let out to visitors when we weren't there, but prices were ridiculously high and it didn't seem worth the hassle. David said that he wouldn't want to use it if I were not there, so we abandoned the idea.

We discovered that the owners of the large house in the trees under the big round hill at the centre of the Daymer golf course had converted a number of outbuildings into holiday flats. The previous spring we'd booked one of these for a week, and looked after ourselves. It was cheaper than staying in the hotel, and was convenient for the golf course, though we did miss the sound of the sea and the view.

On the farm we were being faced with possible changes in the Common Agricultural Policy of the EU, which, if they came, would do away with farm subsidies on growing crops in favour of a system of making a single annual payment based on farm size, with additional payments for doing things to improve the environment. Neither Daniel nor I thought that this would make much difference to our farm profits, as we'd be well qualified to benefit fully from any environmental payments that were going. By good management of the breeding policy and more efficient grazing Daniel and Ian had continued to increase the milk yields each year. This was just as well, since the price we got for the milk was considerably less that it had been when I was in charge.

The year before we had reorganised the beef production and converted the buildings behind Ian's house, which had previously been used for rearing calves, into a new unit. Here we kept the pure-bred Holstein bull calves that we had hoped might be female. We did not castrate them, but fattened them up for what was being called 'bull beef'. With the number of visitors that we had to the farm it would not be safe to let a bunch of growing bulls graze out in the field. So they were kept in strawed yards and fed a high-energy diet from the mixer wagon that was used to feed the dairy cows.

It was quite an expensive ration to feed but they grew very fast, getting up to the right weight for slaughter at about twelve months of age. They produced very lean meat, which is what supermarkets were demanding for their customers, and Daniel negotiated a lucrative contract with one of the big four to provide eighty well-finished carcases each year.

The other crossbred male calves were castrated and finished on a conventional grazing system at about two years of age. This utilised the grass formerly grazed by the sheep, and gave a more reliable financial return. What on earth would grandfather have thought about all this intensive farming if he could return to Earth? I think Dad would have been a bit surprised, too, though I felt sure they'd both approve of what we were doing, as they had both been expansionists in their time. Even I was astonished at how fast farming had changed within my short lifetime.

David and I made another trip to the States to stay with

Charlotte, who'd moved into an apartment nearer the centre of the city with a fine view of the harbour. Sadly, her eyes had deteriorated further, but the General was still in excellent form, and appeared to enjoy taking us to places we'd missed on our first visit. This included one excursion across the border into Mexico at Tijuana, a dusty, run-down looking place swarming with tourists, and touts trying to make a living out of them. We were glad to get back into the cleanliness of the USA. From there we 'did' America with a flight over the Grand Canyon, a day in Las Vegas and a return visit to Yosemite. From there it was Washington, the Niagara Falls and three days in New York. We decided we preferred San Francisco.

That proved to be our last visit as, sadly, Charlotte died the following year. It would have been an anticlimax to go back without her vital personality, which had so coloured our view of the States, being there to greet us.

The ten-acre wood and the wide shelter belt at Barnfield had established well by now, and the trees were growing remarkably fast, especially the conifers, in our relatively warm, moist climate. The land, having been well-farmed previously, was in quite a high state of fertility, which helped to speed the growth. All the work that I'd put in since I'd dug the first pond was now beginning to pay off, as we were in the top band for environmental payments, and the annual cost for maintaining the improvements was quite low.

Winning the Silver Lapwing Award five years previously had increased the number of parties that wanted to come round the farms, and the nature trail was also in demand. The small charge we made for parties covered the annual cost of making new noticeboards and signs, and Janet, now that the three children were at school during the day, more or less took over the administration of the trail. I was occupied during the summer months with taking parties round as Daniel was increasingly tied up with his political work. So we were kept busy, and I enjoyed the work, even if it did mean saying the same things over and over again. But the feedback was always different, which kept it interesting, and there would always be testing questions to be answered. Daniel didn't particularly like this sort of work and passed it on to me as often as he could.

Quite a few of the parties were from the general public, and not from farming, and these often proved to be the most interesting. I felt them to be especially important, because getting across to the public and to housewives what farming was all about was bound to be valuable as a public relations exercise, if nothing else.

Janet's family of two boys, Charles and John, and Maud, the eldest, were growing up very fast, as children seem to do nowadays when compared with my generation. The two boys were very different in character, though they got on very well together. They were about as different as Juliet and Caroline had been in our family. Charles had darker hair and a thinner face, and seemed more serious minded, rather as I had been at that age. John was fairer-haired with quite a chubby face, and was full of life as his grandmother had been; he was far the more extrovert of the two. They were now seven and eight years old, and John was already showing an interest in the animals on the farm. He was always asking me to take him up to Barnfield to see the calves being fed. While Charles didn't show a great deal of interest, he was quite content to go along with what his younger brother wanted. He was often happier with a book in his hands than walking the farm.

It was early days yet, but it was beginning to look as if it might be John who'd step into his father's – and his namesake's – shoes when the time came. In any case it was encouraging to think that there might be someone there to carry on the family farming line for yet another generation. Both boys enjoyed going round the new plantings with me in their holidays, and it was fun for me passing on the knowledge of wildlife I'd gained over the years. They loved using the field glasses I carried with me, trying to recognise the different birds and their songs.

It was then that I regretted not having a son, or sons of my own – now my only real regret that I'd been born gay. But then I'd console myself with the thought that, if I'd married, the children might have turned out to be a problem, and not the paragons I had wished for. As it was, I had these two fine boys as surrogates, who had already adopted David as an honorary uncle, which pleased us both. Janet and Daniel seemed very happy for them to spend time with us on their holidays. Maud, being that bit older, already had girlfriends of her own to keep her occupied. Janet had turned out to be a very sensible and caring mother whom they all adored.

On the cliffs near Polzeath, where David and I would often walk in the afternoons after a morning in the sea, we had found a small hollow away from the cliff path where we could lie sheltered from the wind, listening to the sound of the surf on the rocks below. It was there, not long after we'd got back from the States, that David suddenly said:

'Do you think that it might be about time for us to think of living together? It's something we always said we'd discuss when we got older, isn't it? Here I am, approaching sixty and just retired, and you in your late fifties, so what would you think about it?'

'I'd been thinking about it, too. Every time we get back from holiday when we've been very close and sharing a room for a couple of weeks, I do seem to miss you a great deal and feel quite lonely. Then, when you come to think about it, where's the sense in both of us having to get our own meals when we get home in the evenings in our separate houses? It would be nice to be able to share the household chores, just as we do when you come to stay overnight.'

'I felt just the same when we got back this time. I really missed you, and that's when I decided we should think about it again.'

'I've never brought it up, because I thought you wouldn't want to leave your flat and all the personal things you've got there, like books and photos, and that you'd lose some of your independence if you moved in with me. If we did decide to move in together, I think it would have to be in my bungalow, as I'd still need to be on the spot at Barnfield in case of emergencies.'

'Of course, I've always assumed that I'd come to live with you. I'd certainly miss having all my usual things around me after so many years, but losing them would be a small price to pay when set against the other advantages. I wouldn't mind leaving Norton anyhow, as it's getting very crowded, and I'd like living out in the country.'

'I've just had a bright idea which might get over the problem of losing some of your personal life. It'd be quite possible to build an extension to your bedroom out at the side of the bungalow. It would mean losing a bit of the garden, but that bit's not of any value anyhow. Then you could have a sitting room-cum-study of your own, and all your personal things. You could retreat there if you wanted to be on your own and to get away from me for a time. It could be almost like having your own flat still.'

'That's a brilliant idea, Mark. Let's look at it when we get home, and see how it'd fit in. It would get over the feeling of losing independence when living in someone else's house, which has always rather bothered me. But if we do it, you must let me pay for half the cost of the building. I can easily afford it or more, if necessary.'

'It's a generous offer, and I'll certainly accept it, but it'll increase the value of the bungalow, so I'd definitely want to pay part of it. We've always shared everything, so let's agree to go half and half on it, shall we?'

'Yes. I shall obviously miss the flat a bit to start with, but I'd like to live in the country again. I love that big room of yours and the patio on a summer's day with that marvellous view, watching the sun go down. It's my idea of heaven when we're there together.'

'Mine, too.'

So that was that – the major decision in our lives taken at last. I got in touch with the architect who'd done the plans for the first extension five years before. He designed an extension with a bow window jutting out into the garden, which gave David a much wider view, and which fitted in surprisingly well with the rest of the building. It incorporated the former bedroom, and David moved in to sleep in my room. This was quite large enough for two beds, leaving him with a room almost as big as that in his former flat, into which he could fit most of his possessions, so that it still felt like home for him.

In all, it took about six months to complete. It had taken us twenty years to take that final step, but we both felt that we were ready for it. When the move was complete, we commemorated it with a good dinner and a bottle of wine to celebrate our new life together.

As we lay in bed that night, David said: 'Do you remember the first time we met, when I came out to treat those three cows?'

'Of course, I'll never forget it. But why?'

'Well, beforehand, I'd asked one of the partners about your farm, as I always did when going to a new farm so that I'd know roughly what to expect. He said the farmer was a young chap who'd been a journalist and who'd recently come back to take over following the death of his father. He lived with his mother, and they were a very nice family who farmed well. I thought to myself that if he was living with his mother, he might not be married, and I might make friends with him.

'I was feeling very lonely at the time, having only just come down, and realising that the years were passing me by with no one to care for in my life. This youngish farmer might possibly be in the same boat, though it'd be too much to hope for that he might be gay. At least he might be there for friendship, if nothing else. So you see, I was ready for you, in a way.

'When I drove into the yard and saw how good-looking you were, my heart nearly missed a beat. Then I saw you looking straight at me, and you held on to my hand for those few seconds longer than you should have done. I think I knew then that it might be a defining moment in my life.'

'It wasn't me that held on to your hand, it was you holding on to mine, and the stare you gave me told me that it might be possible that you were like me. All the time you were dealing with the cows, I was thinking to myself that this could be it at last. It was just so lucky that you were late, so that I saw you instead of Ian. That gave me the chance to ask you down to lunch so that I could find out more about you. Then you having played squash provided a wonderful excuse for seeing you again. I suppose that sooner or later we might have got together, but it would have taken so much longer. As it was, we were able to get off the mark straight away. By the time you drove off, I knew it could be the real thing for me.'

'I'd decided that before we'd even gone down to lunch, and was trying to think of excuses for meeting you again. Then when I saw your house and met Mother, who was so kind, I was quite determined to keep things moving. When I saw you wave as I drove away, I was already pretty sure about you. Why did you take so long to ring me up about the squash date? I was beginning to think that I might have got it all wrong.'

'It was only three days. I wanted to ring sooner, but I wasn't completely sure about you, and I didn't want to appear to be chasing after you in case it put you off. If I'd been wrong about you, it might have turned you off for ever, and there was no way I could risk that, as I'd already decided that even if you weren't gay, it'd be nice to have you as a friend. You see, I was lonely as well, having only fairly recently come back to Devon myself. Thanks again, love, for being late that day.'

It felt quite strange having him sleeping in my bedroom, for up until then he'd always slept in the spare room when spending the night. But it was good to know he was so close as I drifted off to sleep, and then to awake in the morning to find him there, just as if we were on holiday together. Even better sometimes to be woken up with a cup of early morning tea at the weekend, or to get one for him. It was nice, too, to come down to find breakfast ready on the table instead of having to get it for oneself each day. Married life, if that was what it was, certainly had its advantages.

'How do think it's working out?' I asked him after the first week. 'Have you any regrets?'

'None at all. I can't think why we didn't do it years ago. I don't feel any loss of independence at all, and it's so nice to be able to share everything between us, quite apart from having you there all the time. I realise now how lonely I used to feel sometimes coming back to an empty flat, and having to get down to cooking and the household chores all on my own with no one to talk to about what I'd been doing all day. I just love it here with you. Even if we don't have much to talk about at times, it doesn't matter. We don't really need to talk, as long as we know the other one is there.'

It was soon after David had moved in that the telephone rang one morning just as I was going down to the farm. It was Cynthia.

'Mark, I'm afraid I've got some bad news. Jack died yesterday evening. He was out working in the garden in the morning, and when he didn't come in for lunch I found him collapsed in the rose garden. He was still alive, but it was his heart, and they were unable to stabilise it. He died very peacefully at about six o'clock, and we were there with him when he just drifted away. Thank goodness he didn't linger on, as he would have hated being an invalid.'

'Cynthia, dear, I'm so sorry. You must be devastated. He was such a lovely man, and I was very fond of him. He was always so calm and unruffled, with that nice dry sense of humour, and he was so understanding about Simon and me when we first met. I was so grateful to him for that. I'll always think of him in the garden he loved, and the pair of you together in such a happy marriage. You're bound to miss him terribly, and it's awful that you've had to cope with two sudden deaths of the people you loved. How old was he?'

'He'd have been eighty-six at the end of the month, so he'd had a good run. It was sad that he was never able to see Simon grow up, as he was immensely proud of him in his quiet way. But we still had Margaret and the grandchildren, and the two greats now, which gave him great pleasure.'

'Have you any idea about what you might do now?'

'I certainly shan't want to go on living here alone. It's far too big, and I don't need the garden. We'd already been discussing moving to a smaller place. It's quite possible that Margaret and Harold will take over the house, which would be fine, and I'll try to find a cottage in the village. I don't feel ready for an old people's home just yet.'

'I should think not. You're far too active for that, and I hope you always will be. Will you let me know about the funeral?'

'Of course, perhaps you could give me a ring tomorrow evening. We should know by then.'

The village church was packed, and David and I only just got seats. Inevitably memories came flooding back of the last time I had been in that church, and the dreadful ordeal of Simon's funeral when I had to struggle not to break down. I thought of how I'd suddenly felt his presence during the Principal's address, and how he was laughing at what was being said about him. I thought, too, how lucky I was to have David sitting beside me, who meant as much to me now as Simon had done then. Perhaps if I'd been able to look into the future on that occasion I might have been assured that the life ahead of me was not to be spent in loneliness. It wouldn't have alleviated my grief at the time, but it would have given me more hope for the future.

Cynthia, who I knew was now eighty-three, bore up remarkably well at the funeral, which was attended by many of Jack's professional friends and former clients. At the gathering afterwards Cynthia's daughter Margaret introduced me to her uncle, Will, the one who lived in London that Cynthia had told me about after Simon's death and who was gay. He was a very charming, cultured man in his late seventies; I could well understand why Simon had been very fond of him. It seemed that he was now devoting his life to his older partner, who was suffering from Parkinson's, and needed almost constant attention. He said that David and I must call in to see them when we came up to London next, as he wasn't able to get out much. I promised to come over for lunch with Cynthia as soon as things had settled down.

I did so three weeks later. It was to be the last time that I'd be in the house which held such happy memories, both of Simon and of her. It was good to see that Margaret's family had brought the tennis court back to life again and used it quite a lot. She and her husband had decided to take over the house, and Cynthia had put in an offer for a cottage not too far away which was for sale after an old friend had moved into a nursing home.

'I'll never forget meeting you that first time,' I said as we sat down to lunch. 'I was very nervous as I wanted to make a good impression for Simon's sake. But you made it so easy for me by giving me that hug and a kiss on the cheek. It was something we'd never have done at home where I'd been brought up in a much more formal atmosphere. My family had never entertained much so I was not used to socialising, and was afraid I'd make some stupid mistake that would make you think I came from the backwoods, and was not worthy of Simon's friendship. You and Jack made it easy for me by asking questions about the farm and things like that, so that I was never out of my depth.'

'I guessed you might be a bit shy from what Simon had said about you, but actually you never gave us that impression at all.

You seemed quite at ease, and we were both pleased that you were so nice and presentable, and we could tell that Simon was very fond of you. It was very different from a rather scruffy type that he brought home once, who was brash and loud, whom we didn't like at all. Luckily Simon saw through him and dropped him soon afterwards. We took to you straight away, and were happy for you both, especially when you got the tennis court going again and you taught him to surf, which he loved. It was a comfort to think, after he died, that he'd had a wonderfully happy summer with you.'

'It was certainly quite unforgettable, as was the way in which you made me feel part of the family. That meant an awful lot to him. I know that, as he told me so during the holiday. I almost felt as though I'd got two mothers.'

'So how are things with David? Are you living together yet?'

'Yes, but only recently. We built an extension on to the room he used as a bedroom, and it's given him a large sitting room where he has all his things from the flat, so that it still feels like home for him. He can bury himself there when he feels like it. It seems to be working amazingly well, as we're still in love and always will be now. I've still got a lot of work on, especially with Daniel getting so involved with farming politics, and I need to be back on the farm more. David plays golf about three times a week, and does some time with a charity in Norton, so we're not on top of each other all the time. Then we go surfing in the summer and abroad most years for a fortnight's holiday. I never dreamed that I could be so happy after losing both Simon and Guy.'

'Do you ever hear from Guy? We did like him, too, that time you brought him over to see us, and felt so sorry for you when it broke up.'

'No. We agreed to make it a complete break, so as to be fair to his new partner. But I did make him promise to ring me up if he ever lost Peter. I've still got very tender feelings towards him, and would love to see him again, and to know whether he's happy. It wouldn't get in the way of my love for David, and I think we could still be friends, but it's probably better left as it is.

'Now, what about you? It must be terrible for you after so many years with Jack beside you. How are you coping?'

'I do feel dreadfully lonely, of course. The evenings and nights are the worst time. I do miss having someone to talk to about what I've been doing during the day, and what I'm planning for tomorrow, and an occasional kiss and cuddle, and not having him sleeping beside me at night. When you're young, you don't think that things like that are going to mean anything when you're old. It's just not true, as they are really just as important, if not more so, as you get older.

'One of the worst things is the feeling that you've got absolutely nothing to look forward to but old age and infirmity which you'll have to face alone. I'm a lot luckier than some as I've got Margaret and the grandchildren quite close, and they've been marvellous, but they've got their own lives to lead, so I can't expect too much of them. I suppose I'll settle to a routine in time. Most widows seem to, so there's no reason why I shouldn't. You can't really share grief, as I'm sure you realised when Simon died.'

'I'm sure it won't be long before other things come into your life to take your mind off the past. You're very resilient, and once you're settled into the cottage you'll find plenty to do around the village, and you've lots of friends as well as the family. I'm sure Jack wouldn't want you to sit and brood on the past at home. You've still got an active mind, and that's really the most important thing. Then if you get too depressed, there's always the telephone, and you can ring me and I'll come over to cheer you up.'

'You're awfully understanding, Mark. Simon was as well, and so is Will. It must be something to do with being gay, I suppose. Perhaps you've some feminine genes lurking in your make-up, which make you more caring than heterosexual men with higher levels of testosterone. I'm so glad you met Will at the funeral. He's a lovely person, and you really must look him up next time you and David go to London. He does feel cooped up looking after his Richard, and he'd be delighted to see you, as he knows all about you and Simon. They've been very happy after that police court case that nearly ruined him all those years ago.'

'He gave me his phone number, and we'll certainly look him up, though we probably won't be going up there for another six months or so. Gay people like us have got a lot to be thankful for now. David and I met up with an elderly gay couple in Italy some years ago. The older one, who's about ninety now, was telling us about the dreadful risks he used to run leading a promiscuous life looking for a partner he could settle down with. Fortunately, like Will, he finally found one. They were together for forty-six years, until the younger one died suddenly from a heart attack. It's amazing to think that if Simon and I had stayed together we'd be notching about forty years now. It does show that loving same-sex unions can last, and that there's more in life for us than gay bars and clubs.'

'I don't think many people realise that unless they know a couple personally. It's so sad that the media seem to focus entirely on the gay scene and its excesses. But then the sort of life that you and David lead isn't at all newsworthy, so you can't expect it to get much publicity. You wouldn't really want it to, would you?'

'That's very true. We certainly wouldn't.'

It was time to go, and I felt miserable at having to leave Cynthia, whom I loved dearly, to her loneliness. But, as she had said, grief should be borne alone in private, and there was nothing I could do to help, except to promise that I'd be over to see her again before long.

It seemed that death must have been abroad at about that time, because I had a call quite out of the blue from my old friend Robert to say that his partner, John, had died from cancer after six months of illness. He was missing him terribly after the thirty three years they had been together. John had left the flat to Robert, but he couldn't decide whether to stay on in it or not. He still had two years to go before retirement, but there were so many memories there that he didn't know what to do.

'Would you like me to come up to stay for a couple of nights, Robert, so that we could talk things over? It might help you to make up your mind what to do, and I'd quite like a couple of days or so visiting some of my old haunts. I'm not very busy at the moment, and could spare time the week after next. David's going to be away then visiting his sister, so it'd fit in quite well.'

'I'd just love to see you. When can you come?'

'I'll come up for a couple of nights on Tuesday week, when David's away.'

He'd aged quite a lot since I'd last seen him, and was going grey at the temples, but was still the slightly extrovert character that I knew, though obviously now rather subdued. We resumed our relationship as if we'd parted only the week before – a sign of a true friendship, I felt.

It was quite nostalgic driving round and seeing the places I'd got to know so well, like the tennis club, and my old flat, which looked just the same – I wondered who was living in it now. It brought back memories of Guy, and I suddenly had a strong desire to see him and even sleep with him again, though I felt guilty at the thought.

I looked in to see Eric, who had been so good in giving me the chance to really find my feet in journalism. He only had two more years to go before retirement, and was looking forward to a time when he could sit back and write at leisure. Gillian had retired two years earlier and gone back to Wales, which was a pity as I would have loved to see her again. On the second evening, Robert invited some of the other residents in the flats whom I'd known to come in for a drink. It was fascinating to see how much some of them had changed, while others looked just the same.

After a meal, and over a cup of coffee, Robert nearly broke down.

'I just don't know what to do, Mark. I feel so completely lost without John. We'd become part of one another, and he was always there for me. I took it all for granted, and it wasn't till he was gone that I realised just what he'd meant to me. I feel so guilty that I wasn't always faithful, or as kind and loving as I should have been. I feel now that I never made him as happy as I should have done, and that I caused the silly little rows that we had sometimes over trivial things. I just want to be able to tell him I'm so sorry, but I can't because it's too late. I don't know how many times I've said those four little words – "It's too late now" – to myself since he died.'

'Robert, you simply mustn't blame yourself like that. It's the most natural thing in the world when you've lost someone you loved to feel that you let them down. It's all part and parcel of the grief you feel at their loss. But it's all so negative. What happened in the past is gone now and there is absolutely nothing you can do about it. It's more than likely that some of what you blame yourself for was not your fault at all, but his. If he hadn't been so possessive and maybe jealous, you probably wouldn't have had the rows in the first place. He loved you too much, I expect, and that can be dangerous when it comes to personal relationships.'

'That's probably true. He could never rid himself of the fear that I might leave him for another man. He'd never been as promiscuous as I had been before we met, and I was the first person that he fell in love with, so naturally he was afraid of losing me. Of course I could never have left him knowing how much he loved me, but I could never convince him of that. I still can't rid myself of the feeling that I could have been more loving and caring than I was.'

'That's not what Angela told me about the relationship. She said that you were extremely loving towards him, and that's what some of your neighbours said this evening when they told me how devotedly you had nursed him over the last six months. They admired you tremendously for how you'd cared for him.'

'That was a bit different. He knew that he hadn't long to live, and naturally I wanted to make his last days as bearable as possible. He worried terribly at the thought that I was going to be left alone. He begged me to find another partner when he'd gone, and he left me the flat in his will, to make it easier for me to find someone.

'But I'm awfully mixed up about that. The thought of spending the rest of my life as a frustrated old gay, haunting the clubs ogling younger men who wouldn't be seen dead with an old man like me, appals me. On the other hand, it'd be terribly difficult ever to find a man I'd want to live with after all those years with him – and could I be happy if I did, living on in the flat which holds so many memories of him? Sometimes I think it'd be the best thing to sell up here and move away, and possibly try to find someone. I just can't decide what to do.'

'I think you ought to stay on here for the time being anyhow. I'm sure you could live with someone if you found the right man, and it could give you a new lease of life. When I split up with Guy, I never really expected to find someone to love again, but he did turn up eventually, and now I'm as happy as I've ever been in my life.

'He won't be another John, of course, but the fact that his

ways are different shouldn't matter a scrap, if you're prepared to make allowances. The important thing is that you should be compatible in bed, and that you should have more or less the same interests in life. At our age, looks don't matter very much, and you mustn't be too choosy and set your sights too high. No Adonis is going to look at you unless he is after your money, so you'll have to settle for second-best in the looks department. As you get older, it may be more difficult to adjust to other ways when you're living together, but I'm sure it can be made to work.'

'You may be right. The problem would be to find him, though. I do miss the sexual side of it. For the last few years, that had become less important for us, and we'd only share a bed about twice a week. But it's not being able to cuddle up against him and to feel his body against mine, and his response as I touched him where I knew he'd be most aroused, as he did to me, that I miss so much. For the last few months of his illness he had lost interest in sex, and I couldn't bear the thought of going out to look for it with him lying there, so I've been starved to add to all the other problems.'

I knew just what he was suggesting. I hadn't had sex with anyone except with David for some twenty years. I'd looked at other men from time to time and thought it might be quite exciting to be in bed with them, but I hadn't ever been tempted to rat on him. I knew it was the same with him. But this was rather different. I was fond of Robert and guessed how much he must be longing to be in someone's arms again, and I wanted to help him because of his loneliness and our past friendship. I thought that was probably one reason he'd asked me to come to stay.

Almost against my will, I suddenly felt a strong desire to be close against him, fondling those parts of his which were so unlike David's, and to feel his arms about me. Surely David would understand, wouldn't he? We'd always said, since meeting Arnold that we wouldn't mind if one of us were tempted to stray momentarily for a brief fling. It could only be a one-off anyhow, and there'd be no risk of either of us forming an attachment. After all, Robert and his John had done it, and yet had remained committed to one another.

'Would you like me to go to bed with you, Robert? Real bed this time, of course. I don't think David would mind me being with you, as I've told him all about you, and that we'd had quite a bit of casual sex together in the past. He'd understand how much you might be needing it now that John's no longer there.'

'I'd love to, Mark. I didn't want to tempt you to be unfaithful to David, if that was how you might see it. That's why I didn't suggest anything last night. I wouldn't want you to feel guilty, but I would love to actually be in bed with you. I always did find you very attractive, but I couldn't let it go anywhere without feeling unfaithful to John. In any case, I knew you still had Simon in your system so it wouldn't have worked.'

'No, it wouldn't have done. I wasn't ready for it then. It can only be a one-off now, as I'm very much in love with David, and always will be. So we've only got tonight. What are we waiting for?'

'I'm not waiting.'

With that we moved to his bedroom, and in a second his arms were crushing me to him, and all his pent-up emotions were released in a passionate embrace. I suppose I should have remained calm, but I found that I, too, was suddenly completely carried away by sudden desire, with all thoughts of David obliterated in the pleasure of having a strange body close to mine. We stayed there for several moments locked together, and then, undressed, found ourselves in bed. It was clear that he had, indeed, been starved of love, for he was passionate in the possession of my body, and I was equally aroused by the feel of the strange hands caressing every part of me.

As a result it was all over very quickly for both of us; but as we lay together afterwards, relaxed in each other's arms, I suddenly thought of David and felt guilty. It was not so much that I was lying in bed with Robert, but that I'd enjoyed the experience so much and been so carried away by it instead of just regarding it as a way of helping him.

The feeling of guilt was further exaggerated by the fact that we stayed together in bed until the small hours, and repeated our lovemaking all over again, but this time at a more leisurely pace, when we could relish to the full the pleasure we were experiencing in the enjoyment of each other's bodies. When I awoke in the morning in the cold light of day, I felt ashamed at how much I'd enjoyed the experience, and resolved to come clean to David as soon as I got home.

At breakfast Robert was very different from the depressed uncertain person he had been the night before, and more like the Robert I remembered from the past.

'I can't thank you enough for last night, Mark. You've helped me to find myself again. I've decided to stay on here, and I'll just have to find someone to share it with, though goodness knows how I'm going to meet him. I know now that I need to have love in my life again, and my dear John was quite right when he told me I should find someone else and not let the memory of him stand in my way. It's just marvellous how you seem to have liberated me. I do hope you're not feeling guilty about David.'

'Well, yes I am, I'm afraid – not because I went to bed with you, but because I enjoyed it so much, and found it exciting as well, which I really shouldn't have done. I must make my confession as soon as I get back.

'Anyhow, I'm so pleased that it's helped you, for that makes it easier for me. I'm sure you're right to stay on here to find a new partner. I don't like the idea of you cruising round the pubs and clubs looking for him, because I think you'd be unlikely to find the right person in that environment. The people there are mostly loners who are looking for a quick fix, and have no interest in the possibility of making a long-term commitment. You could try a dating agency, or the 'Kindred Spirit' columns of the *Times* or the *Telegraph*. There do seem to be a few very genuine middle-aged or rather older men in the market there apart from those looking for a toy boy or a sugar daddy. You might find someone in the same boat as you who's lost a long-term partner.'

'I think you're right. I'll take the plunge. It can't do any harm, and the right one might be there for me.'

'If you do find him, you must give me a ring and bring him down for inspection.'

I'd much enjoyed seeing Robert again, but as I drove home I began to feel even more remorse at how much pleasure I'd derived from our encounter. Did it mean that there must be something missing between David and me? Then I recalled how convinced that wise old bird, Arnold, had been that his relationship with his John had been strengthened in some way by occasional sexual encounters with other men, and that it had brought some kind of stimulation to their relationship.

Perhaps he was right, and it did help to bring a new freshness to a long-term sexual relationship, as long as neither partner was carried away, and tempted into doing it too often. I remembered what Simon had said soon after we got together – that there were two aspects to a loving partnership, physical sex and spiritual, emotional love. The latter was the essential ingredient that would stand the test of time, while the former was ephemeral – highly enjoyable and satisfying at the moment, but of no long-term impact. The more I thought of the previous night in those terms, the less remorse I felt, even though some sense of guilt remained.

David got back two days later with the news that his sister, Mildred, and her husband were definitely moving to Devon so as to be nearer to their son and his wife and the first grandchild, who had just moved to Plymouth. I had met them a couple of times when they'd been down to Torquay on holiday, and liked them, especially his sister, though I found the husband a bit stuffy. It would be good for David to have them near, instead of having to traipse up to Norwich to see them. He'd told me that there was no problem there over our relationship. Mildred had accepted it from the start, and was very happy for him.

I'd decided that I would postpone telling him about Robert until we were in bed that night, so I was caught by surprise when he said over supper: 'So you did have sex with Robert, didn't you?

'Yes. I was going to tell you all about it when we were in bed tonight. How on earth did you guess?'

'Well, ever since I got back I had a feeling that you were tensed up somehow, and rather defensive – a bit like a dog that's been out on the loose, and knows he's done wrong and is expecting to be punished, going around with its tail between its legs. You see, I know you so well by now that I can spot anything unusual straight away. Anyhow, did you enjoy it?'

'Yes, that's the awful thing about it, and why I feel guilty. Robert was very upset, grieving for John, and blaming himself for all sorts of things he needn't have been worrying about at all. He was obviously very lonely, and all mixed up about whether he should stay on in the flat, saying that as he was getting old, no one would want to have sex with him again, so there wouldn't be any point in trying to find someone to share it. I felt so sorry for him and wanted to help him.

'I asked him if he'd like me to go to bed with him, as I didn't think you'd mind under the circumstances. He jumped at it, saying that he'd always found me very attractive, but couldn't do anything about it because of John, who had been very possessive, and anyhow I'd refused to go to bed with him as I still had Simon in my system.

'I thought that I'd do it just to satisfy him, and I'd not be aroused because I'd be thinking of you. But when he got close, it wasn't like that at all. I suddenly found that I wanted it as much as he did – and that's saying something! We had our clothes off in no time, and I forgot all about you in the excitement of this different body in my arms. He'd been starved of sex for so long, and I was so aroused that we both came far too quickly. We stayed there in bed, and repeated the lovemaking, and I found it just as exciting as I had done the first time.

'I feel awful about it now, as if I'd betrayed your trust, somehow.'

'That's rubbish, Mark dear. Of course you haven't. We've always had that agreement since we met Arnold that either of us would be free to have a casual fling if the opportunity offered itself. I remember that you tried to encourage me to do it when we were in the Canaries that time, and I wasn't having it then. I'm just so pleased that you enjoyed it so much. We both know that we're together for life, and if you want to go to stay with him again I wouldn't really mind, as I know you'd come back to me.'

'I'm glad to say that it seemed to have worked for Robert. He said next day that I'd liberated him. He knew now that his sexual days weren't anything like over yet. He'd stay on in the flat and somehow find someone to share it with him, as John had told him to.'

'That's marvellous. Now I've a shock for you, too, which I hadn't meant to tell you about till the lights were out tonight. I was naughty as well when I was away, which may take away those guilty feelings of yours.

'As I was leaving Cambridge, I was flagged down by a hitch-hiker. I took a good look at him before I stopped and he seemed perfectly presentable – a student, I guessed. It turned out that he was doing research in the university and wanted to get to Norwich. He was very good-looking with a nice friendly face, and probably in his late twenties. We hadn't gone far before he asked me what family I had. When I told him I wasn't married but had had a long-term partner for over twenty years, he asked, "Why have you been together for as long as that and not got married?"

'"I couldn't do that. My partner's a he and not a she."

'"Oh, so you are gay, then. I had a sort of hunch you might be by the way you looked me up and down when I was getting into the car. Don't worry, I'm the same." With that, he looked hard at me, and moved his right leg over the gear change till it was almost touching mine, obviously inviting me to do the same. I didn't rise to the bait immediately, though I was tempted, feeling myself suddenly getting stiff. I glanced down at him, and he had an obvious erection which he was stroking with one hand.

'"Do you both have sex outside your marriage then?" he asked.

'"No, we've never done it yet, because we care for each other too much. But we've agreed that we could have a fling if the opportunity arose, though I'd feel guilty if I did."

'"You oughtn't to feel guilt you know. I'm friendly with a gay couple, and they tell me that they both play away sometimes, and it reinvigorates their relationship no end." With that he took hold of my left hand, and pulled it down until it was covering his erection. He obviously had something quite big hidden away and it was very hard to the touch. I felt that I was in danger of coming off involuntarily, and quickly withdrew my hand.

'"There's nothing to be afraid of. For all you know, your partner may be up to it at this moment, too. I do like older or married men, as they're generally much more caring and tender. Younger ones tend to be too rough and greedy, just out to satisfy themselves as quickly as possible and never giving a thought to the other person. To be honest, I do find you attractive and I'd really love to be in bed with you. You're just my type. Take the next turning off. There's a forest and a parking place a little further on. It's perfectly safe there, as we can get deep into the woods, and there's plenty of cover."

'So that was how it happened, love, and I'm sorry I gave in so easily. But I do have to admit that I enjoyed it probably as much as you did, as he had a body rather like yours and was very tender and loving – so it didn't feel at all sordid as it might have done if he'd not been so attractive and with such a nice personality.'

'I'm so glad you enjoyed it so much. It's amazing that we both fell for it at the same time, and that we can both admit we found it exciting. You know, I think Arnold was probably right. I do feel liberated in some strange way, and yet feel that I love you even more than ever, if that were possible.'

'I feel the same. Just very close to you and it's marvellous to be together again.'

In bed that night, it was as if nothing had happened. We'd both enjoyed a new experience, but were more than happy to get back on to familiar ground.

'You can do it again, my love, if you feel the need,' I said. 'But not too often, or I might start to get jealous. Fortunately, with Mildred moving down here, you're not likely to be on the road to Norwich again, and if you began to go over to Cambridge frequently I really would smell a rat.'

'No risk of that. He was lovely, but a bit too young for me, I'm afraid.'

He needn't have been concerned about Robert and me, either, because about a month later Robert rang me up.

'Mark, it's worked! I took your advice and found him in the *Telegraph*. He's two years older than me, a retired schoolmaster who lost his partner three years ago. He's got no close family and has been only too happy to move in with me. We're very compatible in sex, and he's young for his age and quite nice-looking. To add to that, he's more domesticated than John was, so he's really looking after me. I'm sure it'll last, as we seem to share so many interests. I think I'm happier than I've ever been before, and he says that he is, too.'

'I'm so glad, Robert. You deserve some happiness after the

way you looked after John. Do come down soon, as we'd both like to meet him. I could put you both up if you'd like to come for the night.'

As time went on Daniel became more and more involved in his political activities, and I found that I was having to spend more time than I really wanted standing in for him on the farm. He'd been elected to chair one of the union's main committees in London, which meant that he had to travel all over the country instead of just the South West. He'd always try to get home the same night, but if it wasn't possible, I'd have to be on the farm to get the men to work for the day – something I wanted to give up as I got older.

I didn't mind it too much as he'd always leave a list of jobs to be done, and he did all the planning. In any case, if I hadn't got something on myself, I'd usually walk up to the calf unit to see that everything was all right at Duncan's end. I would enjoy walking back along the new shelter belt, now growing very fast, to hear the birds singing and to find that David had breakfast on the table. I felt that life couldn't be much better then.

Most of the farm supervision could be done in the mornings, and I'd fill up the rest of the day in reading to keep up-to-date for my writing of the fortnightly articles, going out to farming events in the county, committee meetings and recreation with David. This might be having a game of golf, or going down to Cornwall for surfing or cliff walks. The time seemed to fly by. If it hadn't been for my farm commitment, we might have made more effort to find a base down in Cornwall, but it still wasn't worth it for the amount of time I'd be able to spend there.

Lying together in our little hollow on the edge of the cliff one day late that summer, after a good bathe in the morning, David suddenly brought me down to earth, rather as Simon had done so long ago at Grindelwald.

'Have you ever thought what it'd be like if one of us were to die?' he asked. 'We're both in our sixties and, though people seem to be living much longer now, there's always the possibility that something might happen to one of us. I've not left you any money in my will, incidentally, as you've got plenty already, and I thought it ought to stay in the family, but I'd like you to have anything of mine in the bungalow that you might want.'

'I've done much the same for you. I've said that I'd want you to stay in the bungalow rent-free for as long as you wished, and it'd revert to the family if you died or gave it up. But why on earth bring up the subject on a beautiful day like this when we're so happy?'

'That's just it. It all seems to be too good to be true, but fate has a habit of striking back when everything in the garden is lovely. I'm not suggesting that we should make ourselves miserable by fearing the worst, but that we ought to be aware that it might end suddenly one day, leaving one of us alone.'

'I've no intention of letting it worry me. I've had it all once, and it wouldn't have made the slightest difference if I'd worried about it beforehand. It would have been equally traumatic. So for goodness' sake don't let it enter your mind. We should be living each day as it comes and enjoying it to the full, and hope that we've still got many years in front of us – like Arnold and his John had at our age.'

But it did worry me just the same that David should have been thinking about the possibility of something happening to ruin our lives. Had he some premonition of trouble ahead? I resolutely decided to put it right out of my mind. A life without him now was too dreadful to contemplate. No dark cloud came into the sky as it had done in the Alps, and I took that as a good sign that history was not going to repeat itself.

Chapter Thirteen

Farming got no easier over the next two years, and it was becoming quite a struggle to make the sort of profits that we'd enjoyed twenty or thirty years previously. It was fortunate that we'd managed to buy the farm at Barnfield when we did, as it had enabled us to expand the business sufficiently to pay off a proportion of the bank loan each year as a result of the higher turnover. The loan was down to manageable proportions, and coming to the point where we had to decide whether it would be sensible to bring it down any further, if we could find a better use for the money to generate more off-the-farm income. Neither of us could see how under the present conditions we could expect higher income from the farming operations, unless prices for our main products – milk, beef, surplus cattle and wheat – increased. We thought this was bound to occur before too long, but for the time being it was a matter of holding on until that moment arrived.

What we'd managed to do was patch up two of the barns on the farms we'd taken over in the past, for which we had little use, making them suitable for the storage of industrial products. In the eighties, a smallish industrial estate had been developed on the edge of Norton (from which, incidentally, Caroline's husband, Geoffrey, had made quite a pile) and a number of manufacturers had moved in. Two of them needed storage space for their products, and we managed to let our two barns at quite good rents for the purpose.

So by now, in the early years of the new century, quite a proportion of our overall income was not coming from farming at all, but from holiday cottage rentals, industrial storage and all the environment payments for which we now qualified as a result of the planting and wildlife measures I'd started as soon as I'd taken over from Dad. At the time, I didn't do them from a desire to make a profit, but it was pure luck that the farming pendulum had swung away from straight farming towards the environment at just the right time. We were now being paid for doing things that cost us very little. Most of the maintenance work could be done during the winter months by our own farm staff, whose wages we'd be paying anyhow. The supermarket contract for the beef animals had been a profitable move, and the market was looking up slightly, so it was really the dairy unit that was not showing the profits it should, owing to exceptional low prices.

Since we'd discovered the holiday flats in the grounds of the big house in the middle of the golf course, we'd taken one for a week on two occasions. It was a good base, not too far away from Polzeath for bathing, and good for cliff walks and an occasional game of golf which David so much enjoyed. David suggested that it might be a good time for Charles and John to learn to surf, so we asked Janet and Daniel whether they might let us take them away for a week during their summer holiday, when we'd book one of the holiday flats at the big house.

They were delighted to have them off their hands, as they couldn't get away over harvest, and Daniel said he could get along without me on the grain dryer for a week. Maud had been invited to stay with a school friend, so it all fitted in rather well. The boys, of course, were rapturous at the thought of going away for a whole week with their uncles (David had become one long ago), and at the prospect of lots of bathing and being away from their parents for a change. They were now eleven and twelve, and very mature for their age, so they'd be no problem to look after.

Janet filled up a large hamper of food to keep us going, and I was reminded of Cynthia doing the same for Simon and me all those years ago. There were the two twin-bedded rooms, the boys having one and David and I the other. On the first morning we took them over to Polzeath and kitted them out with wetsuits and surfboards, and it was marvellous to see their excitement when we got down to the sea. Fortunately for the beginners, the surf wasn't too strong, but just enough to get quite good runs up the beach. The main trouble was that it was a fine day and the sea was packed. I marvelled at how popular it had become since that day when Simon and I had enjoyed a virtually empty beach.

David took John and I took Charlie, and both of them got the hang of it fairly easily, with enough successful runs to whet their appetites for more. Rather as it had been with Angela at her first visit, it was a job to get them out of the sea, and it was only the promise to come back the next day that got them back up the beach to change at the car, and to buy some pasties and bottles of Coke. David and I preferred plain water.

'That was brilliant, Uncle Mark,' said John. 'Can we go in again this afternoon?'

'Not until you've digested that food. You shouldn't bathe on a full stomach. What we'll do is have a good walk on the cliff and come back and see what the surf's like. I don't think it'll be up to much by then as it'll be about high tide, and right up the beach, and it's never much good then. Anyhow, by the look of the mob here now I shouldn't think there'd be room in the sea for you.'

We walked some way up towards the headland, and lay down on the warm scented turf to rest while the boys chattered away among themselves.

When we got back to the beach it was packed as the rising tide had pushed all the holiday makers up on to a limited area of sand. I was right about the waves, too, for the tide was on the turn, and what had been waves had turned to ripples.

'I just don't think it's worth going in. Let's go home and get a cup of tea. Then David and I want to go up to the golf club and sign in for a week, so that we can go out and play if we want to in the evenings, and have one or two rounds during the week if you two wouldn't be too bored.'

'We'd love to go round with you, wouldn't we, Charlie?' John said. 'We've not seen you play before. Could we pull your trolleys for you?'

'I should think so, but you'll have to learn where to stand, as we don't want to go cracking you on the head with a club if you're in the wrong place.'

At the club, we booked a time to play on the following afternoon at about three o'clock so that we could get a bathe in the morning.

They quickly learned where to stand while we were playing our shots and how to hold the flagsticks, but after a few holes they'd had enough of pulling the trolleys up and down the steep slopes, so we let them off that duty. It was halfway round that they really proved their worth. David had been playing rather well, and was four holes up on me, when he suddenly had a rush of blood to the head and hit a drive wildly to his left. It sailed over a bit of marshy land, cleared a small stream and clattered into thick bushes round the base of the hill where we had our flat.

'Damn, why on earth did I do that? It's new ball. I only bought it today before we came out, and now it's gone.'

'Can't we go and look for it?' Charlie said. 'We might be able to find somewhere to squeeze into those bushes. Those balls are quite expensive, aren't they?'

'They certainly are. OK, off you go, and see if you can find it. Catch us up on the next hole.'

It was three holes later that two excited boys, looking extremely dishevelled, finally caught up with us again, with the pockets of their shorts bulging and scratches on their legs and arms.

'We've found six balls in those bushes and others further on, and three of them look new. I expect one of them is yours, David, isn't it?'

'That one looks like mine. That's brilliant of you. If you don't need them, give three to Mark and I'll have the other three. I hope you're not too scratched. You must have been crawling by the look of you.'

'Some of them were in a bit deep, but once we'd seen them we couldn't leave them there, could we?'

'I'd like to learn to play golf,' John announced when we were eating supper that night. 'Would you teach me to play, David?' He'd obviously selected David as his coach, as he'd beaten me quite easily in spite of that wild drive.

'We'd have to see what your mother and father think about it,' I said. 'I don't think it'd be a good idea just yet, as we haven't got a course near the farm where you could practise, and anyhow you'll be far too busy when you go back to school. Perhaps when you're a bit older we might think about it.' Then I had a good idea.

'If you really want to have a go at it, we could take a club and some balls down on the beach here at low tide, provided there's nobody about, and we could tell you how to hold and swing the club. How about that? What about you, Charlie?'

'I'd love to give it a try,' John said. 'The tide will be out in the morning before we go to Polzeath. Could we go down then?'

'I don't see why not. Either David or I will take you.'

'I don't think I'll come,' Charlie said. 'There's not much point as we wouldn't be able to do it again till next year sometime. But don't worry about me, I've got the book I'm reading, till we go bathing.'

David took John down to the beach quite early the following day, when there was nobody about, while I stayed in the flat doing domestic jobs and keeping Charlie company. He was just getting into serious books, as I had been at his age, and was quite happy to be left on his own. On their return, David said that John had shaped up quite well for the first time, and had hit just enough reasonably straight shots to encourage him to persevere.

And so the week passed in a flash, bathing, walking, playing another round of golf or a few holes or climbing up to the top of the hill in the evenings, and then a game of cards to keep the boys amused after supper. The weather was kind, and the surf reasonably good, if not brilliant – quite enough for the boys to enjoy it anyhow. They had the time of their lives, and so did we, if we were honest, since both of us would have liked to have had families. During the week, they'd managed to find another four golf balls for us, which helped to pay for their keep.

'That was an absolutely fab holiday,' Charlie said when we dropped them off at the farm. 'Thank you so much, Mark, for looking after us. Mum, we had a really great time.'

'Can we do it again next year, please, Mark?' John added. 'Thank you so much, David, for the golf on the beach. I can't wait till next year.'

In the middle of September we took our usual fortnight's holiday on the Continent, driving down to the Italian lakes for what would be our sixth visit to Bellagio. We could never equal Arnold and his John's nineteen stays there, but it was nice to be welcomed each time now as favoured guests. Sadly, the matriarch from Oxford had died, but Maria was still on the desk, and the son was running the hotel.

Maria obviously remembered Arnold, for on our arrival she

said: 'I've given you the same room that Arnold used to have each year. They always used to book it early in the season as soon as they knew they'd be coming. Is Arnold still alive?'

'Thanks so much for the room, it's certainly one of the best we've had. I spoke to him about six months ago, and he was pretty good then, though getting very lame. But he's over ninety now, so it's only to be expected, and he misses John a lot after they'd been together for so long.'

On our customary visit across the lake to Menaggio, we bought another terracotta pot to put into the boot for the patio at home. We'd done this each year after David had got the first one for Mother's garden. I grew different types of fuchsia in them, and even in the depth of winter at home the five of them reminded us of happy days eating our picnic lunches on the seats under the oleanders by the lakeside. We'd also discovered a very scenic spot high up in the mountains, where we could park the car, and climb higher to a sheltered spot to eat our lunch to the accompaniment of tinkling cow bells from an adjacent pasture. It wasn't quite as scenic as Grindelwald, but it was sheer happiness to lie together there drinking in sunshine and the view of the mountains without a care in the world.

Three days in the Dolomites, and three in Interlaken revisiting our by-now-favourite haunts, and two nights in Lucerne on one of which there was a Mozart/Brahms concert, completed one of our most memorable holidays. Again, it seemed almost too good to last.

In October, Mildred and her husband moved down to a small house they'd bought in a village on the edge of Dartmoor, and we helped them to move in. The more I saw of her, the more I liked her. She had a number of David's mannerisms, with a very active mind and being full of energy. She'd been a school teacher before her marriage, and had continued to work as a supply teacher after her two boys were away at school. She was widely read, and liked to keep up with current affairs, so we got on well. She had been very fond of David, and seemed pleased that I was giving him happiness in life after a worrying start.

Barry, her husband, I found more difficult. A local government official all his life, he seemed to be one of those people who find it difficult to maintain a conversation, and I did rather dread being left alone with him as I would have to be continually thinking of something to say next. But he was a nice enough character and we got on perfectly well together. It was quite clear Mildred was the driving force in the marriage, though never in a bossy way.

Their eldest son, Gerald, and his wife, who'd moved down to Plymouth, were a nice easy-going couple, with a delightful little girl of eighteen months, and another due in six months. I was pleased for David to have his family so close, though we didn't actually see very much of them.

The following spring we had a bad fright on the farm, when one of the older heifers being reared at Barnfield gave a positive result at the annual Bovine Tuberculosis test. Everything had to be shut down until it was confirmed, with no cattle allowed to be moved on or off the farm. Fortunately none of the cattle down at home had tested positive, so that farm was not affected. We couldn't really believe that it could be a valid test, as we had no contact with neighbours and there were no traces of badgers which might have transmitted an infection. We waited with bated breath for the result of the compulsory re-test. When it came through, it was still giving a doubtful reading, so Daniel decided to play safe and send the animal off to be slaughtered. We just couldn't afford to take any risks.

We had the carcase inspected and they could find no trace whatsoever of an infection, so it was just one of those cases that showed that the current test was by no means accurate. This had been known for years, and no one had yet been able to devise a more accurate one, though one was rumoured to be on the way. I felt sorry for the animal that had had its life cut short unnecessarily, and blamed it on a past government which had failed to eradicate the disease thirty years before when success was within its grasp. The whole episode made us even more careful in measures to prevent infection getting on to the farm.

That summer, Angela came down to stay, saying that it was definitely the last time she'd go bathing, but we had the usual happy three days with her staying in the hotel and going over past times. At seventy-five, she was beginning to show signs of slowing down, but mentally was just her old self. The boys had also had their week with us in the same holiday flat, bathing and golfing which they appeared to have enjoyed hugely, and which had been great fun for us. John continued his golf lessons on the beach, and had decided he'd definitely like to learn to play properly as soon he had an opportunity. In October Charlie was to go as a boarder at Daniel's old school under the same house-master as his father and was very excited at the prospect. John was due to follow him the next autumn. They seemed to be growing up at an astonishing rate.

It was in March the following year that I noticed that David seemed to be showing signs of a limp when we were getting to the end of a round of golf.

'Are you all right?' I asked him. 'You look as if you're in a bit of pain.'

'I am getting a little pain in my right hip when I've been doing a lot of exercise, and it gets a bit stiff after golf. I expect it's just a touch of arthritis starting as a result of strains in the past from handling your heavy dairy cows. It's not too bad, and it doesn't worry me most of the time, and it's not worth doing anything about it for the time being.'

In May there was a phone call from Robert.

'Mark, Phil and I are going down to Devon and Cornwall for a few days holiday in June, and I wondered whether we might look in to see you. I'd like you to meet him, and it's about time I met your David as well. Is there anywhere handy where we could stay?'

'Why don't you come to stay with us? There's room for two in the spare bedroom, though one of you would have to sleep in a camp bed, I'm afraid. It'd be great fun if you wouldn't mind mucking in with us.'

'We'd love to if you're sure it wouldn't be too much trouble having us in the house.'

'Of course not. You won't get Ritz service, but I've got enough spoons and forks for the four of us. When were you thinking of coming?'

'The eighteenth to twentieth would suit us best, if that's all right with you.'

'I'll just check the diary. Yes, that's OK. Give me a ring beforehand for instructions about how to find us.'

They arrived about six o'clock.

'Meet Phil,' Robert said as they got out of the car.

'Meet David,' I said, as we shook hands all round. 'We thought we'd go out for a meal tonight and then I'll cook something tomorrow. You might be a bit long for the camp bed, Robert, or you can toss up for it.'

'I'll have it,' Phil said. 'I'm shorter by a couple of inches.'

Over drinks before we went out the talk was a bit stilted while we were sizing each other up. I was naturally curious as to how Phil might compare with Robert's previous partner, John. He couldn't have been more different. Quite broad and chunky, he had a round face, very blue eyes and rather mousy-coloured brown hair with traces of grey at the temples. A smooth, pinkish complexion, and a mouth always ready to break into a smile made him look younger than he actually was. I was taken by his personality, and could well understand why Robert found him so attractive. John had been introspective and rather stand-offish, and I'd always found him slightly intimidating. Phil was just the opposite.

'I love your bungalow,' Robert said. 'Did you build this extra bit on?'

'Yes, this room was a bit dark and poky before. David and I had always thought that we might like to live together sometime in the future, so it seemed sensible to do it straight away. When we finally took the plunge five years ago, we built the other bit on so as to give him a place of his own, so that we wouldn't be too much on top of one another.'

'Very wise,' Phil said. 'Have you ever regretted moving in together?'

'Not for a moment,' David interjected. 'I can't think why we didn't do it a lot sooner. Mind you, I'm sure it was a good idea for me to have a sizeable room of my own. You don't want to be on top of one another all the time, however much you love your partner.'

'I must confess it was a bit difficult at times with John, if he was in a bad mood after a difficult day at the hospital, when I'd have liked a place of my own. That's probably why we'd have occasional rows when we got on each other's nerves. I still feel awful about that, as I'd sometimes wind him up out of sheer frustration. What do you feel, Phil? Should we try to give each other more space?'

'It's early days yet as we haven't been together for very long, but I can't see it happening with us. I love you too much, and I don't want to be left alone again. When I was living with Adrian, my previous partner, whom I did love dearly, we did have occasional rows, but that was because he could be jealous when he saw me with another man. That annoyed me because it made me feel he wasn't trusting me. Once or twice, after a row, I'd go off and have casual sex as a kind of revenge, I suppose. I can't explain it, and I bitterly regret it now, of course.'

'How do you feel about casual sex, when you're in a close relationship with someone? We've got a very wise old friend who had a loving relationship with his partner for about forty-five years, who maintains that it does no harm at all, and in fact can prevent sex from getting stale, bringing partners closer together as a result. I expect Robert's told you that we used to have it off occasionally if John was away, in the old days when I was single. Did it help then, Robert?'

'I'm sure it did. It relieved the tension, and afterwards I would feel more loving towards him. I can't explain why, but it did.'

By the time we were sitting down to a meal at a restaurant in Norton, we were all more relaxed, and spent much of the time talking about foreign trips. Phil recounted stories of his life as a master in one of the larger public schools. On our last trip to London, David and I had been to see Alan Bennett's play *The History Boys*, and Phil had seen it as well.

'What did you think of it?' David asked him. 'Is it at all realistic?'

'Not really, though I enjoyed it as a play. There's a big difference between the sort of day school depicted there, and a boarding school like mine, but I wouldn't envisage a similar situation arising, from my own experience. Of course, in any school – boys or girls – adolescents will get crushes on one another. It's all part of growing sexual identity, and it can happen, not only with the boys themselves, but between a senior boy and a young master, I imagine. In my sort of school, there was an unwritten rule that masters should never allow themselves to become emotionally involved with boys in their care. In my time that old dictum of being "in loco parentis" certainly applied.

'I can recall being physically attracted to several boys, but I never allowed it to get beyond thinking, gosh, he's beautiful, but he's forbidden fruit. It's not always easy for a gay man, of course. Boys these days seem to be clued up about sex from a young age, and any master who's not married by the time he's about thirty is suspected of being gay. I suppose that in a day school, you could have a situation of a precocious eighteen year old being attracted to a young master as in the play, but I'd think it unlikely in a boarding school. Such boys tend to be attracted to younger boys, and not to a master, and this has to be watched for very carefully.

'Anyway, I suppose that I was lucky in that I've always been attracted to men of my own age and not to young chicks.' As he said this, I caught him looking quite intently at David across the table. That wasn't the first time either; I had noticed it when we were sitting with our drinks before going out for the meal. To make it worse, I'd caught Robert doing the same to me, and I'd found myself picturing his naked body, and thinking how good it'd be to be in bed with it again. Had I been wise in inviting them to stay, I wondered? I knew that Robert had been pretty promiscuous before he met John, and from something Phil had said I suspected he might have been as well. Might they be thinking that it was an ideal opportunity to swap partners for a change? They seemed perfectly happy together, but you could never really tell.

Back at the bungalow, the talk came back again to fidelity in gay relationships. They both expressed surprise that David and I had spent over twenty years together without either of us straying from the straight and narrow path.

'Do you mean to say that neither of you have been tempted?' Robert said.

'No, not really. Of course, I've looked at other men and thought it might be quite fun to go to bed with them but, as I said once to David when we were in Gran Canaria, the grass on the other side of the fence isn't really any greener, and even if it were a quick bite wouldn't really get you anywhere in the end. It wasn't till Robert and I had our fling before he met you that I felt really aroused, and even then I said that I'd never do it again, as I felt it wasn't fair on David.'

'The thing is,' David said, 'neither Mark nor I had ever slept around much before we finally met up. Mark obviously had his first love so deeply embedded in his system that for years he couldn't contemplate sex with anyone else, and then he had the unhappy experience of being dumped which made him feel he didn't want to risk of that happening again. In my case, my earlier experiences were not particularly happy ones, and then I was in a job where I just couldn't risk any possible exposure, so I inclined to shy away from it. So we tended to lead pretty celibate lives.'

'Of course in my situation, I had to be very careful, too,' Phil said. 'When I was younger I used to take ridiculous risks. Then I met Adrian and settled down to a domestic life, though I still felt I needed a bit on the side occasionally. Perhaps the truth is that I didn't love him as much as the two of you love each other. Maybe the same applies to Robert and John.'

'It's not a matter of loving them enough,' I said. 'It's far more likely to be a matter of complete sexual compatibility, which David and I have. You can love a person very deeply emotionally just for what they are, and yet not be completely compatible in bed to the point of a lifetime commitment to sex with them alone.'

'I think you've hit the nail on the head there, Mark,' Phil said. 'That's exactly how I feel.'

'Time for bed. I thought you might like to see the farm in the morning. Janet's giving us lunch and then we could do a little sightseeing perhaps. Does that sound OK?'

'Admirable, and thanks so much for the meal. See you in the morning.'

'Is Phil after you?' I asked David as we got undressed.

'So you did notice it, did you? I was wondering whether you had. I got the impression that Robert's got his eye on you as well. Do you think they've got the idea of a swap in mind? If they have, how would you feel about it? If you'd like to go to bed with Robert, I'd let you off the lead.'

'What would you feel about Phil, then?'

'To tell the truth, I do find him quite attractive as he's rather my type, and I like him as a person, so I wouldn't say no if the situation arose. It's very much up to you. Of course, we may have misread the situation entirely, and they mightn't have it in mind at all. They seem very happy with each other, so we may have got it wrong. Do you want Robert?'

'One half of me does, and I've already mentally undressed him and would be excited to have him in bed again. But I don't think it's on as the thought of you being with Phil in the next-door room would be unbearable. Picturing you with your hitchhiker didn't worry me in the least but this feels quite different. That was just a case of a quick sexual relief, but the idea of you lying naked in bed with him is quite a different matter. Even if I was with Robert, I'm sure I'd still be thinking of you in someone else's arms, instead of in mine where you belong. I'd be intensely jealous, and I'd certainly not enjoy being with Robert, which would hardly be fair on him either. It just doesn't seem right somehow.'

'I quite understand. It seems silly, but I wouldn't object to you and Robert getting together somewhere else, but I wouldn't like it if it was in the same house. I wouldn't be comfortable with Phil either, if you were next door. I think we ought to talk it over with them tomorrow evening. In the meantime, let's see how they react tomorrow. I won't give Phil any encouragement.'

They seemed to enjoy the trip round the farm. Phil, having taught chemistry, was full of questions about the scientific feeding of the cows and the use we made of fertilisers, while Robert, the economist, was equally probing about the financial aspects of the farm and the use of the computer. Over lunch, Janet, who was still working part-time as a supply teacher, got involved with discussions with Phil over educational policies, both of them lambasting the Government over its frequent changes in policy. During the day, Phil seemed to be making the most of his chances of getting close to David.

Comfortably settled down in our armchairs with a cup of coffee after supper, seemed to be an appropriate time to take the bull by the horns.

'We may have got this completely wrong, Robert, and if we have, you'll have to forgive me, but both David and I have got the impression that you and Phil might have thought about the possibility of swapping partners for an evening. We talked about it last night as David knew that you and I had both enjoyed that little fling we had before you met Phil. He said he would let me off if we felt we wanted to repeat it. He thought that Phil might be happy to get together with him at the same time. If that was so, he'd be happy as well. Had you thought about it?'

'To come clean, yes, we had. As I told you last time, I've always found you very attractive, and when you stayed with me I realised just how much I'd enjoyed having full sex with you, and I'd love to do it again, if it didn't upset Phil too much. We'd both enjoyed a small amount of casual sex in our previous relationships, so I was pretty sure he wouldn't mind me having a one-off – but he must speak for himself.'

Phil did so. 'Robert had told me about you two getting together, and how it had helped him, so if he'd like to repeat it, I'd be very happy for him, as I know it wouldn't make any difference to our relationship. The only problem was that it would leave me on my own, unless there was a chance with David… having seen him, the picture is now quite clear. You get that feeling of instant attraction sometimes, and I got it with him. He's just my type, and I've hardly been able to take my eyes off him. So if you and Robert do want sex, I'd be absolutely delighted to pair off with David. But the question then is, does he want me?'

'That seems to put the ball back into my court, then, doesn't it?' David said. 'I'm sorry, but I just don't think it's on. It's not that I wouldn't want to sleep with you, Phil, because I find you attractive, too, and one day perhaps we might get together if Robert would let you off the lead. But I just don't feel that any of us could relax completely, knowing that the one we really deeply love is in bed with someone in the next room. It's just not right, and I'm sure that Mark feels the same as I do.'

'You're dead right, David. Much as I'd enjoy sex with you again, Robert, I'm sure this isn't the time or place for it. I do hope you can both agree on that.'

'Yes, of course I do understand, with you and David being so close still. I don't think it would have bothered both of us, but then we do come from rather different backgrounds.'

'I'll accept it, too,' Phil said. 'But I've had an idea. Why don't you come up to Westerton to see Robert in the autumn, and I'll come down to stay with David for a couple of nights. I'm sure we'd all enjoy the change, and then be pleased to get back home again to the familiar routine.'

'You've got something there, Phil. What do you think, Mark?'

'I rather like the idea. We could do it after we get back from our three days in London.'

'I'll hold you to that,' Robert said. 'I'll be giving you a ring in October to fix it up.'

So the visit ended with us going to our separate rooms. As I snuggled up to David in bed, he said, 'I do love you, Mark. I'm so glad I'm with you and not with Phil tonight. I'd quite like to sleep with him once, but only if you're 200 miles or more away. That's quite irrational, I suppose, but it's how I feel.'

'It's how I feel as well, so we're a couple of stupid old men, I suppose.' We'd enjoyed their visit, but it was nice to get back to a regular routine again.

Chapter Fourteen

For the previous two years I'd been under a certain amount of pressure to open the farm for a demonstration of what we'd been able to achieve in biological conservation. A date for this had been fixed for the end of July just before the start of harvest. So we were kept very busy preparing for it, as several hundred people were expected to attend.

It meant getting out noticeboards for the twelve sites where we reckoned there was something worth showing. It would be too far for people to walk, so we'd have to collect several more tractors and trailers from neighbours, to transport visitors around not only the home farm, but Barnfield as well. We thought we'd do three trips, one in the morning and two in the afternoon, which meant having something on display to keep people entertained when waiting for each tour to start. Fortunately several other organisations were happy to get in on the act and provide static demonstrations in the farmyard of what they did. Add to all that the provision of catering and portable loos, and it amounted to a lot of preparation.

Members of my Farming and Wildlife Committee agreed to man the different sites and answer questions if Daniel or I were not on the spot, so they had to be given the appropriate information beforehand, which added to the work.

We'd given it a lot of publicity in the press and on the radio beforehand, and to our astonishment well over 800 people turned up through the day, which put a severe strain on the transport. In the event it all went well, and it was good to report authentic figures from the bird and butterfly surveys carried out by the university. I couldn't help feeling rather proud at the success of my efforts over the years, and thought that Dad and Grandfather must be, too, if they were looking down from up above, as I felt they were. The other good effect was that it further helped to establish Daniel's reputation not only as a budding politician but as a good farmer as well.

With all that safely out of the way, we were more than ready for the annual week with the boys surfing, walking and playing golf in Cornwall. The only thing to mar the enjoyment was the increasing pain that David was getting from the arthritis in his right hip. It didn't worry him surfing, but it was beginning to bother him quite seriously on the hilly holes on the golf course. It was clear that something would need to be done about it during the winter. For the moment, we decided to make the best of what we'd got, the week with the boys being now the highlight of the year.

We didn't go to Italy that September, David saying that he thought it was a bit too far for the hip, but we did have ten days in Switzerland and the Black Forest instead. Those lazy, carefree holidays abroad with him were some of the happiest days of my life, comparable only to that first unforgettable holiday with Simon, when life and love were young and when, in retrospect, the sun shone every day from a cloudless sky.

We hadn't been back long before there was a phone call from Robert.

'We did enjoy our trip in the summer, Mark, and especially those two days with you and David. When are you coming up to see me? Phil says he's about ready for a short break, if that arrangement we discussed is still on. I hope it is, as I'd like to see you again before long.'

'I'll have a word with David this evening and give you a ring. It won't be just yet anyhow, as we're going up to London for our usual three days of culture the week after next, and then Daniel will be away for a couple of days at meetings, and I'll be holding the fort on the farm. We do like to go to the theatre and a concert now and again, which we don't get much of an opportunity to do down here. I'll ring you tonight.'

David was a bit dubious when we talked about it over supper.

'I don't know that I really want to do it, love. We're really very happy as we are, and I don't know that there's much point in possibly upsetting ourselves. The thing is whether you'd like it. I'll go along with what you decide.'

'Shall we try it just this once, and see how we feel about it afterwards? In a way I'd quite like to put Arnold's theory to the test. It can't do any harm, can it, and you are quite attracted to Phil, aren't you?'

'OK, just once then, and we'll have an inquest afterwards.'

I rang Robert and we agreed that I'd come up for two nights at the end of October, and Phil would come down to stay with David at the same time. In the meantime we had a good time in London, fitting in a visit to a theatre, a performance of *The Magic Flute* at the Coliseum and a concert at the Albert Hall, and some sightseeing during the day. Though we always enjoyed these jaunts, it was nice to get back home again to the farm, and the comfort of the bungalow, of which David was now such a major part, so much had we grown together over the years.

'Good to see you,' Robert said as I entered his flat, where he put his arms around me in a tight hug. It was clear that he was not going to let any thoughts of Phil interfere with his enjoyment of the next two days. 'I hope you didn't find it difficult to decide if you'd come.'

'It was a bit. David was pretty unsure about it, but we decided to give it a try, on the clear understanding that if either of us was unhappy about it afterwards, we'll not do it again.'

'Fair enough. I'm certain that Phil and David will get on well. He's amazingly adaptable, and is certainly very taken with David, but you needn't worry. We know that we're together for life now. He's not likely to fall in love with David now he's got me.'

'I still find it a bit difficult to get my head round it, but it was so good last time that I'll put David out of my mind, hoping he's doing the same when he's with Phil.'

I managed to do just that when the time came for bed, as I felt Robert's arms around me, his body pressing against me once more. It felt so different from David's and especially the silkiness of that organ of his which had always aroused me so much in the past. It did the same again, and I had difficulty in suppressing a premature ejaculation as I felt it harden to my touch.

'God, you do work me up, Mark. You've still got a wonderful body. It's so strong and soft without a sign of the fat which you should have at your age. How do you manage to keep it so trim?'

'Hard work and exercise, I suppose. You've kept yours in pretty good shape too, though I do detect a little flab creeping in about your waist. But I like it, as you were always a bit skinny before. It's the silky feel of your cock which really sends me up.' All thoughts of David banished, I could hold it back no longer, and pulled out a tissue just in time. It was only as we lay relaxed together that I thought of David, and wondered how he'd felt, or even now might be feeling, with Phil. I hoped he'd been as aroused and carried away as I had been, and hadn't thought of me at all.

Just as happened on the last occasion, we stayed together and repeated the experience.

'How do you feel about it now?' he asked, as I got up to go to my own bed. 'No guilty feelings, I hope?'

'Not really. I was so carried away, I never thought about David until afterwards, and then it was really just wondering how he and Phil had got on, and hoping he was not feeling any guilt either.'

I thoroughly enjoyed the two days with Robert. Our association went back a long way, and I regarded him as a close friend, and not in any way as a lover. The fact that we enjoyed occasional sex together didn't mean that I was emotionally attracted to him in any way. We simply got on very well, and our past experiences drew us together and provided plenty about which we could reminisce. Getting back to Westerton was a nostalgic experience, for I'd been very happy there on the whole, and I could now even look back on the interlude with Guy in a pleasurable light.

'Thanks so much, Robert. I really did enjoy it,' I said as I got into the car to go home after another successful night in bed. 'I wonder now how David and Phil got on. If it worked out well for them, I'd be more than happy to repeat the experience next year sometime, but it'll obviously have to depend on them, won't it?'

'Of course. If either Phil or David were unhappy about it, it clearly wouldn't be on, as we mustn't do anything to upset either of them. We'll have to wait and see. Drive carefully. We must keep in touch, Mark, and thanks for coming.'

Driving back down the motorway, I kept wondering if I was passing Phil on the other carriageway, and what he might be thinking about it – and what was David feeling, waiting for me to get back. I could only hope that it hadn't been a disastrous two days for him. Somehow I didn't think it would have been.

He was waiting in his room in the bungalow when I got home, and we fell into each other's arms in a passionate embrace.

'Oh, God, it's marvellous to be back home again, with you waiting there for me, my love. I can't wait to hear how you got on with Phil.'

'Very well, really. It was rather difficult to begin with, as we were both nervous and buttoned-up. But Phil's a really nice guy, and I suppose being a schoolmaster has taught him how to get through to people. So it wasn't long before we felt comfortable with one another, and were talking away about our past lives and experiences. By bed time we were completely at ease. I'd been dreading it a bit, not because I didn't like him, but because it wasn't going to be you and I'd feel guilty if I was enjoying it. But I didn't feel that at all. He's got a lovely body, and is very well endowed, but he's very tender with it and not aggressive, and I found we were very compatible in what we liked to do. I was so completely carried away by the excitement of this strange body beside me, that I never thought of you at all. It was obvious that he was very aroused by me, too, so we both came very quickly. It was the same last night.'

'I'm so glad you got on so well, it's a tremendous relief. I had thought it would work out all right as I liked him as well, but I couldn't help thinking how awful for you it would have been if you didn't get on.'

'I certainly do like him, and he kept telling me that if he hadn't got Robert, he could get very fond of me, which is pretty silly at our age. I used to assume that when you got up to about sixty, sex wouldn't be interesting any longer. But it's certainly not like that at all, is it?'

'It doesn't seem to be with us does it, or with Robert and Phil? And then think of Arnold and John, with Arnold well over eighty, and still enjoying it with John even if he had been impotent for years. So what do you feel about our little escapade now we've given it a trial run?'

'I wouldn't want to do it very often. Now that we know that we both enjoy it, and don't feel guilty with it being out in the open, I'd be quite willing to do it again, perhaps about every six months or so. We know perfectly well that neither of us is going to fall in love with either of them, or they with us, so there's no risk there. So, yes, I'd certainly like to get to bed with Phil again.'

Cuddling up in bed that night, I suddenly realised just how much I loved him, and was almost overwhelmed with emotion.

'It's marvellous to be together again. I just love you more than I can say, dearest David. Do you know, I believe Arnold's right. Being with someone else brings it home to you afresh just how wonderful it is to be able to share two lives together as we do.'

'You're quite right. I couldn't understand how it could be done when Arnold first talked about his relationship with John. But I think I can understand it now. It jolts you out of a rut, and stops you from taking everything for granted, and makes you realise just how incredibly lucky you are to have it. The awful thing is that it's bound to come to an end one day. We must make the best of it while we can. Hold me tight, Mark.'

I did, and it was just as if we'd never held each other before.

It was at the end of November that he went to see the doctor about his hip. Several times in the past I'd suggested that he should take out a private health insurance policy. But he'd always say that the NHS was perfectly capable of dealing with an emergency. I think he regretted it when he was told that he'd have to wait until after Christmas to get an appointment with a consultant. I suggested that he go private, but he said he felt he'd be jumping the queue, and he'd wait.

We had an enjoyable Christmas with the family at Janet and Daniel's on Christmas Day, and with Caroline on Boxing Day. David went over to stay at his sister's for a couple of days before his appointment with the consultant.

As we had expected, he recommended a hip replacement; but there was quite a long waiting list and as it wasn't especially urgent he'd probably have about six weeks to wait. In fact it was the end of February before he was told there was a bed. Neither of us was particularly concerned as we both knew people who had undergone the operation successfully, and said that they'd forgotten all about it after about six months.

We packed a bag, and I drove him in the evening before, and saw him settled in. We had hugged each other before we left the bungalow and had a last kiss, as I knew we probably couldn't say goodbye properly in a public ward. I wished once more that he was having it done privately, but it was too late now.

Everything went well and he was sitting up in a chair when I went to see him the day after the operation. He was very cheerful and talking about being back on the golf course in three months.

I had a meeting the following day at the college, and didn't go in to visit. But I was rather alarmed when Mildred, his sister, rang up in the evening to say that she'd been in, and he was not very well, and running a temperature. The hospital thought he might have a secondary infection. They had rung her as his nearest relative, and not me, as I was not recognised as one of his family. We had discussed entering into a civil partnership when they were introduced, but decided against it as we didn't see much point in our case. We knew we were together for life, and didn't need a bond like that, and both of us were financially independent so money didn't come into it.

I went in to the hospital late the following morning.

'I'll just ask Sister if it's all right for you to see him,' the nurse said. 'He's poorly as he's still got a very high temperature.'

She came back. 'We're just going to move him to a separate room, where he'll be more comfortable. You can have two or three minutes with him now, but no more.'

I was quite horrified at his appearance. His cheeks seemed to have fallen in, and his face was flushed, and with his eyes closed I hardly recognised him.

'David, love, what have they done to you? It's Mark. You must be feeling awful.' He opened his eyes, and stared at me for a moment as if he didn't know who I was.

'Oh, it's Mark. I'm feeling terrible. They're stuffing me full of antibiotics and I think they're making me feel worse. I keep having horrible nightmares all the time. Thank you for coming in. Thank you for everything, my love. You've been wonderful. I hope I'll be better by tomorrow. Come in to see me then, if you can.'

'Of course I will. I'll go now as they're coming to move you to another room.' I bent down and kissed him on the forehead, which was hot and feverish. 'Goodbye, my love.' I had a premonition then that I might not see him again.

I rang Mildred as soon as I got home. 'I'm terribly worried about David. I've just been in to see him and he's looking ghastly. They're moving him to a private room, which is a bad sign, as I suppose they're trying to isolate him. Are you going in later? If so, could you find out what they really think? They wouldn't tell me anything.'

'I'm very worried, too. I rang earlier and they were very cagey, saying they were trying a different antibiotic, which they hoped might work. If it didn't, the prognosis would not be good. I'll give you a ring this evening.'

She rang later. They had told her that if the latest antibiotic didn't work within twelve hours, it would be very serious, as his heart couldn't stand the strain much longer and they thought the infection had got into his lungs. The next twenty-four hours would be critical. There was nothing we could do, as he was now comatose most of the time and probably wouldn't recognise us if we were there, as he'd gone downhill so quickly. We should prepare ourselves for the worst.

I hardly slept that night, worrying about a possible future without him. My morning's premonition that he might not be going to pull through became more of a certainty with each passing hour. I drifted off into a fitful sleep at about half past three, but then woke suddenly at about five thirty, convinced that he was no longer with me. So when the phone call from Mildred came through at seven o'clock to say that he'd died peacefully at the very time that I had woken up, I was in a way prepared for it.

It didn't alter the feeling of utter desolation and loneliness I felt. That same numb feeling of loss that I'd experienced when Jack had told me of Simon's death took over. I just couldn't believe that it had really happened when he'd seemed so fit and strong the day after the operation. It must be some awful nightmare. But all the time I knew it wasn't a dreadful dream, and that from now on I'd have to face life alone once more.

Life had to go on, so I rang Daniel to say that I wouldn't be down on the farm that day. He was, of course, terribly shocked, as I'd not told them how serious it might be. I just wanted to be alone until the afternoon when I had told Mildred I would drive over to discuss the funeral arrangements.

It was as if I were on autopilot for the next few hours. I made myself some breakfast, and wrote out a list of the things I'd need to discuss with Mildred. Then I went into his room and sat down at his desk, and it was only then that the tears came. I didn't sob uncontrollably as I had done when Simon died, but just let them stream out as I told him how much I'd loved him, and always would, and how I couldn't contemplate a life without him being there with me. After a time, I felt that he was there in the room with me, telling me that I must get on with that life, and not to grieve for him, as he wouldn't want that. I should get on and learn to live without him, as I'd had to do when I lost Simon. That made me feel a little better.

At my own desk, I drafted out obituary notices for the *Times* and *Telegraph*, which I thought his veterinary colleagues and other friends might see. Then I rang Cynthia, who was devastated at the news.

'Mark, dear, it must be awful for you coming almost out of the blue like this. I just can't believe it. He was always so fit and strong. To be struck down by a thing like that at his age is terrible. He should have had many years ahead of him. These things shouldn't be allowed to happen. You and I do seem to have terribly bad luck, don't we?'

'I'm afraid we do. For it to happen twice to both of us is pretty hard to bear, especially at this time of life when there is so little left to look forward to.'

'You mustn't think like that, dear. You've still got a lot of years ahead of you, and there may still be some good times to come. I know it must look bleak and lonely for you now, but if nothing else you'll have so many happy memories to look back on.'

'That's true, but memories are a two-edged sword. They can certainly recall happy times, but they can also bring deep sorrow that the one you could share them with is no longer there. I learnt that only too well after Simon died, as I expect you did.'

'Yes, of course I did. But after a time when the wounds have healed, you see more of the happy side of them.'

'I'm going over to see Mildred, David's sister, this afternoon to discuss the funeral, and I'll let you have details as I hope you'll be able to come.'

'Of course I will, dear. You'll need support, as it's bound to be an ordeal for you.'

'I know it will. I'm dreading it.'

Mildred gave me a big hug when I got there, and it was a relief to know that she was there to share the grief. David had confided in her soon after we'd met, and told her how much I meant to him, and she was grateful to me for giving him happiness. So fortunately there were no barriers to be broken down.

'His heart just couldn't take the strain,' she said, 'and he apparently just drifted away at half past five. I wish I could have been with him, but they were so scared of his bug getting loose that they asked me not to come. But I don't think he'd have been conscious by then, so I suppose it didn't matter so much.'

'I wanted to be with him, too. I don't think anyone should be left to die alone, even if they're not really conscious. I was with both Mother and Dad when they went, and I was glad that I was there. With both of them, I felt their spirit was released to move on to a different plane. I think the same happened with David last night, as I woke up suddenly at half past five, and somehow knew that he had gone.'

'He did want to be cremated, didn't he? I meant to confirm it with you this morning. The undertaker has already been on to the crematorium to book a time.'

'Yes, he did, and he asked me to scatter his ashes at a favourite place of ours on the cliffs in Cornwall, where I want mine to be as well when the time comes, so that we can be together again.'

'We thought that the service ought to be in the parish church at Norton, as I expect a lot of his farmer friends will want to be there. I've had a talk with the rector this morning and he's quite happy about it. He thinks the church service should be timed for an hour before the cremation. Does that sound about right?'

'No, it's too tight. I think you should have at least an hour and a half between the two. It always seems to take longer than you think to get to the crematorium. We found that out when my dad died.'

'I'll ring up, then, and see if we can get a later slot. About the address: would you do it for us? I don't know who to ask otherwise.'

'No, I'm sorry. I couldn't face it. I'd probably break down completely. The right person would be Andrew Tweedie, the senior partner in the practice, who's just retired. He had a very high opinion of David, and would be sure to do it well. Would you like me to ask him?'

'Yes please.'

'There is one more thing. What would you like me to do with all the things in his room, which were his personal possessions. Would you like to have them?'

'I haven't had time to think about it. I'm afraid. It's possible that they might like one or two bits of furniture for the house in Plymouth, but could we leave it for the time being?'

'Yes, of course. I'll keep them as long as you like.'

As I was leaving she gave me a great hug and a kiss. 'Mark, we do have some idea of what his death must mean to you. It must seem like the end of everything that's meant so much to you both. You still have the rest of your life ahead of you, and he wouldn't want you to spend it grieving over what you've lost. He'd want you to get on with things, and just remember from time to time the love he had for you, and the happiness you gave him. Don't forget that we're here, and you must keep in touch when all this is over.' I was quite unable to speak for a few moments. What was it, I wondered, that caused me so much emotion at times like this? Were all gay men like this?

Returning to the empty house, the full force of what had happened hit me again, especially when I saw the open door of his room full of the things he cared about, and his desk by the window where he worked, which would never see him again.

After some supper which I barely tasted I could stand it no longer and rang Angela. 'I've got some dreadful news, Angela. David died early this morning.' I couldn't say another word, as the lump in my throat was almost choking me.

'Oh God, Mark dear, what on earth happened? He was so fit and strong.'

'He went in for the hip replacement operation and everything was going fine, but an infection must have got in. After the second day his temperature just shot up, and he didn't respond to any of the antibiotics they gave him. Finally his heart just gave out and he died at half past five this morning. It was so awful that I couldn't be with him. I'm absolutely devastated.' We talked for nearly an hour and I felt less alone.

'Would you like me to come and stay for a couple of nights over the funeral, dear? You'll need support, and it'll help to keep your mind off things a little.'

'I'd love you to. I'd been hoping you might suggest it, but didn't like to ask. The funeral is next Friday. Could you come on Wednesday evening? I'll expect you in time for supper.' It was typical of her understanding and sympathetic nature that she should have thought of what I'd be going through when she offered to come and stay. How lucky I'd been to have been given her friendship in the early days of our acquaintance.

The worst moment of all came at bed time when I saw his empty bed beside mine, all made up for his return when I'd have been nursing him. As I turned off the light, grief got the upper hand once more, and I cried at the thought that I'd never be lying there in his arms again and feel his heart beating and his body against mine. The fact that I was well over sixty seemed irrelevant, and I felt just as I had when I'd lost Simon, and I had been only twenty then. But this time, strangely, I didn't rail at God for depriving me of my happiness as I'd done then. What would have been the point? There was no question in my mind now about whether his death was some kind of punishment for an illicit love, as had troubled me then. I'd seen enough of the world by now to know that that idea was rubbish. I did say in my prayers, though, 'Please God, what have I done to deserve this to happen a second time? Please help me to get through the next few days.' This time it was a plea for strength, rather than an accusatory tirade against injustice.

In the morning, I made a resolution to try to look forward and not back until the worst of the trauma of his sudden death had passed. After breakfast, before going down to the farm, I telephoned the obituary announcement of his death through to the *Times* and the *Telegraph*, and to my former paper, the *Western Times*. I then went to my desk to look up a verse that I'd once heard read at a funeral of one of Dad's friends, and which I liked so much that I intended to ask Andrew Tweedie to include it in his address.

> If I should die, and leave you here awhile, be not like others, sore bereft, who spend long vigils by the silent dead, and weep. For my sake turn again to life, and smile, nerving thy heart and trembling hands to comfort weaker hearts than thine. Complete those still unfinished tasks of mine, and I perchance may therein comfort you.

Reading those lines again brought tears to my eyes, but somehow told me that I should not be wallowing in my own misery, but be looking outwards to helping those worse off than me. It was almost as if he were telling me to pass on all the love he had for me to others who might need it.

The announcements in the papers next day brought letters and phone calls that I found difficult to deal with. The first one was from Phil, who always read obituaries to check up on boys from his school who had died.

'Mark. This is terrible. I just can't believe it. Whatever can have happened to him? It must be just ghastly for you. We're both so, so sorry.'

'I ought to have rung you yesterday rather than let you read it in the paper, but I just couldn't face the ordeal – it was the hip operation.' I told him the full story. 'I wasn't allowed to see him for the last day and a half, which was awful as I couldn't be there with him to hold his hand to let him know that I was with him at the end.'

'Poor Mark. I can't begin to think what an ordeal it must be for you after all those years together. I'll miss him terribly myself, as we had so much in common. If things had been otherwise, and we'd met years ago, I think I'd have fallen in love with him myself. I felt he was so much me, if you know what I mean. I wish there was something we could do to help, but I suppose there isn't?'

'Not really, I'm afraid. The next few days are going to be awful, but tell Robert that Angela is coming to stay for three nights over the funeral so that I shan't be entirely alone. She was very fond of David.'

'We're intending to come down for it, and I'll look forward to seeing you there. In the meantime, try not to take it too hard. Now, Robert would like a word.'

'Dear Mark, what can I say? It's so unfair that you should have lost two people you loved so much from sudden deaths. I do feel so much for you. At least when my John died I had time to prepare for it, but coming out of the blue like this is so cruel. There's so little I can say that'll be of any help. At least you must be thankful that he didn't have to suffer pain for very long, even though he was far too young to die. Do let me know if there is anything we can do to help.'

I had hardly put the phone down when it rang again.

'Mark, it's Arnold here. I've just seen the announcement in the *Times*. How on earth has it happened? He always seemed so fit, I can't believe it. It must be awful for you.' I felt as if I were a gramophone with a needle stuck in the groove, as I went through the details still another time.

'I'm so sorry, Mark. It must seem like the end of the world for you. I'd supposed that you'd have had almost as long together as my John and I had. He shouldn't have gone so soon. The spread of these bugs in hospitals is getting very worrying and I can't see things getting any better.

'I know only too well what you're going through. My John died at a moment's notice when he was undressing for bed, and he wasn't found till the next morning. It was hard to bear that he was alone, and that I wasn't there with him, however traumatic it would have been. It's the emptiness they leave behind that is so difficult to cope with, but the feeling does gradually get less, though it never goes away. I can't remember whether I told you this, but he has come back to me four times now through different spiritualist mediums. I'll tell you about it one day. It's quite astonishing, but I have found it comforting.'

'I'd like to hear about it, though I don't think it'd be for me, as it doesn't fit in with my religious beliefs. Can I come over to see you when all this is over? I'd really love to see you again. I'm dreading the next few days.'

'I know. I nearly broke down at John's memorial service, and still don't know how I got through it. Yes, do please come over. It might help you to be able to talk about it to someone who's experienced what a sudden bereavement's like. I wish I could be there to support you, but I've had to give up driving at last.'

'Thanks so much for ringing, Arnold, I do appreciate it. I'll see you soon.'

I was surprised at the number of letters I received over the next few days. It made me realise for the first time that our close friendship had been widely acknowledged and accepted by so many in our professional lives. It showed just how much public opinion had changed for the better for people like us over the past few years. I could not believe that I would have had so many kind letters twenty-five years before when David and I had first met. I simply wished that he was there to read them – but that's the trouble with dying, you can't know what people thought of you in life. Unless, that is, there is some form of afterlife from which one can look down, which is what Arnold obviously believed.

Of all the letters I received, the one I treasured most was from Daniel's two boys, both of them at boarding school now.

Dear Uncle Mark,

John and I were awfully shocked when Mum told us in a letter that Uncle David had died. It must have been very sudden, as he was always so active and full of beans apart from getting a bit lame last summer. We both thought he was a lovely chap, and we did enjoy those wonderful holidays with you and him down in Cornwall, and the walks round the cliffs, and on the farm at home. It was very nice of him to teach us to surf three years ago. It won't feel the same next summer without him if we can go to Polzeath again with you. I'm sure you're going to miss him an awful lot as you were always such close friends. We hope you won't feel too lonely without him up in the bungalow.

John has settled down very well, and is enjoying his first year at the school. We both like it here very much.

With love from us both,

Charlie and John

I thought how much David would have enjoyed reading that letter, if only he'd been there. He had grown very fond of both of them, and was looking forward to taking John out on to the golf course before very long. Now he was going to miss the pleasure of seeing them growing up and making their way in life – which was one of the few things left for me to look forward to. There seemed precious little, otherwise.

During the next few days before the funeral, I kept myself as busy as possible, to avoid brooding on the emptiness I felt. Letters had to be answered and phone calls dealt with. They were the worst, for every now and again that lump would rise in my throat so that I could hardly speak. Luckily the caller at the other end could not see the tear that might be running down my cheek as I spoke.

I spent a further afternoon over at Mildred's going over the final arrangements and each time liked her more, as she was so like David, with her warmth of character and no-nonsense approach.

It was good for me that I had to get the house ready for Angela's visit, with food to be got in and the bed made up. She arrived in time for a cup of tea, and it was lovely to have company again in the house. Though now well over seventy, she was wearing well and grey hair suited her, softening her expression and giving her almost a maternal look which hadn't been there before.

She greeted me in her usual effusive way with a kiss and a great hug. 'How are you coping, Mark dear? I do hope you're managing to bear up. It must be a frightful ordeal.'

'Just getting by somehow, I suppose, though it's not been easy. There are the bad moments when the full force of it hits me again, and I feel that there is nothing to live for without him. But those moments pass when I get involved in something and have to concentrate on what I'm doing. So I try to keep as busy as possible, which seems to help.'

'That's the best line to take. I expect you've had a lot of letter-writing and things like that to keep you pretty busy.'

'I've been astonished at the number of people who've written. I'd no idea that so many people seem to have known about our relationship. He'd have been astonished, too, at how popular he was in the farming world.'

'You always said that he was a very good vet, didn't you?'

'Yes, he was awfully good at handling animals, especially dairy cows. They seemed to trust him, somehow, and didn't play up as some do with other vets. There was a very tender side to him, which was one reason why we got on so well.'

'That's because you're like that, too, even if you do pretend otherwise if you want to make an impression on people. I imagine that you're going to stay on living here, aren't you, even if it will be rather lonely for you?'

'Yes, of course. I was alone here till he moved in, so I'll just have to get used to it again. It's not so bad during the day, but the worst time is going to bed at night and seeing his empty bed, and knowing that I'll never share it again with him – or with anyone else for that matter. I suppose it'd be better if I took it away altogether, so it wouldn't remind me of the past. But I can't steel myself to do it just yet, as I'd feel as if I were trying to forget him, and I couldn't bear that.'

'I wouldn't take it away yet. The time may come when you can do it, but I don't think you're at that point yet. Everything's far too recent for that, and it may help you to grieve for him properly if you can think of him in an intimate way each night. It's a bit like having an open wound that hasn't yet healed. The worst thing you can do is to bind it up tight. It needs to be left open, and dressed each day till it heals itself naturally – and that can take a little time.'

'I'm sure you're right. If I can think of it in that light it may make it easier to look at it in a more positive way, and remember the good times and thank him for the love he gave me. That's more or less how I coped with Simon's death. I had that lovely photo of him in Switzerland, and I'd talk to him as though he were still there, which seemed to help. Perhaps he was there, if there is indeed some kind of spirit world that enables those we loved to come back to us, even if we can't see them.'

'I had a spiritualist friend once who firmly believed that. She used to tell me quite extraordinary stories about some mediums who appeared to act as a kind of transmitting station between the material and the spiritual world, so there may be something in it.'

'Our friend Arnold was telling me much the same when he rang last night. He got involved with it after his partner of forty-seven years died, and came back to him through a mutual friend who'd been to a service in a spiritualist church. I intend to ask him more about it when I go up to Oxford to see him. It all sounds a bit spooky to me, and I know that the Church doesn't approve of it. But then the Church doesn't approve of us either, so it doesn't always get it right, does it?'

'It certainly does not. As you know that's why I became an agnostic many years ago. I just couldn't accept that a group of people who preach that we should love one another should try to stop us doing so. The whole thing was so abominably hypocritical that I couldn't stomach it. Anyhow, I've never been able to accept that a group of mortals can possibly know, with the degree of certainty they claim, what God, if he does exist, intends for the human race.'

'I admit to losing some faith when Simon was taken, but I do still feel that there must be some power that determines our lives – though I accept that there is no logical reason for thinking so when one looks at the world today. But it does give me some comfort to believe in it. I suppose that losing David like this is again a test of faith in the existence of a loving God, but I don't think that I want to join you in your disbelief.'

We carried on with discussions like this until bed time, and it was wonderful having someone like Angela, with whom I could relate, to take my mind away from the imminent ordeal of his funeral.

Two days later I sat in the second pew with Janet, Daniel and Angela, behind David's family, and was glad this gave me a degree of anonymity. It also meant that if I had to wipe away a tear it would not be quite so conspicuous as it would have been in the front row. I just couldn't bear to look as the coffin was brought in, and clenched my jaw in an effort to keep control. I told myself that it wasn't David lying there, but just the lifeless envelope that had once enclosed the spirit that had made him the person he once was. That was now far away, or might be in the church with us, or even right beside me. I suddenly felt that he probably was there, just as I had thought Simon was there on that other occasion, when he'd told me that he was all right, and that the Principal was talking nonsense in his address.

During Andrew Tweedie's address I found my mind wandering back to that sunny afternoon three years earlier, lying in our favourite hollow on the cliff, when David had suddenly asked me if I'd thought what it would be like if one of us died. Had he some premonition then, I wondered, and wanted to warn me that it might happen? I'd replied then that we shouldn't worry, but take each day as it came. I was still sure that I was right in saying that, for what good would it have done to make ourselves miserable when all was well? None at all. We'd gone on having happy times which I could look back on with nostalgia.

I missed a little of what Andrew was saying while my mind had wandered off, but was brought back by hearing my name. He was paying a tribute to a friendship which he knew had meant much to David ever since he'd joined the practice over twenty-five years before. I felt slightly embarrassed about the effect this might have on some of those present, but told myself that they would all be friends and acquaintances of his anyhow, and would therefore know all about us. I felt grateful to Andrew for I was sure that David would have wanted it to be put on record what we'd meant to one another. It couldn't have been said twenty years ago, and it was good that it could be said in public now.

After the service I was spared the ordeal of having to stand and greet people, as we had to make a quick exit to the crematorium for a brief committal service. The dreaded moment came, as the curtains closed and I knew that he was finally gone for ever. A few tears did fall then, but Mildred and Janet were wiping their eyes as well, so I didn't feel so bad about it.

By the time we got back to the hall for the refreshments I'd regained my composure, and was able to cope with the expressions of condolence from many of his farmer clients and other friends. Angela, who knew virtually no one there, had sat with Cynthia, as they had met three or four times over the years when she'd been down to stay with me, and they'd always got on very well. She'd been quite surprised to see Robert there with Phil, as I hadn't told her about his new partner, or that we'd met up again quite recently. I could see that she was intrigued and expected to be quizzed about it later on.

It was also a pleasant surprise to see that three of his golfing friends, whom I'd not got to know at all well, had also come. They knew that we quite often played together at weekends, and said that I must give them a ring if I ever wanted a game. I thought I'd have to decide soon whether to play more, or else give the game up completely now that he wouldn't be there. It would have to be one or the other. If young John remained keen, I'd probably continue to play, as David would have liked me to bring him on.

Eventually it was all over, and I took Angela and Cynthia back to the bungalow where we could relax over a cup of tea; my two oldest and dearest friends. I was so thankful to have them there so that I didn't have to return to an empty house with no one to talk to about the day's events.

'I thought that was a lovely send-off for him,' Cynthia said. 'He seems to have been very popular in his profession.'

'Yes, he was. He was wonderfully good with cows, even the most difficult ones. He had a gentle touch and they seemed to trust him. It was something I noticed the first time he came to the farm, for that's often the difference between a good vet and a less caring one. I used to wonder whether it might be because he was gay, as women and girls are often good at looking after animals. David loved cows, which is why he came down to Devon, thank goodness, for that made my life the happy thing it was for twenty-five years. His farming clients were dismayed when he decided to retire a bit sooner than he need have done. They gave him a very big party then, and it brought it home to him how popular he was. He was really a very modest person, and hadn't realised till then how much they valued him.'

'You were lucky to find him,' Cynthia said. 'But you deserved that happiness after losing Simon and then Guy. You really mustn't give up hope. You're still young at heart and good-looking, and there are probably quite a lot of older men about who may have lost partners or who want to settle down, if only you could find them.'

'Possibly there are, but not in rural Devon, I'm afraid. Anyhow, I'd find it terribly difficult after such a loving partnership with David. Can I come over to see you soon after all this is over?'

'Of course, dear, just give me a ring when you want to come. I must go now, as I don't like driving in the dark in my old age.'

'I do like her,' Angela said after she had gone. 'She's so motherly and caring. She told me all about you and Simon, and how you became a second son to her when he was killed.'

'I always felt that she was a second mother to me, even before the accident. She was so grateful that Simon had found someone so compatible, and made him so happy with his life. It was wonderful to have her at hand then, as I couldn't turn to my parents who didn't know that I was gay. It was her, too, who told Mother about people being born gay, which made it much easier for her to accept the situation, even if Mother didn't let on that she knew all about me for nearly twenty years, and Dad never let on that he knew either. It's one of the regrets I have that I wasn't able to talk to Dad about it before he died. But that applies to many other things as well – regret that one never got to know one's father properly, and one doesn't realise it till it's too late.'

'I never really got to know my father at all, and I don't think either of them ever suspected that I might be lesbian. They had both died by the time I was twenty, and I think it's just as well they didn't know, as I suspect they wouldn't have approved of it. Now, tell me all about Robert and his new partner. I hadn't even heard that he'd lost John.'

'He died of cancer, and apparently Robert nursed him devotedly until he died. He left the flat to him, and told him he must find another partner. Robert got into a pretty bad psychological state, blaming himself for the rows they'd had, and full of remorse that he'd been unfaithful to John in having casual sex, feeling terribly lonely and getting a stupid idea into his head that he was too old to find another man in his life. He couldn't decide whether to stay in the flat, or sell it and move somewhere else. It was all part of the grieving process, and finding out that he'd really loved John more than he'd realised. I suppose it made it worse that John, being older, was a bit of a father figure, and he was missing that support as well.'

'Yes, we always had that impression in the flats. John was quite a strong personality, and a dominant figure in the partnership, so it's not surprising that Robert was left rather high and dry when he was no longer there. But Robert shouldn't have felt any guilt as John was no angel, and could be pretty cantankerous at times, and quite trying to live with, I'd think. To make it worse he could be jealous as well, which you'll remember I warned you about when I suspected the two of you might be getting up to something.'

'Yes, I'd already got that impression. Anyhow, Robert rang up and asked me to stay with him for a couple of nights. He really was in quite a mess, and I felt sorry for him, as he was obviously missing sex. So I offered to go to bed with him, though I felt a bit guilty as I'd never slept with anyone but David since we'd first met. Robert leapt at the idea saying that he still found me very attractive.'

'Yes, I knew that. He talked to me about it once, and I advised him strongly not to get too involved with you, as I knew it could cause terrible trouble between them if John ever found out. It could have wrecked their relationship, which would have been dreadfully hard on John.'

'Thank you for that. It would have been hard for both of them. I always liked Robert a lot, but I wouldn't ever have fallen in love with him. Anyhow, we did go to bed, and it seemed to liberate him in some way, as next day he said he'd decided to stay in the flat, and try to find a partner, as he'd come to realise that he still needed sex, and the companionship of someone to care for him.

'I advised him to try the 'Kindred Spirit' columns in the *Times* or the *Telegraph*, and after one or two false starts he found Philip, a retired schoolmaster who had lost his partner. It was an immediate success, as Philip was free to move in with him.'

'So that's what happened, is it? But why did they come down to David's funeral?'

'It's quite a long story, and not a very creditable one, I'm afraid. Briefly, Robert and Phil were going to Devon and Cornwall on holiday, and asked if they could look in so that we could meet Philip, and they stayed with us in the bungalow for two nights. Phil was instantly very taken with David. We'd already had quite a long conversation about whether an occasional sexual fling outside a loving relationship was disloyal or, as our old friend Arnold claimed, could help to freshen up a marriage. Both Robert and Phil had been quite promiscuous at some stage of their lives, and thought nothing of a casual fling if the opportunity presented itself.

'But neither David nor I had been promiscuous, and we'd been faithful to one another, until my night with Robert had proved to be so exciting – and in the meantime David had had a quickie with a hitchhiker, which he, too, had found liberating. So when it became obvious that the two of them would like to swap partners for a night, we had to decide whether to do it. I didn't like the idea, nor did David, of us having sex with different partners in adjoining rooms, so we turned them down. But we did agree to go away for a couple of nights to each other's houses to see how we felt, and we did this last summer.

'I'm a bit ashamed to say that we did both find it very stimulating, but it was lovely to be back together again, even more convinced of our love for one another. Phil was almost besotted with David sexually, though he's completely committed to Robert, and we'd agreed we'd try it again later on this year. That's why they were both at the funeral, as Phil was dreadfully shocked at David's death. So that's the sordid story, I'm afraid. But I'm very happy that we did it, as David had become fond of Phil, and it's good to know that he'd enjoyed it so much without feeling any guilt.'

'I don't think it was sordid at all. I agree with your friend Arnold. I've played away in my time, and so has Janet. It's only a matter of getting temporary bodily sexual satisfaction with someone who is quite different, like having a treat of strawberries and cream once or twice in the summer. You wouldn't want it every day, and it's nice to get back to rice pudding again. It has no bad effects on a loving relationship at all. Arnold's right; it can freshen things up no end, and I'm so glad that David enjoyed it. You mustn't let memories of him stand in your way if you're tempted to have it in the future. You're still too young for celibacy!'

'I won't, but I don't expect to get the opportunity.'

Over supper that night, she asked whether I'd have time the next day to show her the nature trail and some of the other plantings that I'd done over the years.

'I'd love to. I've got to go down to the farm first thing to get the men to work, as Daniel's off to London for a meeting, and then I'll be back for breakfast. We could go round after that. You can stay for lunch, I hope.'

'Yes, I told Janet I wouldn't be back till the evening.'

'How is Janet, by the way? I should have asked you as soon as you came, but I'm afraid I forgot with all the other things I had on my mind.'

'She's fine, apart from a little arthritis. We give each other a bit of room, but we've learnt to live together very happily – better than I expected, to be honest.'

We both enjoyed the tour of the farm next morning. Some of the trees were in bud, and the birds were just beginning to sing. Angela with her active mind was full of questions, which kept me on my toes. I wouldn't admit it in public, but I was rather proud of what I'd achieved over the years, and it was satisfying to be able to show it off to someone who really appreciated it, as she obviously did.

After lunch, it was time for her to go, and as we said our goodbyes I was almost crying at the thought of the empty house and lonely years ahead.

'Thanks so much for coming and helping me over these last few days. I just don't know how I could have faced it without you there. It's been so good to have someone to talk to who under-stands. You've been a wonderful friend to me ever since that first day in your office, when you more or less took me under your wing. I'm eternally grateful. Come back and stay again before long. It's an open invitation.'

'I certainly will, Mark. I'm only so glad to have been able to help you over such a rough patch. You've been a good friend to me, too, you know. The next few weeks will be difficult, but it won't be long before this will be just a memory, and you'll settle down to a new routine.'

After a farewell kiss and a close hug she was gone, and I was left alone to face up to a different life once more.

Two weeks later Mildred and her son and his wife came over to see if there was anything that they might like to have from David's room for their new house in Plymouth. Their visit had spurred me into taking down his bed and moving it from my room, which was a harrowing experience. They took it away, and two of his armchairs, but left his desk in the window, for which I was thankful. The room looked a bit bare after they'd gone, but there was enough left to serve as a reminder of him, and I decided to leave it as it was for the time being. Perhaps one day someone might want it.

Charlie and John were home for the Easter holidays soon after, and came up to see what had been going on at Barnfield almost immediately. It was good to have them there to take my mind off things. They seemed to spend more time with me than they did at home, and John was often up at the buildings helping Duncan with the calves.

We were all together at a family gathering on the Monday when Janet said, quite out of the blue: 'What you need, Mark, is a dog to keep you company up there instead of being on your own all the time.'

'We'd thought of getting one several times, but held off because we didn't like the idea of having to leave him behind in kennels when we went abroad on holiday – and we didn't want to ask you to look after him, as you've quite enough to do already. But it's a good idea now, as I shan't be going abroad again, I'm afraid.'

'You could get an older rescue dog, which wouldn't need training and would probably be quite happy being left alone if you were in a meeting. Or alternatively you could drop him off here for a day, if we were going to be in.'

'Yes, do get one, Mark,' John said. 'It must be awfully lonely up there for you without David, and it'd be fun taking it out when we go round the farm with you, wouldn't it, Charlie?'

'Yes, I'm sure you should have one, Mark. What sort would you like?'

'You're all in such a hurry for me to have one, I haven't really had time to think, It'd probably be a Jack Russell, as they're intelligent and full of energy, or perhaps a Labrador, because they're soft and easy-going and would probably be happy to be left alone. Anyhow, let's go to the rescue centre in a day or two to see what they've got to offer. Would you be free on Wednesday, Janet? I'd like you to come along to help me choose.'

'Yes, in the afternoon, I'd love to come.'

I found it quite harrowing the way almost every dog seemed to look at us with pleading eyes as if it were saying, 'Please take me out of here, I want to go home.' I'd decided I wanted a dog and not a bitch, as I'd like to have a man in the house. As it turned out, the decision was almost made for me. It seemed that Labradors were popular for re-homing and the last one had gone out a few days before. They did have one six-year-old Jack Russell, who'd apparently been such a tearaway when he'd been picked up that they'd finally decided to castrate him in the expectation that it'd calm him down and make him more acceptable for re-homing. The kennel manager said that it had worked and he was now a very quiet and amenable little dog.

When we got to his cage, he turned out to be big for his breed, with quite a roughish coat and a wonderfully alert look about him. He looked at me pleadingly, and I could almost hear him saying, 'I want to come and live with you, please take me home.' And I felt as if we had been made for one another.

'I hope you like him, Janet, as I'm sure he's the one for me.'

'He looks very intelligent. I don't think you'd go far wrong with him, Mark. What do you think, boys?'

'He looks a lovely little dog. Do take him, Mark.'

That settled it, and next day I came back to collect him, having bought him a new bed. His name was Lenin, which I thought was a strange name for a dog, but he seemed to like it, so we decided not to try to re-christen him.

When I got him home he went from room to room in the house finding his way around; and then, apparently satisfied, jumped into his new basket, snuggled down into the old blanket I'd put there for him and lay there watching my every move. That evening after supper as I sat reading the paper, I felt a nudge against my leg as he asked if he could come up on my lap, where he lay happy and content to have found a safe home at last. And I felt happier than I had done since David died. I wished then that we'd bought a dog when he came to live with me, as he'd grown very fond of them from treating them in his practice, and I think he'd have loved Lenin.

In a way Lenin transformed my life, providing a loving companionship that filled the emptiness caused by David's death. He hated being left alone in the house, but was perfectly happy to be left for hours in the car, if I was out at a meeting or playing a round of golf. But he had one fault I could never rectify. He would always expect the cows to play with him – or the young animals, for that matter. It wasn't that he wanted to chase them around in a malicious way, but simply that he expected them to play with him, as the boys would play with him with a ball on the lawn or would throw sticks for him. It meant that he had to be on a lead if cattle were grazing on the farm, which we both found frustrating. But that was a small price to pay for the affection he showed me when he would lie in his basket, chin resting on the raised side, gazing at me lovingly, or when he lay contentedly in my lap. That made me feel happy.

As spring gave way to summer, I found that I was thinking less about David, though he'd still come back several times a day, and I'd speak to his photograph as I went to bed each night. It was a good one of him taken on a boat on Lake Como with Bellagio and our hotel in the background. With his tanned face, hair slightly ruffled by a breeze and a broad smile, he looked completely happy, and that was how I liked to remember him. I had the photo enlarged to the same size as Simon's, and the two of them on the dressing table were a constant reminder of how supremely lucky I'd been to have been loved by both of them – and to have had them to love in return.

With committee work and the farm, I was kept reasonably well occupied, but I did regret the decision I'd taken some years before to give up writing my fortnightly articles, and I was missing the mental stimulation that talking with David had provided. I felt I needed more intellectual challenge in my life if I were not to sink into a rut. I was sitting out on the patio enjoying the sunshine with Lenin one evening in May when I suddenly decided that I'd write a novel.

It was an idea I had toyed with, before deciding that I wouldn't have the time. That was no excuse now, though. It wouldn't be a technical book about agriculture and farming, though that might form some kind of a background. It would be about a farmer's son, who grew up to realise that he was gay at about the time he left school. It would deal with the problems that resulted from it, and the difficulty young gay people might have in finding a partner in isolated areas. I'd start the book as he was leaving school and going to college for the first time, and lead on his acceptance that he'd not marry and have a family life ahead of him. I got out a piece of paper and roughed out a synopsis.

The following evening, I sat down at the computer and keyed in the first line: 'Dad looked up from the paper he was reading. "I reckon you've been working on those books long enough, lad, and that you could do with a break."'

I had got as far as that when the phone rang.

'Hello, Mark Harper speaking.'

'Mark, your voice hasn't changed at all. It's Guy, and I'm sticking to my promise.'

Printed in the United Kingdom
by Lightning Source UK Ltd.
121342UK00001B/18/A